Black Hat/White Hat

Black Hat White Hat

A Novel of Good ~~and~~ *is* Evil

Black Hat / White Hat

is

A Tale of Good ~~and~~ Evil

Glenn Della-Monica

Published by
Glenn Della-Monica
373 South Willow St, #159
Manchester, NH 03103

www.gdellamonica.com

Publisher's Note: This is a work of fiction. Names, characters, businesses, places, events, and incidents are either the products of the author's imagination or used in a fictitious manner. Any resemblance to actual persons, living or dead, or actual events is purely coincidental.

Cover designed by Danielle Smith-Boldt

Frontispiece designed by Nona A.Smith

ISBN 979-8-9850639-0-5 (MOBI)
ISBN 979-8-9850639-2-9 (EPUB)
ISBN 979-8-9850639-1-2 (paperback)

Library of Congress Control Number: 2021921119

This is dedicated to my wife, Sue, who put up with me, stuck on the couch with my keyboard on my lap for revision after revision. Her encouragement got me through to the end.

Let us not become gloomy as soon as we hear the word 'torture':
In this particular case there is plenty to offset and mitigate that word
– even something to laugh at.
— Friedrich Nietzsche: On the Genealogy of Morality

Chapter 1

Robocaller Edward Gets a Most Unwanted Call Himself

This was Day One of a new era.

Shortly after Alex and Lara arrived at his apartment in the middle of the night, Edward Trellenby found himself in an awkward position. He was trussed up in network cable on the food-stained burnt-orange shag carpet of his computer room. Alex and Lara, a pair of sinister-looking intruders dressed in hooded black leotards, mirrored goggles, and surgical gloves, were kneeling beside him. Edward favored his left wrist as he gingerly tested his bonds. It was sprained from the wristlock Lara had used to subdue him.

The apartment wasn't much—just two bedrooms, a living room, bathroom, and kitchen. One of the bedrooms was filled with computer equipment. The walls were covered in heavy metal band posters and pictures of sports cars.

Dressed in gray cargo shorts, sweat socks, and a Def Leppard tee shirt, the twenty-nine-year-old scammer appeared to be in uncharted territory as the two finished tying him up. Alex imagined Edward was regretting whatever the reason was for this unscheduled visit.

Through his tears, Edward whined, "Why are you doing this? Take anything you want."

Alex insultingly patted him on the head. He showed their victim the chef's knife he'd obtained from the kitchen on the way in. Edward cringed.

Lara left the room as Alex answered Edward's question: "Well, Edward, my friend, we don't want money or any of your other crap. No, you are special. You see, you have the honor of being the first in what I am sure will be a long line of examples. Our employers have had it with your kind. You interrupted the boss's poker game, and there's nothing to take the jam out of someone's full-house doughnut like getting a call from a scam artist. The organization feels that scammers like you are a blight on society. You pester hundreds of people with calls they don't want, and when someone is foolish enough to believe that you can help them with a nonexistent problem with the IRS, you steal their money."

"But I … but I …"

"Butt you?" Alex laughed. "Okay! We'll butt you."

Alex rolled Edward onto his stomach. He used the knife to slit Edward's shorts and underwear open.

Alex heard Edward gasp in terror, and he realized that Edward could be imagining any one of a hundred horrible things that could follow what Alex had just done. Alex knew the fear of not knowing was as powerful as experiencing any of those possibilities, and he let Edward contemplate his sins in terrifying silence. He laughed to himself that no one yet could imagine why making phone calls would result in being tied on their floor with their pants cut open. Soon they would.

Lara returned from the kitchen and held up a slim flip phone in her right hand. She had a quart can of something in her left hand.

With an ear-to-ear grin, she announced, "Look, honey. I found this on the kitchen counter. Perfect candidate, and it's even has a working SIM card with an active number."

"I'd say that is just about the right size, sweetheart. I'm not sure we could have done it with his iPhone 8. A little big. We should probably carry a small burner phone in the future just in case our subjects don't have one small enough. If you hadn't found this, we probably would have had to use something else, maybe his computer mouse. After all, we don't want to kill him."

"Good point for future reference, honey," Lara commented before she turned her attention to Edward.

She walked in front of him so he could see her clearly and said, "Edward, dear, when you call people, the first thought that goes through their mind is, 'I wish I could cram that asshole's phone up his butt.' I want you to know you are going to be the test case for that. Our employers want to see if that can actually be done. If you tell us all your passwords, I'm going to ease it in with the shortening I just found in your kitchen. If not … well, let's just say this won't be nearly as pleasant."

She held up the can. Crisco. She held up the phone in her other hand and frowned comically as she asked, "Which is it going to be, Edward: Plain or frosted?"

Edward cringed in terror; eyes as wide as silver dollars. Lara showed him the contents of one hand and then the other a couple of times. Edward appeared to finally grasp his options. He nodded toward the can of shortening. Lara smiled and went to the computer desk.

As Lara worked Edward's computer, he grudgingly gave her all the passwords and filenames she needed. Once in a while, he hesitated, and she dangled the phone over him. He relented each time. Finally, she had unlocked evidence of all his scams, bank accounts, Dark Net identities, and contacts. She printed out lists of sites and files along with their passwords.

When she was done, she turned to Alex and asked, "Honey, do you think he earned the Crisco, or do we do this neat?"

"Sweetheart, without the shortening, you'll need a hammer to pound that thing inside him."

Before Edward could weigh in with his own opinion on the matter, Alex had stuffed one of Edward's socks in his mouth and was applying duct tape to hold it in place.

The following new experience Lara gave Edward was the sensation of the slim phone covered in vegetable shortening going where he really didn't want to feel a cellphone. He screamed against the gag until she had the phone securely in place.

"Sweetheart, tell him the bad news."

Lara hunkered down next to whimpering Edward's ear. She whispered, "Well, bunky, by comparison, Mr. Telephone is a comfortable joy next to what will happen to you if you ever use a computer or phone to bother someone again … ever. What we found on your computer should be enough for the cops to put you away for at least a little while, and when you get out, you will be carefully watched. One more spam call or scam attempt, and we'll be back to kill you. Unpleasantly."

Alex added, "We know you visit your parents, Myrtle and Gary, on Thirty-Ninth Avenue in Oakland. We know you have a friend on Tropicana Boulevard in Las Vegas that you visit every few months when you go there to gamble and visit strip clubs. We know you order empanadas at the Mexican restaurant down the block. We know you like to hang out with your sleazeball friends and play pool at Drago's on Third Street. In other words, we know everything about you. We own you."

Alex pinned a wire to Edward's shirt. He warned, "That wire is attached to a grenade tied to one of the legs of your desk. We'll call the cops in a couple of hours to come to rescue you. Move before that and die. Oh, by the way, don't try to take a dump. It would probably kill you. You can tell the cops a pair in black did this to you, but that's it. Give them any details about us, and it leads to that second visit. Just lie there and relax. But take heart, Edward; you're so screwed that only doing something to bring us back could make it any worse."

The wire was tied to the leg of Edward's desk, but there was no grenade. This visit wasn't intended to kill, just punish. Alex took Edward's cell phone and dialed the flip phone's number. He and Lara laughed when a muffled ringtone played through the slit in Edward's pants.

Alex took a business card with an odd image resembling a caricature of a head with a red nose and placed it on the computer keyboard. Lara took some items out of a plastic bag and scattered them about the apartment. As quickly as they had invaded Edward's home, the pair disappeared into the night, leaving the sobbing and confused Edward on the rug of his computer room.

Day One of Papa Paul's new enterprise had just concluded.

Chapter 2

Sasha Trumps the FBI

Two years, three months, and seventeen days after Edward received that pair of unpleasant visitors, FBI Special Agent Cody Smutters got out of a Russian government automobile in front of a nondescript rowhouse in Pushkino, a town on the outskirts of Moscow. He ran a hand through his sandy hair as his brown eyes narrowed to assess the scene.

It was a drizzly gray day. Cody had been sitting in the back seat of that crappy gray government car in a gray concrete and stone neighborhood, looking at a man in a gray sports coat walking toward him. Everything about his current surroundings summed up his feeling about his chances of getting any meaningful information from this latest episode.

Along with him was his partner, Special Agent William Washington. William hated the nickname Bill, preferring his full first name. He was distantly related to William Washington Browne, an African American Union Army soldier in the Civil War, and he was proud of the name William because of that. He hated the diminutive Willie even more.

About five-eight, William was shorter than Cody by several inches, and unlike Cody's runner's physique, William looked more like a rugby player. His mocha skin stood out in urban Moscow, but it had been his confident stride and striking good looks that attracted attention more than his skin color when they checked into their hotel. William could be the most charming man at a party but could turn on almost movie-villain intensity when interrogating a suspect.

The bookish-looking driver provided by the Moscow police stayed in the car, apparently uneasy about meeting the hard-looking plainclothes cop who had been leaning on a black sedan when they pulled up. He wasn't very talkative, either. He and the agents hadn't exchanged more than a nod or two since his superior told him where to take the two Americans. The back of his slicked-down black hair and the gray eyes in the rearview mirror was about all of what the two agents saw of him during the ride.

Cody and William walked over to Criminal Investigation Department Lieutenant Alyosha Sokolov, the Russian detective with whom he had arranged this meet. The man was about six feet tall, muscular with short, graying black hair and a reasonably nice sport coat over navy-blue slacks. Cody extended a hand. The gesture was returned with a firm grip as the detective smiled a rattlesnake-thin smile, a lit cigarette dangling from one corner of his mouth. From Alyosha's expression, Cody suspected he knew what was going to come out of the detective's mouth along with the cigarette smoke.

"This is perfect case for you to be working, Special Agent Zhmutters; involves kiddie zhmut."

While the Russian lieutenant's accent was passable, Cody soon discovered some words were horrible. It was a version of a Muscovite accent, with almost guttural l's and a w pronounced somewhere between an English v and w. English i was more like ee. Surprisingly, he had some English words down pat with only a slight accent. It made them sound eerily odd in the middle of the accented speech, but it was annoyingly inconsistent.

Once in a while, Alyosha mixed in a Russian word with his English, a habit Cody also had when speaking to an English-speaking Russian.

Cody winced at the lieutenant's remark. He'd heard that same weak "kiddie smut" pun about his name from two-bit, small-town cops in the States, and now he was getting the same crap from a Russian detective! Well, at least this guy spoke English well enough that he could make the pun. Cody gave a little perfunctory laugh.

"Yeah … right. Good one. This is my partner, Special Agent William Washington."

William and the Russian shook hands as the latter said, "Alyosha Sokolov. Welcome."

Cody was a pretty good judge of character, and he knew when to roll with it and when to tell someone to screw. He saw that Alyosha had the bearing and confidence of a good cop.

Cody said, "Your name means one who helps, right, Alyosha? So, let's get to helping. When did you get the call?"

The Russian cop looked at him with surprise, inquiring, "Vi gavareetye pa Russki?"

"Yes. I do speak a little Russian. My maternal grandparents were from Kyiv. They taught me some Russian and a little Ukrainian, but my partner doesn't speak it. Since your English is pretty good, let's just stick to that so I don't have to translate for him. Shall we get to work?"

Alyosha smiled at the compliment. Cody guessed Alyosha hadn't been assigned to many cases involving English-speaking foreigners over the years because of his really odd accent. Cody was used to the Muscovite pronunciation and caught most of it, but William looked as if he would be straining a bit to make out what Alyosha was saying until he got used to it.

"Da. We will work hard to solve the case, and then maybe we go nightclub. I will show you best places for vodka!"

"Okay, my drook, we're here to help you as much as we can, and if that means helping you empty a bottle of vodka later, we're in."

"Khorosho," the Russian replied, indicating that what Cody had said was fine. He smiled at being called "drook," or friend, by an American cop.

"So, when did your department get the call?"

"His neighbors call for odd noise in house. They said breaking of things, maybe. The local cops come to house, find no force entry, but call for my office's assistance when they realize what this is. Victim was tied up like doktorskaya kolbasa with gag."

"Tied up like a sausage, eh? Perp used computer cords?" Cody asked with a chuckle at the sausage image.

"Da. Computer cord, like you say. With ... ah ..."

"Something stuck up his ass?" William prompted.

"Ah, yes. You know this thing already, though."

Cody replied, "If the card matches. You got it? Show me the card."

Alyosha opened the trunk of his car and pulled out a worn black faux leather briefcase. Cody saw the PP-2000 submachine gun strapped to the back of the trunk as he did so. He guessed that his new drook, or friend, was carrying one of the reasonably new PYa Grach double action semiautos, too. Cody missed the old Makarovs, but his Russian counterparts certainly did not. While not as compact or romantic-looking in a James Bond kind of way, the Grach was a superior weapon. It was far more powerful and way more accurate.

Cody was behaving as most FBI special agents he knew did when assigned to a foreign country case. They fairly assessed the personnel they were going to work with. If the cops were professional, they treated them like pros, not third-world mooks asking for help from their American big brothers. On the flip side of the coin were the arrogant, corrupt officials American law enforcement officials sometimes ran into in foreign countries.

He knew that his gut feeling was correct; Alyosha was a pro. A hardworking, no-nonsense cop who was good at getting answers. Cody wasn't sent to these foreign cases to solve anything, per se. He was there to gather any information that would help his US counterparts solve their domestic ones. Alyosha would be helpful in that pursuit. Cody was also there to share information that would assist the foreign cops.

Alyosha pulled out a plastic evidence pouch, and in it was what Cody expected to see. It was a white business card with only one thing on it, a funny-looking black-outlined head-shaped scribble with a big red dot toward the right side. The standing joke back home was that it looked like part of a drunk test where someone way over the limit was asked to draw a clown head and put a red dot on the nose. Twenty-three cards so far in two-and-a-quarter years, and no one could figure out what they were.

Closing the trunk and then leaning back against it, Alyosha lit a cigarette and asked Cody in Russian, "I have read what reports I could find on your criminals. Can you tell me what you and your American police have discovered so far?"

It had stopped drizzling, so Cody leaned on the trunk next to his new Russian friend. He told William, "This is going to be faster if I explain it to him in Russian, okay?"

"Sure, Cody. I'm going to walk the perimeter while you two talk."

Cody turned to Alyosha and continued in Russian, "Every case is the same. A scammer of one stripe or another was found tied like a sausage with a gag in his or her mouth. Every one of them had two problems. The first was a small cell phone stuck up the victim's ass. The second was that they were all bound for jail.

"All the victims were found amid vast amounts of evidence that they had been using computers or phones for fraud. Scams involving fake IRS agents, you know, people asking for tax money, the Microsoft Help Desk, or some other pretense. Even in fairly corrupt cities or foreign countries, every single one was arrested and convicted because of the orgy of evidence found at the scene."

"Like the documents we found, yes?"

"Exactly, Alyosha. When victims were interviewed in the hospital or jail cell, they always said the same things. The suspects—there were always two—tied them up. They never asked any questions other than to obtain passwords and account information. They always said that the victims were about to experience the pain that their own victims felt. That pain came in the form of the rectally inserted phone and the subsequent treatment by the police.

"The victims were always left with a warning. If they ever returned to scamming, they would be killed. The ones who dared talk a bit more about the suspects mentioned something about being told they were completely screwed or something, too."

Alyosha laughed and said, "That explains it. Gleb, the victim here, kept saying, 'I'm screwed, I'm screwed!'"

"Well, it sounds like he got the same speech. So, the suspects' descriptions have all been exactly the same: a man and a woman. Always dressed from head to toe in black stretch material. Always hooded and wearing tinted goggles or oversize mirrored sunglasses and surgical gloves. They apparently know how to pick locks and disable alarm systems to get in if necessary. They only use weapons belonging to the victims. A kitchen knife is the usual weapon used to intimidate the victims and slice clothing, and it is always left at the scene."

"Any evidence left by the suspects?"

"No, the suspects are good. They never left as much as a discernible spot of their own DNA behind, but you are going to love this: They carried in all sorts of random fibers and cans and bottles. The containers each had different DNA and fingerprints. The stuff was thrown all over the crime scenes. The first four crimes cost over twenty thousand dollars to analyze. There were fibers from suits and dresses, underwear, pot holders, a treated sun awning, and several sofa cushions. Hair strands had also been left, but they represented more than thirty individuals and several dogs and cats."

Alyosha was laughing now. He doubled over when Cody added, "The fingerprints and DNA from saliva on bottles came from people who lived all over the place, and every one of them that could be traced belonged to someone who could prove they were hundreds of miles away at the time of the break-in. The best guess from the crime lab was that the suspects bought used clothing and other fabric items at estate sales or flea markets, shredded them to get fibers and hairs, and then carried the evidence in to be planted. The bottles and cans appeared to be from trash barrels, as some had dried food or condiments on them."

Cody was laughing now, too. "While aggravating to the police departments that processed those first four scenes, most cops thought it was insultingly funny of the pair to go to that much trouble."

"We wouldn't go to that much trouble for what is basically a mugging," Alyosha chided. "Money is better spent on more serious crimes."

Cody agreed. "When the subsequent crime scenes were processed, and similar mixes found, a few early evidence collections were still kept but not analyzed, and almost no one bothers to collect fibers anymore. The crime lab supervisors guessed that the suspects had a pretty good laugh about the useless bag of shit they left behind."

Cody looked at the card in the evidence pouch again before he handed it back to Alyosha.

He pointed to it and said, "Then there is always that card. That damned aggravating, ugly clown head with the red nose. No one can figure out what the hell it is."

"Well, it's famous enough even here, Cody. Your American press and now some other countries are making big fun of the police to boost ratings. The suspects have gone viral. When our cops arrived at scene, they saw the card and other famous crimes' trappings. And most were rooting for the vigilantes. They reported it to Chief, and that is when they called your FBI as a courtesy. There wasn't any pressing need for us not to pause until you got here, so we paused as your office requested. Now, do you want to tell me why you made that request?"

Cody shrugged and replied, "My boss's idea. If there was no urgency in processing the scene beyond what your guys had already done, he wanted fresh scene observation for me. He's big on that intuitive cognition stuff. And I'm the sucker who got stuck with coordinating all our domestic cases."

Alyosha put his hand on Cody's shoulder and said with mock sincerity, "You must be honored to have been put in charge of such important, history-changing case."

"Yeah, thrilled," Cody shot back with an equal lack of sincerity. "Maybe if I solve these, they'll put me on something even more important. Maybe interstate parking violators. Fucking pressure from the press."

William had returned by the time Alyosha stopped laughing. The latter finished his smoke, went to his car's back seat, and returned with surgical gloves and paper booties for them all to wear.

Alyosha explained, "For the odd chance the suspects actually tracked something in that is obvious or left a fingerprint this time. More than once has a surgical glove caught on something and torn. It caused me to leave my own fingerprint at one murder scene. Criminals' gloves no better."

As they walked, Cody gave William an inquisitive look. William just shrugged to indicate he had found nothing unusual in his cursory search of the exterior. Based on the US cases, Cody expected this.

* * *

The trio entered the two-story cinder block and stucco housing unit. The computers inside were still running. There were lists of Dark Web identities and passwords in a printer tray. The Russian CSI team had already photographed them, and their cybercrimes division was currently working on following the leads. The team had since been standing by to finish processing the site as soon as the Americans were done. The find was a treasure trove of information about Gleb's scams.

William called for Cody and Alyosha to come upstairs, and he pointed out lurid pictures of young teens in the bedroom.

"That's what Alyosha's name pun was about, partner. Most of the cons he'll be in with won't take kindly to Gleb if they find out about this," he added with a wry chuckle.

Cody and William looked for another twenty minutes while Alyosha watched and made notes as they went. Nothing in the house appeared to have had been disturbed by the intruders other than a bookcase, a cheese grater, a can of cooking grease whose lid was still in the kitchen, and a chef's knife, all of which were next to where Gleb had been found. The MO was pretty much the same as in every other case.

Alyosha commented, "We expect to have days of work ahead. Our technical men are—what is expression—drooling to get back to work. This case is a small fish, but my bosses are eager to catch it because it has eluded the American police for so long."

Cody nodded and shrugged as he admitted, "Bragging rights, eh? I guess you will deserve them if your guys solve this. Well, Alyosha, thanks for holding your guys back until we could get here. They on the way?"

"Da. They be here soon."

"We'll just take one more look around and let them have the place to themselves. William, anything you want them to look at?"

William held up a USB drive and said, "Yeah. I just did a quick peek at the hard drive on his desktop computer with this. There are discreet sectors that look recently scrubbed. Scrubbed hard. Not just erased from the directory but overwritten with random ones and zeros. Alyosha, have your guys see if they can recover anything."

"Sure. I will tell them to look. See what made noises that alerted neighbors?"

"Yeah. Pretty funny," Cody said. "This is a new one! Rather than calling the police themselves this time, our pair of funnymen just tipped that bookcase full of ceramics."

Alyosha nodded his head and pointed to a cord still tied to the top of the bookcase. "Attached to Gleb's feet. Sometime after the suspects left, Gleb moved his feet just enough to send the bookcase crashing to the floor. So much noise next to the shared wall that the neighbors called the cops. My investigative team wants to put it on the Internet. They expect it to go viral."

There was a bit of an outline in the debris where Gleb had been lying. If he was not cut outright by the breaking pottery, Cody thought, he would have had the piss scared out of him by the noise.

Just then, two vans pulled up, and technicians started to bring in evidence collection supplies. Alyosha conferred with two of them, and they nodded back.

Alyosha walked to the FBI agents and confirmed, "My guys say you are good. They look last night, too. Erased blocks that have no new data overwritten but just noise. Same four empty spaces on backup drives. Very suspicious. They do work now."

He slapped Cody on the back as he said with a smile, "Let's get lunch. I know good place. You buy."

"You're on, drook. The two of us are on per diem. You know per diem?"

"Da. 'Gravy train' my brother-in-law calls this about foreign diplomats who eat in his restaurant."

"Yeah, that's it exactly. Heck, we'll even buy for the driver."

"Really? I expect that will make him very happy. He usual eats lunch from bag in car."

The two agents had their driver follow Alyosha to a local restaurant. It was a pleasant but plain-looking storefront with a simple neon sign in both Cyrillic and English that said, "The Old Troika Fine Food." There was a painted logo featuring a three-horse cart, or troika, next to it. It was in a retail block surrounded by the massive apartment blocks that made up most of Moscow's urban housing. The four of them entered, and the owner came to Alyosha with open arms. They gave each other a hug and a kiss on each cheek.

"Fellows, come meet my brother-in-law. Owner of best restaurant in area."

The agents were introduced to Vasily, a slender, mustached man dressed in a snappy brown gabardine suit. He was impressed that two FBI agents were in his establishment with his hotshot cop brother-in-law. He said he would treat them all to lunch until Alyosha explained the per diem in Russian.

"It is not their money, Vasily. If they do not spend it, they do not get it."

"Gravy train?" Vasily replied in English with a smile that indicated the expectation of a fat meal check.

"Da. Government per diem gravy train," Alyosha emphasized.

Cody commented, "Vasily, your accent when speaking English is excellent. There is a bit of a Muscovite accent, but minimal."

"I took a few courses, and I watch a lot of American shows on the Internet," he explained. "English-speaking tour companies stop here. I give them a good deal, and they know I can answer their customer's questions about the food and the surrounding city sights. I have good ratings on TripAdvisor from English-speaking tourists and diplomats. I actually have to put on a bit of an extra accent for the tourists to add a little local color. I've been working on Alyosha here. He knows English, but his accent and grammar are terribly spotty. I have been able to get him to pronounce some words properly, but it's an uphill battle."

Cody laughed and replied, "That explains the way he talks. Keep it up." He turned and addressed Alyosha, "Your English vocabulary is good, but sometimes your accent is like listening to bad shortwave radio, and you keep forgetting to use articles." When Alyosha gave him a curious look, Cody explained, "You know, words like *the* and *a*."

"Da," Alyosha laughed. "Vasily tells me the same thing."

Everyone laughed at Alyosha's emphasis.

Their driver, Sasha, did indeed seem to be glad that he was getting a free lunch. When he spoke, though, it surprised both agents.

"Thank you both. This is most kind. This is far better than the cheese sandwich and tea my wife made for me this morning."

Cody and William were flabbergasted. Sasha might have been from anywhere in the Midwest!

"Where did you learn such good English, Sasha? You speak English better than William here with the remains of his South Boston accent!"

Sasha explained, "I wasn't always an interpreter and driver for the police department. I used to work with diplomats. I was at the consulate in San Francisco for a couple of years. Several other places around the world, too. They made sure I was fluent in English, French, and German, and conversant in a couple of other languages."

"What made you gave that up?"

"My wife and I had a child. Well, two now, actually. We talked about it and decided that it would be better to not be away so much anymore. For most assignments, I couldn't take the family with me. The pay is a little less, but I get to raise my two boys. They see me every day."

"Well, that's a pretty good reason. So, the police use you when they need someone who speaks English?"

"Sure. Driver, interpreter, you know, anything they need."

"Okay, what was with the shy driver act?"

Sasha gave Cody a look, and the agent laughed. William slapped Sasha on the back.

"Got us!" he laughed. "Get the two of us in a car, pretend not to know what we're saying. Yeah. Pretty good. So?" William said with a chuckle.

"You two talked about the case on the way to the house. I could tell you were genuine. You showed respect for the Moscow police and didn't seem condescending at all. I let my supervisor know while you were in the house with the lieutenant. After the lieutenant came to the same conclusion, there was no more point in pretense. He signaled me at the window while you were inside."

Alyosha grinned at the two and ribbed, "Big investigators from America, and you didn't guess?"

"We didn't need to, drook. Nothing to hide. We both want this thing solved as much as you do. When you have nothing to hide, you don't care who is listening. But I have to admit, Sasha here is pretty good at his act."

"Thank you. From the FBI, that is something. Lieutenant, maybe you can say that to my supervisor to get me a raise."

"A lot of good that would do," Alyosha scoffed. "Say, Cody, how long have you been in FBI?"

"About fourteen years now. I was a sergeant with the Lincoln Police Department while getting my master's degree part time. That's up north in the state of Nebraska. When I finally finished it, I applied to the FBI. William was a cop in New Hampshire for a bit before he joined nine years ago. How about you, Alyosha?"

"Twenty-one years in Moscow police. I make lieutenant three years ago. I miss directly working cases. I get this case because lieutenant is rank needed to babysit big-shot FBI agents. Mostly now I do boring paperwork and supervise personnel. I think sometimes I did not become a policeman to approve vacation schedules."

"That is why I never put in for supervisory special agent. Same as you, I prefer straight fieldwork. Why did you take the promotion?"

"No choice. My boss make me take it," Alyosha said with a smile.

"Your captain?" William asked.

"Nyet, captain. Wife. She wants to be Missus Lieutenant and get bigger apartment. Now she rubs noses with Missus Captains and other Missus Lieutenants at parties and has Missus Officers and Missus Sergeants uh ..."

He leaned over and whispered something to Sasha. Sasha laughed and turned to Cody and William.

"He says the other wives have to kiss her ass now. Some of the sergeants he used to work for as an officer now work for him."

The FBI agents laughed, too.

"William here gets the same thing from his wife, Abby. Our current special agent in charge is married to a sweet woman, but some of the past ones were married to snooty wives or husbands. You know snooty? Uh, vysokomernyy."

"Da, da. Many wives of high-ranking officers snooty. Nice to see it is same everywhere."

Cody said, "I have to ask. Your government does not condone what the suspect is doing, or they would not have asked us here to consult. What is the opinion of the rank and file?"

Alyosha leaned over to Sasha and asked in Russian what "rank and file" meant. Sasha answered, and Alyosha laughed.

"What do real cops think? The enemy of my enemy is my friend. Most cops think would be better if victims are being left dead."

Sasha, Cody, and William all laughed.

Food being on his mind, Alyosha hadn't gone back to the briefcase in his car's trunk. He still had the evidence pouch with the card in it. He took it out of his pocket, looked at it again, and passed it to Cody across the checkered tablecloth.

"Is it true you have had so many look at cards? And no one has an idea?"

Cody looked at it with idle curiosity and put the pouch back on the table.

"Not a clue. That screwed-up clown face has everyone baffled."

Alyosha appeared not to understand that last word, and Sasha leaned over to repeat it in Russian. As he did so, he glanced at the card.

"I have been to this place. Why is it in an evidence pouch?"

The three cops looked at Sasha in stunned silence as he picked up the pouch and looked at it closer.

"What do you mean you've been there, Sasha?" Cody finally asked.

"Special Agent Smutters, that is sort of a crude map of Dawhat Al Qatar, I believe. I drove some of our diplomats there once. One of our embassy men drew me a crude map that looked like this, but with the roads drawn, too. Very nice Marriott there. Why? Is this important?"

"My new best drook, what you just said, if it pans out, might just get you part of a twenty-five-thousand-dollar reward if we use it to catch the two who have been committing all these crimes. They leave that card at every crime scene to taunt us. No one realized it is a map of Qatar."

William used his cell phone to access Google Earth, and there it was: The map verified that the card looked like a rough outline of the Qatar Peninsula with a red dot where Dawhat Al Qatar was located. The simplistic way the image on the card was drawn eliminated the jagged coastline. What remained looked like the outline of a clown's face, or maybe the snowman, Olaf, from the Disney movie Frozen. It was open at the bottom, omitting Qatar's southern border and the country's bottom quarter.

"Let's call it in," a mystified Cody mumbled.

Both Alyosha and William were on their cell phones before Cody could get his out, letting their respective departments know what the card meant. Now that they had a map to compare it to, it looked obvious, but the outline had no detail that previously indicated that it was a map. It was only part of the outline of Qatar, anyway. How many people would recognize some random part of the outline of their city or state?

Sasha had been anxiously following the conversation. He put a hand on Cody's arm and asked, "Special Agent Smutters?"

"Sasha, call me Cody. You just earned that."

"Thank you. Uh, is there really a reward?"

"There sure is. Ten thousand if the suspects are positively identified and twenty-five thousand if they are arrested and convicted. Probably something just for this clue. Sworn officers are not eligible, but you're a civilian, right?"

"Yes. I don't have a gun or a badge. I just drive and interpret."

"Well, drook, I think you are going to be eligible. And if it pans out, some of the American tabloids might pay for an interview, too. It really is our first big lead, but just what the hell does Dawhat Al Qatar have to do with someone going after cybercriminals? If this was a couple who were committing cybercrimes, I could see the connection. But stopping them? Not a clue. Anyway, this deserves a toast. Alyosha, have your brother-in-law send over vodka."

When Vasily arrived with well-chilled shots of Stoli, the five of them toasted to their new friendship. Cody chuckled to himself when he later paid the check and saw the top-shelf drinks in the count.

* * *

After lunch, the agents called Washington, DC, again and fully briefed their special agent in charge, or SAC, and their supervisory special agent. They were told to stay two more days if they needed it and work with the Russian tech team. Their SAC told them to promptly report anything new they discovered, as the director would want immediate news. If this amounted to anything, the FBI could take the credit for bringing the clue back to the local jurisdictions in America.

* * *

The four drove to the Moscow Police Department, where the most recent victim, now a suspect himself, had been deposited after having his ass taken care of at the hospital. A broken edge on his phone had nicked him on the way in and on the way out. He hadn't been able to take a dump with the phone in there, and as soon as it was out, he let loose. Apparently, that wasn't a good thing to do, even with minor rectal lacerations. The three of them were almost on the floor with laughter when Sasha read them the medical report. Gleb was on sufficient pain medication to allow him to sit on his sutured rear end, but only on an inflatable donut-shaped pillow.

Cody asked Alyosha to see if he and William could meet with Sasha's supervisor. Alyosha made the call to a nearby part of the building, and a minute later, Andre Lada arrived at Alyosha's office, eager to meet the FBI agents. Cody explained how helpful Sasha had been and asked him if they could have Sasha tag along with them until they departed for the States. When Alyosha added the bit about Sasha finding the clue, Andre called his supervisor. Two hours later, the four of them were in the chief's office getting their picture taken.

This was going to be a big media story. An employee of the Moscow Police Department discovered a clue that had stumped the FBI and many American police departments for over two years. Alyosha had been right. The Moscow police now had the first real nibble from the small fish, and they wanted to gloat. Cody thought about it and came to the conclusion that Sasha's discovery deserved a little gloating. After another call to his SAC, he had permission to pose with the Russian driver who had one-upped the Bureau. The nature of the clue couldn't be revealed at this time, but the picture of the Chief, Alyosha, and the two American FBI agents congratulating Sasha was worth a million rubles.

When they were done getting grip-and-grin pictures with the Chief in his large, ornate office, the Chief asked a question that none of the cops had thought of before.

"Sasha, with stories about these intruders all over the news, why hadn't you seen the card before? It has been on television here many times."

Sasha looked a bit embarrassed as he explained, "My wife watches the news, but when she is doing so, my face is usually buried in a book. I heard about the card but never put my books down to see it on the screen."

Cody admired his new friend, who seemed to live life without much of a care in the world.

* * *

After the Chief's session, the four went to a section of the complex with holding cells and interrogation rooms to pay a visit to Gleb Froylenko, the man with one mighty sore ass.

Cody, William, and Sasha watched through a large one-way mirror as Alyosha questioned Gleb for two straight hours. Despite Alyosha's very effective interrogation skills, Gleb didn't reveal much more than they already knew. The suspects who assaulted Gleb behaved exactly as others had described them. Beyond that, Gleb wouldn't give answers, even to otherwise innocuous questions, as he squirmed uncomfortably on his air-filled seat cushion.

The interrogation room was typical of such rooms throughout the world. The paint was drab, and the floor was a depressing mottled brown that would have looked dirty even after a good mopping. Gleb sat in his jail uniform on a worn metal chair at the far side of a very plain metal table with U-bolts for securing handcuffs, though Gleb's hands were free. Alyosha sometimes sat in a similar chair and occasionally got up to ask questions over Gleb's shoulder. Gleb seemed to be uneasy about Alyosha's constant movement. The greenish-white light from the fluorescent bulbs in the single ceiling fixture made Gleb look even paler than he actually was now, to Cody's amusement. Cody knew the tricks that well-crafted interrogation rooms could play on suspects' minds.

When Alyosha finally asked about files that possibly were scrubbed from Gleb's computer, Gleb looked shocked. Cody translated for William.

"He just read a list of files from one directory. That's when Gleb looked surprised. Alyosha asked him if there should be four more files in that directory. That's when Alyosha gasped and shook his head."

William turned to Cody and offhandedly asked, "Why did the pair in black want us to know about the files anyhow, Cody?"

Cody was confused and asked, "What do you mean 'they wanted us to know'?"

William looked at Cody with surprise, as if everyone should have known what he was talking about. He raised an eyebrow and asked, "You mean you really don't know what the drive looked like when we graphed its contents?"

"No, William. I don't really know, but I would be fascinated if you would tell me," Cody responded, beginning to feel a little foolish at his lack of computer knowledge.

William explained, "Okay. You have a chalkboard full of information. You erase four squares, leaving just the blackboard showing. Anyone who comes along sees four erased areas on an otherwise full board. They know something was erased. If you fill the erased spots with more data, it's harder to see if there was something erased. Normally, when you delete a file, just the pointer to the file gets erased. The data remains until you empty your Recycle Bin. Then the computer allows other data to overwrite the deleted data."

Cody asked, "Where would I get the data to fill the space I erased?"

William shook his head in pity as he replied, "The disk they erased the files from was full of other data. They could have used a program to just keep copying its own files until the disk was full. The four patches would disappear. Figuring out what happened would be harder than finding a needle in a haystack at that point. And they made a point of doing this to Gelb's laptop and backup hard drives, too. Pretty clear message."

Realizing that the cover-up would have been so easy, Cody asked, "Could they have just forgotten to do that or have overlooked that step?"

William thought and then said, "Yeah. Could be they hadn't done this before. Glad they didn't, though. We would have missed this show. I kind of like watching Gleb's tender asshole pucker every time Alyosha asks a question."

Gleb indeed looked terrified every time Alyosha asked him about the four blocks of missing data. He shook his head each time. Even William understood what nyet meant. Alyosha left the interrogation room and joined the other cops in the observation room. He asked Sasha to step outside and then spoke to Cody in Russian.

"Gleb is afraid to reveal something about his computer being recently tampered with. The files were, indeed, not just erased. They were wiped completely clean. Overwritten as in random code. As you say, bleached. Our computer guys tell me that after you erase files, in short order the space they were in looks like swiss cheese with bits of new data. When they are freshly erased, they look to them like white paint on a black wall. Neat blocks of white noise."

Cody nodded as if he had known that all along. He looked at William and translated, "He agrees with you on the computer files that are missing, and this does not happen by accident. So why did our two miscreants bleach files for the first time on this particular computer? No previous files have been erased that we know of, and now this. Gleb is scared shitless to reveal what was in them."

Alyosha asked in English, "How important is it that you learn what was in files?"

"No clue. It could point to our mystery couple, or it could mean nothing. See if you can work Gleb."

"Please not to worry. Gleb will be a special guest here."

Cody, William, and Alyosha moved back to Alyosha's office. It was utilitarian, though Alyosha had pictures of his family on the desk and several marksmanship trophies and other awards on the bookcase and the walls. Cody also noted three framed commendations for bravery from the police department and a picture of Alyosha in the army with a couple of medals in a shadow box. It was nice to see that he rated a window. Unlike most of the patrol lieutenants, who had cubicles or desks in a shared office, Alyosha had this small one to himself. The view was just the central courtyard of the building. With fifty thousand cops in the Moscow police force, even a tiny office would be a prized perk, Cody guessed.

* * *

Two days had now passed, and the most significant finds were still the Qatar map and the four missing files. The latter were utterly unrecoverable, Gleb was still mute on the subject, and his interrogations had tapered off. A behavioral specialist watched him once when Alyosha and two other detectives questioned him. The specialist's opinion had been that something frightened Gleb so much that it would be almost impossible to get him to reveal what was missing short of torture, some kind of deal to hide him, or drugs.

The special agents and detective talked about the situation and decided that the files were probably related to a criminal organization. There were plenty of crime-related files that were recovered from Gleb's computer, but the erased ones had to be something that would result in his death if he let on what they were. Not that he might not get a visit from someone in the night regarding what his computers already revealed if that information ever got out, of course.

The only employee of the Moscow police who significantly benefited from the case during those two days was Sasha. He got two more free lunches from Cody and William and the official commendation from the Chief.

The final decision was that getting Gleb to talk was not worth any more effort. He was already looking at a good percentage of his remaining years behind bars, so maybe sometime down the road, he might want to make a deal. They left it at that.

It was time to leave. The mystery of the card had been solved, but the solution only led to another puzzle. There wouldn't even be enough new information to keep Cody and William busy on the plane a quarter of the way home. Sasha drove Alyosha, Cody, and William to the airport, where Alyosha sped the agents' exit process.

* * *

Back at the Bureau, Cody hosted a videoconference with the agents around the country working the domestic cases. Their respective local police departments were invited to join, and most did, along with Alyosha and his counterparts in the Czech Republic, Pakistan, and India. The victims were in fourteen states and now four foreign countries with the Gleb case. All the attendees were happy that the ugly clown card had finally been identified as a map of Dawhat Al Qatar. Now they had another mystery to solve: Why Qatar?

It was time to contact the CIA. Unfortunately, Langley's answer was that no one there had a clue, either, but they were working on it. Working between jokes about the FBI and their former "clown face" description of the card, that is.

Chapter 3

Alex and Lara—Two Crazy Kids from Cicero in Moscow

Precisely five days and eighteen hours before Cody met Alyosha, two Americans strolled hand in hand down a picturesque boulevard in Moscow. Lara and Alex Cutter were from Cicero, Illinois, and they were in town to do something other than the antique dealing they pursued under their real names. They had just showered and changed after a day of sightseeing and decided to get something to eat. They were taking a week or so to see historical sites, buy some antiques for legitimate export, take in the ballet, and enjoy Moscow's food and culture.

Lara called from the bathroom, "Honey, did you get the plans yet?"

"Yeah. They came in while you were in the shower. And by the way, the dress you bought today is stunning. You look fantastic in dark green. It accents your lovely eyes."

Compared to Alex's six-foot, muscular build, Lara was a trim, athletic five-foot-seven, with strawberry blonde hair and hazel-green eyes. His sandy hair and blue eyes adorned an oval face, while Lara had a more heart-shaped face.

"Thanks. We'll hit a club after dinner, and you can feel me up in it while we dance."

"Deal. We can go over the plans at dinner. Downloaded 'em to your tablet."

"That's so sweet. Borsht and bloodletting. You're so romantic."

"That's me. Remember when we had dinner in that restaurant in New Orleans while we were waiting for Billy G to show up? You wanted to do him so bad because of what he did to your friend's cousin. We'd just finished our entrées when he came in. You left to take him out on his way to the bathroom."

"Oh, that was fun. I came on to him in the hallway to the restrooms and got him to follow me out to the back. He was such a perv. He was, what, sixty? Hell, I was well less than half his age. So I capped him with that cute suppressed Sig twenty-two you gave me for my birthday that year—I love the rainbow titanium finish so much—and I stuffed him in a dumpster under some other garbage. Those subsonic twenty-twos were actually silenced, but I had to manually work the slide to pump the second and third shots into his ugly melon. No one heard a thing. When I returned, you had bananas Foster, and a single red rose waiting for me. Swept me off may feet once again!"

"I knew you'd want to celebrate. That made ten for you. Milestone. I wanted the evening to be all about you."

"And I loved it. Oh! And do you remember when the call girl he hired came into the restaurant while we were still eating dessert and the staff couldn't find him? She was so pissed! Made everyone know that he was such an asshole for calling her service and then stiffing her. God, was that funny or what?"

"Well, she probably felt a little better two days later when the Dumpster service emptied the container, and he came tumbling out," Alex replied.

If there was one constant in their lives it was that they loved to reminisce about their past assignments. Laughing, they left their room and headed for the lobby, where the concierge called a cab for them.

* * *

After a short cab ride, they were seated at the restaurant Alex had picked. After they ordered and the waiter was gone, Lara pulled out her tablet and studied the plans. She frowned.

"This is a better security setup than I would expect for a lowlife scammer such as Gleb. That's a red flag. After dinner, let's make a call to Siggy. I smell a next-level connection involving poor Mr. Froylenko."

Sigmund "Siggy" Fressman was their primary contact in the Lenetti family. Papa Paul Lenetti used this Jewish business associate to oversee the legitimate businesses that now almost wholly represented the Lenetti family's wealth. Hidden deep within Siggy's organization was the specialized department that kept Alex and Lara supplied with bullets, rental cars and frequent-flyer miles. Alex and Lara could never be traditionally made members of the Lenetti criminal organization because neither was Italian. They were prized associates of the Siggy-run organization for two reasons, though. The first was that they were good. Really good. The second was that they had saved Pappa Paul's life and those of his wife and grandchildren.¶

Chapter 4

How to Turn Your Hobby into a Career

A decade and a half before sitting in the Moscow restaurant, Alex and Lara met during high school in Savannah, Georgia. They both were taking karate at the same dojo when they fell in love. It wasn't just a physical attraction, either. They both had a fascination with movies about hitmen, and they played the game of squirt-gun assassin with friends from school. The competition involved stalking and "hitting" a single victim or opposing team member with a squirt gun or sometimes a Nerf gun. They would talk about the hitman trade endlessly, comparing actual historical hits to one another.

Between assassin matches, the two played first-person shooter games online. Their strategy was never to rack up the most eliminations, but to hide, snipe, and outflank. The total score wasn't their objective. Practice in outwitting others was the goal. They played under many gamer names, and they developed a personality for each identity. One of their favorite tactics was to bait an opponent by intentionally having Alex's avatar walk into a cul-de-sac with only one kill-shot vantage point. At the same time, Lara covered that vantage point with a sniper weapon.

Their favorite movies were those like Léon: The Professional, Hitman, Sniper, and The Mechanic. Of course, when they were in the mood for a laugh, they couldn't watch Grosse Pointe Blank enough times. They absolutely loved John Wick but laughed at the multitude of gaffes in the plot.

* * *

Their families were getting a bit annoyed with their obsession by the time they were seniors. To resolve the issue, they both decided to go to college out of state. Away from watchful parents, they could enjoy their hobby to the fullest. Both were accepted at the University of Illinois at Urbana-Champaign, where Lara took computer science and Alex studied electrical engineering. They found an assassin club on campus and soon earned a reputation as formidable opponents.

In college, they both continued their martial arts training, taking a few interdisciplinary classes, too. They learned knife throwing and archery, though they were only fair with the latter unless it was with a scoped crossbow. They loved to go to the range, and they both became experts with both handguns and rifles.

They joined a fish and game club that hosted target and quick-draw competitions. Lara decided they could save money by reloading their empty cartridge cases. They bought a press they found on sale at Bass Pro one weekend. It allowed them to make new cartridges out of the spent brass by adding fresh powder, primers, and bullets. She soon became an expert at manufacturing extreme-accuracy loads, low-noise subsonic rounds, and other specialty ammunition. Lara was fascinated by the books, online data, and variety of components and equipment available, and she spent many enjoyable hours perfecting her new hobby.

One thing led to another with their hitman obsession, and they started to role-play their hobby outside the assassin club. Unlike the assigned-victim squirt-gun game, this really crossed the line. They would plan and execute mock hits, first on fellow classmates of their own choosing and then on well-known people around town. Instead of a squirt gun or Nerf gun, they used a camera to record their "hits." They went so far as to actually stalk their victims, including breaking into places where their hit was planned. They snuck into homes and businesses undetected, and by the time they graduated college, they had become experts at defeating security systems and lock picking.

They also learned about crime scene processing and how to avoid leaving clues and traces. They decided to leave false trails, including fibers and objects with random people's fingerprints and saliva. They often picked up freshly discarded beer and soda cans when out of town, though they never actually left anything behind that a "victim" would recognize as out of place. They planted micro evidence but only photographed the larger items, such as beer cans, before removing them at their exit. They looked at the photos later and laughed about some guy in a town fifty miles away being questioned by the police after the prints would be found.

After graduation, they found work in the southern suburbs of Chicago. They both had nine- to-five jobs in their respective degree fields with reasonably good pay. That gave them the time and money to continue their hobby to its fullest.

Alex actually proposed to Lara at a lakeside mansion where they had just executed a hit. It was on a stockbroker who was swimming in his pool at the time. They had just taken the photo of their victim from a dark alcove when Alex got on one knee and pulled out the ring. Without a sound, Lara nodded her head and kissed him. Later, when their parents asked where he had proposed, they just said it was while enjoying a romantic view of Lake Michigan.

They traveled back home to Savannah for their wedding and were married at a family friend's summer beach home on Tybee Island. Both sets of parents and most of the guests were disappointed that the couple intended to settle up north permanently. They understood that four years of college and a year's employment there regrettably had gotten them attached to the Windy City.

* * *

They continued their hobby after their wedding but changed the focus to match their developing personal sense of justice. They started to concentrate on the lowlifes they read about in the papers. They decided that if they ever actually became real hitmen, those were the people who would be more likely to be their targets, and those targets deserved it in Alex and Lara's personal philosophy. Their surveillance of their victims led to ever-increasing revulsion toward those people. Without law enforcement's constraints of warrants and constitutional rights, they were able to uncover the most unspeakable sins of their subjects. Hacking computers, planting bugs, and hiding video cameras became second nature in this obsession. The more they discovered, the more their hatred of the worst ones grew.

The palpable danger of stalking dangerous people fed their passion for their invented sport. The threat made them even more careful, and they concocted elaborate schemes to carry out their quests. Far more intricate, in fact, than prudence required.

* * *

One day they cracked the security system of a well-known thief in Tinley Park, a town twenty minutes east of where they lived. The thief's name was Stanislav "Packy" Shipkowski, and they were going to plan and execute one of their mock hits on him. They decided to gather information in his home, so they broke in and planted two bugs to start recording his plans and movements for a couple of weeks. They connected the bugs to an unsecured home network in the neighborhood. Now they could listen to them on a computer at their house that was continuously recording. To their surprise, they learned that their mark was planning a hit himself on a well-known Chicago figure, Papa Paul Lenetti.

* * *

Papa Paul was the head of a once-major crime family, though now involved mainly in after-hours gambling joints. Gambling might not be as lucrative as other criminal activities the Lenetti family had run in the past, but it was far less risky than those other enterprises. Most of those had been passed on to former capos who now ran their own families. All of the Lenetti income came from legitimate businesses and investments these days, with the exception of that last sliver of the old shady operations and the specialized enterprise Siggy oversaw. That arm of Papa Paul's organization was so far outside the old Lenetti operations that the feds and even most of his old capos didn't have a clue about them. Siggy kept the Lenettis insulated from exposure to everything but the after-hours establishments. And the fix was pretty much in for those. Papa Paul found the gambling business too entertaining to let go of yet.

For no apparent reason other than an old grudge, a far more violent Eastern European gang involved in gambling, prostitution, drugs, and union racketeering wanted the otherwise insignificant gambling controlled by the Lenettis. They were behind the hit on Papa Paul. Because he was getting his family out of the rackets, the other mob saw him as weak, and its leader hated Papa Paul.

* * *

At the computer in the gun and equipment room concealed in their basement, Alex and Lara listened as Packy and two associates planned the hit. They were going to break in during the wee hours of the morning in five days and murder Papa Paul, his wife, and two grandchildren who would be sleeping at Papa's house while their parents were in Paris.

Lara turned to Alex in horror and said, "Honey, we can't let Packy kill those two little kids."

"So what do we do? Turn our tapes over to Papa Paul? We could make some real dough out of this."

The horror turned to something else in Lara's eyes as she thought for a moment. "Alex, we can get a lot more out of this than money."

Alex saw that Lara was breathing hard. "What else can we—?" he began.

"Alex, we can do what we've only dreamed of," she blurted out. "Don't tell me you actually want to spend the rest of your life as an electrical engineer. I would rather use my computer science degree for something other than a life in a cubicle. Cracking alarm systems and hacking marks' computers, for instance. Tell me you don't secretly want it for real."

Alex's pulse was pounding now, too. The love of his life actually wanted to go through with something they had fantasized about for eight years!

He was out of control. They grabbed each other and ripped off their clothes. He carried her upstairs to the bedroom, where they had the most intense, adrenaline-fueled sex they had ever experienced. Even the sex they had after their first mock hit wasn't close.

As they lay there in the glow of that beautiful passion, Alex turned to Lara. He propped himself up on one elbow. "What do you want to do?" he asked.

"Well, if we tell Papa Paul, I'm sure we'll be rewarded somehow, but if we do something more … involved, well, I think that might act as a better résumé."

Alex was breathing harder again. "You want us to actually take out Packy and his accomplices, don't you?"

"Yeah. I want Papa Paul to wake up and find all three dead and us standing over them. I want him to hire us."

"I love it. And I love you, honey. Yes. I'm in!" Alex exclaimed, sealing it with a kiss.

They only had five days to plan. Fortunately, their bug caught Packy and his friends talking their way through the security system at Papa Paul's house. Alex actually found a flaw in their plans to disable the security system, and he made notes to correct it for their own entry.

Their plan was to wait inside Papa Paul's house. It hinged entirely on their killing Packy and his team without being discovered beforehand. If they were caught before Packy got there, they would likely be dead before they could explain anything.

* * *

Two days before Packy's hit, Alex and Lara made a dry run to the planned entry point. As Packy indicated in one of the bugged conversations, there were no security personnel at the house. The alarm system and CCTV cameras appeared to be the only security.

Lara surmised, "Since the Lenettis are pretty much out of the rackets, I guess they no longer think it's necessary to have their guys physically on duty at the house."

"Yeah, the Roberson hit we planned in May had two goons to take care of before we could get in the house. We had to quit after we took the pictures of the bodyguards. This may be one of the reasons the Hungarians think he's weak."

* * *

Back in their basement gun room, Lara and Alex needed to decide what kind of weapons they would use. They agreed on Sig Sauer Mosquito .22-caliber semiauto pistols with the pair of homemade suppressors Lara had read about and constructed months ago. With subsonic bullets and the suppressors made from truck fuel filters, the sound of the slides cycling on their pistols made more noise than the discharge.

As an experiment, they bought the relatively inexpensive pistols with threaded barrels. They had the filter adapters made at a local machine shop. Lara had experimented with Quiet-22s from an ammo company called CCI. The subsonic rounds barely made a sound from a rifle, but from an unsuppressed pistol, they were about the level of a loud handclap. The suppressor made them whisper quiet. As the packaging noted, though, they would not operate the action of a factory semiauto weapon. Because of that, Lara modified the springs and reduced the mass of the pistols' slides with relief cuts for fairly reliable functioning.

They both agreed that nine-millimeter pistols carried in quick-draw holsters would be their backup weapons in case the little low-velocity .22s didn't do the job on Packy's crew or the Mosquitos jammed because of the unorthodox modifications. Lara's amateur gunsmithing involved a lot of trial and error to get it right, and there were still occasional malfunctions.

The fact that each gun/adapter/filter combination constituted a federal felony didn't seem to faze either of them, as their breaking-and-entry and hacking activities to date probably added up to a couple of hundred years apiece in prison if they'd been caught. And so far, they had risked all of that for mere fun.

For quick hits on three or four people at close range, these seemed like the ideal weapons. "Like shooting rapid-fire at steel plates at the range," Lara quipped with a grin. "They'll be dead before they hear the noise if all goes well. If not, the nines will do the job, but the noise will leave us in the hallway with our pants down."

"I'd rather chance it with that than risk having a jammed gun while facing down Packy and his goons," Alex replied coldly. "I'd rather deal with a startled Papa Paul and his wife than a murderous, wounded Packy."

* * *

On the night of the hit, they broke into Papa Paul's house by disabling the alarm from the outside keypad in the garage. Their plan was working perfectly. They put the alarm system into its daytime mode so that Packy's incorrect procedure wouldn't set it off when he got there. They went to Papa Paul's office and ensured that the closed-circuit TV cameras were recording correctly. This would give them video evidence to back up their story if they needed to convince Papa Paul. Then they went to their observation point and waited.

Papa Paul's house was a large but not overly pretentious home in the suburbs. He lived in a Federal-style two-story with an attached garage and a stone wall with an electric gate. All the bedrooms were upstairs. The couple knew the complete house layout from Packy's description. They anticipated that the grandkids would be in the bedroom at the end of the hall away from the master bedroom, as that guest room had its own en suite bathroom.

At 2:34 a.m., they were rewarded. They heard the faint sound of Packy and his two accomplices coming into the house through the garage, as expected.

Alex whispered to Lara, "They must have thought Papa Paul was getting senile for not setting the night mode on the alarm."

Alex and Lara were in the guest bathroom between the girls' bedroom and the master bedroom. The door was cracked open, and the night-light in the hallway was bright enough to let Alex and Lara see what was happening. They had their pistols loaded and ready. The thugs, all dressed in jeans, sneakers and, and black hoodies, went toward the master bedroom door but stopped midway. The one leading the way, Packy, motioned to one of his confederates to go to the far guest bedroom.

Alex and Lara heard Packy whisper, "Remember, Buzz and I go into Paul's room. We turn on the lights and cover him and his wife. When you see the lights go on, open the kids' door. We let Paul and Lucy hear you shoot their grandkids. Then we give it to them, too. On the way out, Lester grabs the security camera hard drive from the old man's office. It's in that metal cabinet. Code for the door is six-three-five-four."

When Lester passed the guest bath, Alex stepped out behind him in stocking feet and pointed his pistol at Lester's head. Lara stepped out behind Alex and silently walked toward Packy and Buzz. The door to the master bedroom opened, and Packy reached for the light switch.

Before Packy touched the switch, Alex fired twice into the back of Lester's head where it met the spine, and Lester dropped like a sack of potatoes. There wasn't a lot of noise, but enough to make Packy turn around. Lara's pistol was aimed upward, directly at the taller Packy's startled face, and she pulled off two quick shots, the first in his left eye. This was followed by two more to Buzz as he started to turn, too. The first was with Lara's muzzle almost touching his right ear.

Papa Paul was awake and reaching for the nightstand. Lara threw her gun down and raised her hands as the nightstand light came on.

"Don't shoot! You're safe now. Don't shoot."

Papa Paul had a revolver pointed at her, and she knew that it might be the last thing she ever saw. Her heart was racing from the adrenaline rush. She loved it!

"Don't shoot. These guys were here to kill you." She added, "I stopped them."

Papa Paul looked at her with a furious expression. Lara didn't know if his rage was going to overcome his intellect, but they had decided to take the risk when they planned this.

"You better start talking. One move, and you're dead," Papa Paul shouted.

"My husband just killed the man who was going to kill your granddaughters. He's in the hallway, and he will come in with his hands raised when you tell him to," Lara replied, breathing hard as she spoke.

By now, Paul's wife Lucy had a Glock .40-caliber semiauto handgun aimed at Lara.

Papa Paul motioned to Lara and ordered, "Go sit in that chair with your hands behind your head."

Lara sat.

"Call your husband," Papa Paul said, now behind Lara with his revolver barrel touching her skull.

Lara called out, "Alex, you can come in now with your arms raised."

Lucy, still dressed in a mauve cotton nightgown, was waiting behind the door, and as Alex came in, she put her pistol to his neck.

Her dark eyes seemed to be evaluating the situation for a second before she turned and spoke to Lara, "Okay, sister, you better explain what the fuck just happened."

"In Alex's breast pocket is a recorder. Play it."

Lucy reached into the pocket and retrieved his digital recorder. She turned it on. It was cued to the part of the recording where Packy was briefing Buzz and Lester.

"... the boss wants them dead yesterday, and he wants to send the message loud and clear. So we do it next Wednesday. His son is leaving his grandkids with him to babysit when they go to Paris. We hit the old man, his wife, and their grandkids. The boss wants them awake to hear you ice the kiddies, Lester. We let them know what you did, and then Buzz and I put two in their brains."

Lucy turned off the recorder. There was ice in her voice as she put her gun in Alex's ear and hissed, "Who the fuck are you two?"

Papa Paul lowered his gun as he said, "Calm down, dear. I think it's pretty clear that these two kids just saved the two of us along with Maria and Theresa. You, uh, Alex? Go sit in that other chair while I call Petie."

Papa Paul made the call for Peter "Petie" Tagliani and a crew to come over and clean up the mess. He checked to see that the girls hadn't been awakened and then returned to the bedroom. He turned to Alex.

"So, talk."

Alex and Lara briefly explained their hobby. They explained the events that led from the recording made from the bug in Packy's house to where they were now sitting.

Fifteen minutes later, Papa Paul admitted, "I'm impressed. Lucy, that is some tale! These two plan things for fun better than my guys do for real. So, you two, why the events tonight if you only play at this?"

Lara spoke for the two of them: "We decided when we heard that they were going to kill your grandkids that they had to be stopped."

Papa Paul laughed and shook his head. "The two of us being whacked would have been okay, but not the grandkids, eh? Okay, maybe. But you could have stopped them with a phone call. Why are you here?"

Alex replied, his voice tense and cracked, "We ... we decided that this could be our audition."

Lucy looked at Papa Paul in disbelief and said, "Papa, I think these two want a job."

Papa Paul laughed again. "Well, isn't this the damnedest thing you ever heard? You two ain't ever been in the life, and now you just want jobs killing people for me?"

"Well, uh, yeah," Lara replied.

"This I gotta think about," Papa Paul mused. "Lucy, this has gotta be the weirdest fuckin' night I've ever had."

* * *

Shortly after that, Petie arrived, and his crew began working quickly and quietly so as not to wake the girls. Papa Paul and Lucy put on robes and ushered Alex and Lara downstairs to the ornately decorated dining room. They talked over some wine at the dinner table. Alex looked at the furniture and guessed that it was at least a couple of centuries old. His hands were still shaking, but he was careful not to spill any wine on the table.

This was the first time Alex and Lara were calm enough to closely observe their hosts. Papa Paul, at fifty-six, was even more dashing than he appeared to be in the photos they saw when planning. Square-jawed with a thin mustache, he looked like a boardroom executive, even in a robe and pajamas. He was a few inches taller than his five-six wife.

Lucy was just a tad plump, but not fat by any means. Her black hair was matted a bit from just having been awakened, but it looked like it would be a stylish coiffure when brushed and hair sprayed. While Papa Paul had put his revolver away, Lucy was still carrying her pistol. She was holding it with the familiar ease of someone who viewed it as a part of her everyday life, not as an emergency tool that was handled infrequently.

Lara wondered if she had been involved in the active side of the family, not merely the housewife of a mob boss.

Alex and Lara explained everything in great detail. After almost an hour, Papa Paul was convinced that they were on the up-and-up.

He leveled with them: "You two killed three guys in my house, and you knew the hallway where you did it was on camera. You didn't turn off the recorder, even though you knew where it is and knew how to do it. You could have killed both of us, but Lara here dropped her gun as soon as she capped Packy and that other moron. You apparently don't mind me having the recording; in fact, you intended it to be your audition video. I have to say I believe you if for no other reason than that the enemy of my enemy is my friend."

Lara let out her breath and took Alex's hand. He met her gaze and smiled before turning back to Papa Paul and Lucy and asking, "So how did we do?"

"Pretty good. But with fair hair and blue eyes, my guess is that you two aren't Italian."

"No, I'm mostly English and Belgian, and she's mostly French and German with a little Irish."

Alex took a leap of faith. He gave Papa Paul their real names, adding, "Mr. Lenetti, Lara and Alex Cutter are aliases we have used in the past. We would prefer that we only be known in the Lenetti family as Lara and Alex Cutter. One extra level of security for all of us, if that is okay."

"Sure. We have a number of associates known only by aliases. But if I brought you on, you two would be the only ones at your level who could never be made. Could be a problem."

"Oh, dear, they just saved our lives. And more importantly, they just saved the girls! You can just give them to Siggy rather than Angelo if they really want in." Turning to Alex and Lara, she asked, "Do you two need any time to think this over?"

"Mrs. Lenetti, we don't need to think it over. Alex and I have talked about little else this past week. We made our decision before we disabled your alarm."

"That brings up another question. How did you accomplish that?" Papa Paul asked.

Alex played another part of the taped conversation from his bug. When Buzz asked where the alarm information came from, Packy said he had someone inside Papa Paul's organization.

They heard Packy explain, "The kid runs errands, and he gave me the name and model number of the alarm system, where the sensors are located, and what the codes are."

Alex stopped the tape for a second to explain, "He described the codes later, but he actually mixed up the away and daytime code sequences. We simply put it into the daytime mode for when they arrived. Lara is a computer whiz, and I'm an electrical engineer, so we could easily have defeated it ourselves. But they gave it to us on a silver platter."

Packy's taped voice continued when Alex pushed the play button again: "He also gave me the video system details and where the server is that records it, along with the location of the upstairs bedrooms. When he's sent out for food, he gets extra and sits to eat with Paulie's crew that maintains the system. And you wouldn't believe who convinced the fucking mook to betray Papa Paul."

"Dominic! How could Angelo's nephew betray us like that?" Lucy said between clenched teeth.

"Money," Lara answered. "He did it for a lot of money."

"Well, he can spend it on his funeral," Lucy said with ice in her voice. "Did they ever say who got to Dominic?"

Alex replied, "No, he never gave the name in the range of our bugs or on the phone."

Papa Paul was furious. He took a big gulp of wine to calm down.

"I'm going to call in Angelo. He's going to have to clean up the mess he brought to me."

"Uh, excuse me, Mr. Lenetti. That's what Alex and I ... well, we're here because, uh, of that sort of thing."

Lucy laughed and said, "Dear, I think what this young lady is trying to say is that they would like to close our little loophole."

Papa Paul replied, "You are probably right, Lucy, but I have to offer it to Angelo to clean up his own mess. If he wants to use these homicidal lovebirds, that's his option."

Lucy got up from the table, placed her pistol on a sideboard, and walked around to Alex and Lara. They stood as she approached. Neither knew what to expect and were amazed when Lucy hugged Lara. When she broke the embrace, she had tears in her eyes.

"The two of you saved Maria and Theresa tonight. The two of us will always be in your debt."

She gave Alex a hug, too.

Papa Paul stood and shook their hands. He said, "Lucy is right. With almost none of our activity left on the shady side, we figured that no one would think they needed to come after us anymore. We let our guard down enough that a traitor like Dominic could be used to get to us. Your little enterprise saved both of us plus the kids. Come back this morning at eleven. Go home and get some sleep."

* * *

With that, Alex and Lara headed home. As excited as they were, though, sex that night was out when they got home. They were physically and emotionally exhausted. They were asleep as soon as their heads hit their pillows.

Chapter 5

In Part Two of the Audition, Dominic Has a Horrible Day

Hoping that their new adventure would require their full attention after the Packy elimination, they secured a few personal days off from their respective employers. They arrived at Papa Paul's before ten, but Papa Paul had them wait in a room to the side of the main entrance. They were apparently meant to overhear Papa Paul as he explained the events of the previous night to Angelo. Angelo Caparelli was a former Lenetti capo who had been given permission to form his own family and take over some of the cast-off Lenetti rackets

Shortly after they arrived, Alex and Lara heard a car pull up outside the window of their room. A late-model silver Mercury Grand Marquis pulled to a stop. The driver ran to the rear passenger door and opened it. An older man in a gray suit, snap-brim fedora, and brush mustache got out and walked briskly to the house.

Alex turned to Lara and said, "That must be Angelo."

After Papa Paul greeted Angelo in the next room, Alex and Lara heard Papa Paul explain to Angelo what had happened the night before.

Angelo was furious. "My sister's own kid!" he ranted. "It must be that good-for-nothing rat bastard Natalie married after Dominic's real father died. He didn't give Dominic no moral upbringing! Family! He got no loyalty to family, and especially 'cause I been giving them money for years and I gave that rat bastard Dominic a job. Papa Paul, I'm so glad you weren't hurt. You said someone stopped Packy? Who was it? I want to thank them and maybe give them something like a car or money or something."

Lucy, who had been waiting with Alex and Lara, brought them in and introduced them to Angelo. "This is Lara, and this is Alex. They are the two who saved us."

A smile appeared on Angelo's slightly pudgy face. He hugged them both and said, "You two saved my life, too. Hey, I wanna do sumthin' for you. What kind of car you like? I can get you whatever you want for lettin' Papa Paul know what Packy was up to."

"Angelo?" Papa Paul interjected.

"Yes, Papa Paul?"

"They want you to let them do something for us all as their reward. They didn't just warn us. These two actually did Packy and his crew."

"No shit? These two kids?"

Papa Paul assured him, "Yes, these two youngsters did it, and they want to help again."

"Huh?" Angelo grunted. "I don't get it."

"You agree that Dominic has to go, right?" Papa Paul asked.

"Yeah. No question, Papa Paul. Nephew or not, he crossed the line. And I need to find out for sure if his fuck-up stepfather put him up to it."

"Well, how would you like a way to accomplish that unpleasantness without your sister being able to connect it back to the family?" Papa Paul asked.

"Well, sure, Papa Paul. So?"

"These two have offered to take care of everything for us," Lucy explained.

"No shit? You two could do this thing? I mean for money? I'd pay ya."

Without hesitation, Alex replied, "Yes. And we can make it look like whatever you want."

Angelo thought for a second and smiled, suggesting, "Can you make it look like Packy turned on him? Make it look like his stepfather, Bruno, set him up for the hit, and Packy's people did it? My sister will divorce him, and we can take care of him later after things simmer down. Or maybe she'll just want me to hit the mook."

Lara looked at Alex, then back at Angelo. She said, "Mr. Caparelli, we have been planning this sort of thing for the last eight years. We could make it look like the mayor did it if you want."

"If you can get a plan together by tomorrow that satisfies me and Papa Paul, you got it. We got to act before Packy gets missed."

"Then do it," Papa Paul said as he held out his hand to Angelo. Angelo kissed it.

Papa Paul held out the hand to Alex and Lara, who took the cue and kissed it too. Both of them knew that they had just crossed a line more severe than the previous night's killings.

* * *

Lara and Alex followed Angelo to his home. They quickly got down to business in his office, a room decorated in a somewhat heavy-handed Mediterranean style with a lot of dark wood accents and a thick red and black carpet. It had a small conference table where Lara and Alex set up shop after Angelo provided the Wi-Fi password for Lara's laptop.

She laughed when she heard the password, "Angelina82," and said, "Angelo, please change it. Your daughter's name and birth year are too easy to guess."

Angelo started to ask how she knew it was his daughter's name but caught himself and blushed. "Yeah. Okay," was all he replied. It was obvious that Alex and Lara had done their homework.

Two of Petie's crew, Rocco and Tony, arrived to help plan the operation. Angelo and the two worked with Lara and Alex over the next sixteen hours. Angelo and his guys were shocked at the speed Lara hacked into Bruno's email account and created emails between Bruno and Packy. They indicated that Bruno would take care of Dominic for Packy to tie up that last loose end after Papa Paul was out of the way. After all, "Dominic ain't my real kid," one of the emails noted.

A lot of other incriminating evidence was created in addition to that. Angelo was genuinely impressed that they could deposit money into Bruno's checking account from an anonymous Bitcoin wallet. These were things that Angelo's sister, Natalie, could be shown if needed.

When Angelo asked if they needed to call work to get another day off, he laughed when Alex replied, "We told our respective managers that we had someone terminal to take care of for a few days for a family member. We have the rest of the week."

* * *

The following day, Alex and Lara were with Angelo when he called Dominic and instructed him, "I need you to meet two of our Los Angeles friends' couriers to fetch some important documents. It's hush-hush, so the pickup is in a secluded spot. We don't want any unnecessary eyes on this deal."

Lara and Alex, posing as the couriers, met him at a lonely spot in a local park. The couple had parked their car on a utility access adjacent to the park, not in the park's lot.

They saw a lanky young man in a green windbreaker, striped polo shirt and, chinos leaning against a nearby tree. From the photos Angelo had shown them, this was Dominic. His demeanor as they approached was indifferent as if he were bigshot in the organization, not an errand boy.

Dominic introduced himself casually as if nothing was amiss. Alex saw this as evidence that Dominic had been given information about the hit on Papa Paul, but not the date. Dominic appeared to be unaware that anything had happened to Packy.

Lara reached into her briefcase, but instead of documents, she pulled out the stone-cold Sig Sauer P220 pistol with a suppressor that Angelo had thoughtfully provided.

"Dominic, the documents you were sent here for today may be an airline ticket out of here, your hospital admission forms, or your death certificate. Your choice. March!"

The bewildered Dominic was walked to their car. Alex drove them to a shuttered furniture factory that one of Papa Paul's corporations bought years earlier with the intent of tearing it down and building condos.

* * *

They walked Dominic to what had probably been a foreman's office, a space with no ceiling on the main factory floor, where he was deposited onto a dusty metal swivel chair. Lara closed the door and stood in front of it with her pistol trained on Dominic.

In the dingy light of the long-unwashed skylights high above them, Alex calmly announced, "Dominic, we're going to have a little clarification session. Who goaded you into contacting one sleazeball named Packy?"

Dominic looked like he had just been given an ice-water enema as he insisted, "I don't know anyone named Packy. What are you talking about? Do you know who I am? I'm Angelo's nephew. Do anything to me, and you'll be dog food by tomorrow."

Alex pulled out a little Sig Sauer P938-22, also untraceable and provided by Angelo. He made a point of slowly screwing on the suppressor in front of Dominic, though it was just for effect. It was a meme from the movies intended to convey impending doom. It appeared to be having the desired effect, as Dominic held his breath during that ominous procedure.

In all reality, Alex or Lara could have used Dirty Harry's forty-four Magnum, and there would not have been anyone within earshot of that office to hear it. Rocco had assured them that the building would be cleared of any possible transients, though most of the homeless in the area already knew not to squat on mob property. Word traveled quickly among them about what happened to the few who tried in the past.

As Dominic's widening eyes were fixed on the silencer, Alex explained, "Dominic, Angelo sent us. My lovely wife is holding a nine-millimeter loaded with hollow-point ammo. A shot to your head will kill you instantly. A shot to your stomach will take a while, and it will be painful. On the other hand, this is a twenty-two. I can shoot arms and legs, feet and hands all day, and you won't die. Now listen to this."

Lara played the recording of Packy talking about Dominic delivering alarm specifications to him.

"Now, for the record—and please be honest here—was it your stepfather, Bruno, who told you to see Packy?"

"I never ..."

The first shot hit Dominic's left foot, and he tumbled forward to the concrete floor in agony. The next shot hit his right forearm. He looked at Alex in horror and held out his left hand in a defensive posture. He was shaking his head in panic.

"Dominic, you have two options. You set up Papa Paul, Lucy, and their grandkids for a hit. Your options are having either my wife or me killing you and whether she gives it to you in the head or stomach. Do you understand these options?"

Dominic whimpered, "What about the plane ticket thing? Wait! Don't kill me. Please."

Alex aimed his pistol at Dominic's left foot, replying, "Well, maybe they'll let you live if you give everyone up. But seriously, I can use the target practice, so please deny everything one more time."

Dominic covered his injured foot instinctively and pleaded, "No! Wait … wait … I can tell you who in Packy's mob wanted Papa Paul out of the way. It's … it's Mickey. Yeah … uh … it was Mickey. Send me away. I'll disappear. I'll never come back."

"Sweetheart, he's going for Door Number Three. Dominic, there is no Door Number Three," Alex said as he pumped two more shots into Dominic's left foot. Dominic hesitated, so two more bullets hit the same now-pulpy spot. Dominic grimaced in agony, unable to speak.

"You're going away, all right, but not on a plane. One last time before I start on the gonads. Was your stepfather involved? Yes or no?"

"Y-y-yes. He g-g-got me to do it!"

Lara gave Dominic a shot of morphine, applied a local anesthetic on the wound sites, and tied on tourniquets. Clot packs stopped the bleeding. They waited until Dominic was stable enough to sit back up in the chair in relative comfort.

Lara set up a video camera as Alex explained, "You are going to look into the camera and say exactly what happened and who you spoke with."

Dominic began, slowly at first: "Bruno promised me that the other mob would pay me a ton of money. He said they were going to make me more than a fucking errand boy, too. They gave me five large as a taste of what was to come."

He began to speak at his usual pace as he continued, "Bruno arranged the meets with Packy. Packy told Bruno exactly what he wanted me to observe about the security camera and alarm systems, and he said to note what Papa Paul's schedule was and what their plans were."

After Dominic's confession, Lara gave him another shock. Turning off the camera, she said, "Thanks, Dominic. All that bullshit about Angelo sending us was just that. Mickey sent us."

She turned the camera on again.

All this was digitally recorded in full 1080i with Alex and Lara carefully standing behind the camera during the confession. Lara would run their voices through voice-changer software during the planned edit, and Alex was careful to zoom in on Dominic so that only Lara's gloved hands would show when she touched him. Any hint of their identities would be edited out, and they intended to shred the original, unedited SSD card.

"WHAT! I don't ... who ...?" Dominic sputtered at Lara's last statement.

"Well, Mickey and Bruno. He said that you were a liability and would rat at the slightest pressure," Alex said. "He was right. A few lousy twenty-twos to the foot and one to the arm, and you sang like a canary. Just like Bruno said you would. He said that if you were his real son, you would take it like a man and be a stand-up guy, but if you folded like a cheap suit, then we should kill you."

"That asshole stepfather of mine set me up to be killed? After he used me to get the goods on Papa Paul for Packy? I'll kill that son of a bitch! How the fuck can he have his own stepson killed? Wait! You're passing up a fortune! Call Angelo. He'll pay you more than Mickey or Bruno. I swear!"

The next sound was the report of Lara's pistol and the thud of the shot hitting Dominic's stomach. It was aimed not to sever the aorta or any other large artery or vein. Angelo's instructions were that it was to be the opposite of quick and painless. Even the morphine couldn't dull the pain of a stomach wound like that. They grabbed his arms and taped them to the chair.

Alex and Lara watched with detached curiosity as Dominic slowly succumbed to her shot. The kills the day before were quick. This was different. It was lingering and personal. The two of them discussed what was happening to Dominic as the young mook writhed in pain.

"Good shot, hon. Guts, but no severed aorta, no liver, and no big vein. Open his shirt so you can see the involuntary contractions. They cause as much pain as the bullet itself."

She pulled open the moaning and writhing traitor's shirt and poked around the wound a bit.

"Yeah. Every time I feel something move inside, he screams."

While she was poking, she decided to add a little to the drama that was still being recorded. "By the way, Dominic, that part about Angelo sending us being bullshit was bullshit. We're going to edit out everything but the part where you just talked about Bruno sending us to kill you. We'll show that to your mother. If she doesn't kill Bruno, she'll have Angelo go to Papa Paul to do it. Thanks. You were perfect. Say, does this hurt?"

She pressed the side of his abdomen next to the entry wound. Dominic's moaning turned into a scream.

She looked him in the eyes as she pronounced, "Alex, this is what someone looks like when their karma about killing kids catches up to them."

When Dominic didn't die after ten minutes had passed, Lara suggested, "Hon, he's not going fast enough. Try a few with your twenty-two. See what happens with various torso shots. Experiment a little."

Even with the unbearable pain of a gut shot, the morphine, and the blood loss, Dominic still looked up in fear at her request. The horror on his face peaked as Alex tried one to the right chest and one to the liver.

Seconds later, the blood loss from the shredded hole in his liver added enough to the loss from the gut shot to drain away the last of poor Dominic's life.

Lara casually walked over and turned off the camera. Alex pulled out a burner phone and called a number programmed into it. While they waited for the crew to arrive, they mopped up the blood with rags that would accompany Dominic, picked up all the shell casings, and opened a couple of bottles of bleach. The crew arrived, bringing Dominic's car with them. Dominic and the bloody rags were stuffed in the trunk of Dominic's own car, now bound for the metal shredder at a scrapyard owned by Angelo's family. Lara doused the entire office floor with the bleach after double-checking for any remaining evidence.

When the crew departed, it was also time for Alex and Lara to go home. They were shaking, but not from fear or horror at what they'd just done. All they had aspired to do had been realized in the last hour. They were being paid to kill another human being, a disgusting, traitorous one who had conspired to kill children. They were filled with emotion, proud of what they had done.

* * *

After a passionate lovemaking session back at their house, Alex turned to Lara. He looked pensive as he asked, "Penny for your thoughts, honey?"

"Alex, we did it. We killed three people two days ago, but that was an actually-justifiable homicide. We stopped three assholes from killing four innocent people. Well, two innocent and two mob members. And we did it on our own for free. Today we killed a man for money. We crossed the line. How do you feel about that now?"

"The same as I did half an hour ago when I tore your clothes off. Why? Are you having second thoughts?"

"Not in the least. Dominic was just a piece of shit who helped set up a hit on those innocent kids."

Lara looked like she was deep in thought for a moment.

"Okay … okay … but what if we get assigned to kill a truly innocent person? In all our role-play, we always made up stories that we were after some nefarious criminal. I think we were telling ourselves that we have some sort of moral compass," Alex suggested.

"Well, I think that no kids is a good start. What else?"

Lara nodded. "Yeah. Good start. No kids. Torture to get information like today, but no rape. I couldn't do that to a woman, and I certainly don't want you doing it, either, buster! And how about no one unless they are crooks or corrupt?"

They decided to discuss their preferred boundaries with Papa Paul the next day. They hoped he and Lucy would respect them, though they knew they were now bound to do whatever the mobster demanded.

Chapter 6

Bruno Winds Up Wishing His Day Went *As Well* as Dominic's

The morning after Dominic went for a ride to the scrapyard, Alex and Lara met at Papa Paul's house. It was there that they met Siggy for the first time.

Papa Paul introduced them to their new handler. "Siggy, this is Alex and Lara, the two who saved our lives. Take good care of them."

Offering his hand was a short man about the same age as Papa Paul. He was dressed in an obviously bespoke suit, and he wore it with the casual manner that conveyed that these were his everyday clothes. His thin face, close-cut hairstyle, and brown eyes behind steel-rimmed glasses were softened by a broad smile.

Siggy shook their hands and said with the slightest trace of a Yiddish accent, "I'm so happy to meet you two. Papa Paul and Lucy are my two oldest surviving friends, and you have no idea how relieved I am that you were there. I told this old coot that he should never have given up having a couple of the guys around all the time. Maybe he'll listen now."

Papa Paul had explained who Siggy was and what he oversaw, but the "old coot" remark instantly framed him as a friend and confidant to Papa Paul, not an employee.

Papa Paul gave a nod to acknowledge that Siggy had been right, and then Siggy continued, "Papa Paul, here, told me to bring the two of you up to speed on the organization and how you will fit in. He also let me know about your desire for relative anonymity. No problem. The two of you have met a few of the guys, and you will meet a few more, but that's it. You are outside hired talent to all but the small circle that Papa Paul and Lucy personally pick. Anyone else is going to forget you even exist.

"Now, whatever you guys need, come to me for now. Advice, questions, whatever, okay? Once you two are up to speed, there are a couple of my people buried in my organization who handle the day-to-day contacts in your line of work. From time to time I think I may just have to put myself in the picture, though, from what Papa Paul says. You two are too interesting not to."

Alex and Lara nodded and thanked him. A bit later, while the three were at the antique buffet in the dining room helping themselves to some of the breakfast offerings laid out for the group, Alex asked Siggy if he had a minute to answer a question in private.

"Sure," Siggy replied, "Let me get some coffee, and we'll take our plates to the back porch."

* * *

Sitting in the wicker furniture on the screened porch beneath the second-story balcony, Lara explained their moral boundaries and asked if Papa Paul could be approached on that subject.

Siggy gazed in amazement at his two new employees and shook his head. "You two are for real, aren't you? Well, I think what you want is doable. Papa Paul and Lucy have some views on the subject, too.

"The guy behind the hit on Papa Paul, Lucy and the grandkids is a world class asshole named Donat Vayda—mad-dog killer who worked his way up to head his own mob in part by wiping out whole families, innocents included. No one can prove it, but Papa Paul suspects it was Donat who torched the previous head of Donat's organization on Christmas Eve, incinerating the guy, his wife, kids and three grandchildren."

Lara, teeth clenched in hate, asked, "Do you think we can do him?"

Siggy nodded slowly as he said, "If the next phase works out, that's a strong possibility. To be in on the elimination of the head of another family, though, your performance, your next move, is going to have to be spectacular."

Siggy returned to the subject of Papa Paul's code, explaining, "Unlike Donat, anyone in Papa's family who kills a kid will be taking a dirt nap himself. When all of this current mess is over, sure, I'll go to him with you and see what we can hammer out. Papa Paul's own organization doesn't do much muscling anymore, and we can pick and choose what outside contracts we assign to you.

"Papa Paul is almost completely legit now. He dabbles in things that amuse him, but I suspect even that is going away eventually. What you two are going to be doing for me is a tiny fraction of one percent of the operation I oversee for him, and it's the only wiseguy piece of it there is. It's our insurance policy. We keep it running to let the other organizations know this dog still has teeth. Sure, the capos who have their own families now have muscle, but mine, the one you are now part of, carries the old Lenetti brand name, so to speak. No one knows where the retribution comes from, but screw with Papa Paul and someone shows up at your doorstep to make your day unpleasant. You two know computers. It's like Papa Paul has guys like you stored in the cloud. Most of what we do is outside contracting to keep the brand alive, but once in a while, we need to do something to protect Papa Paul and his family."

Lara asked, "How often do things like Packy's hit happen?"

Siggy pulled a face and replied, "That was the problem. The last time anyone tried to move on Papa Paul personally was about six years ago. He thought he had nothing left on that side of the line that anyone would put any effort into seizing anymore. I told him not to let his guard down, but he didn't count on Donat trying to go after something not really worth it. For some reason, Donat just hates Papa Paul. I've looked into it, but I never could figure it out. It must have been some trivial insult when Donat was still just a knockaround guy in the Hungarian mob. The guy never let go of it, the vengeful prick."

Lara asked again, "So you think you can assign us to work in line with what we explained?"

Siggy laughed and replied, "Well, since the two of you are really just extra ammo in my arsenal, yeah, I'm pretty sure the answer is yes."

"Thank you so much, Mr. Fressman. We were worried sick that we might be obligated to do something we didn't want to sign up for," Alex said with noticeable relief.

"Don't count it out completely, Alex," Siggy admonished. "You're in, and that means obedience, but you two seem to be different. Papa Paul gave me some instructions. I don't know how to explain it other than to say that you two are now family. I don't mean like I'm part of the family. I mean, you two are part of Papa Paul's actual family."

He raised his eyebrows and said, "Lucy has it in her head that you were sent by God to protect them. You call Papa Paul 'Papa Paul,' like everyone else, but you don't call Lucy 'Mrs. Lenetti' like the other guys below the capos here. You call her 'Lucy,' and you use my first name and those of the other capos and bosses in the families on the rare occasions you meet them. They have all been instructed. You two might as well be Lucy's kids. Congratulations. You now have a third set of parents. Don't be fooled by the way they treat you, though. When they need to, both of them can be tough as a cheap steak."

Lara said, "That sweet woman, too? I mean, she acted a bit rough after we took out Packy and his crew."

"That sweet woman made her bones three months after she and Papa Paul were married. Some mook came into a restaurant to hit him, and she had her gun out of her purse before any of Papa Paul's guys even saw the guy coming. One to the head and two more to the chest before the hitter even started to drop. My advice is never fuck with Lucy."

Lara froze, her mouth open and a fork full of scrambled eggs poised to enter when Siggy said that last bit. Earlier that week, a furious Lucy pointed a gun at her.

Siggy laughed and said, "Don't worry, Lara. She's taken a liking to you, so you would really have to do something to piss her off for anything bad to happen. I think the two of you are smart enough to avoid that."

Lara let out a breath and finished her bite. They chatted about their place in Siggy's organization until their plates were clean and the coffee was gone. One bit of information during that chat really shocked Lara.

Siggy said, "The nice thing about your being part of my crew is that the feds don't even know I have one. Like I said, you two are part of an organization that is off in the cloud. Our guys in the PD tell us that they all have a vague idea about the button men that Angelo, Petie, and the other former Lenetti capos have in their families now, but the feds are certain that I'm one hundred percent legit. They don't know that Papa Paul and I were friends from when we were kids. I went into business, and he went the way he went. When he wanted to get out of the rackets for his kids' sake, he looked me up. Everything he and I do with that one exception has paper trails, audits, SEC oversight, and the whole nine yards."

"When Pauli Jr. and his sister Connie inherit everything, they will be as clean as a preacher's sheets. Pauli Jr. works with Papa Paul and me managing the legit businesses. He will take over the business end when Papa Paul fully retires, and Connie will probably stay the head of their charitable foundation. They could become trust-fund kids, but their parents instilled in them a desire to be useful."

"Wow, that's quite an achievement. Not too many mobsters get to walk away. Kind of like Mayer Lansky. So, Alex and I can't be traced back to Papa Paul?"

"No, Lara. Not the way we've set this up. After this current situation is settled, you two will have no more official contact inside his or his former capos' organizations unless he changes things. You meet anyone at a Christmas party, you're just friends of the family."

Lara turned to Alex and said, "Cool! Talk about next-level gaming."

The three rejoined the rest.

Papa Paul addressed Siggy, but some of what he said was obviously for Alex and Lara's benefit. "Siggy, I was impressed with the way Alex and Lara planned things so far, but I want to see if you can get them to set up something really complicated. The objective is to take out Packy's ultimate boss, Donat, hit one of his top lieutenants, and make the whole thing look like something other than it is. You said you wanted to see this one planned, not run it through your two guys. Okay. Take Angelo with you. Use the room in the basement."

* * *

Siggy and Angelo took the pair down to the den. Alex and Lara asked a hundred questions. Who were the players? What was their relationship with each other? What properties did they own? Who likely got to Bruno? They even asked what the geography was at various locations. Seven and a half hours and two take-out orders later, they finally came up with a well-thought-out, very precise plan. It was about as convoluted as Siggy or Angelo had ever seen, but it looked like it could work. The two veteran mobsters just shook their heads as they called Papa Paul down to review the plan.

Siggy explained, "Papa Paul, I want you to be patient. These two came up with a doozy that none of us have ever seen."

Alex started, "Donat Vayda hates you, Papa Paul. Always has. For some reason, his hate is visceral. Lara and I feel that we can work this to our advantage.

"Now, in our exit interview with Dominic, he claimed that the lieutenant who ordered the hit on you was Mickey Movitz. Reviewing the tape, everyone questions whether or not Bruno had even told Dominic who had contacted him from the Vayda mob. It looks like Dominic just guessed to save his own life."

Papa Paul said, "Yeah, I got that feeling when Lucy and I saw it, too. So how do we find out?"

Lara explained, "We encourage Bruno to tell us. Angelo says that Donat's son Leo is far more reasonable than his piece-of-shit old man. If he was in charge, a truce could probably be forged. The problem is how to push a button on Donat and the lieutenant who set up the hit and still leave little Leo alive. The key is convincing Bruno himself to set it up."

Papa Paul asked, "How the hell are we going to get Bruno to cave? Not likely. He's twenty times tougher than Dominic was."

Angelo replied, "Papa Paul, these two kids go at it like a Doberman on a pork chop. I've never seen two people so engaged in planning a hit. It's a game they have to win. They cover every angle, and I think they have that angle covered. If this thing works, they will have proved that they could be very, very valuable."

Papa Paul looked at the pair. Alex and Lara were beaming as if they were kids who had just gotten an A-plus on a term paper.

Papa Paul said to Siggy, "I've been around for a long time. I know that look. Properly channeled, these two would be deadly. Lots of hitmen are good, but few actually live for it. This isn't just the vocation they want to have; it is their avocation as well."

He turned to Angelo and calmly said, "Okay. I'll listen. Spell it out for me."

Angelo continued, "Natalie came to me because Dominic was missing, and she asked for my help locating him. Yesterday I told her I had terrible news. I said that Bruno was involved in Dominic being whacked, but not to let Bruno know we knew.

"I showed her the proof the kids recorded, and she wants him dead. I suspected that she'd actually wanted him dead for years. She was more than happy to set him up; enthusiastic would be more like it."

"Nice," Papa Paul mused. "So, what's next, Angelo?"

"As soon as you okay it, Natalie is going to ask Bruno to come to my house for help in locating Dominic. There, the kids're going to, uh, encourage him to give up whoever contacted him at Donat's, and the kids have a way to get him on the line with whoever that is. The next part of the plan is pure genius."

Papa Paul looked at the rest of the details outlined on a whiteboard and laughed, "Okay." He turned to Angelo and said, "The kids' plan is great. Set it up. And I want to see if the kids can work it out to get me to the hit location with Donat and whoever the other guy is."

* * *

Angelo set the wheels in motion. After his invitation, Bruno couldn't get to Angelo's house fast enough. Three of Angelo's guys, Pete, Rocco, and Tony, met Bruno at the door.

Angelo's guys looked like they could be brothers—medium height and build, dark hair, brown eyes, and chiseled features. They were dressed casually in short-sleeved shirts and jeans. Bruno, by comparison, was taller, with coarser features, and a bulkier frame.

While not fat, he shopped in the large men's section of stores. He was dressed in a leather jacket, long-sleeved shirt, and chinos.

Bruno had been an enforcer prior to marrying Angelo's sister after her first husband's death. Now he was the manager of one of Angelo's social clubs. While an imposing figure, he had gotten a bit soft in the last decade.

Bruno worriedly asked, "You guys know what happened to Dominic? Angelo said something about you guys helping me find him. Natalie is driving me nuts. Personally, I hope the fucking weasel got hit by a truck, but Natalie's gonna kill me if I don't find him."

"Sure," Tony replied. "Ropey Joe from the club phoned in just now, and he said Dominic's holed up in the Motel 6 off Interstate 80. He's going there now to pick the jerk up. I guess he got scared because Packy broke in the other day. Talk about unsuited for the life! No spine at all. Come on downstairs and have a beer with us while we wait. We just got in a case of Smuttynose IPA from back East. C'mon and get a cold one before they're gone."

Dominic visibly relaxed and exclaimed, "Damn, that's a relief! I'm gonna whip that wimp from here to next Tuesday! The grief his ma gave me when he flaked! Didn't call her or nothin'."

Bruno was smiling as they led him downstairs, but his smile evaporated when the door opened, and Pete and Rocco grabbed him. They shoved him down into a wooden armchair and used zip ties to strap his wrists and ankles to the chair.

Tony cut Bruno's black leather jacket from the right wrist all the way up to the shoulder with a pair of heavy scissors.

"What the fuck is going on? That's a four-hundred-dollar coat!" Bruno yelled, trying to break his arm free.

Alex and Lara, who had been listening and watching in an adjacent room, stepped through the door. They were wearing white Tyvek coveralls and the kind of face shields dentists and hygienists wear when examining patients. Bruno turned white when he saw their attire. Lara had a plastic toolbox. She extracted a syringe and a vial of fentanyl.

She smiled at Bruno as she tapped the syringe and said, "Bruno, don't worry about the coat. If you don't cooperate, you won't be needing it anymore, anyway."

"Who the fuck are the painter twins here, anyway?" Dominic nervously laughed. "Where's Angelo. I wanna talk with my brother-in-law! Let me the fuck up!"

Lara inserted the syringe into the vial. A dose dozens of times more than lethal was extracted as Lara explained, "This is fentanyl. A few drops will kill you."

Alex grabbed the arm with the slit sleeve and cut the exposed shirt with the gutting hook of a hunting knife from the toolbox. He swabbed the inside of Bruno's elbow with an alcohol prep.

"Bruno, we don't want you getting an infection," he reassured him.

"Honey, this is fentanyl. He won't get an infection," Lara chided.

"Why not, sweetheart?"

"Well, 'cause an infection would take hours or days to develop. This will kill Bruno in about eight seconds," Lara said in a matter-of-fact tone.

Alex patted Bruno's arm and said with mock concern, "Oh, dear. Get that, Bruno? Eight seconds. You'd better listen to her. She knows these things. Very smart lady. Studied learning at the education place. Got a degree and everything, you know?"

"Who are you two? Guys, I wanna talk with Angelo! He don't want me dead. He's my brother-in-law," Bruno pleaded. The nervous laughter had turned to trembling speech as he looked in terror at the syringe.

Alex pointed back and forth to himself and Lara to comically ask who should explain the situation to Bruno. Lara laughed and addressed Angelo's trussed-up brother-in-law. Their sarcasm bit into Bruno like a blast of cold wind. His bravado disappeared utterly.

"Angelo doesn't want to have to kill you," Lara said. "Natalie lost her son, and we don't want her to lose her husband. Yeah. Dominic's dead. Mickey got him. No, we don't want you; we want your contact in the Vayda mob. If they tied up Dominic's loose end, how long before it is your end they come to tie up?" She teased the needle over his arm.

Bruno knew what was in the syringe and what it would do. Angelo told Alex and Lara the evening before that Bruno had been with his guys when they used it for a hit. He had been holding the victim down when Rocco injected it. The mark in his hands went limp in seconds and was dead almost as fast.

Also, in the dozens of questions Alex and Lara asked Angelo, one of them was what fears or phobias Bruno might have.

Angelo answered, "Needles. Natalie says he nearly passed out the last time he got a flu shot."

Bruno knew he was one jab and a few seconds from that same fate. The woman dressed in creepy white Tyvek nicked his skin with the needle once, and he audibly gasped. Lara looked him in the eyes and giggled! Bruno was visibly terrified: eyes wide open, head tilted back and frozen in place, fingers splayed.

Another tiny prick with the syringe's needle, and Bruno gritted his teeth, tightly shutting his eyes in anticipation of the poke that would end his life.

When the tip of Lara's needle caught skin once again, Bruno's will evaporated, and he confessed. "It was Jerry. Jerry Cambric. He came to me. Offered me money and a job with them. He said the old man was weak and that I could help get rid of him, or they would get rid of me along with Papa Paul."

Jerry Cambric was another lieutenant in Donat's mob. It wasn't Mickey, after all.

All of this was being taped, with the shot tight enough on Bruno not to show anything but the occasional hand and needle in the frame.

Alex explained, "Bruno, did you ever hear of the adage that if someone cheats with you, they will cheat on you? Well, in your case, it means that the Vaydas would have you cheat on the Lenettis with them, but then would probably cheat on you by whacking you. What benefit would they gain by leaving a loose end like you alive?"

"Now, Bruno," Lara insisted, waving Mr. Fentanyl in front of his face, "we need you to call Jerry and give him a message. We're going to go over a script we want you to say to Jerry. We'll go over it several times. In return for your cooperation, I'm going to put this syringe away. Papa Paul said we are to leave you alive if you say what we tell you to. Otherwise, well, not so much."

Bruno nodded enthusiastically in relief as Lara put the syringe down. Sweat was dripping from his forehead now.

They went over the script several times, with Bruno reading it aloud until he had it down pretty well. Lara reminded Bruno what was in the syringe from time to time to motivate him. When Bruno could give a good rendition, they had him call Jerry on Bruno's own phone. Bruno's voice was rushed and showed stress, but that is what it would have been if the message was the truth, too. It added authenticity.

The phone was on speaker as Bruno began, "Jerry, the hit on Papa was botched. I'm at Angelo's right now. Papa Paul is onto you. I heard Angelo and the other guys talking. Papa Paul called Donat. They're going to make a truce, but Papa Paul insisted on Donat giving up the one who set up the hit. Angelo says that Donat is giving you up as payment. They're going to call you to a meet at Rossi's tomorrow evening so to whack you."

Jerry shouted, "Those sons of bitches! After all I've done for Donat!" He paused for a second and asked, "Rossi's? The place on Fifth?"

"No, the one out of town in Lemont. Quieter out there, I guess. They're going to take you when you arrive at the parking lot and drive you out to your warehouse there for the hit. They're all going to be there, Papa Paul, Donat, and the guy that hit Packy and his crew. They're going to take you out in front of Papa Paul. He's furious that his grandkids were going to be killed, and he wants you … well, you know."

"How do I know you're telling me the truth? You're the guy that got me into this mess in the first place with the shit info you must have had Dominic give Packy."

Lara quickly wrote something and showed it to Bruno.

"Uh, 'cause if they ask you to meet at Rossi's in Lemont, you'll know."

"Okay. Shit! I can't believe he would do this to me just to make Paul happy. Fuck! So, if what you said pans out, I know it's legit. I gotta take Donat out. I got some boys I can trust. We'll ambush them. I'll get that asshole Donat myself. You and my boys take out whoever else he's with. Son of a bitch!"

"Hey, I'm no hitter, Jerry. I—"

"Look, you piece of crap. You botched it. Dominic's information was for shit. Paul lived, and Packy and his boys are probably under the foundation of a building somewhere by now. Donat is coming for me because he wanted Paul dead so bad, and I failed. The deal is on. You help me take out Donat, or so help me God, I'll come after you next. Do it, and I'll take you in. Don't do it, and I put you under. You follow?"

"But ..."

"Damn it, Bruno, grow a dick, you piece of shit. Be there with Papa Paul for the meet!"

Jerry ended the call with a few more obscenities. Bruno looked up at Lara with a smile.

"I did what you wanted. You're not going to kill me now, are you? I did it, right? I get to go back to Natalie?"

Lara tickled his chin as she laughed. "Sure. We're not going to kill you. We know that Natalie really does want you."

Bruno sighed in relief and slumped forward a bit as he relaxed. He held up his palms in a gesture he expected would get the zip ties cut. His relief was short-lived. Alex went to the partially open door and opened it all the way.

Standing there were Natalie and Angelo. Bruno looked at her and smiled briefly. The look on her face wiped the smile off his face.

Natalie looked to be in her mid-fifties. She was almost as tall as Bruno but was thin and wiry-looking. She had her brown hair up in a tight bun, and it gave her narrow face a severe look. Alex imagined that she was really beautiful, but her mouth and eyes were contorted in an expression of hate that masked that.

Angelo, Alex, and Lara shook hands as Angelo said, "Thanks, you two. Impressive. Most impressive. The needle thing worked better than I expected." He turned to Tony and the rest and instructed, "Guys, get ready."

He looked at Alex and Lara and added, "You two are welcome to watch, but if not, I'll meet you upstairs in the dining room. I got a nice bottle of wine breathing up there if you want to go now. You're dressed for the job, so like I said, feel free to watch."

Angelo's men were spreading a large plastic tarp on the floor along with some absorbent liquid-spill material to stabilize the body fluids Bruno was expected to lose shortly. They put on raincoats and rubber gloves.

Bruno was sobbing uncontrollably as he watched the preparations. He was begging for mercy: "Please, Angelo. Don't do this. Natalie, don't let him. I love you. Please, please!"

Natalie walked calmly to him and slapped his face as hard as she could, spitting out, "What you get now is payback for years of living with you and payback for Dominic."

Angelo's men lifted Bruno's chair and placed it on the plastic. Bruno saw Lenny "The Magician" Brillo enter the room with his toolbox. The Magician could make people vanish without a trace. Bruno's face lost any shred of hope.

Natalie hissed, "Bruno, in about an hour, I'm going to be a widow for the second time." Then, in a chilling reminder that Bruno's body would never be found, she looked into his eyes and said, "The difference is that I'll have to wait seven years for you to be declared legally dead. Lenny, process the body before, not after."

Lenny replied, "Sure, Natalie. For you, anything. Bruno, you know what that means? No fingers and no teeth. You got a preference for what goes first? No? Then I'll take the liberty of starting with the teeth."

He placed his toolbox box on the table next to Lara's plastic one and extracted various-shaped dental forceps and a small ball-peen hammer. He explained to Lara, "The forceps are there if he stays still.

The hammer is there for if he doesn't. 'Before' never goes a smoothly as 'after.'"

After the first of Bruno's teeth were extracted to the sound of his howls, Alex and Lara excused themselves to go upstairs and get some wine.

"Sure, kids. Go have a drink," Angelo said. "This isn't for everyone. I need to stay here for my sister, and she wants to use my knife to finish the job herself if he survives what Lenny is doing."

* * *

As Alex tasted the respectable Bordeaux waiting on the table, Lara smiled at him and raised her glass, toasting, "For the female of the species is more deadly than the male …"

Alex almost choked with laughter as Lara recited the entire Rudyard Kipling poem, The Female of the Species. At the end of each verse, they saluted the recurring line with a raised glass and a sip.

"Alex, did you see the look on her face as she whispered in Bruno's ear after the tooth was pulled? I've never seen hate like that. If Bruno lives through the processing, she's going to make his death slow."

"Yeah. By comparison, Dominic had it easy. Sucks to be Bruno today, I guess."

"But he brought it on himself," Lara reminded him. "He should have gone straight to Papa Paul when Jerry approached him. He opted for the greedy path rather than the honorable one. He's getting no less than he deserved."

"Remind me not to cross you, sweetheart. Kipling was right! Now, when Angelo gets back up here, we need to have him call Papa Paul and get the rest of the plan in motion."

"I'm dying to see this work. There's nothing more satisfying than having your enemy bite himself in the butt," Lara said, punctuating the last word with a giggle.

Chapter 7

Triple Cross—A Craftsman's Best Résumé Is Showing Off a Finely Crafted Piece of Work

The following day the next part of the plan was simple to initiate. Papa Paul had a fixer who handled delicate matters, a gentleman by the name of Marvin Smalls. Marvin was given a carefully edited audio track from the tape Lara made to take to Donat.

The meeting was set at Donat's house. Marvin had done numerous errands for Papa Paul, but he wasn't part of his or any other family. He was one of the people in Chicago who knew people. Siggy had filled him in on what he was to offer Donat in exchange for peace. He and Siggy talked about where the peace offering on Donat's end should take place, too.

Papa Paul was using someone neutral to set up the hit, but Marvin was not knowingly part of the scheming. In the final analysis, Donat's own organization would do most of the heavy lifting. Marvin would never know he was carrying anything but factual information to Donat. Marvin's reputation as a neutral party would be preserved. In any event, when people in Marvin's position transported information, all parties made their own judgments about its veracity. Caveat emptor was the operational norm.

Marvin, a highly successful sixty-year-old African American lawyer, was driven to Donat's mansion by one of his own employees, who waited in the car. The front door opened as Marvin approached.

He was ushered into Donat's office by Andras Nagy, an up-and-coming Vaydas soldier. Andras poured Marvin a whiskey while they waited for his boss. After a ten-minute wait, which Marvin knew was only to stress how important Donat was, the mobster, manicured and dressed in a beautifully tailored suit, entered the room with his son, Leo.

Marvin had to stifle a laugh, as he knew Donat back in the day when Levi's and a sleeveless tee shirt were his best clothes. Over thirty years, Donat had scratched and clawed his way to the top, and he loved to remind people how far he had come. He was also continuously compensating with ostentatious behavior because of an unfortunate circumstance surrounding his last name. When his grandparents came over from Europe, their name was Vajda, meaning war leader. When Donat's grandfather pronounced the name, it sounded like "Vayda," and that Americanized form was written on the immigration documents by the staff at Ellis Island. Vayda was a girl's name that meant pretty as a flower but strong willed.

In contrast to his father, Leo was an unassuming fellow. Dressed in a sport coat, gray slacks, and an open-collar shirt, he had a reputation as a rational leader—at least as rational as anyone could hope for in Donat's organization. At thirty-eight, the stocky heir apparent to Donat's empire looked pleased to see Marvin and interested to know what occasioned the distinguished go-between's visit that day.

Marvin stood for Donat, and they gave each other a perfunctory hug. Leo shook Marvin's hand and then dismissed Andras. Donat invited Marvin to sit as he walked around his polished walnut desk to the high-back, button tuft leather chair behind it. Leo sat in the chair next to Marvin's, both facing Donat's desk.

Donat smiled broadly and asked, "Well, Marvin. What can we do for you today? I hear that you have an important message from a mutual friend. Any reason your meeting is just with me and my son?"

"Mr. Vayda, as you know, I'm here on behalf of the Lenettis. They are aware of who was behind the hit on Paul and his family. An educated guess would be that they have a mole in your organization, and the information I brought could not be shared with certain of your people, the reason you will shortly understand. They do not want a war, and as a token of their sincerity, they want you to have this. I haven't heard it myself yet."

He pulled a recorder out of his pocket and played the conversation it contained, the voices being very identifiable as Jerry and Bruno:

"I gotta take Donat out. I got some boys I can trust. We'll ambush them. I'll get that asshole Donat myself. You and my boys take out whoever else he's with. Son of a bitch!"

"Hey, I'm no hitter, Jerry. I—"

"Look, you piece of crap. You botched it. Dominic's information was for shit. Paul lived, and Packy and his boys are probably under the foundation of a building somewhere by now. Donat is coming for me because he wanted Paul dead so bad, and I failed. The deal is on. You help me take out Donat, or so help me God, I'll come after you next. Do it, and I'll take you in. Don't do it, and I put you under. You follow?"

"But ..."

"Damn it, Bruno, grow a dick, you piece of shit."

After considerable swearing from Donat, who was now stomping around the deep-pile maroon carpet, Marvin continued, "Paul would like you to know that Jerry approached him to make a deal after Jerry botched the hit. Jerry told Paul that he figured if Paul had someone buried deep enough in your organization to warn him of the hit, Paul was smarter than you, Mr. Vayda. He wanted to make a deal before Paul started taking out your top people to get revenge. Paul stalled him for a few days but had his men bug Bruno, who Jerry identified as your traitor in Paul's organization. Listening to this, I'm guessing Jerry has since decided his only option is taking you out before you take him out."

"He should know I'd never do that over just a botched hit," Donat insisted.

The look Marvin saw on Leo's face betrayed that assertion, but Marvin stood mute. His position wasn't to judge, just convey information.

"So, what is Paul offering?" Donat asked.

"Paul pledges not to take revenge for the hit on him and his wife and grandkids. You take out Jerry, and all will be forgiven if you pledge to leave Paul's operation alone. What he has left in Chicago is chickenfeed compared to your operation, and he pledges not to go after any of your territories."

"Anything else?"

"Yes. One other thing. He wants to watch you take out Jerry," Marvin replied.

"Okay. Usual arrangement?"

"Yes, Mr. Vayda. He'll go with your men, unarmed, and you leave someone with his people. He suggests your son."

Donat thought about it for a minute and then conferred with his son. "What do you think, Leo? You'll have this chair someday. What would you do?"

"Jerry has to go, but he's going to be nervous, Pop. The botched hit sent him over the deep end. We can't tip him off."

Donat replied, "Sure. Business as usual. Give him something to do. Tell him about some new business and then have him meet the clients somewhere."

"Okay. Where?" Leo asked.

They turned to Marvin, and Leo asked, "Any suggestions for a neutral location?"

Marvin had been given a location that Siggy said would offer privacy and security for Papa Paul. He asked, "You have a pretty secure warehouse in Lemont, right?"

"So?" Leo asked.

"Set up a meet somewhere public nearby. Someplace open and neutral. Snatch him and take him to the warehouse. What's near the warehouse?"

Donat pressed an intercom button and said, "Get Mickey in here with someone who knows Lemont."

A minute later, Mickey entered with two men, Andras and another soldier, Vanosh Sandu.

Donat asked, "What's out by the Lemont warehouse?"

Mickey answered, "Not much. I don't go there much. It's agricultural and industrial. Guys?"

Vanosh said, "When the guys go to the warehouse, they eat at that place on the highway, Rossi's. Only place for miles. Good food. I recommend the meatballs."

"Vanosh, for heaven's sake, we're not going to go inside to eat, just meet someone. But Rossi's is a good suggestion."

"Sorry, Mr. Vayda."

"That's okay. You two can go. Mickey, stay here." When the other two were gone, he continued, "The suggestion for the parking lot at Rossi's is good on my end. Marvin?"

"Excellent. Just pick the place for Paul to meet you and do the exchange."

Donat picked a very public pub downtown, and the wheels were rolling. Donat filled Mickey in on the particulars.

Mickey was stunned. "You sure, Boss?"

Donat had Marvin play the recording again. Mickey got redder and redder as the recording played. In the end, he just nodded resolutely. He was being instructed to set up the hit on his oldest friend in the mob. He was visibly shaken as he walked out of the room.

* * *

Mickey couldn't bear to meet with Jerry, afraid he would display a tell that would warn his old friend. He sent his best guy, Andras, to pass on the message about some new business and Donat's instructions for Jerry to meet the new client at Rossi's parking lot an hour or so before closing the following evening. As far as Andras knew, the instructions were legitimate.

* * *

The next evening, Papa Paul showed up at the pub, and after some overly dramatic backslapping between himself and Donat and apologizing on both sides, Donat got into a car with three of his men. Papa Paul got into a second sedan with three more armed goons and they followed Donat's car. Leo, went with Angelo to wait out the events in the office of one of Papa Paul's gambling joints.

As they neared Rossi's a little over forty-five minutes later, they could see about ten or fifteen cars in the lot, with one at the end farthest from the restaurant's entrance. The rural restaurant closed at 9:45 p.m., and Papa Paul knew there would be few, if any, new customers showing up this late.

There were fields on three sides of the lot, with the restaurant on the right side of the property and the parking lot on the left. Papa Paul could see a few diners through the windows facing the lot, but Papa Paul knew they would be face down on the floor in a pool of their soup and pasta in a few seconds.

Jerry was leaning on the driver's door of the lone car at the far end of the lot, and he waved as the two vehicles approached. Donat's car stopped about twenty-five feet from Jerry. The sedan with Papa Paul parked in a slot near the restaurant as Jerry would expect only one car to meet him.

As Donat and his men stepped out of their car, Jerry pulled a shotgun from his open car window and opened up on Donat, just as Papa Paul predicted. Three of Jerry's men began firing from another car closer to the one Papa Paul was in.

The three hoods from the second car jumped out and began running and firing at Jerry and his men. Papa Paul opened his door and rolled out, crouching behind the engine block of the nearest parked car. He peeked around the hood from time to time. He didn't want to miss anything. He was finally going to get rid of the thorn in his side, and the danger was worth the joy of watching Donat's men take out each other.

The lot wasn't particularly well lit, but Papa Paul could see that the driver who brought him was down. The two other men from Papa Paul's car were now alongside Donat's car to protect their boss, who had been wounded by the first shotgun blast. Donat was firing from behind the trunk of his car, with his men firing at Jerry's guys over the top. One by one, men started to drop. Jerry and his three guys and Donat and his men traded shots until all except Jerry, Donat, and one of Donat's hoods were down. A series of pops from the cornfield nearest Jerry's car reached Papa Paul's ears as he watched the remaining three fall to the ground. The battle had lasted no more than thirty or forty seconds.

Alex, Lara, and Rocco ran out of the woods, nine-millimeter carbines slung over their shoulders. Dressed in gray-and-black camo with hoods, they were careful to use the parked cars as cover from the field of view of the single security camera on the side of the restaurant. Until they reached the areas of the closest cars, their clothing would just look like background pixilation in the darkness at the far end of the lot.

They quickly took guns from the members of each faction and used them to finish off wounded members of the opposite side. In the unlikely event that the cops even bothered to do ballistics in such a slam-dunk case, there might be three bullets that wouldn't match pistols, but it would just be an unsolvable mystery. Even Papa Paul, who was now looking for their arrival, couldn't see anything but muzzle flashes from behind cars. The carbines would be melted pools of slag in a few hours.

Papa Paul scooted back to the car that brought him and hopped in behind the wheel. As he slowly passed the end of the aisle, the others jumped in on the side opposite the restaurant and piled onto the back seat and floor before the car left the lot. It took a couple of minutes to drive all the way around to the other side of the field, where Alex and Lara's car was parked.

* * *

The mood in the car was elevated. Papa Paul praised the plan, saying, "You guys built so many outs into that plan. If everything worked, Jerry and Donat are dead, which they are now. If Jerry decided not to go to the meet to ambush Donat, Donat thinks he's a rat and puts out a contract on Jerry, or Jerry finds a way to kill Donat. Either way, a partial win for us."

Lara laughed and said, "We figured Jerry would be cautious. We saw Jerry's guys look in every car in the parking lot before Donat got there to make sure Donat didn't have extra guys planted. We were in the field under camo netting a half hour before Jerry got there."

"Alex, where did you learn tactics like that?" Rocco asked.

"Gaming. In games, you have almost unlimited virtual resources and time compared to the real world. You can over plan things to help ensure success. We are known in the gaming world as devious, underhanded, sneaky little shits. In shooter situations, we hide and snipe. In tank games, we flank and hit from the rear. Success comes from being where the enemy thinks you can't be."

Lara added, "As Sun Tzu wrote in The Art of War, 'Making no mistakes is what establishes the certainty of victory, for it means conquering an enemy that is already defeated.' That's how we play."

"Damn! If what you two just did was play, remind me not to piss you off enough for you to go to work!" Rocco said in awe.

Papa Paul asked, "Any tips on the next phase, Alex?"

"Just one. When you meet with Leo, do your best to look sincere when you are consoling him. Sincerity is the key to everything, and when you can fake that, you've got it made."

Papa Paul laughed, "Sincerity. Yeah!" He added with a grin, "I could get an Oscar for how sincere I'll be. Sincerity … oh, you two."

He dropped Alex and Lara off at their car, hidden at the far edge of the field. He dropped off Rocco at his car a mile away on the road back to Chicago.

Chapter 8

Papa Paul Turns a Lemon into Lemonade

Alex and Lara got into their car and kissed to celebrate their success. Then they casually drove back to their home with Lara's head on Alex's shoulder. In his rearview mirror, Alex could see a half dozen or more police cars with flashing lights heading in the direction of Rossi's.

* * *

Papa Paul drove to where Leo was being held. It took a little over an hour, including the two stops he made to drop off the others. By the time he'd gotten back to Chicago, reporters had begun live broadcasts from the scene. Leo was in shock at the news, and Papa Paul's men were consoling him over a stiff drink. Leo stood and looked at Papa Paul, speechless, with a look of anguish distorting his face.

Papa Paul embraced Leo just as the television reports broke to a long-winded press statement from the senior police official at the scene. A Lemont PD lieutenant was obviously enjoying his fifteen minutes of fame as he addressed the press. "Our community has, to the best of our knowledge, just experienced a deadly internal struggle between factions of the Donat Vayda crime organization. This is a preliminary evaluation based on what we know at this time. We have interviewed several witnesses and reviewed the video from the single security camera on the parking lot side of the building here at Rossi's restaurant. While the witnesses stated only that gunfire broke out at the far end of the parking lot before they moved to safety, the video shows men searching the parked cars approximately an hour and twenty minutes ago at the direction of a man now identified as Jerry Cambric, one of Donat Vayda's lieutenants.

"Minutes later, Mr. Vayda's car pulled up to Mr. Cambric's car. Almost immediately, shooting began. Three men from another car that pulled into the lot ran to the fray, and within a minute and a half, all were motionless. Eleven men were involved in the shootout, and all have been pronounced dead by the coroner.

"Most of the action was at least partially obscured by the parked cars already in the lot, but there was an image of one man near the third car. The man never looked toward the camera and was impossible to identify. We assume he was an unarmed driver as he did not appear to be involved in the altercation. He escaped in the third vehicle, a white or tan full-size late-model sedan. We're not releasing any other names until next of kin can be contacted.

"This appears to have been a dispute between factions of Mr. Vayda's organization that erupted into deadly violence. There is some damage to the building of Rossi's from stray bullets, but we are relieved to report that there were no injuries to the patrons or staff."

The longer the statement dragged on, the worse Leo appeared until he was in tears. He asked, "How could Jerry have known that he was being sent to Rossi's to be hit?"

Papa Paul put his hand on Leo's shoulder and replied, "I'm so sorry, Leo. My guess is that he was nervous about meeting anyone at this point because he botched the hit on me. He knew your father's temper and was likely anticipating the fallout from that failure. He came to me, you know, to make a deal, but I didn't trust him. I had Marvin bring that to your dad. That's why I thought I might have been able to forge a truce with him. Anyway, Jerry may just have been paranoid about the meeting at Rossi's and called someone at your place. Maybe to see if your father had left the house with anyone. Only a few people knew what he was doing, so it would have been seen as an innocent question. Someone probably told him that your father left with two carloads of men, and Jerry figured it out. I know your dad liked to play his cards close to the vest."

"Yeah. Dad was kind of like that. Should've made sure everyone knew not to say anything to Jerry, even something that simple. Jerry was smart enough to wheedle something out of someone in the crew. When I find out who was responsible."

Papa Paul interrupted him in a fatherly tone. "It was probably an innocent answer, Leo. Take some time to grieve and then get back to normal. Don't be rash. Be strong. You're in charge now. You have friends, and I'm one of them now if you want. The bad blood between our families can be over. Call your guys to come get you."

"Did, did you see my father …?"

"No, Leo. Your dad's guys made me wait in the second car while they were going to snatch Jerry. It was supposed to be quick, with four guys against just one. I saw Jerry fire the first shots, and then his guys opened up out of nowhere from behind another car. I tried to see what was happening, but as soon as I saw the guys down, I got in the driver's seat and took off. They didn't let me bring a gun, remember? I couldn't do anything to save him. It was a hail of bullets. Over before I even left the lot."

He repeated, "Go ahead and call your guys, Leo. The cops are going to be coming to see you. My best advice is to tell them your father and Jerry were having problems, and your father set up a meet at Rossi's to resolve it. And call your lawyers."

Leo shook Papa Paul's hand and said quietly, "I guess we're quits. I never understood my father's obsession with your family. There's nothing you have that's worth any more dying to get."

Papa Paul agreed. "Those are the words of a man who cares about his family. I'm truly sorry for your loss. Jerry, the man who targeted my grandchildren, has paid the price, and I'm satisfied."

Papa Paul could have taken Leo out instead of letting him go. The original plan was a hostage exchange, Papa Paul for Leo to ensure that Papa Paul got back alive. Now Papa Paul was back, and Donat was dead. By letting Leo go, Papa Paul showed that there would be no attempts at revenge as long as the Vaydas kept the truce.

* * *

The next day was Saturday, and Papa Paul invited Lara and Alex over for dinner. Angelo, Siggy, Petie, and a few others were there, as well. After a round of hugs and the two of them kissing Papa Paul's ring after formally pledging their fealty, they all adjourned to the library for a predinner drink.

Papa Paul saluted Alex and Lara with his bourbon glass. He almost had tears in his eyes as he said, "Your plan has paved the way for the Lenettis to peacefully run our last few wiseguy operations until I'm ready to let them go.

"The whole affair, from saving Maria and Theresa to planning the massacre that eliminated the man behind the hit, permanently cemented you two with Lucy and me. We didn't know if that first night was a fluke, but your efficiency and skill have been proven.

"Well, efficiency may not be the most accurate term. I've seen Hollywood movies with less convoluted plots, but the escapade at Rossi's was sure enjoyable," he added with a smile.

Lucy said, "There's never been anyone that I know of who just showed up in the rackets like the two of you did. Usually, that kind of behavior results in a one-way trip somewhere deep and wet, but the two of you were different somehow. Saving the girls was a start, but Paul, Angelo, and I talked about you for hours. Siggy did a background on the two of you, and you had no connections anywhere. Both the names you are known by here and your real names—nothing in the life and no criminal records. I guess we gave you a chance partly out of gratitude and partly out of pure curiosity. We do have one question for you, though."

Lara replied, "Ask away."

"How do you see yourselves? I mean, what do you think about how you want to live? Any remorse?"

"The two of us have discussed this since we decided to make our move," Lara said. "Remorse? Not a bit. Ever since we started to seriously exercise our inclinations, we've talked about removing evil people from society. We've set limits to what we're willing to do, such as no hitting kids, and we're happy with what we've done so far."

"How long have you had these, uh, inclinations? Have you ever talked to anyone about them?"

Alex chimed in, "We've talked about this since high school, but not with anyone else. We've never felt the need to see anyone about what we like. We know most people would think we're a bit, well, different. But we're completely comfortable with who we are. We have a good moral compass, and we decided only to remove those that society is incapable of removing. I hope it doesn't shock you, but we actually find it a bit of a turn-on."

Siggy interjected, "The two of them talked to me about what they would prefer to do and not do. I told them that we could accommodate them. In my opinion, I want them fully motivated for each assignment."

Lucy thought for a second and said, "Thanks, Siggy." She turned to Alex and Lara and continued, "So as long as what we give you to do doesn't violate your moral compass, you'll do it willingly? How about the job on Dominic? That wasn't a straight hit. We asked for some incidental punishment."

Alex replied, "Of course, Mrs. Lenetti …"

Lucy scolded, "It's just Lucy to the two of you."

"Oh, right. Lucy, we'll do it willingly. It's an honor and a pleasure to serve the two of you. The Dominic hit was just a case of the punishment fitting the crime. After all, there are few greater sins than disloyalty. To God, family, country, or employer. Period."

That last statement struck a chord with Lucy, and she smiled. "Uh, one more question: If you hadn't overheard Packy, would you and Lara have sought employment in the field of your inclination?"

Lara looked at Alex and then back at Lucy, saying, "I think we may have tried to figure something out, Lucy. Maybe some freelancing. We have some contacts on the Dark Web, and some of them may have led us to something. We felt it to be a bit risky so far, though. Packy solved that problem."

Papa Paul weighed what they said and remarked, "Well, I hate to say it, but I have to thank the dear departed Packy for that. I'm glad we found each other and that you're not working for a competing firm. We can use you, and I'd hate to be up against you."

Lara blushed as she said, "That's about the highest compliment I have received since Alex proposed. We chose to physically help you instead of just making a call to warn you because your family is no longer involved with drugs or some of the other crimes we disapprove of. Both Alex and I love to play poker, so we can see the attraction of your after-hours clubs. We both know that we will be farmed out to assist organizations involved in trades we don't condone, but we're not going to be in bed with them, just removing the worst of the worst."

Just then, Tony came to the library and announced, "Dinner is served, everybody. Come get it while it's hot."

The party adjourned to the garden, where a barbecue dinner awaited. They ate, drank, and talked for hours, and none of it concerned business. Papa Paul watched Alex and Lara closely and appeared confident that the pair had found a home for their pursuit at last.

* * *

After a couple of hours, Alex and Lara left for home. Lucy sat down next to Papa Paul on the porch swing. Angelo and Tony were sitting in wicker chairs opposite them.

Papa Paul asked Tony, "Are we clear out here tonight?"

Tony laughed and said, "Yeah. Every organized crime cop in three counties is working on the fracas at Rossi's. The two morons who park out on the street behind us aren't' there tonight. It's the only line-of-sight vantage point of the back yard. Besides, the stereo speakers at the pool are between us and the back wall. Guido has been sweeping the house for bugs since the Donat thing started, so, yeah, we're clear."

Angelo asked Papa Paul, "You think they're completely what they represent themselves to be?"

Before Papa Paul could answer, Lucy replied, "Everything and more, Angelo. Not only do they have the craziest skills, but they have the drive to do it, too. What's more, they have been an organism looking for a host. I've seen it before. What they craved as much as being able to kill bad men was finding a world in which it was not only acceptable but prized. When we valued their work and praised them, it was like a drug. We're providing that alternate universe where what they're doing is not only condoned, it is highly prized."

Lucy thought for a moment and added, "As long as we channel their energy properly, we have a formidable tool. Did you see the detachment Lara showed when poking and prodding Dominic? The two of them look at this as a real vocation, with knowledge gained essentially by the scientific method. Angelo, if memory serves, you threw up when you made your bones. You couldn't even carry the newly departed Mike Zitti out to the car. The guys Papa's dad sent with you had to do it. And when Matty Genolo said you had back-splattered blood on your face, you threw up again."

"You knew about that?" Angelo asked, blushing slightly.

"Are you kidding? I was Papa's fiancé at the time. Those macho fucks who took you to the hit were laughing about it in the kitchen when Papa and I got home from our movie date that night. They joked about you praying at the porcelain altar after you made your bones. And don't give 'em no crap. You did the same when anyone under you folded the way you did. Rite of passage.

"Anyway, these kids are the genuine article. Smart, overly careful, clinically efficient hitters we can mold any way we want. They're motivated by the good they think they are doing, and if I read Lara correctly, by the sexual turn-on it gives them. That's a strong set of incentives."

Papa Paul hugged her and gave her a kiss on the cheek before he added, "My Lucy is right once again. My grandfather and then my father had Salvatore Demanincor. I've had some pretty good ones, too—like you, Angelo, after you toughened up a bit, and Tony here."

Tony looked deadly serious when he replied. "Papa, I'm not too bad, if I do say so myself, but those two scare the crap out of me. I painted some houses for you because the family needed me to," he said, referring to the blood-splattered walls where hits occurred. "Those two do it because they love the setup, and their favorite house paint is red. Same as Sally."

Papa Paul looked at his wife and asked, "Lucy, do you think …?"

"Yeah. Old-fashioned drive with twenty-first-century smarts and technology. Where Sally was a blunt instrument, though, I think we found a stiletto."

* * *

Back at their house, Alex and Lara were elated beyond words. Their new jobs assured; they tendered their resignations at their respective places of employment the following week. Papa Paul's offer eclipsed their salaries by quite a bit. That was an unusual state of affairs for people so new to the organization, but both Lucy and Pauli Jr. insisted on it.

As Lucy said when they were told about the salary, "You two wouldn't take a dime for saving the girls and us. This is Papa's and my way of saying thanks. Quid pro quo. For life, too. Pauli Jr. is even more adamant about it. You saved his kids."

Siggy mentored the pair at first. He explained who was who in the organization and explained jargon and protocol. Alex and Lara soon found out that things were often not how they were portrayed in the movies, though some were.

Most hits were just someone walking up to someone else with a gun and opening up, not elaborately choreographed ballets with the hitman rappelling down from a skylight and then taking out twelve disposable goons in hand-to-hand combat before reciting a long monologue and killing the mark in some obscure way. If a boss wanted someone dead, he didn't say, "Kill him," and then leave so the tied-up victim could overcome the goons holding him and get away. The boss said, "Kill him," and the guy was dead.

From their hitman research, Lara and Alex already knew much of what Siggy told them. When Siggy described the organization's early years and clashes with other outfits, they found some of the brutal reality of the more violent, out-of-control gangs disturbing.

On the other hand, the movie explanation that when someone said "my friend" it meant someone who wasn't a made associate and that "our friend" meant a made wiseguy who could be trusted was pretty much the real thing.

Siggy got a good laugh, though, when Lara sheepishly admitted one day that some of their complex shenanigans were derived from movie plots they had seen as teens.

"Just go with it," Siggy advised. "Papa Paul gets a kick out of it, and it makes a lot of your work look like anything but what the cops expect. Sometimes bizarre can be camouflage, I guess."

Over the next couple of years, Alex and Lara became the most feared hitters in the organization, even if only a few knew who they actually were. Siggy contracted them out for hits all over the country. There was the occasional local job for one of Papa Paul's split-off former capos, too. They were used in third-party contracts to provide a buffer for sensitive hits. In, hit, out, and disappear like they were never there. More than once, a targeted mob blamed an internal power struggle for a member's death just as in the Donat Vayda elimination. They built an impressive résumé and were sought after for difficult situations.

* * *

From the first day of their new venture, Alex and Lara knew they needed a cover occupation and a way to launder their salaries. Lara was the family expert on eBay and other online auction sites, both buying firearms accessories and reloading equipment and selling no-longer-needed items. They decided to try using that to launder their salaries, but it proved impossible to move that much money or cook the books so that the cash flow from Siggy was hidden. They found that legitimate buying and selling of eBay items took far too much time and effort for the amounts they needed to launder.

Siggy made a suggestion: "You know, Papa Paul, Lucy, Petie, and most of the others at their level love antiques, like the furniture in Papa Paul's house. The markup is incredible, and who's to say what something is actually worth? Why not buy things they want on the legitimate market and then just mark them up so the profit matches your salary? Maybe add jewelry to your line, too. The retail markup is eight hundred percent or more. That way no cash comes to you that can't be accounted for. We have dozens of businesses and associates we can funnel the money through."

He explained, "You buy legitimately, sell like a wiseguy, and the family gets stuff they want in return. Now that Papa Paul is going legit, he can use the paperwork to show the feds that his house isn't furnished with stuff that fell off a truck. The IRS was always a bigger fear than the FBI to him. My lawyers can set you up with legit corporate papers, a tax ID, and the works."

Alex and Lara were quick studies, and within months they had a thriving business, complete with a storefront and a few employees. A year later, quite a few auction houses and antique dealers knew them on a first-name basis.

After a couple of years, Papa Paul finally decided to completely retire from the rackets. Angelo and Petie were given the remaining gambling operations. Papa Paul and Lucy moved south and turned the legit business completely over to Pauli Jr. That included everything he had managed with Siggy except the wiseguy side of the specialized department Lara and Alex were a part of. Pauli Jr. decided he didn't want the risk, so Siggy continued to report to Papa Paul when it came to painting houses.

Papa Paul wasn't directly involved in that operation, looking at it more as an insurance policy to be used internally only in case of another Donat incident. Siggy ran the operation independently with a two-person staff at the end of a corporate maze of legitimate companies. He just briefed Papa Paul from time to time as necessary. Besides, that department was so well hidden in Siggy's otherwise sterling organization that the feds still didn't have a clue about it. When not arranging the now-infrequent hit, the two employees sourced dried cranberries, chocolate, and other ingredients for a regional chain of Lenetti-owned dessert bakeries in the Southwest.

In this circuitous chain of command, Alex and Lara theoretically would have kissed Papa Paul's ring, not Pauli Jr.'s. In reality, though, their only direct interactions with Papa Paul and his family were social, something they all cherished.

* * *

About two years after Papa Paul retired, Siggy had Alex and Lara met with Papa Paul and Lucy at their retirement spread just south of Nashville, Tennessee. They had a most special operation they wanted the two to start. That they were initiating a new charitable hobby was all Alex and Lara were told. It was one that would prove entertaining to the pair and, as it turned out, quite beneficial in general for the removal of irritating pests from humanity.

That was what made them perfect candidates for the first visit to Edward and the string that followed. And that was why they found themselves sitting in a Moscow restaurant contemplating a security system diagram.

Chapter 9

Lubov Has a Special Request

In that Moscow restaurant a few days before Cody and William met Alyosha and Sasha, Lara handed the tablet back to Alex. She pointed to a few security features.

"Way too sophisticated for a mere Internet scammer. Connected? Russian Mafia? Maybe just paranoid?"

"Lara, when you did your research on this mook, you didn't find any connection, did you?"

"Nothing in police files. Not with FSB or local Moscow cops, and there's really nothing about him on the Dark Web other than that he sells stolen credit card and identity info and makes some ransomware attacks when victims believe he is from the Microsoft Help Desk and they let him establish a remote session on their computer. If there's a connection, it's hidden."

Alex took Lara's hand and smiled lovingly. "Darling, you are the best with a computer I have ever seen, so if your sixth sense tells you to, send a message to the cranberry buyers. I have no idea who they contact, but their presence on the Dark Web is really next level. Ask them what we should do if a link on Gleb's computer leads to anyone the family does business with. The dons that split off from Papa Paul's family have a lot of Russian, uh, imports."

The restaurant was not more than twenty years old but had been decorated in pre-Revolution style, with gold trim, red flocked wallpaper, and lights made to look like old-fashioned gas lamps. The menu was old school, too, with classic entrées. Lara had skewers of lamb shashlik, and Alex went for the stroganoff.

The couple picked that particular restaurant not only for the traditional food but also for its musical program. There were singers and dancers on a small stage.

Alex had the interesting ability of polyglotism. He was able to learn languages with extreme ease. It was discovered when he was a young boy. His parents took him on vacation to Mexico, and they were amazed when he read a phrasebook on the plane and then spoke to Mexico's customs officials in broken Spanish. His parents had him tested, and his unusual ability was confirmed. With the encouragement of his father, he subsequently learned half a dozen languages. He learned more now as he needed them. One of them was Russian for their antique import business, and it came in handy again on this trip.

At one point, a singer with an accordion strolled through the audience as he sang "Ochi Chyornye," or "Dark Eyes," the most famous Russian romance song. The singer encouraged the audience to stand and participate. Alex stood with the rest of those singing and sang to Lara in Russian. The first verse's English translation was "Dark eyes, burning eyes, passionate and splendid eyes. How I love you, how I fear you. Truly, I saw you at a sinister hour." Except for the color of her eyes, the words fit her perfectly.

The performer saw Alex, likely a tourist, standing and singing to his lover in excellent Russian. Alex was overly dramatic, using grand hand and arm movements to accentuate each verse. The performer strolled to Alex, and together they finished the song, to Lara's delight, though she only knew a few of the Russian words. The audience stood and clapped as the performer shook hands with Alex.

He said to Alex in Russian, "That was very good Russian, my friend. Does your lovely companion speak Russian, too?"

"Oh, no. Just enough to order at a restaurant," Alex replied, also in Russian.

"Do you know Russian folk dancing in addition to folk songs?" the singer asked.

"No, but I have seen many dances and have always wanted to learn," Alex replied.

"Please come to the stage. Our troupe is next."

Alex again amazed the singer when he could dance a few kazatsky steps, squatting and kicking a leg straight out in front. Most tourists couldn't do it, even with a dancer holding them up from behind. The conditioning and balance from his martial arts practice gave Alex the ability to perform the difficult dance step.

After a round of applause from the dance troupe, Alex returned to Lara to finish his meal.

Dance music was next, and the musicians took requests. At one point, Alex asked if they could play a tango. He and Lara learned the dance after they watched True Lies and Assassination Tango. It had become their favorite.

Several other couples joined them on the dance floor, and there were a few excellent dancers among them. Alex and Lara mainly stuck to the basic eight-step tango but threw in a few figure eights and a dip at the close. Alex felt her lithe body under that silky dress as they danced, and he loved it.

* * *

Returning to the hotel after dinner and dancing, they checked for messages at the front desk.

"Yes, sir, you have one. A Miss Lubov Vasilyeva will be here in the morning at eleven to take you sightseeing."

They thanked the desk clerk and went to their room.

"Alex, Siggy's guys must have found something. This is getting interesting."

When Lara fired up her VPN network connection and checked emails, there was one from Siggy, as she expected: "To my overly cautious, anal-retentive, paranoid control freaks. Thanks! Your hunch panned out. The upgrade you mentioned at the client's building was required by the friend of a friend, who says 'thank you.'"

Alex read the email and remarked, "The security system upgrade at Gleb's was a third-party requirement. I can't wait to meet Lubov. Siggy didn't say to cancel our appointment with Gleb, so I guess he's in deep doo-doo with whomever Lubov represents."

* * *

The following day, Alex and Lara were sitting on two green velvet couches facing a central coffee table in a small alcove off the hotel lobby. The thick oriental carpet and curved, burnished wood trim gave the impression that it was designed for the kind of confidential conversations among persons of substance that Alex and Lara expected to have presently with the mystery woman, Lubov. They were having hot tea, served in a glass inside a silver-handled holder in the traditional Russian way, when they saw the concierge wave to them.

"Sir and madam, your guest has arrived," he called out.

A well-dressed woman in her forties was at the desk. Alex stood and approached. They exchanged the traditional air kisses on both cheeks.

She spoke in English, with a slight Muscovite accent. "Welcome to Moscow. Some mutual friends have asked me to take you sightseeing today. My name is Lubov."

"Come sit with us and have tea, Lubov." Then in a low tone, he added, "Did Siggy brief you?"

"Yes. To my people, Alex and Lara Cutter only."

Alex and Lara knew what the message the night before from Siggy meant. It was an emergency protocol. Siggy had contacted a Russian counterpart who did business with one of Papa Paul's former capos. Lubov, either a capo, a counselor, or a fixer, would be the only other member of that person's organization who would know their cover contact information. Alex guessed she was the Russian equivalent of Marvin Smalls, but mob etiquette did not permit him to ask. That Siggy had vetted her was sufficient.

The pair joined Lara, who rose and exchanged kisses with Lubov. Alex motioned to a waiter to fetch them another glass of tea.

"Tea from a glass and not a big mug of coffee? How un-American," Lubov joked.

"Lubov, when in Rome. The two of us like to get as much local color and custom as we can get when we travel," Lara replied.

Lubov laughed and sat, saying quietly, "Your observations were most appreciated. Your Mister Siggy called my employer on behalf of one of your employer's past associates. We do a little business with that associate's firm, and he had our friends check with a number of your friends. It appears that a certain acquaintance you may see later this week has represented himself to one of our friends as something he is not."

Alex nodded that he understood as Lubov continued, "Our friend has given this acquaintance some business, and he may be in the possession of certain spreadsheets containing lists of products. Once we're alone, I'll give you a list of files our friend does not want your acquaintance to continue to possess any longer."

"And what would be the desired disposition of this acquaintance?"

"Deal with him how you like. He is no longer of any concern to our friends once those files disappear."

Alex and Lara understood every word. Lubov was a member of an organization that was probably importing or exporting black-market goods or involved in some similar activity. Apparently, something impacted someone involved with one of Papa Paul's former capos.

One of the American organization's Russian partners had given Gleb some work. Alex and Lara's inquiry apparently revealed that he was also engaged in the unauthorized extracurricular phone-scam activities that brought Alex and Lara to Moscow. It could jeopardize some small portion of the mob's work if he was exposed.

"Let's go see some churches, our new friends," Lubov said in a louder voice as she stood.

Alex and Lara followed her to her car. Lubov gave the driver instructions, and they departed. In the front seat next to the driver, Lubov turned to speak to her passengers in English.

"Your employer informed me of what you are here to do. It is a most humorous business. I will be watching to see how it turns out."

Once they were away from the hotel, Lubov handed Lara a USB thumb drive. Lara pocketed it immediately.

"There is one encrypted file and a program. The password is 'Laika1957.' Capital L. Please reformat and then physically destroy the stick when you are done."

Alex mused, "Ah, Laika, the first dog in space back in 1957. Easy to remember."

Lubov raised an eyebrow and smiled as she said, "I see you know your Russian history. But back to our little problem associate. As I said, one of our friends hired him as an outside contractor because he knows the Dark Web extremely well. He was hired to do some trivial work, but it should still not be made available to the authorities. It is my understanding that you will leave him very exposed."

"Oh, yeah. Lara and I will leave him with his zipper down. You know this expression?"

"Yes. It is most appropriate. I know you will be leaving him with something uncomfortable placed somewhere sensitive. My employers have asked if you could make that something likely to do damage."

Alex and Lara laughed, and Lara offered, "Yeah. I'll have Alex hold him down, and we'll use something with sharp edges. Will that do?"

Lubov smiled and replied, "Yes, that will amuse them. The man you are seeing has no stars. Those who do will be watching him."

Alex knew that she was referring to the tattooed stars of the vory v zakone, the original, prison-spawned Russian Mafia. He guessed that after the vory had a good laugh over what he and Lara were going to do, Gleb would be killed in prison.

They toured Moscow for several hours. Unlike the commercial tours they usually booked through the hotels, Lubov took them to places with special meaning for her and her family. She described areas in terms of pre–Cold War and post–Cold War. Lubov treated them to some delicious smoked fish for lunch at her favorite restaurant.

After ordering, she explained, "Under the Soviet regime, only those in power came here. The food was of better quality than most places, and food of that quality wasn't plentiful. You had to be someone or know someone to come here. Now you just need money."

As they pulled up to their hotel after the tour, she reached into the back seat to shake their hands.

"I will most likely not need to contact you again. On the chance that you do need further assistance, you can reach us through your employer. Are you sure you do not need anything else? Weapons? Tools?"

"No. We have that covered already."

"I was told of your antique business. You know we can get you antiquities, too."

Alex said, "Thank you for the kind offer. We only buy them if they come with proper documentation and all the export papers. Most of my clients are high-end, and they insist on everything being proper and legal. Not to mention, of course, that the paper trail for this visit has to pass muster if I ever get audited."

"Very well, then. Not too many of our suppliers have that kind of genuine paperwork available. Good luck and, again, welcome to Moscow."

* * *

Back in their room, Lara unlocked the file on the USB stick. It had a list of file names, people, and organizations to search for. A few essential contents of the spreadsheets were also given in case Gleb had renamed any of the files. The program was a hard drive cleaner that could scrub a whole hard drive, a specific disk sector, or just a single file. It was bulletproof when it came to erasing files, but no one in Siggy or Lubov's organizations could have anticipated the unintended consequences of using it.

* * *

For the next few days, they enjoyed themselves and made some antique purchases from dealers they knew. Soon enough, it was time to go to work. Lara had been in communication with Gleb for some time on the Dark Web. She purchased blocks of credit card numbers from him to establish credibility. She used a Dark Web identity that had access to deep levels of several Dark Web sites trafficking in such things. It had taken her years to develop the trust among denizens of those chat rooms to access levels that deep.

She contacted Gleb and said she would have some Bitcoin coming in at 1 a.m. his time. She asked if he could sell her some more card numbers if it wasn't too much trouble to stay up that late. She already knew that he was usually on the computer between 8 p.m. and 3 a.m. Moscow time.

Gleb responded that he would be in a particular chat room at that time, and she could contact him there.

Chapter 10

Gleb Wishes He Hadn't Been Quite So Greedy

Later that week, Alex and Lara rented a car. Alex told the hotel concierge, "We decided to do some sightseeing outside Moscow for a day and a night. We're going to leave some of our luggage in our room here. Can you recommend a hotel near Zelenograd? We want a tour the area northwest of Moscow."

The concierge replied, "Of course, sir. I can make a reservation for you and handle all the paperwork you will need if you will permit me."

Alex said, "That would be very nice of you," as he rewarded the concierge with a handsome tip for his efforts.

The Zelenograd hotel was many kilometers farther from Gleb's suburban residence than their Moscow hotel was. Gleb's town of Pushkino was northeast of their Moscow hotel, while Zelenograd was to the northwest. The path to Gleb's apartment building from their new hotel would now be along suburban and rural roads, not those from the center of the city. They would swing around and approach his house from the A113 highway on the side opposite urban Moscow.

They did some sightseeing, taking lots of pictures to show back at their Moscow hotel. They shopped and ate along their sightseeing route, being sure to use credit cards liberally. The photos wouldn't provide an alibi for the exact time of their visit with Gleb, but they would reinforce their touristy cover. They stopped at several shops offering handicrafts and local foods. At one souvenir shop, they returned to their car with a large shopping bag.

They checked in at the Zelenograd hotel and unpacked. After dinner at a nearby restaurant, they returned to their room and dressed for the evening's main event. Both had light leotards with long sleeves and hoods. They donned them but kept the hoods down and put their street clothes on over the leotards. Under a colorful babushka in the bag from the souvenir shop were a few items they had been provided that were not generally associated with tourist businesses. There were two tool bags and some other materials. One bag contained some electronics, zip ties, a few tools, leather gloves, and a nylon climbing harness. The other held a small rubber ball, surgical gloves, a roll of tape, goggles, and a thin cloth stuff bag. There was also a license plate, garbage bags, and a gallon of chlorine bleach.

They left through a back door, carrying the shopping bag. There was one security camera at the back of the hotel. The pair switched their car's plates as soon as the vehicle was outside its view.

***

It was just before midnight, and they were near Gleb's house forty-five minutes later. They parked in an area with other cars on the street and walked the remaining two blocks to Gleb's residence, the end unit of a block of two-story townhouses.

There were very few detached houses anywhere near metropolitan Moscow that were not for the wealthy. These townhouses were a luxurious oddity.

"Lara, Gleb must be doing pretty well with his scams to be able to afford this."

Lara chuckled and predicted, "The bigger they are, the harder they fall. A prison cell will feel worse because he's used to this."

They ducked down an alley that led to the lightless parking area behind the apartments. There they took off their outer layers and stashed the clothing in the stuff bag, which Lara slung over her shoulder. They pulled up the hoods and put booties over their shoes. They donned goggles with mirrored lenses, keeping them on their foreheads until they were inside. Lara put on surgical gloves, and Alex put on the pair of thin leather gloves. They saw a shadow on a shade in one of the first-floor windows. It moved every now and then, illuminated by what looked to be a computer monitor or television screen.

Alex went to work on the security system. Gleb was home, so Alex knew the motion sensors inside would not be activated. On the other hand, the perimeter sensors were most likely in night mode, so he had to deal with that. He went for a window on the second floor. Alex scrambled up the one-and-a-half-inch main electrical conduit from the street to the window and attached a seat strap to it so he could work in the dark in relative comfort.

He worked from the plans drawn by the company that upgraded Gleb's security system. They had been obtained for rubles in a paper bag given to a security company technician by Siggy's Russian friends. Alex located the window sensor and put a meter on the outside wall just above it. The alarm sensors downstairs were very sophisticated, according to the security company records. The second-floor window sensors, on the other hand, were old school. People often failed to upgrade second-story devices, figuring that if anyone was going to break in, they'd do it from the first floor, where the access was more straightforward. The people who had given Gleb the files and the business that came with them probably insisted on better security, but Gleb had gone cheap when it came to the second floor. Alex read a small current on the alarm wire in the wall. He used a one-inch neodymium magnet to keep the inexpensive reed switch of the sensor closed.

He loved security systems as bad as this that didn't require Lara to design electronic bypasses or cell phone jamming. He told Lara that fancy systems with weak points this vulnerable were akin to putting a hundred-dollar lock on a two-dollar hasp.

It was a simple task to jimmy the casement lock and open the window an inch. The meter did not register a change in the alarm wire current. He opened the window all the way, and he was inside in a flash. He put the meter in his tool bag and reached out to unhook the seat strap, pulling it inside and wrapping it around his waist. He took off the leather gloves and placed them inside his tool bag, too, replacing them with surgical gloves.

He looked around and realized Gleb was a pig on several levels. He was in a bedroom. Dirty clothes were all over the floor. Porn was posted on the walls, including child pornography. There were used tissues that Alex was careful to avoid. Kiddie porn would certainly get Gleb even more notice from the police.

He went to the stairs and heard Gleb on the first floor, at his computer in a back room. There was a video playing, and someone in it was doing a lot of moaning. He silently crept down the stairs to the kitchen, where he found a large carving knife with a fair edge. He looked in the room where he heard the noise and saw Gleb from behind. He was watching porn with his hand obviously in his lap. This was going to be even more enjoyable than Alex had thought. He walked up behind Gleb and put the knife to his neck.

Gleb gasped and started to jerk forward until he felt the blade against his flesh. He froze.

Alex knew it would get his message to Gleb more effectively if he spoke Russian even though Gleb spoke fluent English. He told Gleb not to move. Gleb stayed still. Alex pulled out a zip tie and bound Gleb's hands behind him.

"What is the alarm disable code?" Alex asked.

"One three seven nine one six," Gleb repeated at the point of the knife.

"Repeat it backward."

"Uh, six … one, nine … seven three one."

Alex had him repeat the code, both forward and backward, faster and faster. It was almost impossible to make up false codes and get them right time after time like that.

When Alex was reasonably sure that he had the code, he marched Gleb, still unzipped and exposed—but now flaccid—to the alarm panel and entered the disable code. They went to the back door next, where Lara was waiting in the shadows.

She laughed when she saw Gleb exposed.

They marched him back to the computer room and tied him up on the floor with various computer cables.

Lara spoke to him in English.

"You understand me, don't you, you scheming crooked bastard?"

"Yes, I understand, and you two are in huge trouble. Do you know who I work for?"

"Used to work for. The vor you took money from is very upset that you are doing work on the side that could expose him. You had a good thing, but you got greedy and decided to do something your partner did not think was an acceptable risk."

"I do nothing to be exposed," Gleb protested, suddenly looking even more worried that his attackers knew something about who had given him the files.

Lara took the knife from Alex and gestured toward Gleb's open fly. Gleb tried to move away but couldn't.

"That, my perverted friend, looks awfully exposed to me. Honey, can I cut it off? I don't want to touch it, and it just bothers me hanging out like that."

The terrified Gleb rolled over to protect his groin.

Lara laughed and said, "Gleb, that is just the pose we want you in."

She went to one of the computers and began a file search. There were several password-protected files and directories. Gleb didn't want to cooperate at first. Lara cut through the back of his belt and sliced his trousers down to his crotch. She did the same to his shorts.

She said, "Gleb, we're going to have a little clarification session. We want to know codes and passwords. By the time I'm done back here, you will want us to know them, too."

She started poking his butt with the knife tip.

Gleb squirmed as she went to town on him. At first, he resisted and wouldn't give any information. She slapped his butt with the flat of the blade and prodded for a few minutes before he realized that she wasn't going to stop. There were only a few pinpricks with a couple of drops of blood. Lara was trying to encourage cooperation, not wound him seriously.

"Please stop," he pleaded. "They will kill me if I give you what you want."

"Gleb, they sent us here. If they wanted you dead, you would be dead already. I want you to know I'm the nice one. If you don't tell us what we want to know, my honey here is going to roll you over and go to town with, with something terrible. What are you going to use, honey?"

"Well, I found a cheese grater in the kitchen and a pair of pliers over there on the server rack. I haven't made up my mind yet. Gleb, do you have a preference?"

When Gleb didn't answer, Alex rolled him over and held up the cheese grater while Lara held him down.

"Let's go for some grated nuts, shall we, Gleb?"

As Alex reached out with the grater, Gleb started to sob. Alex and Lara had subjects in the past that held out for as long as half an hour. Gleb was a wimp.

"I'll tell you codes. Don't, please not to do that."

He gave each password as Lara found files. Eventually, the list on the USB stick was exhausted. She had found four files containing their associate's data. She used the eraser program to do multiple scrubs on the target files.

Then they had another question-and-answer session about backup disks, drives, and web-based storage.

Lara asked, "Would you care to describe your backup system and tell us where any laptops or other portable devices might be?"

"No … I don't have any. No backups."

"And no laptops or tablets, either?"

"N-no. No such devices."

Alex held up the cheese grater and smiled.

"Okay. I believe you, Gleb. As a token of my appreciation for being so honest, I think Mr. Shred-All and I will have a party, and you're invited. Actually, I don't think you heard my questions correctly. To improve your hearing, I think I'll take the liberty of grating off your left ear. I understand that when one sensory stimulus source is lost, the body makes up for it by heightening the senses elsewhere. Maybe after your left ear is gone, you'll hear my questions better with your right ear."

He reached out slowly with the grater toward Gleb's left ear. As soon as the metal touched the ear, Gleb started crying.

"I'll tell you. Stop! I'll tell you."

Now Gleb was ready to give up his backups, laptop, account names and passwords for the child pornography sites, and many other things.

Lara found the two backup drives and a laptop with the same four files, but nothing belonging to Lubov's people on any of Gleb's cloud storage. She erased every copy of the files, scrubbing them all thoroughly.

When she was absolutely sure that Gleb had given her everything she and Alex were after, Lara told him why they were there.

"Gleb, you are an asshole of the first order. You steal from the wrong people. In addition to the usual scams to bilk old people out of their savings, you planted ransomware that wound up infecting a hospital. One of their shit-for-brains employees answered your phone call from the 'Microsoft Help Desk,' and you put a virus on his home computer. When he used a USB drive from it at work, you were notified by the virus, and you forced the hospital to pay to unlock their files. Well, it happens that our employer donates money to that hospital. He thinks they do good work, and you froze their files for a day. You broke the ransomware code of conduct: no hospitals, charities, or safety services. That was very naughty of you. For that, you will be punished."

Gleb looked back at her with a blank stare. He apparently couldn't believe that anyone would go to this kind of trouble over something as trivial as scam phone calls and ransomware that only cost a hospital five thousand US dollars in Bitcoin.

"Is there more? Did Rodion not send you?"

"No, we don't know anyone named Rodion. You have simply been bad, and you need to be punished," Alex reiterated.

"But why?" Gleb whined.

Lara huffed impatiently and scolded, "We told you. You are a pest—a pain in the ass. You bother people and screwed up a hospital for a day, so some of them sent us to bother you back. Now hold still, or this is gonna hurt even worse. My honey here is going to put a rubber ball in your mouth now and keep it there with tape. I suggest you bite down hard on it."

She got some bacon grease from a jar next to the stove along with a spatula to coat the slim burner phone they had brought. Gleb's own cellphone was far too large to insert.

"Get ready for Mr. Cell Phone, Gleb," Lara cooed as she patted his butt and applied lots of lard. She made a face and looked at Alex.

"Eew, honey. I really hate this part when their personal hygiene isn't the greatest. Gleb, you stink. I mean physically, in addition to your naughty activities. Better think about something to take your mind off this."

Alex got down next to Gleb's head and patted his cheek. While Alex distracted Gleb, Lara broke the cell phone's corner, leaving a jagged edge.

Alex explained, "She's right. This can cause some small degree of discomfort. Think about happy things, like what other prisoners do to people convicted of child pornography. This is probably going to be the first of many happy backdoor encounters."

She went to work as Gleb screamed against his gag. When she was done, the cell phone was buried painfully inside him. There wasn't much blood, but enough to know that the sharp edge had done minor damage. Alex and Lara knew that it would hurt even worse coming out, as the broken edge was pointing mainly in that direction.

Alex whispered to Gleb in Russian, "We are going to leave in a few minutes and report back to our employers … and yours. Your employers have paid the police a lot of money to report back to them exactly what you say to the police. Whatever you say will be known to your employers. Some of them, I'm guessing, started in the old vory v zakone and now work with your employers. You do not want them to hear anything disturbing. Vory v zakone started in prison. That is where you are going, and their presence there today is undeniable. You have no choice now. They will make sure that you die painfully if you tell."

He sternly added, "I have it on good authority that if you tell the authorities about those four files or say more than that two people in black came in and tied you up, you will be tortured to death. Personally, I think they will cut your skin all the way round your waist and pull it up over your head. You'll suffocate before you bleed to death is my guess."

Lara got down next to Alex and said, "Okay, Gleb. I don't know what my honey there just said, but I hope it was entirely horrible. We're going to leave you tied up here for several hours so you can contemplate your sins. Whatever you do, don't try to take a shit. It would kill you. I just printed out a list of all your file locations and passwords for your friends in the Moscow police to find.

"Now, you may be tempted to free yourself. That would not be wise. See the wire attached to this safety pin I'm putting on your collar? It's attached to the pin of a hand grenade. Unless you lie here perfectly still, you will die. Okay? Maybe move your feet a bit, but not your torso. Nod your head if you understand."

Gleb nodded. He didn't know that the wire was merely attached to the far leg of the desk. So far, none of their previous victims had tested it, either.

On this trip, Lara decided to add a special touch. She pointed out a bookcase loaded with ceramics and glassware. She motioned to it and tilted her arm to indicate something falling. Alex grinned and nodded. They tipped it forward until it was just about to fall over. Lara placed a drinking glass under the rear to keep it precariously balanced. Alex tied a network cable to the top of the case and then to the cords binding Gleb's legs.

"As soon as Gleb moves his legs, the bookcase will come crashing down," Lara whispered. "No one can keep entirely still for hours, after all. The bookcase will miss him, but he'll be covered in ceramic fragments."

"The noise will probably scare the neighbors and save Siggy's contacts from having to call the police themselves. I'll notify Siggy to have them monitor the dispatches just in case," she added.

Alex turned to Gleb and said in Russian, "We will send someone here to disarm the grenade. If you don't move, you will be fine. Now promise us you will be good from now on. No more bilking old people out of their savings or messing with hospital computers, okay?"

Gleb still apparently couldn't understand why this had happened and why the pair were leaving without doing anything more than roughing him up and erasing four files. His face was a mix of terror and bewilderment.

"Gleb, pay attention. Was that a yes to being a good boy from now on? Nod your head again for yes—or would you prefer the cheese grater?"

Gleb nodded and was rewarded with another condescending pat on the head. Alex looked at the pathetic figure on the floor and said, again in Russian, "Relax, Gleb; you're so screwed that only talking to the cops could make it any worse."

Alex took out a little plastic zip pouch and placed its contents on the keyboard. It was one of his calling cards: Qatar's outline with the red dot. They didn't use the random DNA, fingerprint, and fiber gag much anymore because the American cops had finally gotten the joke and put the word out. According to Siggy's well-informed sources, many departments didn't even send a CSI team for DNA and fingerprints anymore. The cops' teams were there more to collect computer data and other evidence against the scammers themselves, not the assailants.

Chapter 11

Having an Exit Strategy Is Critical

Lara and Alex's setups for a hit, whether a lethal one or one of the robocall punishments, always tickled Papa Paul's funny bone, but what really got him in stitches were the elaborate getaways and evidence disposal the pair often planned. This time it wasn't the most complex scheme, but the foreign setting gave it a certain cachet. It started in Gleb's kitchen as the couple shed their black tights, booties, and hoods and put their street clothes back on. They exited through the back door. Alex left the magnet on the window sensor, as he'd wiped it clean before initiating the evening's events. They placed the tights in a black garbage bag with the goggles and then poured the gallon of chlorine laundry bleach into the bag. The plastic bleach jug was the last to go in before they sealed it with tape. They walked back to where the car was parked and put the tool bags and garbage bag into the trunk.

They drove to a small shopping area and parked behind it. It was the one that their contacts identified as having no security cameras in the rear. They searched the garbage cans for one that had the same type of garbage bag as theirs, and they placed theirs under one that was already in the can.

Their last stop was the alley behind the souvenir store where they had picked up the tool bags earlier. There was a metal box near the back door. They switched the plates again and then put the bogus plates and the tool bags in the box and locked it with a padlock they found inside it. They knew the security camera above was disabled from midnight to 3 a.m. just for this occasion. Alex and Lara also knew from the cranberry buyer's pre-trip briefing that more than half the merchandise for sale in the store "fell off a truck." It was owned by the mob and used for disposing of stolen cargo and laundering money.

Just before they got to their hotel, they stopped, and each gargled with and then spit out a couple of good swigs of vodka from a bottle they had purchased at one of the food stores they visited earlier that day. They poured out two-thirds of the contents of the bottle, a little of it onto their clothing. They parked and took off their gloves, putting them in their pockets. They staggered up to the night clerk's desk.

Alex slurred his speech as he asked where they could get some breakfast when they woke up. Both of them made a point of breathing the fresh vodka at the clerk, so he got a good whiff. He gave them a recommendation for a nearby cafe, saying that was where he ate himself. Alex reached into a pocket, pulled out a wad of crumpled bills, and gave it to the clerk without counting it as thanks for the recommendation.

They weaved over to the elevator and pushed the call button. While they were waiting, Alex pulled out the bottle. As the elevator door opened, he unscrewed the cap and raised the bottle in a farewell toast to the clerk. The clerk paused from counting the generous tip, laughed, and waved back.

In their room, they used scissors to cut the gloves into small pieces and flushed them down the toilet in a couple of batches. After, they made love like crazed badgers for the next hour.

* * *

In the morning, Alex and Lara did go to the cafe mentioned by the night clerk. They were pretty happy that they had gotten the recommendation, too. The food was inexpensive and excellent. Any time a restaurant was filled with lots of locals and few tourists, the food was bound to be good.

They took more pictures of churches and other points of interest on the way back to their Moscow hotel. Once there, they made a point of asking the concierge to help them put names to some of their digital pictures. The pair had long ago discovered that cover story elements were not only essential to maintain but could be fun if they chose enjoyable activities.

They stayed in Moscow for the following week. The paperwork for the antique business they did the first two days in Moscow was languishing on some bureaucrat's desk. The export permits on some antiques always took a while. Besides, in their research, they learned that the police would check airline, bus, and train passenger lists for one or two days before and after a crime but seldom searched for three and had neither the resources nor the inclination to do four on anything but the most serious of crimes.

Lara and Alex's contact for their legitimate business on this trip, Yuri Turgenev, had no inkling about their other profession. They invited Yuri and his wife, Irina, to the hotel for dinner and introduced them to the maître d' as business associates. While they were waiting for their table, the maître d' asked what kind of business they were in, and Alex told him about the antique export business.

"You know, our hotel has a specialist to assist you," the maître d' offered.

Yuri replied, "Yes. Your man and I often consult with each other about submitting paperwork. Irina and I have known Boris for years. He is a very meticulous man. Excellent work. These two here have known me for a few years now, too, so they come straight to me. Otherwise, Boris would be a good choice."

Having a good cover was necessary, and doing actual business was even better. The pair kept meticulous records and always paid the taxes on the profit from their company.

In addition to being a great cover that could be used worldwide, Alex and Lara really did enjoy this line of work. They put as much or more effort into it as into their other business. Both had become experts in the field and had become known among many prominent dealers on several continents in the relatively short time they had been in the trade. They discovered early that when you are buying high-end pieces, the better dealers are willing to spend time educating you about them. They had the time, money, and personalities to cultivate those business friendships.

The hitman business was well-paying work, but not that regular. There was a lot of time between hits and scammer visits, and the antiques kept them occupied between the happy little outings they completed on Papa Paul and Siggy's behalf.

The only problem with using one's legitimate business as a cover is that one has to use real names, not only for business but also for

travel. One has to be careful—really careful—about who hears which
name.

Chapter 12

Cody Is Glad He Got Up that Morning

Two and a half years after the first scammer visit by Alex and Lara, Cody heard a voice from the doorway: "Cody, grab William. Teleconference on the Qatar Card thing in thirty."

It was Phil Zelman, his supervisory special agent.

"Your office or the big conference room?"

"The little conference room off Henderson's office. Just the five of us," Phil answered.

"Five?"

"Yeah. You, me, William, Henderson, and someone new. Quantico is sending some private contractor PhD named Haley Briggs. Behavioral psychologist. I think she's the one who gave that training I sent you to a few months ago. She'll be here in a few. She's the reason for the call."

"Thank you! I'll get William," Cody responded, his mood suddenly elevated.

Cody found William in the copy room and leaned against the counter, smiling.

"Well, someone's in a good mood. What's up, Cody?"

"SAC just called a teleconference in thirty minutes. And guess who's coming to join us?" Cody teased.

"From the look on your face, I'd say either the Easter Bunny or a Playmate of the Month."

"Combination of the two. Do you remember that seminar we attended on profiling gang-related murder suspects?" Cody asked with the thumb-over-the-shoulder gesture to indicate the past.

"Yeah. Quantico a few months ago. So?"

"Do you remember a certain PhD named Haley Briggs?" Cody asked.

"The looker?" William laughed. "Sure. How could I forget? You talked about her for two months, even at the barbecue at my place. Abby said you never called her 'cause she's way too smart for you."

"Well, I'd just broken up with Gretchen, and Haley was seeing that National Academy liaison guy."

William shook a scolding finger as he said, "He transferred to San Diego long ago. You never called her because you're a wimp. So, what's with her?"

"Well, in less than half an hour, the two of us will be sitting in a room with her, Phil, and Henderson. Teleconference regarding the Qatar Card case."

"Finally! It's been four months. Just promise me one thing, though."

"Sure. What?" Cody asked.

"Promise me you won't embarrass the two of us in front of the SAC by getting a hard-on every time you look at her."

"Screw you, asshole," Cody laughed. "See you in Henderson's office in ten."

William was done in the copy room, and they walked to the "bullpen," the cubicle-filled office where special agents with similar duties were clustered. Desk, computer, bookshelf, and some personal items. Cody settled into the chair in his little domain and wondered what twist of fate caused the romance gods to favor him so.

Cody didn't want to admit it, but William was right. No matter how many times he tried to call Haley, he just couldn't make the call. The couple of times he started to, the phone seemed to weigh two hundred pounds. He was happy that he now had a reason to see her again. He bucked up his resolve and promised himself he would ask her out this time.

A quick trip to the men's room to make sure his tie was straight and he didn't have a big piece of spinach in his teeth, and he was on his way to the SAC's office.

* * *

She was already in Special Agent in Charge Dwayne Henderson's office when Cody arrived. Her shoulder-length auburn hair framed the oval face and brown eyes that had been in his thoughts for the last four months. She was dressed in business casual style, with a cardigan sweater instead of a suit jacket, but Cody hardly noticed. In low heels, she was his height, and Cody was thankful for every delightfully curvy inch of it.

Before his SAC could introduce them, Haley stood and extended her hand.

"Cody, good to see you again. It's been what, three months now?"

"Yeah. Well, four, actually. How have you been?"

He was aware that his face was probably a little flushed, and he knew it was her profession to detect emotional responses. He hoped she took it in the right way. He was elated when she looked him in the eye for a second and then smiled.

"I've been well, Cody. A lot happening since the seminar. Maybe we could get a cup of coffee, and I'll tell you about some personal updates after the teleconference."

Just then, Phil and William entered, and they and Haley exchanged greetings.

SAC Henderson had everyone sit, and Phil turned on the large monitor. The teleconference software was already running. One by one, the other field offices with Qatar Card cases, as they were now known, appeared on the screen. Everyone introduced themselves. SAC Henderson was the first to talk about the business of the day.

"The reason I called this teleconference was to introduce a new teammate. Dr. Haley Briggs is with us today. Many of you may have met her at one time or another at Quantico. She's a civilian consultant in psychological profiling, and we're hoping that we may be able to get some new insights into these cases. Dr. Briggs, the floor is yours."

"Glad to be here, folks. Just call me Haley. I understand that the Bureau's initial profiling efforts to assist the local police in these cases have run up against a brick wall. My firm was asked to develop a new approach, and I volunteered to lead that effort. I have been reviewing the case files, and I have a few ideas and observations I'd like to bounce off you collectively."

"We're all ears, Haley. The case is pretty much stagnant, and anything new will be a refreshing change," Henderson said.

Haley nodded and started, "Let me begin by saying most of you appear to be correct that this is not a pair of loners who are doing this on their own. All victims who were willing to talk about them in even the briefest detail say they are disciplined and workmanlike, though often sarcastic. They all report the phrase 'our employers' in the threats the pair uses to silence them."

The SAC interjected, "And that points to the reason we wanted a fresh set of eyes on the problem. The suspects' behavior is just too cavalier, and the information they supply to their victims about their employers is atypical of any professional hit team the Bureau has encountered."

Haley nodded again and said, "These two mysterious suspects, while appearing to work for someone powerful and deadly, also appear to be on a lark when they visit their victims. They talk casually and make jokes. They don't seem to have any problems doing or threatening to do terrible things to people. They're apparently not incensed enough themselves about the scammers to do this on their own. It's the people behind them we have to figure out.

"My company's opinion is that these two have been hired by someone who wants to tease the victims they are sent to torture. Someone who has enough resources to hire what appear to be very expensive operatives to avenge what are trivial crimes."

There were overlapping suggestions from all quarters until SAC Henderson asked for quiet so Haley could continue.

She explained, "In this case, the profiling factors are mainly those of a third party or parties."

Several special agents began to talk again, and SAC Henderson held up his hand once more to quiet them before asking, "Haley, can you distill the rationale behind your avenue of attack?"

"Sure. First, the very worst single crime known to have been committed by any of their victims was bilking seventy-five thousand dollars from an elderly couple. That was more than double the value in the next highest case, which was three times the next highest case.

The average is around a few hundred dollars based on what we saw in the scammers' bank records that were left unlocked and open on their computers by our pair. The ransomware case involving the hospital was several thousand dollars, as was the ransomware attack that did not result in releasing the victim's data after the ransom was paid. The fact that they were an attack on a hospital and what the ransomware community would call a dishonest ransom transaction may have been an independent trigger for the visit by our mystery pair. The victims were not even remotely connected, so how the Qatar Card pair knew to target them is still a mystery, though.

"Second, the average fee for a professional hit is between fifteen and thirty thousand dollars. We have over twenty of these cases now. Because they are not actually murders, we guess five to ten thousand dollars per visit. At the low estimate, that's over a hundred thousand dollars, not counting travel and expenses, which in some cases probably exceeds the actual fee.

"Third, the Bureau has a computer analysis of all the scammed victims. There is no correlation between them, and none have the resources to go after the scammers."

Cody agreed. He looked into the camera to address the remote participants and said, "All of you pretty much ruled out scam victims being the perpetrators after looking at what your local police departments found in the records at each scene."

"Right." Haley nodded. "The fourth point is that we think the pair are sociopaths, not psychopaths, who justify their actions to themselves. They show restraint in what damage they do to their victims. They appear to follow their employer's specific instructions, which seems to include ridiculing the scammers they visit. The Qatar cards are intentionally left to link the crimes as a warning to other scammers that any one of them could be next. More than anything, though, the cards look like props from a romanticized hitman movie. We're factoring that aspect into our analysis."

She let this information sink in for a few seconds and then concluded, "Now, ladies and gentlemen, how do we profile something we've never seen before? We have a millionaire, or possibly billionaire, who is willing to spend insane amounts of money to go after people who have seemingly done nothing against him or her. He doesn't physically harm his victims other than having his agents shove something up their ass to drive the point home, so to speak."

That brought a round of laughter from the participants. When it subsided, Haley continued, "Right. No matter how we start, we come up with something incredible. We have stripped away every possible traditional motive. In the words of Sherlock, whatever remains, no matter how improbable, has to be the answer."

She waited for a few seconds. The anticipation was palpable as the agents smiled in anticipation of her punch line. "Whoever is behind this is doing it for fun. He's doing it for a hobby."

The collective virtual assembly erupted in laughter again. Some of them disagreed, but most thought it was at least plausible.

"Listen up!" someone yelled. It came from one of the special agents in the Denver Field Office.

SAC Henderson called the teleconference back to order and asked what Special Agent Christopher Ullery had to say.

"It could be a hobby, but I think it might go deeper. Could someone be doing this as a service? I mean, we have all gotten a call from the phony Microsoft Help Desk, someone selling overpriced auto repair insurance, or Rachel, Heather or Carmen from cardholder services. Who here hasn't secretly wished they could reach through the phone lines and choke out the asshole on the other end or shove his keyboard up his ass? Doctor Briggs, could someone have taken this up as both a hobby and a public service to avenge scam victims in general?"

"Yes. That is a possibility we have examined. A genuine possibility."

"Haley, what are you suggesting we look for?" Henderson asked.

"The suggestion is to start looking for someone with huge wealth, enough time on their hands to dabble in this hobby, and lots of morals but no morals."

"You got me on that last one," Henderson said.

William did the palm-to-forehead "got it" thing and then leaned toward the camera.

"Guys, what she's saying is someone with some moral outrage, but no filter between thinking about slamming a scammer and actually slamming a scammer."

Haley responded, "That's exactly what I meant. We're looking for someone with the moral set that allows them to order terrible things to be done and a sense of outrage at others who do bad things. Could be a mobster, but just as easily it could be a ruthless industrialist or a wealthy dot-commer who went to one too many ComiCons."

Special Agent Harold Smith from the Duluth office asked, "ComiCons would pretty much describe these two jokers."

"How do you mean?" Haley asked.

Cody answered, "Harold there is the one who realized the male suspect was repeating a tagline. You know, the thing about being screwed."

Harold laughed and said, "Yeah, it was always something about being so screwed that only something to bring them back could make it worse."

Haley responded, "Ah, you're the one. Nicely spotted, Harold. It was in the material I received from the Bureau, but who found it wasn't noted. A sort of glib parting ritual on their part. It's one thing that led us to believe that these two may have a superstitious or obsessive side. He repeats that line every time."

Jokes about taglines bounced around the videoconference participants until Henderson held up a hand and said, "People, we could go on for days with the funny stuff, but we need to get some useful Bureau work done here sometime today. Anyone else got any insight?"

No one volunteered anything else, so SAC Henderson thanked everyone for attending and closed the video conference.

Haley looked at Cody and asked, "How about that cup of coffee?"

Cody just nodded.

* * *

Haley led him down to the lobby and out to the street. They walked to a Peet's Coffee half a block away.

On the way, Haley stopped him for a moment and turned to face him.

"You never called," she said after a short, reflective pause.

"I just broke up with my gal, and you were still with what's-his-name, Haley."

"You didn't break up. She got transferred, and you wanted to stay in DC. And what's-his-name transferred out as soon as the National Academy section he was babysitting graduated. That was over three months ago. You must have known there was a mutual attraction between us. When we were both free of entanglements, why didn't you call?"

"Well, I've been—"

Haley interrupted, "Look. I have a PhD, I make multiples of what you make, and I'm still good enough looking at my age that every stud at Quantico wants to nail me. You were a little intimidated, weren't you?"

Cody was used to being on the other end of interrogations. He was in uncharted waters here. Did he have to admit that he could be intimidated by a beautiful woman? He'd bedded a couple of dozen women in his thirty-six years. All the liaisons had been mutually understood as temporary. This seemed different, somehow. Untypical of his gender, he decided to just go with honesty.

"Uh, I guess a little. But there was something else. I was a little confused about what I wanted," he nervously replied.

"Good answer. Coffee. We'll talk."

They sat over their coffees and made a mutually reassuring discovery. Each had thought about the other almost continuously for the last several months.

She revealed, "I dated one other guy, but it just didn't seem right. I haven't dated anyone since. I was hoping you would call. When you didn't, I decided to take the initiative and volunteered to be the firm's liaison for the Qatar Card case. If that hadn't come up, I think I would just have called you."

Cody sat back in relief and exclaimed, "Wow! I kinda knew that there might have been something mutual at Quantico, but I had no idea you were thinking about me the way I was thinking about you. Yeah, I went on a couple of dates, too, but they fizzled out pretty quick. Both ladies sensed I was looking at them but thinking about someone else."

Cody leaned forward and put his elbows on the table as he picked up his cup and took a sip. Haley seemed to sense that Cody still seemed unsure of that afternoon's turn of events. She took the next step and leaned across the little table. Without warning, Haley kissed Cody. The kiss only lasted a couple of seconds, and then she sat back. He didn't move, but he did smile.

"Okay, Special Agent, that awkward moment is past. You don't have to think about when the right time would be. Now we can just talk. I want to see you. I want to see where my instincts are leading me. I'll be in town for two days a week on the Qatar Card case for a few hours each time."

"Okay. We can get together for dinner, maybe?"

"I like steak, Thai, Chinese, and Italian. I like flowers. Roses. Red ones. I like movies, and I like to hold hands. If things work out and you're as nice as I think you are, you may get lucky by next week. Okay?"

She said the whole thing so fast that Cody missed a word or two. At the end of that verbal eruption, she let the rest of her breath out and took a deep one. It was Cody's turn to take the initiative.

"How long have you been rehearsing that speech?" he asked.

She looked down, embarrassed that it came out so fast. "Ever since they agreed to assign me to your team."

"Thought so. So, Capital Grille right after work?"

"Date."

They finished their coffee over a conversation about the seminar where they met. They both remembered the other flirting just a hint at the lunches. And there was a restaurant where some of the class went on the second evening. Haley was with her guy, but they both knew he was leaving in a week or so.

She explained, "He and I had a good time together, but there was never talk of permanence. He was fairly smart, but I think you have him beat."

"What was there that attracted you to me?" Cody asked.

"What attracted me to you first was your ability to think logically. If you had an opinion and someone gave you enough facts to convince you that you were wrong, you dared to admit it. Logic over emotion. I liked that. I thought you were good-looking, too."

That seemed an honest response to Cody, and he reciprocated. "Talk about good looking, Haley. One of the reasons I guess I was hesitant about calling you was that I kind of thought you were out of my league. I've dated some nice-looking women, but you leave them in the dust."

Haley blushed at the compliment and said, "Thank you. I try to keep in shape, but I'm afraid I'm not the same as I was at twenty-two. A dozen years later and gravity takes its toll. So does excess food storage. I watch what I eat and go to the gym, but it still settles where I sit."

Although he was trying to be respectful, his eyes wandered across the table as she described herself, pausing briefly at her breasts before returning to her eyes. "Nonsense! In my opinion, you have the perfect shape. Frankly, I don't want a college kid in skinny jeans. I want someone with a little shape."

* * *

After coffee, they walked back to the WFO, the Washington Field Office, and split up to go to their cubicles. Cody had some work on another case that had to be ready for the federal prosecutor the next day. It was pretty much done, but he and William had to go over it one more time to check a few facts.

When Cody got to William's desk, he was met with a high five and a cheery, "I saw the two of you coming back to the building. I can't believe you manned up and held her hand."

"Yeah. All this time, she felt the same way about me as I did about her. Damn! I could have been seeing her for months. I'm taking her to dinner tonight. But let's get this case out of the way, so I don't get stuck working late."

They dug in, and they finished with plenty of time to spare. Cody went back to his own desk and shuffled papers nervously until it was time to find Haley.

* * *

SAC Henderson found her a vacant cubicle to use when she was in the office, and she was in the middle of an email when he arrived.

"Hey, Cody. Have a seat. I should be done with this in five or ten minutes. I'm sending out some additional details about my theory."

"Anything new from your meet with Henderson?" Cody asked.

Haley replied, "Well, something interesting, in point of fact. We discussed the resources that were being expended on this case. It is a relatively major case with agents assisting local police with way over twenty instances now, but he gave me the impression that there was no political will to solve it with massive resources. Seems the banking world and the politicians are almost happy that these scumbags are being punished and turned over to the authorities. The FCC and most congress members are usually flooded with complaints about scammers and annoying phone calls. These cases seem to make them happy."

Cody countered, "Well, the government goes after a lot of them. The Rachel-from-Cardholder-Services calls resulted in a class-action suit and a government payout to victims, didn't it?"

"Cody, the amount returned to victims was about forty dollars each. And the next set of scammers just started right up after that."

"So, what was the resource outcome? Did Henderson say?" Cody asked. He really was interested in the subject because it had also occurred to him over the last year.

She looked a bit disappointed as she revealed, "I don't believe the Bureau is going to do much more. I was surprised they hired my firm until he told me that a senator put some pressure on them to do something, no matter how limited. I have a feeling it is simply window dressing in case it ever comes out that the government was lax in investigating this large a string of crimes."

"Hey. There's one positive outcome already," Cody offered.

"What's that?" she said, perking up a bit.

"It solved my bullheaded problem about calling you."

"Yes, it did," she said with a laugh. "So, my report will show that paying my firm vast sums of money to provide a dating service for one FBI agent was more than enough justification for the expense."

Cody cleared his throat comically as he replied, "Yeah. Bury that somewhere in your report. See if anyone catches it. To me, it certainly was worth it."

He took her hand off the computer mouse and looked at her. He wasn't laughing anymore.

"Seriously. I have to say this. I'm sorry I didn't call you. I wanted something so bad that I was afraid of rejection if I tried to get it. I want to apologize for that."

She patted his hand. He thought he could see the tiniest tear in her eye as she looked at him. She said, "You know, that is the first time a man ever unequivocally apologized to me in my life. The usual guy format is 'sorry, but.' Do you know what the word 'but' means? It means 'ignore everything before this word.'"

"I'm happy to be the first to redeem my gender. With any luck, I may be able to give you more firsts."

"Looking forward to it." She smiled. "Now, let me finish so we can go have a drink before dinner."

He looked at her but wasn't trying to ogle her, merely trying to figure out what it was that attracted him so much. It might have been her figure, he thought. She wasn't thin, but she wasn't fat, either. She had great curves. Not a skinny girl, but a real woman's shape. She looked athletic, possibly someone who could keep up with him on the Yellow Brick Road running path at Quantico.

Being a guy, of course, his mind wandered to how she would look in the sack. He was staring into space, imagining that when she interrupted him.

"Hey, there, handsome. You look deep in thought. Eyes up and to the right—accessing the part of your brain for constructed pictures. I hope it's me."

Cody snapped out of it and smiled. He was about to date a woman so good that the FBI came to her for advice. She was as good an interrogator as he could ever be. The old, debunked theory about eye direction indicating whether someone was lying, constructing mental images, accessing memories, and so forth was used these days mostly to bullshit suspects. It was that she said it so convincingly, fishing for a reaction, that impressed him.

He responded honestly, "Yeah. You. Nice thoughts, too."

She was finished, and they left the building for the restaurant.

* * *

Dinner at the CG was as good as Cody always expected, and they both enjoyed their steaks. What Cody enjoyed more than the steak was the way Haley spoke. She came right to the point, saying exactly what was on her mind. He hadn't dated anyone like that in the past.

She explained, "I've been concentrating too long on my career. I worked full time while I was getting my master's and PhD, and that didn't leave a lot of room for a social life. Since I got my doctorate, I've been busting my ass to build a reputation. Last year, I realized that I had it all but no one to share it with. My colleagues are all married, and I began to envy them."

She paused for a second and added, "I think I was attracted to you because you fit all the unconscious criteria I had been working up in my head."

"Wow. I can understand the sudden course correction," Cody replied. "I had been enjoying the job, free to go wherever I wanted as a single guy. Since I was assigned here, I've been working a lot with William, and I've seen how rich his life is with Abby ... that's his wife. I guess that triggered something in me, too."

After the pleasant meal, he expected that she would ask him to walk her over to the Metro to begin her hour-twenty trip back to her home in Fairfax, Virginia. Instead, she asked him to find a quiet place for a drink. He walked her to a nearby hotel that had a suitable bar. They sat in a high-back corner booth.

She said, "Maker's Mark, on the rocks with a splash," when the waitress greeted them.

Cody already had a drink before dinner and a glass of wine with his steak. He just ordered a Beck's NA. He knew he wasn't even close to moving the needle on a breathalyzer at this point, but the Bureau had standards, and he was overly cautious around alcohol.

She took his hand. The touch was still exciting and frightening at the same time. Cody had no idea what she was up to.

"Cody, what are you really looking for in life?"

"You mean other than catching bad guys and kicking butt?" he answered.

"Yeah. Off the job. Personally. We talked about course corrections over dinner, but where is that new course taking you?"

Now was the time to put Plan A into effect. He looked right into her eyes and said, "I want to have someone to more than casually share my life and who likes at least some of the things I do."

"Shooting?" she asked.

"You've been asking about me, eh? Yeah. I like target shooting and combat course shooting. How about you?"

"You can't beat an armed woman, as the gun crowd likes to say. My dad was a marine. He liked to shoot, even more so after he retired. He taught Mom, my sisters, and me how to shoot. From all accounts, I'm not nearly as good as you are, but I bet my sister Maryann is. She and her husband, Ricky, are good old-fashioned Southern gun enthusiasts. They even go to competitions together."

"Love to meet them. Do you have a concealed carry permit?"

"Of course, but I don't carry unless I'm going somewhere dodgy, and Washington, DC, is impossible."

"So, what else does your network of paid informants say I like to do?" he chided.

She laughed and ticked off items on her list. "Movies, hiking, swimming, and excellent booze, but in small amounts."

Cody asked, "Your hobbies?"

They traded pastimes and other interests for fifteen or twenty minutes until she retook his hand.

"So, back to the original question. What are you looking for, FBI Special Agent Cody Smutters?"

"Like I said, someone to share life with. Someone romantic. Someone who has at least some of my interests. Someone who likes to cuddle on the couch and watch movies one day and go hiking the next in the mountains."

"Can I be blunt?" she asked.

"You haven't been so far tonight? Damn, I'm in trouble now!" he replied with a chuckle.

"Touché. Okay, I hope you take this the right way."

Cody didn't know whether to expect good news or bad.

"If I read you right, I could take off for home, and you would go back to your apartment and fantasize about me. I would sit at home and do the same. Or you could take me home, and we can cuddle on your couch and watch a movie."

Without another word, Cody paid the check and tip in cash, left his half-finished drink, took her hand, and led her outside to hail a cab.

Indeed, they did cuddle on the couch in his clean but spartan apartment while watching an old movie, To Have and Have Not with Humphrey Bogart and Lauren Bacall. When Bacall said the famous line "You know how to whistle, don't you, Steve? You just put your lips together and … blow," Haley got up and sensuously walked toward the bedroom.

She stopped at the door, turned around, and whistled.

It was possibly the best night Cody had ever experienced. Nothing was rushed. In bed, her personality didn't change. She asked what he liked, and she wasn't shy about telling him what she wanted. Cody could have died a happy man by the time they went to sleep a little after midnight.

The following day, while eating the simple bacon-and-eggs breakfast he cooked, Haley asked if he had a gallon zip bag.

"Sure. Why?"

"I brought fresh underwear in my purse, but I forgot to bring a zip bag to take the soiled stuff home in."

"Damn," Cody lamented humorously as he fetched the bag. "I hate to be seen as a sure thing."

"I was hoping when I left home yesterday morning. By the time our teleconference was over, I was pretty sure. Your blush response and eye dilation were the giveaways."

"Remind me not to play poker with you."

"Oh, I don't gamble," she said with a sly grin.

"But at the seminar last year, you mentioned that you were going to a game."

"Honey, when I play with marks like you, it's not gambling."

Cody was sipping his coffee, and it went everywhere when he laughed.

"Point taken," he said as he mopped it up.

He did have one question that had been bugging him. She'd told him about her house in Fairfax, and he knew the area. It was an expensive area.

"Haley, what the federal government pays is for shit, so where does your company really make its money?"

"From law firms, mostly. Niche market and we're well known in it. They hire us for jury selections, to watch people giving depositions, to watch jury reactions during trials—stuff like that."

"So why do you take chickenfeed federal contracts?"

"Magic," she replied cryptically.

"Okay, I'll bite. What magic?"

"When we put those three little initials on our list of clients, it's magic. Who wouldn't hire a team that the FBI hires? We figure we make a little on consulting and putting on seminars, but the fact that we have those contracts has probably made the firm millions of dollars more than we would have made without them."

"That much, eh. Wow!"

"We actually have a brag book that lists every single case we helped solve, even if it was just a free four-minute phone call to some remote FBI field office. Between you guys actually doing the work and TV and movies making you into supersleuths, having your name on a client list is treasure."

"Geez. Rich, beautiful, and smart. You sure you want to hook up with a lowly special agent?"

"Bub, close your eyes and imagine what my face looked like last night during my second orgasm. Got it? Now ask yourself that same question."

"Speaking of that, that was the acme of sex for me. I've never had a partner ask what I wanted and tell me what she wanted like that. Most people are too hung up to talk about sex during it. My toes curled so hard I was afraid they'd fall off."

"I'm happy, Cody. Last night was everything I hoped it would be," she said with a pleased sigh.

"So, how long were you checking up on me?"

"Oh, a couple of months, I guess. Like I said, I dated after my last guy transferred out. After him, no one seemed right. I kept thinking of that seminar where we met. It was like trying to get the Disney song It's a Small World out of your mind."

"Damn! I knew I could be annoying, but not that annoying," he said with a comical wince.

"In a sense, you were. When you didn't call me! I left that door open when we met. You knew when he was leaving. I dropped a few hints."

"Like I said, I'm sorry. I couldn't work up the nerve."

"You were an Army Reserve lieutenant in Afghanistan. You had people shooting at you, and you were afraid to pick up the phone?"

He looked sheepish when he replied, "Well, yeah."

She got up and went around the table to him. She wrapped her arms about him and whispered in his ear, "Relax. I'm just busting your balls. Personal issues like that often have a stronger emotional impact than physical danger. You didn't behave any worse than most guys. The fact that you were hesitant even shows some respect for me. That's sweet. Don't beat yourself up."

"No?" he asked.

"No. That's my job," she said with a little poke to his ribs.

They held each other in silence for a moment, and then he kissed her before breaking the embrace, suggesting, "Uh, maybe we should get going."

"Yeah. I have to contact the special agents in the cities where the last four cases occurred. I need to see if the local officers who responded to the scenes can re-interview the victims about any small things the suspects may have said or done."

Cody laughed. "It won't be hard finding the victims in three of the last four cases. One is still in jail with bail denied, and the other two have court dates this month. One big-time grifter who is a flight risk and two small fish."

"What about the fourth? I haven't looked up the name or location of that one yet."

"Well, you're looking at the guy you need to talk to about the fourth," Cody said. "I'm the liaison. It's foreign—India. The guy was a phony Microsoft Help Desk operator. You know, they call and say they have detected hacking on your computer then have you fire up a remote access connection so they can charge you money for problems that don't exist, plant a virus, or ransack your computer for financial data. The guy's name is Ankit Chambal, and he ran the operation with his wife."

* * *

They left the apartment building and headed toward the Metro. As they walked, Haley asked, "Anything interesting that separates it from the others?"

"Not much. I'll go over the case file and my notes with you at the office. By the way, a benefit of being the liaison for foreign cases is that I get to eat in a lot of interesting places. India, Pakistan, Russia, and the Czech Republic, so far. Personally, I think that the Bureau is spending money on my travel just to show they're doing something. Window dressing."

"Wow. Lucky you," Haley said.

"So, do you want to go over the files with me before you go to the other US cases?"

"I'd like that, Cody. I do have one question, though, that relates to all of them. I'm not that technical when it comes to computers."

"Ask away," Cody offered.

"How do these guys get tracked? I mean, using a browser like Tor, I thought you were invisible."

"The Deep Web and Dark Web communities and the telecommunications community are pretty open about it. Everyone has an IP address; that's Internet Protocol. It identifies where an Internet query is coming from. Browsers like Tor bounce the request around, and when it comes out, the IP address is now hidden."

"Okay, how does our pair unhide it?" Haley asked.

"So, most of the time, they don't actually have to. The scammers simply give themselves away because of a stupid mistake on the Internet or the Deep Web. Someone with a reason to get them can plant attractive bait, like a porno file with a virus embedded to give a location or a cheap list of credit card numbers with an embedded script file. Sometimes the scammer just makes a silly mistake, maybe bragging to someone they think is a confidant in a secure chat room or forgetting to use a secure connection just once. Many of the less professional scammers don't even use Tor or a similar browser. Their locations are easy to find."

"How else do they get tracked?" Haley asked with increasing interest.

Cody replied, "The funniest ones are the morons who call top-level tech support guys or advanced hackers. I have met several of them who operate machines that can open up a sequestered virtual computer environment. The scammer is looking at what appears to be a standalone computer while the tech guy downloads a virus, deletes files, or does something else to the scammer's computer. They can actually take control of the scammer's computer without the scammer realizing it. It's exactly the reverse of what Black Hats do. You will seldom find a good Black Hat hacker vulnerable that way. Most of the top ones are far too savvy to let that happen, but the lesser clowns sometimes get the tables turned on them. I strongly suspect that some government spooks can track the best of them, too."

"Okay, technology and stupidity. How about phone scammers?" she asked.

"For phone callers, there are some methods of tracking even spoofed-ID calls if you have the resources. I actually don't know how they do it. One of our tech guys tried to explain it, but it was like I was listening to a foreign language, so I can't help you there. But some criminals have poor impulse control in one area or another, and they make impulsive mistakes. It would appear that the guy named Gleb from Russia, who was a robocall scammer, may have been tracked when he bragged to someone that he'd planted ransomware in a hospital."

"That's a no-no in the ransomware community, isn't it?" Haley asked.

"It sure is. A whole bevy of people immediately got on his case from chatter we heard about from the NSA. We suspect one or more of them turned him over to the Qatar Card pair. A similar event happened in the Czech Republic when the ransomware operator failed to restore a victim's computer after being paid the ransom. The ransomware community apparently hunted them down and turned them over to pair in black, too. The ransomware operator is now in jail. I was told by our cybercrimes people that ransomware attackers are trying to become seen as reliable so more people feel comfortable about paying."

They were on the subway by then, and Haley asked, "If some of the information the Qatar Card pair get is from the Dark Web itself, how do you view those sources?"

"It becomes really complicated. Black Hat hackers out there can do some wondrous things with computers and software, but they do it for bad purposes. They are geniuses, but they're evil geniuses from our point of view. On the other hand, White Hat hackers try to secure against or even catch the Black Hats. Black and White sometimes get blurred, though. Some White Hats used to be Black Hats but now work for the government or corporations. If you are a hacker in China trying to burrow into a US site, we would call you a Black Hat, but your Chinese employers would see you as a patriotic White Hat. They probably see our NSA guys the same way. The Dark Web is truly a murky place."

He shifted in his seat and thought for a minute, then continued, "So how do I feel personally? Well, I think about some of them how I would think about a criminal who becomes an informant. I'm happy with the information they provide, even if I believe they will return to doing bad things. Some reform and I'm happier. Some are vindictive rivals. The hackers and gamers who call SWAT teams on rivals by falsely reporting crimes in progress, for example. Or those who find that turning a rival over to a criminal organization is satisfying to them, but it's akin to one mobster hitting another. The difference here is that with the Qatar Card cases, the criminals are subjected to some harsh karma rather than being killed."

"Thanks." Haley nodded. "It helps, but that tech stuff is all magic to me. I use some fairly sophisticated antivirus software. Our firm has a VPN connection and two-step authentication, but I leave the technical stuff to the technical staff. I do know that we have a cardinal rule. Anything with an attachment has to go to IT before we open it. No exceptions.

"I guess that some Black Hats out there are turning information over to our Qatar Card pair about the scammers. They're going after people the rest of us hate, so ..."

Cody finished the thought. "So, the enemy of my enemy is my friend. Who would have guessed? Black Hats doing the world a service. If any of them are actually doing this, I honestly gotta admit I would like to shake their hand. It probably just shows they are human and are pissed off about the same annoyances that bug the rest of us."

They arrived at the WFO and spent the morning going over the foreign cases Cody had worked on. Cody got her on the phone with the police in India who had interviewed Ankit. By lunch, Haley had all the information she needed for the moment.

She looked thoughtful as she said, "I have a vague idea that something about our pair is staring me in the face, but I can't put my finger on it."

"A behavior?" Cody asked.

"That's my specialty, but I'm not sure if it's a behavior or some other trait."

"Well, mull it over and let me know if you come up with anything. Heading back to Fairfax tonight?"

"Yes. I was hoping you could come over."

"I wish you had said that before we left my apartment. I could have packed a bag."

"Tell you what. We'll take the Metro back to your place, and you can pack and drive us both to my place. If we leave after dinner, the traffic won't be heavy, and we can be there in half an hour or so," she suggested.

"I would love to, but are you sure on your end we're not taking this too far too fast?"

"I'm thirty-five, and you are the first man I've even remotely thought about as having a future with me. I have neither the time nor the inclination to go slowly, and I've already waited a few months to get this romantic enterprise on wheels. If this isn't right, we'll know soon enough. I think it is right, though."

"You sure?" he asked.

"Cody, I have a lingerie collection …"

"What time will you be ready for me to meet you?" Cody grinned.

"Five thirty. I have to go. Lunch with a law firm client. Big case coming up."

She gave him a kiss just as William entered the office.

"Hi, William. Nice to see you, but I gotta go. See you at five thirty, Cody. Let's eat on the way there."

As Haley walked out, William looked at Cody with awe as Cody settled into his cubicle.

"Dinner on the way to where, buddy? And, wasn't she wearing that dress yesterday?"

"Shut the hell up. Yeah. We hooked up. I'm serious about her. No cracks, okay?"

"Hey, Cody, I'm just happy for you. Finally, someone worthy of that brain of yours. And it's time you thought about the future. Damn, though. I don't think you could have done better!"

"Aw, I'm not that smart," Cody began to protest.

"Yeah, right. How many other agents in the WFO belong to Mensa?"

"Uh, six, ten, something like that, I think."

"So don't give me that not smart crap. You need someone who can keep up with you upstairs as well as downstairs. Abby and I liked the women you've dated, but we knew they weren't your intellectual equals. Hot, yes, but not women you could grow old with happily. Abby will be tickled."

"Thanks. Lunch?"

The two walked to a Sweetgreen salad location they frequented for healthy alternatives to burgers and talked about what Haley mentioned.

"She said there was something in our reports that looked odd, but she couldn't put her finger on it," Cody related.

"Hmm. Tantalizing. Let's put together another comparison chart. Just the foreign cases. All the known characteristics and actions of the suspects," William suggested.

"Sure thing. We have the data; just have to plug it in and crunch it and hope it means something useful."

Chapter 13

A New Venture

That evening, Cody and Haley went to dinner together as planned. After, they went to his apartment so he could gather some overnight things and get his car. He started to pack a small bag.

"No, honey. Pack for a few days."

Cody stopped mid zip. He put the bag down and looked at her. He really liked the word she had used—honey. And it wasn't just the word; it was the way she said it. The request for several day's clothing also struck a chord. Two days ago, she was just a constant, almost overpowering fantasy, and now she was asking him to stay several days at her house.

He walked over to her and held her. Things were moving far faster than he ever thought possible. He would not have suggested staying with her for days at a time on his own, even though he wanted that from the minute he heard she was joining his team. He would even have considered suggesting that they sleep together on their first date too forward. He was not brought up like that.

But she had taken control of the pace from the outset, and he was determined to follow her lead now. He looked at her for confirmation.

She smiled and nodded. "I want this, Cody. You understand what I'm saying even when I use big words, and we share very similar interests. And you are one of the most thoughtful, romantic lovers I've ever had. So, a few days? Give it a try?"

Cody gave her a little kiss and, without a word, went to the closet. He pulled out his suitcase. When it was packed, they drove to a diner for dinner and then across the Potomac to Virginia and her house. On the way there, he stopped at a market and bought her a bouquet of red roses.

He knew what he wanted, and he hoped that this was the right road to that goal. What he didn't know was that the ensuing chain of events would impact his life in ways he couldn't imagine in his wildest dreams.

* * *

When they arrived at her house, he was duly impressed. It was a mid-1800s Victorian in a district that must have been one of Fairfax's wealthier areas when the house was built. The houses in her neighborhood all had large lots for an urban setting, and from what he could see in the twilight, they were all immaculately maintained.

The house itself was beautiful, with and high ceilings and a rich patina on the interior wood trim from years of cleaning and polishing. A grand staircase led to the second floor, and the hall had a brass chandelier that looked like a converted gaslight. It could even have been initially designed for oil lamps or candles.

While the house was fantastic, Haley was the opposite of a neatnik. There were books and papers in every room, probably individual cases she was working on. Cody thought that he could use some of his organizational skills to clean up the mess and make the house a bit more presentable, but his train of thought was derailed by a welcome interruption.

Haley embraced him and gave him a kiss that left his head reeling. She took him by the hand and led him upstairs. Once in the bedroom, she began to undress him, and he reciprocated. Suddenly Haley stepped away. She walked to a doorway and disappeared into a walk-in closet. She emerged a minute later dressed in the silkiest midnight-blue nightgown Cody had ever seen. Her auburn hair was even more vivid against the dark fabric. She walked directly to the antique bed. She pulled back the coverlet and slid under the sheets, inviting him to join her with a pat of her hand.

He slid in next to her, and they shared a silent embrace that spoke volumes. The smell of her hair, the softness of her skin, the feel of the gown, her breath on his neck, the touch of her skin … these were things he noticed almost as if he had never experienced them in the past. She wrapped a leg around him. The two took their time, and an hour later, they were smiling and sharing little kisses in the afterglow of their lovemaking.

She stroked his hair. It felt good. It was the last thing he remembered before he was fast asleep.

* * *

On the way to work, she took him to a delightful little diner for grits, eggs, and biscuits. Cody looked at her over his coffee mug as he sipped. He was still having trouble comprehending that this was real. It was like going on vacation and waking up in a strange but wonderful place. She was talking to him as if they had been together for years. It took him a moment to center himself and relax enough to reciprocate and enjoy the moment.

For the next two days, they went to work separately and then met back at her house for dinner. After that, they alternated between his apartment and her home a few days at a time.

A little over two months later, they drove to Pennsylvania and stayed at a cute B&B for the weekend. They hiked a nearby mountain on Saturday, saw a movie after dinner, and then made love until the wee hours. Sunday, they went to the Brandywine Museum and spent several hours enjoying its diverse collection of fine art, including some of the seminal Andrew Wyeth paintings. Haley seemed impressed that he knew as much as he did.

"Blame it on one of the humanities classes I was forced to take as an undergraduate requirement. I actually found I liked art," he explained.

That afternoon they began the drive back to her place. On the way, they talked about what was happening between them.

"Cody, what would it take for you to move in with me full time?" she asked.

Cody half expected that question sometime soon. He had rehearsed his answer over and over. He really wanted to make this a permanent relationship, but he needed one more assurance from her. Maybe it was old fashioned, but he needed it.

"What would it take? Just three little words."

"Ah ... I see," she sighed.

He was disappointed she didn't immediately respond the way he thought she might. If she said it then he had been planning to say it, too. He was mulling this over when she asked him to pull over at a café for some coffee. When they ordered their coffee, she also ordered a pecan-covered sticky bun. He hadn't seen her eat many sweets, so he just figured it was the kind of food one ate on the road when calories weren't counted. They sat at a picnic table outside to relax for a few minutes before getting back on the road.

She smiled a playful smile. She pointed to herself then to the bun. Next, she pointed at herself again, made a heart with her thumbs and forefingers, and finally pointed at him.

It took Cody a couple of seconds: "I … my … pastry? … bun …?"

She put her finger on the gooey topping and lifted some to her lips, smiling at the taste.

"Gooey … ah! … sweet! My sweet … I … heart …"

He stopped and looked at her.

"Yes, Cody, I love you, my sweet. I made up my mind at the Brandywine. When you bent down and explained to that little boy and his mother what a painting was about, I didn't see Special Agent Cody Smutters. I saw the loving, caring man I hoped you were before this all began. What you did was spontaneous; it wasn't to impress me. It was just who you were. You had me right there."

Cody felt as if he had just won the lottery. He smiled and took her hand.

"Then, my answer is yes. I love you, too. I'll drop you off at your place and spend some time at mine getting some things together to bring over. My lease isn't up for a few months, so you'll have somewhere to stay over when you work in the city for two days in a row. I'll give up the lease when it expires."

"Oh? How much a month is the rent?"

He replied, "Eighteen hundred a month or so. Plus parking. As you saw, my place is fairly spartan. Good enough location where I don't have to worry much about crime, and close to a Metro station."

"You know, I've always wanted a pied-à-terre closer to downtown DC. Could we keep it?"

"Twenty thou a year for a closer place to stay? Isn't that a bit extravagant? Just how much do they pay you, anyway?"

"Enough, but that's not where my money comes from, mostly. I've dabbled in the market."

"Holy moly! How?" Cody asked.

She replied, "Well, I use my skills in an unusual way. I do a lot of jury-selection work for law firms in corporate cases. I watch juries during important testimony to give one side or the other feedback. I'm usually hired by a third party, so I don't even know which side gets my reports. To put it simply, when I see a slam dunk coming, I bet on the stock market based on the corporation's chances of winning or losing."

"You do know you're talking with an FBI special agent, right? Wouldn't that be insider trading?"

"No, silly. If you were sitting next to me as a spectator, you would have the same information as me. I only use what I observe in open court to predict what the jury is going to do. I get no information from either side. That would skew my observations."

"How often are you right?"

"More than eighty-five percent of the time. The more positive I am about the outcome, the more I risk."

"And you're sure your activities are kosher?"

"Yep. Checked with some of the best lawyers in the business. And I checked with a gal I know at the SEC. She said it would pass an audit. Most people can't invest that kind of time sitting in courtrooms, but I'm paid to do it."

"All right, Haley, I guess it's no different than watching companies closely in the trade journals and predicting mergers and things. Okay. How much have you made, if you don't mind me asking?"

"Enough where twenty thousand a year for a room in town won't make a dent. But that's just with my brokerage accounts. I also have my 'dumb luck account.'"

"I'll bite," Cody laughed. "What's that?"

"One of the tech guys at work talked me into buying some Bitcoin. That was back in early 2011. I had just made a killing on a stock. The tech, a guy named Fred Murray, told me about this new currency and said I should invest in it, as it had gone from a quarter a coin to about ninety cents per in a couple of months. I gave him a few hundred bucks just to get him to stop asking me."

She smiled broadly as she continued, "I completely forgot about the account for years. What're a few hundred bucks in some cockamamie investment, after all? A couple of years ago, Fred came to me and asked me if I ever wanted to do something with it. I asked him if it had doubled yet. I almost had a stroke when he told me how much it was worth. When I bought it, I tracked it for a little while when it was waltzing around at a few bucks. Fred told me it had rocketed up to thousands."

"Holy crap, Haley!" Cody exclaimed after doing a quick mental calculation at today's Bitcoin value.

"Yeah. I cashed it out, paid the long-term capital gains taxes, and stuck the rest in conservative mutual funds after paying off my house and Mom and Dad's mortgage. Talk about found money!"

"Wow. So, when were you going to tell me how much you were worth?"

"Not until you said you loved me, and I was sure enough to say it back."

That was sure a memorable sticky bun! They shared it as they drank their coffee and planned the move. Whenever he saw a sweet bun after that, he remembered the moment when his life changed forever.

Chapter 14

Who Knew India Had Such Fun People to Do?

A few months before that sticky bun was served, Alex and Lara were booked for three weeks in a romantic four-star hotel in southern India. They enjoyed their previous trips to India so much that they decided to add extra sightseeing to their present task. Both had developed quite a taste for curry and those delicious samosas, the fried dumplings that could be vegetarian or meat-filled, so a foodie tour was in the mix.

They booked tours through the hotel's concierge about every other day. They saw temples and scenic rivers, hiked some low mountains, and even took a harbor boat cruise.

They had a few clients who collected Indian antiques, so they did a bit of buying, too. They were having a ball, even on the day they had to go to work work.

Ankit Chambal lived a pedicab ride away from their hotel. He and his wife, Kalyani, were both involved in robocalling. Their main scams were phony computer help desk calls.

The scammers had bilked thousands from their hapless victims over the past few months. It took dozens, if not hundreds of calls before they found a fish they could hook, but it was easy money. Not much from each victim unless they got banking or credit card info to sell later, but a comparatively substantial sum to the victims if they were retired or on a fixed income.

Unfortunately for them, their robodialer had randomly dialed Papa Paul.

Lara had given him a booby-trapped computer for just such joyous occasions. When Papa Paul followed Ankit's instructions and Ankit was connected to it, the computer automatically uploaded a virus to Ankit's computer. While Ankit was busy searching for any sensitive data on Papa Paul's computer, the virus pinged his IP address to another computer. Lara had that computer running at one of Siggy's business locations, and it was dedicated to this one task.

Papa Paul's bait computer had nothing on it other than Windows Vista, a browser, and a word processor, and was quickly restored after the call.

Ankit downloaded a virus to Papa Paul's computer and then "found" it, displaying a dialog box warning as proof. Then he asked Papa Paul if he wanted Ankit to remove it.

Papa Paul later told Lara, "I just said I would have my grandkids take care of it, and I hung up. Then I texted you to let you know I just landed a fish.

* * *

Lara downloaded the information the tracking virus sent her. The IP was a bit cloudy, apparently having been routed through a hijacked small business Wi-Fi network. She ran the IP address through Dark Web contacts she had, and Siggy had one of his guys do the same. Siggy's connections usually seemed to be even better than Lara's own for some reason, even though Siggy himself wasn't a real techie. When other contacts ran down the same name and address for the scammer, she gleefully informed Alex that they would get to see another city in India soon.

* * *

Two days before their official visit to Ankit, they booked a pedicab sightseeing tour of the district where he lived. They had their driver, Pranab stop at an outdoor café that Siggy's sources had pointed out. Alex offered to buy the driver a chai when Alex ordered his and Lara's. While they were sipping, Alex said he wanted to see something in the shop across the street and asked Pranab to stay with Lara to watch out for her. Alex knew that Pranab was on contract with the hotel, so he was eager to please his passengers. The neighborhood was upscale, with other single women sitting alone at the cafe, so the request was just to keep Pranab occupied while Alex scouted Ankit's neighborhood. Besides, if a mugger tried to attack Lara, the mugger's head would disappear in a soft, wet explosion as Lara rammed it into the pavement.

Alex walked over to the shop, which was next to Ankit's address. He glanced at Ankit's house as he walked and noted the electrical service location and the telecommunications lines. He confirmed through an open window what his informants had reported about the alarm system being for shit. It was really just a door sensor, a simple keypad, and a buzzer. Alex could bypass it with what he usually carried in his shaving kit.

He bought a small trinket for Lara, and she made a big deal of it. She didn't do more than put a hand on his for an instant, though. Public displays of affection between men and women were frowned upon in this particular district.

When they got back to the hotel, they gave Pranab a handsome tip and went inside for dinner.

* * *

After dinner, they went over the plans and made a list of things they needed to buy locally. One thing they didn't need was bleach. When they left Ankit's house, all they had to do was leave each piece of clothing in a public trash bin. Each would be gone within a minute, soon to be worn by someone in abject poverty.

Pretty much all they needed were latex gloves of the same color as those used by the staff at their hotel and a bag of zip ties. Instead of the ski goggles they often used, they each had a pair of wraparound mirrored sunglasses. They picked up a small packet of gloves and some zip ties at an open market during their next pedicab sightseeing tour.

They checked with Siggy's two specialists in that obscure department one last time to see if things were set up on their end, and then it was time to relax and have fun until their unsocial call to Ankit.

* * *

The night of the visit to Ankit and Kalyani's arrived. They put loose casual clothing on over their usual tights. They took a pedicab from the hotel's stand to a restaurant about a mile from their targets' house.

They had a pleasant dinner of chicken tikka masala and vegetable samosas, then retired to the lounge.

Lara said, "Let's see if TripAdvisor was right about the bar here having a good selection of Indian single malt whiskey. The stuff is becoming respected, and I'd like to try some. We never tried it on any of our previous trips, and I want to sample at least one."

Alex asked the bartender, Samir, "Do you have any suggestions for Indian single malt whiskeys?"

Samir replied, "My favorite is Amrut Fusion."

"Sounds good. Two, please, over with water on the side."

Alex paid with his credit card and then they took their glasses and found a seat in a dark corner of the crowded lounge. The whiskey was good, but they only had a few sips.

About fifteen minutes later, they disposed of the remainder in the restroom, casually walked out the crowded bar's side door, and took another pedicab to a small grocery store a couple of blocks from Ankit's. They paid the driver, and after he pedaled away, they walked toward Ankit's house.

* * *

As Alex saw on the pedicab tour with Pranab, there was an alley behind the house. They scooted in, shed their outerwear, pulled up their hoods, and donned the sunglasses and gloves. They knew Ankit and his wife would be asleep, as his target victims were on the other side of the world. Ankit's workday would be starting in just a few hours.

Siggy's contracted surveillance showed they were in the house and inactive at this time on weekdays. Alex and Lara were always glad that Siggy had long arms when it came to payouts wherever they were needed. He had unusually useful friends in every country where he had sent Alex and Lara in addition to those in the US.

It took Alex sixty seconds of the ninety-second entry delay to disable the alarm, and only that long because the hinges were squeaky, and he didn't want to make too much noise opening the box's door. They stopped in the kitchen to get a couple of knives, bamboo tongs, and some cooking grease. The pair crept upstairs and saw Ankit and his wife, Kalyani, asleep in bed through their bedroom's open door. The sheets were kicked off, and they were wearing long nightshirts.

Lara put her knife to Kalyani's throat as Alex put his to Ankit's. Alex spoke to them in Hindi, another language he had added to his repertoire before their first trip to India. They quickly gave the usual instructions. Alex took Ankit downstairs while Lara tied up Kalyani on the bed. She followed Alex downstairs.

Ankit was refusing to reveal any of his passwords when Lara joined Alex. They knew that Ankit spoke fluent English, and it was taking too long to convince him to cooperate. Lara said something that made him freeze and listen carefully: "Ankit, you are doing pretty good. Tough guy. I'll give you that. Honey, do something horrible to him."

Alex spoke to him again in Hindi.

"Oh, I'm not going to do anything to you. If I don't get your passwords in the next minute, I'm just going to go upstairs and do something horrible to Kalyani while you listen. If you don't give us the information after that, I'll send my partner upstairs to kill your wife. It will be slow and painful."

Alex had absolutely no intention of doing either of those things, but Ankit didn't know that. He started singing like a bird. In a few minutes, they had passwords, accounts with scammed funds, and the names, phone numbers, and other information of his victims. Ankit even gave up his Bitcoin wallet, which Lara drained in an anonymous donation to a local hospital. It was quite a nice list.

Lara gagged Ankit and then rolled him over and lifted his nightshirt.

"Ankit, this is going to hurt a little. No, I take that back. It's not going to hurt a little. It's going to hurt a lot."

Lara had found a slim, older-model cell phone behind Ankit's computer desk. It was the perfect shape and size. The phone went up his butt, aided by tongs and a lot of ghee, the popular Indian clarified butter Lara had gotten from the kitchen.

When she was done, she looked at her gloves and then at Alex as she laughed. "Since our first trip here, I've loved cooking with ghee. For some reason, this time, I just have no urge to lick my fingers. Hope that thought doesn't last. I really like ghee."

Alex laughed, then turned to Ankit and gave him the usual warning about what would happen if he continued scamming. He set up the grenade ruse and explained that someone would free them in a few hours.

After he delivered the usual "being screwed" speech, he added something that took away Ankit's last hope: "We know that you bribe the local police. Your Bitcoin is gone, so you don't have that to bribe them with. The government is probably going to confiscate your bank accounts, anyway. Our employers have paid them far more than you can pay them. Enjoy your time in prison."

Alex put his usual card on the computer keyboard. The two shed their tights in the kitchen and donned their street clothes before they left. Four trash cans later, the tights and glasses were gone. The gloves were destined for a trash can at the hotel.

* * *

They took a pedicab most of the way and then walked the last three blocks back to the lounge where they had dined. By luck, Lara found another dark booth that had just been vacated. Alex located Samir and got another suggestion. As before, they used a credit card to pay. The whiskeys were pretty good. They had poured out most of their first drinks, but now they could afford the time to enjoy the libations. They tipped Samir well in cash and asked him to find them a Lambro cab when they were ready to leave. From the time they first got to the restaurant to when they departed was a little over two and a half hours.

* * *

Back at the hotel, they dropped their gloves in trash cans in the restrooms by the pool. They went to the concierge to see about their tour the next day.

After their tour was confirmed, the concierge asked, "Where did you dine this evening?"

Alex named the restaurant, commenting, "They had some good Indian whiskey in their lounge, too."

The concierge agreed. "Oh, they are known for a good stock of local whiskeys." Then, with particular pride, he said, "But we have an even better selection at the bar here, sir. Please try the Rampur Select single malt. It has gotten high awards even in your country."

They thanked him and repaired to the bar for a taste. They enjoyed the Rampur immensely, noting that they should bring a couple of bottles home if the duty-free shop at the airport had some in stock.

* * *

At 6:30 a.m., they were in the restaurant having delicious local fruit for breakfast when Siggy sent a message: "Your package was picked up at 3 a.m. The parcel service men were amused that someone was paying them to look, not look the other way."

Checking her phone to make sure they still had time before their 7:15 a.m. tour, Lara enjoyed a few more bites of mangosteen fruit and karonda jam on toast points. She giggled about the previous night's events. "We don't often get to do a couple, honey. That was fun!"

* * *

Five days and a bazillion gigabytes of tourist pictures later, they were on the way back to the States. Before they left, though, they had a good laugh when the news had a small piece on Ankit and his wife being arrested. The story noted that two FBI agents from the United States had flown over to consult with the Indian police and had a photo of the two coming out of the local police office. Their names were not given.

"Look, Alex, it's the same two who go to all our offshore parties. Someday we'll have to send them a note asking them if they enjoyed their vacations as much as we enjoyed ours."

Chapter 15

Cut to the Chase … or Maybe Chase the Cutter

About two months had passed since Cody moved in with Haley. They settled into a pleasant routine, and Cody was thinking of the right time to pop the question. The longer they were together, the closer they became. He now knew she really was the one.

They decided not to keep his apartment after all. Haley found a two-bedroom just as close to the Metro. Cody liked the extra space for the work she brought home on the days they both were there.

* * *

One thing that Haley was curious about was his name, asking one evening, "Honey, I don't care what the answer is, but how did your family get the name Smutters?"

Cody laughed and replied, "Well, apparently one of my forebears in England operated some sort of machinery for sorting the crud out of grain. The crud was called smut, and the machinery was called a smutter. Those who sifted shit out of grain were called smutters. Sorry, but you can't always choose things like your name. How about you?"

"Not a clue. No one in the family knows, and I never had the inclination to have a genealogy done. All I know is that it's English. The package you like to fondle was made by the Irish, British, Swiss, Armenian, Lebanese, Norwegian, and Polish. That's as far back as anyone has family records."

"Well, just tell all of those countries that this guy gives them an A-plus for packaging."

He gave her a kiss and followed it up with a dinner idea: "Any of your Polish relatives ever give you pirogi?"

"God, yeah. Uncle Stan and Aunt Anna used to make them when we visited them in Greenpoint in Brooklyn. I love them."

"I have the perfect place for dinner then."

* * *

They drove to a Russian restaurant Cody knew that made fantastic pirogi. When they arrived, Cody greeted Stanislav, the maître d', in Russian. They exchanged a few words, and he sat them at one of the better tables.

"Russian? That's something you mentioned about the cases you worked on, but I didn't know you were that fluent. I'm impressed."

"I guess I've just never had the occasion to use it around you the last couple of months. Learned it from my maternal grandparents. The other half is English and German. As I said, English is where the Smutters name came from. My parents were second and third generation, though, and never spoke anything but English around the house."

The pirogi were fantastic, just as Cody had promised. He asked one of the waiters in Russian if Chef Ivan had anything special back in the kitchen. The waiter disappeared, and Ivan came out a few minutes later with pelmeni—beef, lamb, and pork dumplings served with a bit of vinegar, pepper, and butter. He spoke to Cody in Russian and put the plate on the table. Cody translated, "He said he made these tonight to feed the staff. He made enough that he could let us have a plate."

"Thank you very much!" Haley exclaimed at the honor.

"Please to enjoy, ma'am. You come here weeth Cody, I make sometheeng special anytime."

They were enjoying the meal until Haley stopped and looked up at Cody.

"That's it!"

"What's it?"

"The missing link! The mystery couple! You told me that your Moscow PD friend said the man spoke in Russian to Gleb. Do you know what other languages he spoke in addition to English in other countries?"

"No. The foreign reports only say that the suspects talked to the victims. I can find out, though. I'll have the guys start working on that. Did I ever tell you that you were smart?"

"Not since yesterday."

"Well, you are. And pretty, too."

Haley paid for the meal, something Cody was finally accepting. She loved buying him things, too, including a Kashiyama hand-tailored suit that she enjoyed seeing him wear. His personal life up that point had been classified using "his" and "everyone else's." Now he was seeing the concept of "ours" creep into his consciousness. The "ours" part of everything was coming into clarity for Cody as he got closer to popping the question.

* * *

The next day Cody briefed Phil and sent out an email to every foreign police department where an incident had occurred. He asked if the suspects spoke anything other than English.

Later that morning, Phil announced that Henderson had called them up to his office. They both walked upstairs.

Henderson motioned for them to sit as he said, "Nice, Cody. How did you think of it?"

"I didn't. I triggered it, but Haley found it. The information in our files regarding the foreign cases is far less complete than in the domestic ones, and our profiles were mainly based on domestic cases. The victims were all reluctant to say any more than they were attacked by two foreigners dressed in black. They were all scared shitless."

"You wouldn't be if someone broke into your house, tortured you, and then shoved a phone up your ass?" Henderson jokingly asked.

"Yeah," Cody laughed. "I might want to follow their instructions."

"Congratulate Dr. Briggs for me and take her to dinner. I like her."

"Thanks. Uh, by the way, something I've meant to ask for a while. Why have the psych-profiling resources been limited to just one outside consultant through our office? I mean rather than all field offices going through the team at Quantico?"

Henderson looked as if he had thought about this very question himself. "It may be a long string of assaults, but upstairs they still think it's chicken feed. Nothing ever stolen. No one killed. Frankly,

Cody, my best guess is that it's better press for the folks upstairs at the cabinet level and Congress if we don't catch these two."

"Makes sense. Thanks for the straight answer. I'll keep plugging away along with my other caseload."

* * *

On the way back to his cubicle, Cody wondered if the papers weren't right to some degree. Of course, he couldn't condone a vigilante, but …

William was waiting for him and revealed, "We got nothing on the polyglot angle so far, here or abroad yet. Sorry. May be a dead end, but let's give it some time. Not to mention that the suspects' descriptions are only that they are a man and a woman, covered head to toe and described as athletic and probably young."

Cody laughed. He put his hand on his partner's shoulder, mocking, "Yeah. That fits, what … three billion people? We don't even know what race they are for sure. We have DNA samples that show white, black, Asian, and Hispanic. They were all planted. There's no DNA from the foreign ones because, as the suspects correctly guessed, those cops wouldn't waste the money looking for it. Heights are relatively consistent, with the man about six feet tall and the woman maybe five seven. Other than the woman calling the guy 'honey' and the guy using 'sweetheart,' they don't give many clues other than they're working for someone who has it in for scammers. Hell, even my sixty-seven-year-old Aunt Gertrude has it in for scammers."

"Yeah, buddy, that just about sums it up. My gut still says the case files spell two professionals who have been hired by someone well-heeled enough to pay for the operation. But my question from months ago still stands: Who in the hell pays zillions of dollars by now to swat flies?"

"A mobster with a sense of humor?"

William looked at his partner. He replied, "You might just be right. Who else has tons of hard-to-launder cash and enough of it to waste on spanking naughty people?"

"Ah, I still like the rogue banking executive who's sick of absorbing bad debt. Maybe a bunch of 'em met at the club and came up with the idea over poker. They may be doing it as a lark, too."

"We'll know when we finally have them in handcuffs, I guess." William sighed.

* * *

The case went unsolved for yet another two months and another two incidents. Information that the shape on the cards had been identified as a map of Qatar had been released to the press for a week now in desperation. The Bureau hoped someone would recognize the connection.

Cody was watching the news, and the anchorman asked what some remote city in Qatar had to do with the incidents. The other talking head mimicked what every other news outlet had reported that week: She suggested that the pair of intruders originally came from there. Of course, that apparent dead end had been exhaustively examined by the Bureau and other law enforcement. This time the anchor's suggestion struck a chord that made Cody vaguely curious, though.

* * *

The next day he visited one of the larger travel agencies in DC. He met with a Middle Eastern travel specialist named Teana Brocklin. She was used to dealing with government officials and had helped the Bureau before.

He asked, "Teana, can you tell me how Dawhat Al Qatar compares to other Middle Eastern destinations?"

"Well, it's been ranked as one of the safest places in Qatar and the surrounding countries for travel if you stick to the resort areas. There are some beautiful spots."

"What can you tell me about this card? Is it a logo from a resort there or something? Maybe used in a tourist promotion?"

He showed her a picture of the now-famous card.

"No, nothing I've ever seen commercially, Special Agent Smutters. It's just a crude outline of Al Qatar. I've seen it on the news, but I have no idea what the significance is."

Cody was startled. She didn't pronounce the name the way most Americans did: "Al ku-TAR." She pronounced it "Al CUTT-er."

"What did you just say? 'Cutter'?"

"Yes. Most Americans say it 'ku-TAR' or 'ka-TAR.' People from that country call it something similar to the English words cutter or gutter. It varies even inside their own country."

"Thank you, Teana. Thank you very much! If you ever need a friend at the Bureau, look me up."

"My pleasure, Special Agent Smutters. Happy to have helped," she said with a little wave as he disappeared out her door.

* * *

Back at the Bureau, Cody sought out William. He found him in the break room, having a cup of coffee.

"William, have you ever heard of a mobster named Al Gutter or Al Cutter?"

"Not specifically. There must be a million people named Al Cutter or Gutter. Why?"

Cody held up the picture of the card and said, "This, my friend, is a drawing of Al Gutter or Al Cutter."

"You lost me, buddy. I thought it was a map of a town in a Middle East country."

Cody explained the pronunciation, and William slowly got the concept. He grinned at Cody.

"Berry punny! We have a comedian hitman? Boy! This is getting weirder and weirder."

They both realized that they had heard Qatar pronounced just about every way possible over the last year, but it had not sunk in until Cody made the trip to the travel agency. Teana was very precise in her pronunciation, and something had just clicked.

They drafted an email to be sent nationwide. It asked for information on any contact that had ever been made with a hitman, mobster, or other crook named Gutter or Cutter. The first name could be Al, Alex, Alexander, Alfred, or any other name commonly shortened to Al.

William called Phil, who called Henderson's office and asked if the SAC was free. He was, and Cody sent the draft to him. The SAC asked everyone to come up a few minutes later.

SAC Henderson read the message on his monitor again carefully, then looked up in disbelief. "Let me get this straight. I have a supervisory special agent and two FBI special agents with thirty years' experience between them standing in my office. They are telling me that a card left at about thirty crime scenes that have cost the Bureau and local law enforcement hundreds of thousands, if not millions of dollars, to investigate, is … is what? A joke? Is that actually what you assholes are trying to tell me?"

Cody looked at William, who gave the "go-ahead-tell-him" look and nod.

Cody sheepishly answered, "Well, yeah, that about sums it up. It's the best idea we have on the card so far."

Henderson looked at his printout of the email and thought hard for a minute. Finally, he said, "Damn. I'm the head of one of the most prestigious field offices in the country. I retire next year. Senators and congressmen will probably come to my retirement party along with the director. It will be at a fancy hotel. Now you two clowns come to me with the cockamamie theory that we have a hitman with a sense of humor planting cards that actually tell us his name? I gotta tell you I want to believe this is true, but if you are wrong, my retirement party will be behind the men's room, and the highest official to attend will be the janitor supervisor."

"So?" Phil prompted.

"So, before you whisper a word of this outside the WFO, I want you to run every possible combination of names you can. Use a Soundex search to find ones that even sound like them. Phil, put Adams, Dominguez, and Margolis on it with these two. Use any technical staff you need in this building. You have two days. Come back to me after you finish. If this pans out, we're all heroes. If it falls flat, we'll never hear the end of the jokes the other field offices will come up with. Hell: That's what our lives will be. Living hell. Now get the hell out of my office."

As they were leaving, Henderson looked up and called out, "Hey, guys. Really. Good luck."

* * *

For the next two days, the team ran names every which way they could think of. They sorted by age and gender until one of the IT techs, Melinda Dominguez, dropped a bomb.

"What if it's Alexandra, or Alexis, or any of the other female names that could possibly shorten to Al?"

Cody sighed and told everyone, "Rerun it without the male-only search term."

It took most of the two days to come up with a relatively good list. There were very few Al Cutters or Gutters in the final analysis. Cody had then run all Gutters and Cutters, regardless of the first name. They excluded hits listing people in jail during more than one case. They eliminated those in the military. They even found some in law enforcement and decided to eliminate them, too, though they kept that list on the back burner if all others failed to pan out. They used the general age filter of twenty-one to forty, as the victim descriptions seemed to indicate that probability.

They looked at everyone with a criminal record: arrests, not just convictions. They made sure that every AKA, or also known as, was included. They also tried to check for customs activity three days before and after each foreign incident.

In the end, they had a list of possibilities that stretched across the country. They did another filter and eliminated people arrested for or convicted of crimes that weren't considered relevant. Real estate fraud, rape, cruelty to animals, and other crimes didn't fit.

The list also included any name matches from the banking and credit card industries they could find, whether they had a criminal record or not.

As a final touch, they searched for anyone with one of the names who had filed a phone or Internet scam complaint. That was the only list without any hits, but access to other law enforcement databases was limited.

* * *

Cody, William, and Phil brought the results to their SAC. They went over the data for an hour. At the end of the briefing, SAC Henderson sat back in his chair and put his hands over his eyes. Thirty seconds or so later, he leaned forward and gave his decision.

"Guys, we're going to go with this. Put this out to the Bureau only. Have them make personal contact with their folks at the state, county, and local levels. This needs to be discreet. At this time, we don't want to connect the names with the case. With something this broad, there could be leaks that could get back to a well-connected suspect or his or her employer if there really is one.

"From what you presented, there are only about five thousand people in the US with the last name Cutter or Gutter. There's a bit more with variations, but still under twelve K. The number of hits with variations of Al is tiny. Start with the last-known addresses of the people we have listed. Contact those PDs first. From what I read, there are no Bureau persons of interest with those names, correct?"

William answered, "Completely. We have a couple of remotely similar-sounding names, but not for anything actually like this."

"Okay. Go with it, and keep me apprised of any info that comes to light on your foreign language thing, but this is not a huge priority. If anyone upstairs rides my ass about this, I want to tell them we're doing it on an as-available basis."

There weren't any Qatar Card cases in the DC area, so Cody and William's main task was acting as a central point of contact for data collection.

* * *

The police in the foreign cases were still slow in getting back to Cody on the polyglot angle. None of them had thought to ask their victims what language the suspects spoke. The only response to come in so far was from one of the cases in India. The locals apparently wanted to impress the FBI, and they sweated one into admitting that the male suspect spoke to him in Hindi. At least that was something.

Haley and her partners continued to work on the profile while Cody and his crew were searching for data.

* * *

Haley addressed the team again in a conference room at the WFO and the other agents around the country by videoconference.

"We have narrowed our profile a bit. Both have intellectual skills, probably college level. That means over twenty-one for starters. They are trusted to do their work anywhere in the country and some fairly exotic spots overseas. That means they have experience and the trust of their employers. They also have incredible efficiency and practical skill. That collection of attributes would take eight to ten years of fieldwork to achieve. Add that to twenty-one, and that puts them right there in the middle of that window you have identified."

"How about speech patterns?" Henderson asked. "Any identifiable accent, Haley?"

"When they speak English, they have flat, Midwestern accents, but with a hint of something else. That bit came from only two victims who thought they briefly caught the possibility of a Southern accent. So, someone who may have grown up in the South or around Southerners but moved some time ago. Too thin to hang your hat on it, but a possibility. I was raised in the South, but the only time I have a discernible accent is right after talking with my parents."

An agent from the San Francisco Field Office asked over the video system, "Any new insights on personalities?"

Haley said, "The most glaring trait is that these two love their work. They have a strong bond between them based on that shared avocation. These two are sociopaths in love, both with each other and with their work. One possible guess is that they may have met in a cosplay or gamer environment as youths and got carried away by the romantic image of the hitman or assassin. They were loners until they found each other, and now they feed off each other's desires. They somehow transitioned from a fantasy obsession to a real-world occupation. How they made that leap is anyone's guess. There is a strong possibility that these two were not brought up in the life."

William inquired, "So you don't think they were raised in a criminal environment."

"No. There's a high probability that they didn't start with roughing up scammers, either. These two are pros. Our assessment is that there's a string of bodies under freeways or fed to pigs because of them. And from the limited descriptions we have of their body language during the home invasions, we would all like to be flies on their bedroom wall when they return from one of their assignments. These two are getting off on their work. Highly sexual."

Henderson added, "And arrogant."

Haley agreed, "Absolutely. They don't hide their feelings toward one another. They use pet names, such as 'honey' for the male and 'sweetheart' for the female. They refer to each other lovingly. They insist they have employers, and they give the reasons for being at the victim's home, bizarre as those reasons may be. They taunt law enforcement with that card, and they intentionally left false evidence in copious quantities at the US sites until the cops stopped wasting their time sifting through it."

Haley paused for a second and then said resolutely, "They also think that they are smarter than we are. The problem is that they are smart. Clever, too. These are the kinds of people who watch CSI and then find out what cops really do in those circumstances. They do research, and they apparently have some pretty good resources available to them to gather information. The Bureau has already identified most elements of their skill sets, which are, unfortunately, impressive, including getting in and out of foreign countries."

Cody remarked, "They may be good, but they have some weaknesses. William found one when they erased files in the Froylenko case in Moscow."

William explained, "Yeah. They scrubbed some files on his computer. They were probably instructed to hide some link to their employer or someone related to him. But they didn't overwrite the newly created blank spots. They could have easily covered their tracks by copying files or uploading dummy files of their own."

Haley asked, "Why didn't they just erase the whole disk?"

William answered, "They wanted the Moscow cops to have all of his criminal activity files. Just not the four they erased."

"Oh, of course," Haley agreed before returning to her briefing material. "They also know how to get to their victims without being spotted. In towns where they have hit someone, store, bank, and ATM cameras have shown nothing."

Cody laughed and related, "Yeah, the only camera ever to catch them was at a 7-Eleven and that showed two shadowy, pixelated figures at night over a block away near the rear of a victim's house. There wasn't even enough detail to tell how tall they were. To add insult to injury, the pair knew where the camera was and waved."

Haley smiled at that. "Their movements show incredible planning. We have seen this behavior in teen role-play participants. Some will plan for hours just for a single move. To carry that depth of preparation to adulthood shows an obsession with detail far beyond the normal."

She had just started to speculate on where the mystery couple called home when the briefing was interrupted by a phone call from the Ann Arbor, Michigan, field office. Another Heather from cardholder services had just been found wrapped in an electrical cord with a little cellphone up her butt, charging cable still attached. The special agent on the line was invited to join the videoconference already in progress. Once he was online with the group, it was evident that he was having difficulty keeping a straight face.

He said, "Hello, everyone. Andy Friender here. I just got back from a meeting with the Ann Arbor PD. Another Heather from cardholder services scammer is now at the hospital. The Qatar Card couple did a number on her. She says she begged the pair to let her go. She said she only worked at the boiler room operation and wasn't the owner. They told her that she was actually doing the work, and the 'we were just following orders' excuse wouldn't cut it."

Friender couldn't keep it together and broke out laughing.

"What's the joke?" Henderson asked, a little impatiently.

"Sorry, SAC Henderson. The pair! They, they," he stammered.

"They what?"

Friender managed to get it together and explain, "They told her that in a bad German accent. You know, 'Vee vas only follwink orters.' Sounded like Sergeant Schultz from the Hogan's Heroes TV show from the way she described it. What's worse was she was babbling it to an Ann Arbor detective in the emergency room while they were fetching the lube and speculum to ease the phone out of her ass. There she is, mimicking the bad German accent, lying on her stomach on a gurney with the USB cable dangling out from under the cloth covering her ass. It was so funny that the cops interviewing her almost peed in their pants."

The rest of the video conference attendees laughed now, and it took a minute for everyone to quiet down.

Friender resumed. "Anyway, this one was a little different. All the pair wanted was for her to immediately tell her coworkers that they would be next if they didn't stop scamming and that they would use a joystick, not a phone, to butt-plug them. They gave her eight hours, or they would start making more visits. Maybe kill some of her coworkers. She gave up the location of the boiler room so the detectives could go warn her friends. The locals got a warrant and went in. They busted the operation. The guy running it already had a conviction from a previous scam. Broke his probation."

Haley asked, "Special Agent Friender, Dr. Briggs here. Did both suspects do the funny accent, or was it one of them?"

"The victim says it was both. After the only-doing-what-she-was-told bit, they made fun of her while they were busy, uh, doing the violation with the phone. They told her that their employers often talked about scammers having their phones shoved up their asses, all in that silly accent. The two apparently laughed their whole way through that delicate procedure. By the way, they used Crisco from her kitchen to get the thing in. Their casual attitude scared the crap out of the victim. The suspects were doing, well, what they did while joking. She thought they had ice water in their veins. They might as well have been making waffles in their own kitchen the way they acted."

Haley was making notes as she said, "Thanks. Now, what was the time between when she was assaulted and the cops being called?"

"About six hours. They did her about three in the morning, and the call came into the PD just before nine. That's why she was in such a hurry to have the detective call her friends. There were only two hours left until the deadline the pair gave her."

William asked, "Did they do the grenade-on-a-wire bit, Andy?"

"No. This time they got a bit more creative. They took one of her lamps and aimed it, turned off, in her face. They told her that a piece of cardboard they slid under her was a pressure switch. They gave her a story about how they had tied the cellphone to the charging cord, and if she moved, there would be 120 volts going directly into her rectum. They said the light turning on would be the last thing she would see. She stared at that dead bulb for six hours. Cruel as it was, you have to admit that was a pretty good gag."

Haley asked, "Anything else?"

"Yeah. You want to hear some irony?" Friender asked with a raised eyebrow.

"Sure, Special Agent Friender. What is it?" Haley asked.

"The pair said she was picked because of her name. She was working as Heather from cardholder services, but her name isn't really Heather, of course."

SAC Henderson seemed to be enjoying the entertaining turn of events and smiled in anticipation as he asked, "Okay, what is it?"

"Carmen. As in Carmen from cardholder services."

Everyone on both ends of the teleconference circuit laughed again. The name was used in a huge number of cardholder services scams.

Cody thought of another question. He moved to make sure the camera was capturing him as he said, "Hi, Andy. Smutters here."

"How are you doing, Cody. Long time."

"Yeah. Hey, any video? ATMs? Convenience stores? Traffic cams?"

"Nothing we can correlate with our pair. We checked every plate we could identify. There weren't many at that time of the morning in the victim's area. Patrol cars, a few delivery trucks, twenty passenger vehicles. All check out. All the vehicles coming from the area where she lives that stopped at the gas stations and other late-night places close to the freeway entrances are being checked, too. That's going to take a couple of days. I gotta tell you that the Ann Arbor Police Department isn't devoting much in the way of resources to investigate this. A couple of uniforms volunteered to take it because they thought it was so funny. If they catch the perps, I think the only thing that will happen will be the Chief giving them a medal. The interview with Carmen at the hospital was videoed. It has been shown at every watch briefing in every police department for fifty miles. Our perps are underground heroes here."

"Thanks," Cody replied.

Special Agent Friender, now part of the team working the Qatar Card cases, stayed on the line. Haley continued her presentation.

"As I was saying, cold sociopaths. They enjoyed torturing her like that. Part of the revenge for the greater good in their minds, I suppose."

Cody looked at his SAC. He hesitated for a second and then asked, "Can we ask Friender to email a copy of that interview. Er, I mean just for training purposes, of course."

He couldn't keep a straight face and cracked up along with everyone else.

"Yeah, go ahead and send it, Andy. But it does not wind up on YouTube from here."

The videoconference ended ten minutes later. Haley left for another meeting and Cody returned to his cubicle. He didn't let the others know, but two days earlier, he had been watching Jeopardy with Haley when he got a cardholder services call on his own cell phone. He missed one of the contestants' answers because of the interruption, and shoving the scammer's phone up her butt was just what he thought at the moment.

He couldn't admit it, but he was glad the Cutters had gotten revenge for him. He knew there were hundreds of thousands like him that were glad, too …

Chapter 16

Fun Things to Do in Ann Arbor after Midnight

At 12:30 a.m. the same day as the teleconference with Special Agent Friender, a car containing an elderly couple got off the freeway in Ann Arbor, Michigan. It pulled up to a McDonald's on West Stadium Boulevard as the crew was getting ready to close. The man driving ordered two coffees and a hamburger.

As he paid, he asked, "How do I get to the Detroit freeway entrance on the other side of town? My wife doesn't want me to eat this tasty snack at freeway speeds."

The cashier told him how to get there, asking, "Why don't you just use the GPS on your phone?"

The driver held up an older flip phone and said, "Maybe someday my wife and I will upgrade, but we really don't do anything but make calls with these darn things."

The cashier laughed as she handed them their order.

***

On the way through town, the car paused in a residential area at a stop sign. The rear door opened, and two figures dressed in black rolled out and ran to some bushes in a park. They used a breathable black tarp to cover themselves. The tarp had a thermal layer, much the same as a mylar emergency blanket. That layer would mask some of their heat signatures.

"We have quite a while, honey. What do you want to do while we wait?"

Alex responded by putting his arms around her.

"Cuddle for warmth?"

They snuggled and kissed for a bit as they talked in whispers about the plan.

Lara asked, "Do you think she will buy the pressure switch thing, honey?"

"Why not? It's just as believable as the grenade trick. Papa Paul really wants to punish this crew. We discovered that they were responsible for eight of the robocalls he got last month. He hopes that staring into that bulb of death will make a lasting impression."

"Yeesh. Looking for six hours at a thing that you think will kill you should do it. I hope she has Crisco."

"Why?" Alex asked.

"We had to do the last one with cooking oil, and it was hard to coat the phone properly. Crisco stays put."

When it was time to visit their victim, they folded and stashed the tarp in a backpack, put on their hoods and goggles, and followed the route through the small park to their target's house.

This time there was no alarm. This wasn't the boiler room where the phone calls were generated. This was a private house where frumpy, unpleasant Carmen Schwatzer lived alone with her two cats. She was single, forty-three years old, and had been working scams such as this for two decades. She moved around every few years when one grift dried up, and she found another through her sleazy contacts.

They didn't even need to break in as she had left a window open at the rear of the modest house. They stopped in the kitchen for a knife and, fortunately, a can of Crisco and then opened her bedroom door. She was in bed snoring when Alex put his hand over her mouth.

She screamed at first under his hand but fell silent when he showed her the knife.

Alex instructed, "Don't move, and we won't use this on you. Scream, and we kill you. Nod if you understand."

She nodded.

"Do you know why we're here?" Lara asked.

She shook her head.

Alex explained the reasons for their visit and the consequences of her or her associates robocalling in the future.

When Alex's hand was off her mouth, she gasped, "You're them? Wait, wait. I don't do anything. I just answer calls. My boss says we help people get lower credit card rates. Really. That's all I know."

The pair launched into comical German accents while trussing her up and looking for a cell phone of appropriate size. Lara found a small one with the charging cord attached.

She slathered the phone with Crisco and then inserted it as the struggling Carmen screamed into her gag. The charging cord dangled out like a tail.

Alex then took a table lamp and split the cord in front of Carmen. He draped the cord over her shoulder and tied the unplugged cord to the charging cord.

He warned, "This lamp, Carmen, is connected to the pressure switch now under you and to the cord of your cute little cellphone. The switch is normally closed, but you lying on it opens the switch. If you roll over or otherwise move, the switch will close, and that lamp will come on. One hundred twenty volts will run through your rectum and cook you like a hot dog. That light turning on will be the last thing you see."

Alex explained, "You were picked because of your name, Carmen. Bad line of work for someone with your name."

Alex patted Carmen's head and stroked her sleep-matted, bleach-blond hair with brown roots. He laughed and said, "When the cops get here in six hours, tell them exactly what you do and where you do it. Give them your friends' names so they can warn them. Remember, eight hours from now, if they're still grifting, we start killing you all one by one. If even one person is still making phone calls with your robodialer, we kill the lot of you. We'll be watching."

He left the Qatar card on her dresser and checked his watch. He gave her the usual ending speech, and they exited the house at the rear sixty-five seconds later. They hopped over a fence to the street behind it and crouched behind a bush.

Twenty seconds later, a passing car slowed down to three miles an hour, and they jumped in, lying down and covering themselves with the tarp once again. The car drove south, heading toward Toledo. The pair stripped off their black garments and put on street clothes waiting for them on the back seat. The black clothing and their burner phones were stuffed into a garbage bag destined for the kiln at a cement plant.

The driver made a couple of unexpected turns, followed by the expected path again.

"Sir, we may have picked up a tail. Far back and trying to look not like a tail, but I think someone has taken an interest," he warned.

"Thanks, Fred. Sweetheart, make the call."

Lara pulled a burner phone from the garbage bag and dialed the contingency number.

"Hey. Yeah. Possible problem. Driver reports a likely tail. Could be a curious local undercover unit … Kansas City Shuffle? Sure. Ypsilanti all set?"

The car pulled off at Ypsilanti and headed to a large all night grocery store near the exit. It parked next to a white SUV that had stopped there just three minutes earlier. A large pickup truck blocked the store security cameras' view. The driver of Lara and Alex's car got out and walked casually into the store. By the time he came out with a warm rotisserie chicken, two bags of potato chips, and a couple of sodas, Alex and Lara had slipped into the front seats of the SUV as the driver of that vehicle got into the other car. The chicken was placed on the back seat of the original getaway car, and the driver started the engine.

The SUV driver had thoughtfully provided a full tank of gas and two cups of hot coffee, one black and one with cream and yellow-packet sweetener. Alex watched as their first ride left the parking lot. A gray sedan that had stopped just inside the grocery store parking lot waited for a few seconds and then followed their first car out. Alex and Lara waited for ten more minutes before leaving.

Alex and Lara didn't stop for the next hour and forty minutes. They parked the SUV in the Amtrak lot in Kalamazoo and went for breakfast. They had plenty of time to stretch their legs and get back to the Amtrak station before the 10:23 a.m. Amtrak Wolverine would depart to take them the rest of the way to Chicago. At breakfast, they chatted with a nice gentleman who lent them his newspaper. When they returned the folded paper, it had the SUV's keys in it, and they had the train tickets it formerly contained.

* * *

Siggy picked them up at the Amtrak station in Chicago. He drove them over to Papa Paul's in-town digs, where the retired gangster and his wife were staying for a couple of weeks on a visit to his kids and grandkids.

"Lara, my love, and Alex! Tell me how it went."

Lara answered, "Papa Paul, it went as we planned it. We had to use one contingency on this one, though. Probably a curious cop."

When they described the vehicle swap they had on standby with the cranberry buyer's operatives, Siggy put his hand to his forehead in mock lament and wailed, "Those plans! Oy! You two are driving my guys nuts with your meshuggeneh plans."

"Now, now, Siggy," Papa Paul chided. "I like their plans. Hearing about them makes it like one of those spy movies. You know how much I enjoy them. Lighten up. It's my money."

"Yes, Paul," Siggy laughed.

Alex and Lara gave them a recount of the operation. When they got to the part where they improvised the comical German accents, everyone was in stitches.

"How about the pressure switch thing? How did that go?" Papa Paul asked.

"She was terrified," Lara said. "We described what 120 volts would do to her insides, and we put the bulb right in front of her face. She had to look at it until your guy called the PD to come to get her. Man! That would drive me nuts."

"Lara, she deserved it. Those assholes called me a dozen times!" Papa Paul reminded her.

"Papa Paul, it wasn't nearly that many, and we keep telling you that you can get a call blocker," she chided.

"Sweetie, if I put a call blocker on I can't have them call me, right? I don't want Siggy's people always selecting these assholes. I want the satisfaction from time to time. I actually enjoy talking with them, knowing that the asshole is going to get a visit from the two of you," Papa Paul said with a wink.

"Okay, Papa Paul. You make the rules. Anything coming up?"

"Yeah. Siggy has something for you. Our Russian friends need some out-of-town assistance. Siggy, take them to your place tomorrow and let them take a look."

Lara hugged the old man and said, "Papa Paul, you are the best. I love you."

"Sweetie, I love you, too. Now let's go take this lovable hunk and get some dinner."

Chapter 17

Searching for Your Roots Is Rewarding

Late the next morning, Siggy drove them to his huge Lake Michigan summer home. One of his housekeeping staff had just returned with a massive bag of takeout. There were no wiseguys here. Just legitimate paid staff with tax withholding and workers' comp coverage. Siggy, Lara, and Alex sat down at the conference table in Siggy's office to eat White Castle burgers and talk.

Siggy explained, "Papa Paul was asked for a favor. One of our Russian friends has a little problem. Remember Gleb? Well, he told the police a little too much. The old-school vory now working in their mob had him killed in jail, but he'd already told the lead detective about an associate. The associate is a mook who has too much information about our Russian friends. They are afraid that he will spill the beans."

"So why don't they take him out themselves?" Lara asked.

"This guy is a government official. He's connected to the mob through graft. We know he is being watched by the police. They are building a case against him before they arrest and interrogate him. If the Russian mob takes him out, it will cause them problems. They want it to look like something else."

"What is our time frame?" Alex inquired.

Siggy replied, "Two weeks. Our friends' sources in the police department think that they will have enough on him by then, and they'll pick him up and start squeezing him in about two weeks."

"Whaddaya think, sweetheart? Couple of days here for planning and then maybe head over to Belgium to see where my great grandparents lived? Always wanted to do that. Then, we meet with our friends for the final planning when we go back to that wonderful hotel in Moscow. Last time we didn't go to Gorky Park, so we make sure we see it this time."

Lara excitedly said, "Oh yeah, Alex! We wanted to see that shopping arcade. What was the big department store called?"

"GUM," Alex said.

Lara continued, "Yeah! This will be fun. Are the police doing physical surveillance on this guy, Siggy?"

Siggy rolled his eyes and said, "Oy, you two! I never can get used to planning sightseeing and a hit in one sentence. But, no. No physical surveillance. With one exception. They are watching who sees him at work, but nothing outside the government building where his office is located. They apparently don't know how much he knows, and they're treating him as small fry. They are building a corruption case on him based on taking bribes."

"Is the guy dangerous?" Alex asked Siggy.

"Nah. Bureaucrat. His name is Semyon Blinov. When the cops go to get him, they'll probably just send a detective or two or maybe a couple of uniforms. Pushover. Lives alone. Divorced. He's a disagreeable, fat fuck, too. A corrupt little weasel gives out business permits for large cash payments. Gleb was the contact who would approach business owners and steer them to Semyon on behalf of the mob. The payoffs were split with Gleb, who passed on most to the mob."

Lara looked at Alex with hate in her eyes. "I want to do him, honey. Up close with a knife."

Alex put an arm around her and said, "I know you do, sweetheart. He's as bad as the guys who squeezed your dad for his business permit. But there may be an even more satisfying way to get him. Siggy, would our Russian friends be willing to do a little digging?"

Siggy answered, "Sure. What do you have in mind?"

Alex said, "We need to get a few names of people who paid him off. Get 'em to testify."

Siggy thought for a moment and concluded, "Shouldn't be a problem. Our Russian friends probably know them from Gleb's payouts. They can visit the business owners and offer to repay their losses in exchange for testimony against Semyon. Last year in Hot Springs, we did that to get revenge on a mook who tried to fleece my commercial property division for a perfectly legitimate strip mall. It cost us three times what the bribe would have been, but the guy's in jail now. Very satisfying on any number of levels."

Alex said, "Okay, Siggy, have them get some names. We gather the bribe evidence and send it to the police. The cops verify it with the scammed business owners and get a warrant for Semyon. We get our friends in the police department to tell us when they will serve the warrant and make sure they're going to do it at his house. We'll figure out the ending when we have more info on his residence. We give him an ambiguous end. No ties back to the mob, and Lara and I were never there."

The pair said they would flesh out the plan and get back to Siggy the following day. Siggy's staff showed Alex and Lara to their rooms. After changing, they spent the afternoon with Siggy, lounging by his infinity pool overlooking the lake.

* * *

A week later, they were exploring Brussels. Alex's grandparents had told him stories of living in Belgium as young children, and he finally got to see some of the places they told him about. His grandparents had been gone for almost a decade now. Alex always regretted never visiting their childhood city with them.

The pair hired a car and driver to take them to the house where his grandfather lived as a small child. They found a couple who appeared to be in their seventies sitting in a nearby park.

Alex spoke to them in French and asked if they knew of his family. They hadn't lived in the area that long, but they said they knew the family in the house next door to his great grandfather's house. They took him there and knocked on the door.

An elderly woman answered the door, and the older couple told her Alex was looking for someone who knew his family.

Alex introduced himself and Lara, again in French. She responded that her name was Philomène.

He pointed to the house next door, asking, "Did you know Albert Desmêt? He moved to America with his parents when he was about nine years old."

"Albert? Yes, I remember him and his parents. He was a devilish little boy. He and I were about the same age. I think he was maybe two years older. He was always playing pranks. I got into trouble more than once because I helped him. I missed him when he moved, but the war did so many things to so many people. His parents saw the chance to go to America, and they took it. Do you want to see the house where he grew up? The owners both work in offices in the city, but they will be home later. About five thirty."

"Philomène, I would be so pleased to see it. My wife and I are going to see some sights here in Belgium, and we would be honored to take you to lunch and hear stories about my great grandfather." Noticing her wedding ring, he added, "Is your husband home, too?"

"I'm sorry to say he passed away a few years ago. I have nothing to do today other than walk to the market for food. Let me get my coat. I would love to talk with Albert's grandson."

While Philomène was getting her coat, Alex thanked the elderly couple and asked them if they wished to join them for lunch. The man declined, saying that the time should be for Alex, Lara, and Philomène. They went back to the park to enjoy the sunshine and feed the squirrels.

The lunch at a nearby café was enjoyable, and Philomène was pleased to find someone who had taken the trouble to search out his family roots. When she asked what they did for a living, he explained that they bought things at antique shops, auctions, and estate sales and sold some of them for a profit through their business and on eBay. Then he had to explain what eBay was.

They had a wonderful time. Alex learned a lot about his family's neighborhood in 1930s Belgium. After lunch, Alex and Lara walked Philomène home and promised to come back at 6 p.m. so she could introduce him to the couple next door.

At the appointed hour, they returned, and he was able to see his great grandfather's house. Lara knew that it was an emotional experience, and she lovingly held his hand as he experienced what his grandfather had told him in stories. Albert's recollections had been reasonably accurate, even though he last was at the house when he was nine.

Alex explained some of the stories as he went through the house. "The cupboard in the upstairs bedroom is built into a gable, and it was where he kept his best toys.

"He loved to run his hand over the railing with the little knobs on top at the second-floor landing. I'm glad it is still intact.

"The back porch was where he used to sit and watch the birds in the oak tree. All of it is still here, sweetheart."

The rest of the tour of Brussels was almost as memorable. Seeing what his grandfather had remembered from so long ago was poignant.

He sighed. "I wish I had brought them here at least once."

"Honey, when we finally had the money, we were so busy, and then they passed away. It would have been nice, but it just wasn't possible. At least you got to see where your grandfather came from. It is really too bad that your grandmother's entire neighborhood was destroyed during the war. It's a miracle that both your grandmother's family and your grandfather's family made it out of Europe back then."

"Well, it was right after the war, and things were chaotic. When they finally made it to America, they settled in New York, and that's where Grandfather met Grandma. One thing they hated, both here in Belgium and then in New York, was corruption. Both had to bribe their way out of Europe, and then there were payoffs to do business in New York. It wasn't just the criminals, either. It was the petty bureaucrats, too."

"Interesting. You never told me the part about the crooked bureaucrats who robbed them. Aw, honey. It's so nice that we have that in common. Your great grandparents would be so proud of you. Coming back to Europe to kill one of the kind that robbed them the same way that asshole in Savannah extorted Dad."

"Yeah. It is sort of satisfying, though I know it is a lot more satisfying for you. Maybe because it is two generations closer to you, you think?"

Lara furrowed her brow and said, "Possibly. I mean, I still remember Pop ranting about that asshole and the permits. You know, that was when I started to think about doing to real crooks what we were doing in the assassin club."

"Funny," Alex replied, "my grandfather's stories are what got me fired up about taking out those assholes, too."

Lara asked, "Do you think that one day we can tell Dad we got some kind of revenge for him?"

"My sweet, the only time we could tell him would be at our trial if we were already arrested. I don't think he would approve of our occupation."

"I guess you're right. Gotta expect that from a straight-arrow retired-Marine ice cream store owner. My sister, too. You know who she does business with."

* * *

The following week went off without a hitch. The Russian mob friends who asked Papa Paul for the favor found several business owners who filled the bill. They paid them what they had lost plus a little extra to convince them to give evidence of Semyon's corruption when the time came. They also ensured that in exchange for their testimony, the business owners would not be charged with bribing Semyon. The mob's lawyers had all the right connections to keep the enterprise's gears running smoothly.

Semyon needed to be at home, not at work when the warrant was issued. This was quickly arranged. Gleb's arrest had left a void in Semyon's wallet. The mob had given the task of finding victims for the permit-application scam to an interim associate, but business was spotty with the new guy, who was still learning how to approach marks.

Shortly after they arrived in Moscow, Alex and Lara met with Lubov, who explained, "We have informed Semyon that we have a permanent, experienced replacement for the man who has been filling in for Gleb. He is to meet the new man in three days. This was excellent news for Semyon, but I insisted the meeting could only be with the new man during the day. Semyon, of course, did not want to see him at the office. He suggested that he call in sick that day and meet our man at Semyon's apartment.

"Our people have thoroughly cased Semyon's apartment and neighborhood for you, and here is the list of features you asked for. By good fortune, he has a first-floor apartment. I will have the driver who takes you there provide the pistol and ammunition you asked for. It will be stolen from a security company and traceable to the original owner, as you requested. It is something Semyon could buy on the black market. Do you need anything else?"

Lara replied, "No, but thank you. With what we have in mind, the case will be wrapped up by the end of that day."

Lara and Alex looked at the layout of Semyon's apartment that Lubov provided and the map of the adjacent streets. They conferred quickly regarding the options they had anticipated, and then turned to Lubov. Lara explained the planned sequence of events.

Lubov laughed. "Your reputation is well deserved. Even if one of the detectives has a suspicion, his higher-ups won't want to waste any rubles on solving what appears to already have been solved."

Lara said, "Looks like everything is good, and we can get this plan in motion."

Lubov replied, "Yes. Our contact in the police department who is following the case is waiting until the appropriate time. He will go to the Criminal Investigation Department and find the detective supervisor in charge of Semyon's investigation, Lieutenant Alyosha Sokolov. It was his discovery of the connection to Gleb that brought Semyon to light. Alyosha has a reputation for being very persuasive."

"What else do you know about him?" Lara asked. "Maybe there is something that will help us set this up."

"This detective, Sokolov," Lubov explained, "is a very determined man. He appears to suspect more in the Gleb matter, and he won't let go. Like a vengeful character in a Russian novel. In fact, when my man in the detective bureau told Sokolov that he was chasing nonsense, Sokolov quoted Dostoyevsky: 'Talking nonsense is the sole privilege mankind possesses over the other organisms. It's by talking nonsense that one gets to the truth!' He is an educated, experienced, and determined man dedicated to his profession. If there is anyone who might question Semyon's demise, it would be him."

Alex asked, "Then do we have anything to be extra cautious about if he is the one at the scene?"

Lubov laughed. "If it was just him, maybe, but Sokolov's superiors are nothing like him. They will close the case quickly and brag that their superior investigation led a corrupt official to justice. They will parade our witnesses in front of the press and again brag that the justice system is so honest that these witnesses had no fear of reporting the corruption. Peace in the Middle East is more likely than getting a bureaucrat to change a story once it is already announced to the press."

Alex asked, "Any details on what information Gleb spilled?"

"What little Gleb said before his untimely demise was vague, but it did include what he did for Semyon. The case against Semyon was developed from there. That is all we know for sure."

* * *

With the timely witness statements provided by Lubov's crew, Alyosha quickly obtained the expected warrant. A check with Semyon's office showed that he had called in sick, so Alyosha took one other detective and drove to Semyon's house for what should have been the easy, uneventful arrest of a fat, corrupt bureaucrat.

He didn't know they were driving to a setup.

Chapter 18

Suicide by Cop

A few hours before Alyosha went to serve that warrant, Alex and Lara were picked up three blocks from their hotel, just outside a café specified by Lubov. Their driver drove them to the neighborhood where Semyon lived. He seemed nervous, but Alex told him to be quiet and drive when he tried to ask questions. He made a mental note to let the clients know that the driver might still be a bit too green to take on such assignments.

The driver let Alex out in front of Semyon's apartment block. He drove Lara around the corner and let her out, too. She walked to the sheltered alley side of the building and waited.

Alex used the main entrance intercom to ring Semyon, identifying himself as the new contact. Semyon buzzed Alex through the street entrance. Alex knocked on the apartment door, and Semyon let him in. As soon as Alex was inside, he pulled the gun that Lubov's people had provided and ordered Semyon to sit in a front-room chair. He opened a side window to let Lara in, and they began to wait for their police contact to call to let them know that the arrest team was on the way.

Semyon, a balding middle-aged man with a round face, was wearing slacks and a red open-collar shirt. The color made his round face look even redder as he sat in that chair, sweating profusely. His large belly fought against the buttons of the shirt. Combined with the color of the shirt and his face, it gave the comical impression that he was a cartoon character about to explode.

Alex spoke to Semyon in Russian. "You are a bad person, taking bribes from people who just want what they are entitled to. You are to do what we tell you to do. Don't worry. We are not here to kill you. We can guarantee that you will not die by our hands. Now I'm going to fire my gun while you hold it. Let me do the work. Don't struggle, or my wife's knife may cut your throat. You wouldn't want us to break our promise, now, would you?"

"Why do you want me to have the gun in my hand when you fire it?" Semyon asked nervously.

"Don't worry about it. We'll explain later," Alex replied.

Lara kept her knife on Semyon's throat. Alex put the gun, loaded with a single round, into Semyon's hand and fired it with the muzzle pressed against the side of a sofa cushion. The little PSM pistol, with its diminutive 5.4-millimeter round, made little noise. Even less than usual, in fact, as Lara had asked for one cartridge to have half the gunpowder removed. The cushion effectively muffled what report the squib load made, and the bullet barely made it out of the other side of the cushion. As Alex pocketed the projectile and the cartridge casing, he noted that the entrance and exit holes wouldn't be noticed unless someone lifted the cushion and looked at it carefully. They didn't know whether or not the police would bother to do a gunpowder residue test on Semyon's hands, but they weren't taking any chances.

The apartment's exterior was painted concrete, so it was perfect for the setup. Lara loaded the magazine, chambered a round, and watched from the kitchen window to signal Alex when anyone walked toward the building.

The intercom buzzed, and without answering, Lara buzzed the police through the front entrance. Then the three in the apartment heard Alyosha knock on the door and announce in Russian, "Mr. Semyon Blinov! I am Detective Lieutenant Alyosha Sokolov of the Moscow police, and we want a word with you."

Alex fired two shots through the door, far too high to hit anyone. It had the appropriate effect, sending both detectives quickly back to their car. Lara peeked through a slit in a curtain and watched as Alyosha retrieved his PP-2000 submachine gun from the trunk. His partner, Egor Garin, drew his Grach and appeared to call for backup.

Lara joined Alex in the front room. Lara held Semyon at knifepoint while Alex broke out a window from behind its curtain and fired two quick shots into the street. From the safety of the concrete wall on either side of the window, they each held one arm of the terrified and now-squirming Semyon. Two short bursts from the

PP-2000 a couple of seconds apart sliced through the spot from which the gunfire had come. They heard a few individual shots, too, with one chipping concrete in the window opening.

The pair felt Semyon tense and freeze for an instant before dropping limply out of their grasp. He lay dead on the floor, six nine-millimeter bullet holes in his chest. They placed the stolen gun next to his hand.

Lara took a second to kiss Alex before the pair exited through a back window. They scaled a low fence and walked onto the street and into the back of the waiting car with the same driver. They stripped off their surgical gloves and put them into the used McDonald's bag lying ready on the back seat. The driver took them to Gorky Park. The pair got out of the car, and on the way to the beautiful main gate, they deposited the bag in a trash can.

Alex and Lara were instantly sorry that they had not visited Gorky Park on their previous Moscow trips. The old, seedy park had been reinvented. The amusement park rides were replaced by a mall and great restaurants. The grounds were beautiful, and they strolled for quite a while before returning to their hotel with several purchases in tow.

* * *

They engaged in their cover business, doing a bit of antique buying while they were in the city. Yuri reported that some of their purchases required additional authentication. The pair welcomed the delay and extended their stay. They never left a foreign country until all paperwork had cleared whatever customs hurdles were necessary.

They enjoyed the city for a few more peaceful days. About a week later, they were home.

Chapter 19

Alyosha Smells a Rat, but the Brass Rats Won't Listen

For four minutes after Semyon's last terrifying moment on earth, Alyosha and his calm and efficient partner, Egor, waited for backup behind the safety of the engine block of their car. Police came screaming in from every direction. They tried to make contact with Semyon, but they received no reply. Finally, a tactical team entered the apartment and found him dead in a pool of blood beneath the window raked by Alyosha's bullets.

The subsequent search revealed a phone message on his recorder that indicated a Russian mob member had found him a new contact to channel applicants to his office for fleecing.

Alyosha conferred with Egor and with the head of the tactical team, Ivan Shupiatski.

Ivan made a suggestion. "Lieutenant, if this sukin syn has just made contact with a mobster and was about to be arrested, he would have known he wouldn't last a week in jail. This looks like suicide by cop to me. I think he knew his options were either nine-millimeter bullets from your PP-2000 or being tortured to death in jail. Agreed?"

Egor agreed, "Boss, this sounds plausible. Maybe there was more to it, but the piece of crap is dead. This will be a brief report. With Ivan's backing, there won't be any investigation of our use of deadly force. A simple report, a press release on the demise of a corrupt official who fired shots at the police, and the case will be closed."

While Alyosha had a nagging doubt about the crime scene, he didn't think it was worth the bureaucratic effort to pursue it officially. He asked, "Ivan, what would you have ordered your team to do if you were here when the shots came through the window?"

Ivan appeared to take the question as possible remorse on Alyosha's part, and he put his hand on the lieutenant's shoulder. He said in a reassuring tone, "Alyosha, our manual says to do just what you did. Don't mourn this sukin syn."

Sukin syn—son of a bitch. Alyosha weighed the value of the dead man against the problems that following his hunch would create. He looked at his counterparts and said, "Ivan, you are right. Moscow is now better by one less corrupt bureaucrat. Write your report as you suggested."

Alyosha turned to Egor and scolded, "You need more time at the range, Egor. I saw concrete chips flying all over the place, but I don't think you got any in the window. Your pistol is more accurate than that."

"Okay, Lieutenant," Egor replied, "but that window was almost thirty meters from our car. Anyway, Ivan will have us both covered in his report."

Alyosha, though, was as good a cop as Cody and Lubov had pegged him to be. He did a little more poking around the crime scene. Later, he sent an email to Cody asking him to call.

* * *

The following day, Cody was on the line to Alyosha. Since Moscow was eight hours ahead of DC, Alyosha was in his office thinking about an afternoon glass of tea, while Cody hadn't yet left for work. They spoke mainly in Russian.

"Drook! What do you have for me?" Cody asked.

"It may be nothing, but there is something odd tied to the case involving Gleb. The computer he owned had four files erased, remember?"

"Oh, yeah! Were you able to recover them?"

"No. They were scrubbed. Gone. It was more than a lowlife like him would normally do. So, we sweated him a number of times after you left. You know this term, sweated?"

"Yes," Cody laughed. "You hurt Gleb's feelings for a couple of days."

Alyosha laughed, too, and said, "Yes. Hurt his feelings. Eventually, he told us who gave him the files but could not tell us in any detail what was on them. His employer had given them to him but had not yet started the task they were meant for. They were shipping manifests he was supposed to examine once his employers gave him what he called a wish list from another mob. He said that the pair who accosted him erased the files. He got the impression that pair were somehow connected to the vor who gave him the files in the first place."

"Vor? As in vory v zakone? I didn't expect to see their involvement in a scam as trivial as Gleb's."

"Yes. They are not exactly what they were before the Great Patriotic War, but some became part of the new Russian Mafia organizations, and some still exist simply as vory v zakone. They are terrible people to cross. They are involved in all manner of crimes. Gleb thought that the gang he was doing business with was associated with vory. That appears to be what scared him so."

"What was that other group? The one they fought with? I remember something about it from some Russian Mafia cases I worked here."

"During the Great Patriotic War, many vory were pressed into military service. Many hardcore vory refused because of their code that forbids any cooperation with the prison or other government authorities. Vory v zakone means thieves-in-law, not because they are related by marriage, but because they have a strict code, a set of thieves' laws. Many did serve, though, in violation of that code. A lot of those returned to criminal life and were sent back to the gulags. The vory who refused to serve called the others suki ... you know this word?" Alyosha asked.

"Bitches," Cody answered in English. "So what happened with the suki?"

"War," Alyosha answered. "The Soviet jailers hated the vory because they would not serve against the Germans. Sometimes they even gave the suki weapons to war against the vory in prison. Over time, the vory were weakened."

"Was betrayal of one of them the motive for the assault on Gleb?" Cody asked.

"Only in part," Alyosha said. "He insisted that the pair who assaulted him were there because of his Internet scam activities. He used ransomware against a hospital, remember? Very strange that something so inconsequential should result in such an action."

"I agree. We are still very puzzled about this, too. Can you question Gleb about the vory connection? He had no vory or other gang tattoos, from what I understand. The made guys in the Russian Mafia cases I worked were covered with them."

"Only the devils in hell can question him now. The criminals found out he had given us information, and one gutted him in jail. They probably saw him as sukin."

Cody smirked as he said, "Too bad for Gleb."

"Yes. I shed a tear for him. But I was cutting onions at the time, so maybe the tear was not for him," Alyosha joked. "Before they got to him, we eventually got him to tell us about other criminal activities. One of them was that he was gathering clients for a corrupt government official. Someone in the business permit bureau. He was extorting money to process permits. A man named Semyon Blinov."

"Have you questioned Semyon?" Cody asked.

"Again, only devils can do this," Alyosha replied. "I shot him two days ago when he fired at me from his apartment when we went to arrest him."

Cody said in surprise, "This case is really leaving a string of corpses, isn't it? So, what's unusual about a corrupt official who resists arrest?"

"The official story is that he knew he was a dead man if we took him to jail because he could give us information about the mob."

"Sure, Alyosha. Suicide by cop," Cody guessed.

"Yes, but it is bullshit because he had the spine of a worm. He would have tried to make a deal. Also, the gun he had was stolen, and this was a—how do you say—a white-collar criminal, not a thief. He was not the kind of man who would have the courage to fire on the police."

"Someone could do that in a panic, I suppose," Cody offered as he gathered his phone, wallet, and keys and took down a travel mug from the cupboard. It was one of Haley's—a bright pink one with "Virginia is for Lovers" emblazoned across it. But he was running too late to notice and just started pouring the coffee.

"It is possible. But there was one shot through a sofa cushion, two very badly aimed shots through the door when we arrived, and two more shots through the window at us through a curtain. He then stood behind the curtain very still while I returned fire."

"Use the PP-2000?" Cody asked, half listening now as he realized what mug he would be sipping from on the way to work.

"Yes. I fired ten rounds. Two bursts of five, I think. A few seconds apart. Six hit his chest."

"He stayed still for a few seconds?" Cody asked as he stopped pouring the coffee. This was unusual.

"Yes. As if he was held steady by something or someone. One more thing. We only heard four shots. Two from the window and two through the door."

"Could the shot through the sofa cushion have been an old one?" Cody asked.

"No. The cushion still smelled of gunpowder. I would guess a few hours at most. And no bullet or casing."

Cody frowned and tried to think of a reason behind that shot. He asked, "Could it have been a test shot? Did he suspect he would be arrested?"

"No, we do not think so. Semyon had no reason to believe we were onto him."

A light bulb lit above Cody's head. "Was he tested for gunpowder residue?"

"No. there was no need. The case was closed. No need for the expense. But it was my thought, too, that he may have been exposed to gunpowder residue in this manner before I arrived."

"I'm beginning to get the picture. You think Semyon may have been set up to make it look like 'suicide by cop' but was held there for you to shoot him. Someone else fired the shots through the door and window?"

"It is a possibility. I have told my superiors about my suspicions, but they are not interested in a closed case solved so easily. They all had pictures taken with bribery victims who came forward, oddly all at the same time. Getting, as you say, the brass who have been in the newspaper to change their story is as hard as getting a statue of a rat to eat cheese."

"Ah. I get it. Brass rats, so to speak."

"Yes. A good term, brass rats. I will use it." Alyosha laughed.

Cody laughed with him. "You have such colorful descriptions of your superiors, too."

"I'm sure you have some for yours, as well, Cody. So, with the brass rats above me, I had to tell someone, and since it is loosely connected to your case because of Gleb and that card, I called to tell you."

"I appreciate that. And that is damned good police work, Alyosha. Even if your superiors don't buy it, I think you uncovered a real possibility. Good hunch."

"Thank you, Cody."

"Speaking of hunches, do you have access to run names of people arriving at and departing from Moscow?"

Alyosha replied, "Of course. I can look at visa data. Why?"

"Oh, just another hunch. Can you look for anyone entering the country in the last six months with the last name of Cutter or Gutter?"

"Six months? Drook, that will cost me a couple of bottles of vodka. At least two of the technicians who process visa data will have to spend a couple of hours pressing computer keys."

"The next time I see you, I will buy you a case of vodka," Cody assured him. "It's worth that and more to scratch an itch like the one you have with Semyon now."

Alyosha responded, "For this reason, I will do it. I will be happy to share the vodka with you when you come. It is good to have a friend who believes in good police work. Too many do too little just so they can get a pension. I suspect at heart you are a real policeman."

"I try to be, and I guess you do, too. Yes. It is good to have such friends."

Alyosha said, "It will take me several days to find the technicians willing to do it, but I will email you when I have checked the visas."

"Thank you. Goodbye, friend. Thanks for letting me know about Semyon."

"You are welcome. Goodbye, Cody."

When Cody hung up, he felt uneasy. Gleb's files were probably from some form of Russian Mafia, if not the old-style vory. Whoever tortured him at his house apparently knew this and wiped those files. That meant that they had some connection to the same gangsters. Everyone was sure that the pair that visited Gleb was American, so what kind of American has contact with people such as vory? Looking at the time, he grabbed the pink coffee cup and dashed out of the house.

* * *

After glancing at his emails at his desk, he decided to check with William about the other foreign cases. He walked over and took a chair until William finished a phone call.

As William put down the phone, he turned to Cody and asked, "What's up? You have that patented Cody, 'Don't think I'm crazy, but I have a question,' look on your face."

That broke the tension Cody was feeling, and he laughed. "Okay, don't think I'm crazy, but I have a question. I was just talking with our friend in Russia from the Gleb case. Got me thinking. Have Any more hits on foreign languages spoken by the Qatar Card suspects?"

"Yeah. Something came in yesterday, but I haven't had a chance to read it. Where is that …? Ah! Here it is. Let's see: Pakistani police, first victim, yeah. I don't want to know what they did to the guy, but he finally gave them some info. The male suspect spoke Urdu to the victim. Let's see, that's English, Russian, Hindi, and now Urdu."

"Great! Can you get ahold of the Czech cops again? We hit three aces. Let's see if we can make it four."

"Come on! That would be too weird. I bet we don't get a fourth foreign language," William insisted.

"You're on. Loser buys lunch," Cody replied.

Sucker bet.

Chapter 20

Well, Isn't Cody Full of Romantic Surprises

Cody went back to his own desk and called Haley. The news about the languages was important, but he needed to check on something else, too.

"Hi, honey. Good news. We have four languages now, English, Hindi, Urdu, and Russian. William is checking with the Czechs. I guess that would be a Czech-check."

"Very funny. Thanks for the update."

"Dinner still on for tonight?" Cody asked, trying not to sound too anxious.

"No problem. Court never runs late. Hey. Gotta go. The judge called a thirty-minute recess, and everyone's going back in now. William and Abby still coming?"

"Yeah. See you tonight."

"Love you," Haley said, making a kissing sound.

"Love you, too," Cody replied, without the kissing sound.

* * *

Cody got a call midafternoon from Mike Westerfield, another special agent in the WFO.

"Hey, Cody. I'm down at DCPD First District Substation. We have two suspects who only speak broken English. They've just been interrogated by the DC detectives, and they called me down because there's an interstate transport charge. Their native language is Russian, and they're about to be put in a hallway with me to wait for transport. Their lawyer and the translator just left, and we want to see if you can pick up any idle communication between the two."

"The suspects already know I don't speak a word of Russian. I asked the DCPD crew if it was okay for me to babysit them until it's time for their guys to pick them up and transport them to the DC Central Detention Facility. Can you stop by on some pretext and give a listen? They'll be picked up in under an hour."

* * *

When Cody arrived, the two suspects were seated on one side of a hallway, and Mike was sitting opposite them. There was occasional foot traffic passing by, mostly uniformed officers and plainclothes detectives escorting suspects. Cody had some random papers on a clipboard in his hand as he approached.

"Mike! Glad I caught you. Henderson wants these filled out. Got a second?"

"Yeah. Have a seat. Waiting for transport for those two," Mike said, gesturing to the suspects with the clipboard.

Cody looked at them blankly.

One of them gave Cody an "evil eye" motion with two fingers and said "Fuck off" in Russian.

Cody responded by raising his voice and speaking slowly, "I'm sorry … I don't … speak … your … language … I'm … Special … Agent … Smutters."

"Don't bother, Cody. They don't know enough English to order at McDonald's." Mike pointed at the pair as he said, "No 'sprecken' English."

Cody just waved at them, and the one who spoke so eloquently before gave him the finger back.

"Not very sociable," Cody said to Mike.

"Tell me about it, Cody."

Mike meticulously filled out gibberish on the paper while Cody checked his email on his cell phone. The two Russian speakers talked to each other sotto voce but loud enough for Cody to make out what was being said.

Fifteen minutes later, the DC cops came took custody of the pair for transport to the central Washington jail.

When they were gone, Cody turned to Mike and grinned. "The bulk of whatever it was they stole is at the little one's house. They intend to call someone named Ivan when they get phone privileges back at the jail so he can get it out of his house and deliver it to their fence. He also thinks you are a son of a bitch, and he hopes to see you on the street someday. I think you hurt his feelings."

"Thanks, Cody. We have them on an interstate transport rap with what they had in their car. The rest of the loot will put them away. Got time to go with me to get the search warrant? I'll tell the DC detectives on the case to call the jail to make sure those two don't get near a phone for a couple of hours. They've already had phone privileges today, anyway."

Cody looked at his watch. It was going to be close, and he really needed to be out by five. Any later might screw up his carefully planned surprise for Haley. He knew he had to verify the conversation with the judge, though, so he agreed. "Sure, Mike. Let me know when you have the affidavit filled out, and we'll go. Have to be out by five, though. Big night tonight. Can we make it? I mean, if we get delayed at the courthouse, I'm screwed."

"When was the last time you ever heard of Judge Zuckerman staying one second after four-thirty? I'll have this ready in fifteen, and we can go with the DC detective in charge of their end. By the way, the pen you handed me ran out of ink two minutes ago."

* * *

Judge Zuckerman was in a meeting that only lasted twenty minutes, but it seemed like hours to Cody as he sat fidgeting in the clerk's office with Mike and Detective Randy Pincher. Mike gave Cody a curious glance when Cody checked his watch for the fifth time.

Finally, Judge Zuckerman's clerk ushered them into the judge's chambers. The judge carefully read the affidavit. He asked Randy about the initial arrest and seemed satisfied that there was probable cause for it.

He and looked at Cody and asked, "The statements made by the suspects in the hallway were voluntary and spontaneous?"

"Yes, Judge," Cody answered.

"They were asked no questions?"

"No, Judge."

"They were in a setting where no expectation of privacy existed?"

Cody was about to pee in his pants from the time this was taking, but he answered, as calmly as he could muster, "Yes, Judge. Agent

Westerfield and I were not only sitting with them in a public hallway with constant foot traffic, but he and I were sitting on the opposite side of the hallway, and the suspects spoke loudly enough for me to hear what they said clearly."

Judge Zuckerman asked, "And why was he in a hallway and not the detention cell area?"

Cody realized that the judge was asking if the suspects were intentionally being set up by being placed in an area where they could be overheard, and was about to speak when Detective Pincher came to his rescue: "Judge, I had something I had to take care of, and I asked these Bureau guys to babysit my suspects for a few minutes until transport got there. You know what the holding area smells like. I thought I would save them the unpleasantness."

The judge had been a public defender at one time, and he had been around the hearty aroma of a drunk tank. He nodded and said, "I didn't know the PD was that kind to the feds. Okay, I'll buy that."

Judge Zuckerman read the whole affidavit once more to make sure he fully understood it, and then, to Cody's relief, he signed it.

* * *

They were out at 4:34 p.m., giving Cody just enough time to get back to the WFO, put on the tailored suit Haley had bought him, and then make it to the restaurant on time. A few days ago, they had made a date with William, who was bringing Abby. They were to meet there at six. Haley hadn't displayed a single clue that she knew Cody was going to surprise her.

Cody got there just early enough to make sure his arrangements were ready. William and Abby got there a little after six, and Haley arrived about 6:10 p.m. Haley knew William from work but had never met his wife, Abby.

Haley was wearing her work clothing, a beautiful brown suit, and a muted orange blouse with a single string of pearls. Abby was wearing a blue skirt and a white blouse. The blouse accented her skin, which was a little darker than her husband's. She was about William's height in the two-inch heels she was wearing. Her neck-length hair nicely framed her oval face.

Haley hugged Abby and said, "Pleased to meet you, Abby. Cody says you're the one who keeps William on the straight and narrow."

"Yeah. It's a full-time job. Cody told me so much about you. I'm happy we finally met."

Haley knew Cody hadn't been over to their house since she and Cody started living together. She was curious. She asked, "Abby, when did he tell you about me?"

Before Cody could stop her, she replied, "Right after that seminar he and William attended. Girlfriend, he was gushing. I kept asking him why he didn't call you back then."

Haley turned to Cody, who was blushing. She gave him a little poke. He smiled at her sheepishly and just mumbled, "Yeah."

"That's sweet, honey. Did you get a table yet?" she asked.

"Yeah," he replied. "Benny! We're ready. The whole gang's here," he called to a waiter he knew.

Benny was the archetypal Italian restaurant waiter—curled mustache, black tie tucked into the top of his black vest, and pleated trousers with a thin black-on-black striped pattern. A long white apron was tied around his waist. He showed them to their table near the center of the room.

On the way, Haley noticed Cody's suit and remarked, "Thanks for changing. I love you in this."

Once they were seated and had their drink orders in, Haley asked Abby, "How long have you two been together?"

"Since college. William proposed in our junior year. I couldn't say no. Put up with his sorry ass when he went to the police academy, and then again when he worked all shifts as a rookie, and still again when he became a baby agent at Quantico. I don't even mind the moves. I can get a job as an RN just about anywhere."

"Wow! Real lovebirds. I love romance," Haley said.

They ordered an antipasto to share. Benny came back in a few minutes and got everyone's entrée orders. Haley ordered her favorite, veal marsala. About halfway through the antipasto, Phil and SAC Henderson came in with their wives. They were seated at a table next to Cody's party, and Haley noticed them first.

"Hey, you guys! Small world. You come here for the marsala, too?" she asked.

"Yeah, we love it. Some coincidence, eh?" Phil responded.

"Want to join us?" Haley invited.

When Henderson nodded, Haley motioned for their waiter, saying, "Benny, these are friends of ours. Can you put our tables together?"

"Sure. We do it right away," Benny said in his charming Italian accent.

The eight had a great time, with the wives telling stories about their husbands. Haley was in stitches over some of them.

William's face flushed when Abby related, "So William comes home after four days of a stakeout, smells like a wet dog, and he's constipated from four days just sitting and eating crap food and bad coffee."

Haley asked, "What did you do?"

William replied, "I'll tell you what she did. She threw me in the shower and then gave me a choice: an enema or the MiraLAX festival. Three glasses of that stuff and there was recoil. That's what she did to me. RNs have no mercy or sympathy for their husbands."

The whole table erupted in laughter. The conversation continued pretty much in the same vein until the entrées were finished and cleared. Haley was reaching for the dessert menu when Benny and the owner, Michael Valenti, came to the table. Michael took the dessert menu before she could get it.

Michael playfully held the menu out of reach above his thin comb-over hairdo and grinned as he announced, "I'm sorry, Dr. Briggs. We're out of everything on the dessert menu. We must have had a rush of sweet-tooth customers. But I think we have an alternative that may please you."

The bewildered Haley turned to Cody and discovered he was down on one knee. He had a ring box out, and when he opened it there was a diamond ring. She put her hand to her mouth as tears started to well up.

"Haley Briggs, will you marry me?" he asked.

Through her tears, she replied, "Yes, you romantic, wonderful man, I will."

He took the ring from the box and placed it on her finger. She was oblivious that everyone at her table and most of the other patrons were standing and clapping.

She looked around and realized that a group was watching her from behind. Emily, Thomas, Mary, and Steven, her partners in her firm, were watching! Their husbands and wives were with them.

She stood, and her dear friends and coworkers all exchanged hugs and kisses with her. She introduced them all to the people at her table, and then Michael, obviously proud and excited that another such event was taking place in his establishment, motioned for her to follow him. Everyone followed the animated restaurateur to a private room. A banner hanging on the back wall said "Congratulations Haley and Cody" in pink letters with a background of red roses.

A busboy brought Haley a bouquet of red roses, and Benny opened one of the bottles of champagne that were sitting on ice next to the table. There were sixteen crème brûlées with little hearts on them waiting at the table, too.

Everyone congratulated the couple. Haley hugged Cody and kissed him over and over.

He whispered in her ear, "Does that mean I get special treatment tonight?"

She laughed and nodded.

After she composed herself, she turned to Henderson and said, "I'm guessing your coming here wasn't a coincidence."

"No, Haley. It was Abby's idea."

"Thank you, Abby. This was as romantic as it gets. Cody here is pretty good about that stuff, but this whole dinner was spectacular."

"You're welcome. And yeah, your fiancé there is pretty romantic. He gave me Steven's number so I could get your friends from work here, too."

Abby turned to the grinning Cody, who raised his champagne glass, toasting, "Here's to my fiancé, Haley!"

Everyone stood and saluted, "To Haley and Cody!"

They had a marvelous time. Cody had previously met Steven and Mary, but not the other two partners, nor had he met any spouses. They spent over an hour and a half talking.

Towards the end of the party, Steven asked, "Where do you two think you'll get married?"

Cody hadn't thought that far yet, and he turned to Haley. "Should we get married here in DC or at your parents' place in Savannah?"

"Wow. Savannah would be romantic, too, but all of your friends and mine are up here."

Cody responded, "Yeah. We have enough room to put up your parents and mine at your place, so let's do Virginia."

"Well, actually, I'd like to put our parents up in a hotel," Haley said. "Can I have my sisters stay with us before the wedding? I don't get to see them very much anymore."

"Yeah. Sure. That would be nice. I'd like to get to know them, too." Cody added, "Michelle is in San Diego, right? And your other sister, Maryann, is in Illinois?"

"Right. She and her husband, Ricky, bought a house there."

Fifteen minutes later, everyone thanked Cody and Haley for letting them share the moment, and all began their trips home.

On the drive to Fairfax, Haley held Cody's arm and said, "That really was romantic. Thank you. God! Fiancé! I like that. We'll have to start thinking about a date. We'll have to check with our families.

They talked about possible wedding plans until they got home. This time Haley made it into the bustier before giving him the wildest ride he'd had in weeks.

Chapter 21

Sometimes You Have to Scratch That Itch, Even If It's Risky

Almost three years had passed since Alex and Lara started Papa Paul's hobby. One evening as they were standing in their kitchen preparing dinner, Lara asked, "Alex, do you ever regret any of the things we've done?"

Without missing a beat in his carrot chopping, Alex replied, "No, not even one day. Well, maybe that trip to Cancun. If it wasn't for Lomotil, I wouldn't have been able to make it on the plane home. I never had the runs that bad."

"No, silly, I meant our work for Papa Paul," she chided.

"I knew what you meant," he said with a playful poke as she passed behind him. "The answer is still no. Everyone we took out deserved it: thieves, rapists, drug dealers, crooked officials. And the ones we roughed up for Papa Paul's little hobby, well, that was a service to humanity. Those scams are down by more than thirty percent. We've saved people millions of dollars, not to mention the aggravation. No, there are no regrets. You?"

"Just one," she said pensively.

Alex was startled. She never expressed a shred of doubt about any of their hits before.

"Which one, sweetheart?" he asked.

She explained, "One we never did. Something I sort of wanted to try but never told you about. We've been taking martial arts for more than seventeen years, and we've always used a gun, knife, or some other weapon. We've never killed anyone with our bare hands."

"You're right," he reflected. "I never thought about that. I guess the closest was that hit we did with a piano wire garrote to throw off the cops."

"Did you ever want to?" she asked.

He dumped the carrots onto the salad he was making and paused for a second before answering, "I don't know, Lara. Most of the people we did wouldn't have been much of a challenge. To face that kind of risk, there ought to be at least a little pride in the outcome."

"How about the Campbell hit? He could have given us enough back to make it fun. Or the Kronketta hit? He was in pretty good shape."

Alex agreed, "You see, that's what I'm talking about. Harshman could have been worthy of the effort, too. We could have taken him, sure, but it wouldn't have been easy."

"Yeah. Probably would have taken a while, too. Whaddaya think? Crushed larynx? Choke? How would you have done it, sweetheart?"

Alex thought for a moment and suggested, "Well, the throat would be a good way, but so would a blow to the base of his skull. Say! … Are you getting turned on?"

She put the casserole she had taken out of the oven on a trivet a few feet away and sidled up next to him. She breathed, "Yeah. Kinda," into his ear.

He put his arm around her and gave her a hug.

She asked, "Do you think we could do it? I mean, ask Papa Paul to let us do one like that?"

"Papa Paul doesn't care, I guess, as long as we do our job. Let's see what Siggy gives us next time. If it's a hit you can do the guy with your hands if you want. You know, we've been training hard blows on that makiwara board downstairs for years. Want to see if you can take someone out with one blow to the nose, Mas Oyama style?"

Lara laughed. "Well, neither of us could take out a bull with our bare hands as he did, but I think I could drive someone's nose cartilage into his brain."

"A lot of controversy over that, sweetheart. Well, let's see the next time Siggy gives us one."

* * *

The next opportunity was a few months after the Carmen episode in Ann Arbor. Siggy had one of their favorites, a revenge hit on a really evil crook. It was, in fact, another hitman, or rather an enforcer.

Lee Doyle was as cruel a piece of work as there ever was. He was part of a gang of thugs in Long Beach, California, called the Cruisers. Their specialty was hijacking trucks, but their sidelines were prostitution and extorting money from small businesses—the protection racket.

One business owner, Carl Destry, refused to pay them, and Lee paid him a visit at his home. He tied up the family and then raped and beat the man's daughter, Shirley, in front of them before killing Carl and his wife, Edna, with a baseball bat. Shirley barely survived but Lee wasn't able to be identified, as she had been blindfolded and he used a condom.

Two of Carl's cousins would ultimately be connected to Alex and Lara, each in a different way. One was Joshua Revauge, who did some shady business with another area mob. The head of that organization, Eli Arcadia, came to Joshua after he got the news about the latter's loss. Eli and his associates in the trucking industry had ongoing problems with the Cruisers. Up to that incident, they didn't want to have to deal with Lee. This was the last straw. He told Joshua that he would seek vengeance for the outrage.

The other cousin was a well-placed woman who Alex and Lara would meet under entirely different circumstances.

* * *

When Siggy's two cranberry buyers got the call for assistance from Eli, Siggy knew just who to turn to. He called in Alex and Lara and briefed them personally.

"He raped a teen and left her for dead?" Lara screamed in disgust when she heard the details. "I want him to die slowly and painfully."

"That's about what the client wants, in fact," Siggy informed her. "Slow and painful would make them happy. What did you have in mind?"

Alex said, "Lara wants to try at least one hit using just martial arts. Hand to hand."

"Lara, Papa Paul would never forgive me if I okayed something that would put you in danger. He loves you as much as he loves his grandkids. Tell you what, if Alex can cover him to the point that he can kill him instantly with a gun, I'll let you scratch your martial arts itch. Remember, this asshole Lee is a hard piece of work. He won't be easy. I don't want your pretty face getting messed up, now."

The two promised they wouldn't take any more chances than necessary. They spent four days going over maps, pictures of Lee's house and neighborhood, profiles of the known gang members, and more. Eli had his people send them whatever details they needed, and Lara got a lot of physical layout information from LA County's public geographic information system as well as Google Earth.

They had several problems to solve. First, they had to either make sure Lee was alone or plan to take out any associates present quickly and effectively. They had already gotten Siggy's approval to take out as many gang members as necessary—and any that were not necessary but just convenient, as a bonus. Eli had been very clear on that score.

Second, they had to make sure that Lee was unarmed or figure out how to disarm him. That was going to be a problem. Lee was known to carry a knife and a handgun most of the time.

Third, they were going to have to get in and out of the gang's territory unobserved.

Fourth, if there was an actual fight, there might be DNA left at the scene in the form of Lara's blood on the floor or even skin under Lee's fingernails.

Lara practiced for half an hour every day on the makiwara board, a rope-covered springboard designed to toughen hands and increase strike force. She reviewed facial and other pressure points likely to disable a person, too.

The pair looked at everything they could about Lee. He wasn't a martial arts student, just an experienced street brawler with seven arrests and two battery and extortion convictions. He had done almost two years total in the LA County jail system, but no state time yet. There were a couple of videos that Eli's people were able to obtain from the jail showing fights he had in the yard with other prisoners. He was a wild brawler, dependent on weight, strength, and speed rather than technique. He did seem to favor roundhouse punches.

Siggy had obtained a crucial piece of intelligence from Eli. He told Alex and Lara, "A typical Saturday night for Lee features a wild party at the gang's private clubhouse. Lee is known to take women home, but rarely. He most often has a gang member deliver one of their prostitutes to his house. He is very frequently accompanied by a close friend in the gang, Riley Dunder, a particularly disagreeable and mutton-headed thug. They usually take turns with the prostitute."

"His house was at the end of an alley, itself off a cul-de-sac, both clearly seen on the Google Earth images we looked at yesterday," Alex noted as the plan began to come into focus.

Lara said, "Yeah. The long driveway with a curve in the middle is going to be a valuable terrain asset. Lee probably chose it for privacy, but it will give us privacy for a kill zone, too."

Siggy showed them the blueprints of Lee's house, obtained from the Long Beach Development Services Department, the local building permit agency. The house itself wasn't huge. Just a three-bedroom, about eighteen hundred square feet.

Alex looked at the Long Beach city GIS system and Google Earth images of the neighborhood. He noted, "The small park on the rear side of Lee's property is deserted after dark and pretty much the same during the day, according to Eli. No one goes there because of the junkies in the area. They use it as a shooting gallery. I can make use of one really advantageous feature, the hill that overlooks Lee's house with a clear view of the driveway."

Lara said, "The I-405 freeway is close to the park, and the area isn't far from the flight paths for the Long Beach Airport. That will prove very useful. I can load up some of those subsonic thirty-caliber rounds you like," referring to the .300 AAC Blackout loading she had developed for extreme accuracy through a suppressor. "The ambient noise will mask the sound if Eli can provide you with a suppressed AR-15 with a Blackout upper."

Siggy reviewed their plan with them one more time and said, "Okay, you two. This looks good. But remember, if it looks like Lara is in trouble, Lee goes away with a headshot."

"Is Eli able to get us everything we need?" Lara asked.

"Yeah, Lara," Siggy replied. "I think so. But anything they lack, we can provide by the time you get there."

The pair gathered what they needed to take with them, along with extra clothing for the cruise they were going to take to Baja California out of the Long Beach Cruise Terminal when they were done with Lee.

Alex saw that Lara was excited on the flight out. She was really looking forward to the encounter. Sitting next to her, he smiled when he saw tiny hand movements that showed she was going over the possible killing blows in her mind.

* * *

They took a cab from Los Angeles International Airport to their designated hotel. Their room was half of a lock-out suite with a connecting door to the other half.

After they unpacked, there was a knock on that door. They opened it to find their contact from the client, known to them only as Greg. He had their weapons and other gear in two rectangular duffle bags. He also handed them a set of keys to an older black SUV parked in the hotel lot.

In his room, he had the latest surveillance information on Lee and his associates.

"The Saturday party: Everything normal, Greg?" Lara asked.

"Yes, ma'am. The weather looks good, and there's nothing to indicate any changes for this weekend."

"The others that hang around Lee's house?" Alex asked.

"Still the same, sir. After the party at the clubhouse, a few who can still navigate usually wander over to Lee's. They hang out on his pool deck. They sometimes swim but usually just drink enough alcohol and smoke enough dope to pass out until morning. The nearest neighbors are several hundred feet away beyond thick hedges and trees, so they can party without anyone calling the cops."

"The hookers: Are they planning to have someone bring them and pick them up?" Lara asked.

"Yes, ma'am. Most women don't want to go there because Lee and Riley sometimes get a bit rough. They are always escorted by someone because of this to ensure they get there. Who brings them changes all the time. Just runners. Lowlife knockaround guys still proving themselves.

"By the way, my associates and I thoroughly enjoyed hearing about your DNA-evidence idea, and the materials you requested are in the back of the SUV. We will recover the SUV back here and destroy it."

Greg departed and Alex and Lara returned to their room. It was Friday night, and they had about twenty-four hours before the operation would begin. Lara was nervous that night, and they didn't do more than cuddle until they were asleep.

* * *

In the morning, she was like a kid on the verge of a trip to Disneyland. She was excited and animated, going over the details with muted glee. When they had exhausted their lists, they hopped the hotel's shuttle for a tour and lunch at the RMS Queen Mary at the Port of Long Beach.

After a relaxing day, they returned to the hotel. Dinner was a simple take-out sandwich from the lobby café and soft drinks from the minibar in their room.

The room was pleasant and comfortable, but the same cookie-cutter layout that was found in most upscale hotel chains. The view of the Long Beach harbor and the Queen Mary was a plus, but other than that, the room was unmemorable among the scores of rooms and suites they had experienced in the last dozen years.

They dressed for their date with Doyle and left in the black SUV that evening at eleven thirty.

* * *

Lara dropped Alex off at the park and then drove to the cul-de-sac. Alex's chosen spot was behind a little exposed knob that was out of view of the thickets and overpass abutments the junkies used at the edge of the freeway.

Several people on the working-class cul-de-sac appeared to have party guests. The proximity to the freeway and airport meant lower property values, and the cars on the street reflected that. Their older SUV blended right in.

When Lara saw Lee's car pull into the alley, she signaled Alex with a text, a single love-eyed emoji. About twenty minutes later, she saw another vehicle with one man and one woman enter the cul-de-sac. She texted Alex with two emojis and followed the car past the driveway entrance with her lights off.

She saw the man and the woman exit the car. She didn't hear the shot that went through the man's brain. Alex, on the little hill, had used the Eli-provided suppressed rifle with Lara's subsonic bullets. The ambient noise masked what little sound the handloaded .300 AAC Blackout rounds made, as Lara predicted.

Lara ran up and grabbed the woman from behind. With her hand over the prostitute's mouth and a gun to her back, she warned, "Don't make a sound. We're not here for you. We want that pig in there. Understand?"

The woman nodded.

"Has he ever hurt you?" Lara asked.

She nodded again.

"Well, I'm here to hurt him. Any problems with that?"

The woman shook her head. Lara pointed to the dead driver and continued, "I'm going to put you in this asshole's car. Stay still, and you will be fine. Make a noise or try to escape, and the guy who just capped that asshole will do you, too. Okay?"

The woman nodded again, and Lara put her on the floor in the rear, gagged, hooded, and bound. Alex ran out of the park and drove the runner's car to the side of the driveway. He dragged the driver's body into the bushes behind the car. Taking a position in the vegetation about twenty-five yards into the park, he could see anyone coming.

Lara parked the SUV back at the corner of the alley and the cul-de-sac. She returned to the bushes at the side of the entrance and took her position.

As expected, two more cars approached the alley. When they stopped, three men got out of one car, and two got out of the other.

A low pop and a soft thud were all that indicated a bullet had hit its mark on each of them in rear-to-front order. In less than two seconds, all five were down. Lara walked over and put two more in each head with a suppressed .22 semiauto. With a borrowed pistol, her favorite subsonic ammo wouldn't cycle the action. She had to manually operate the slide each time, to the horror of the last victim, who was still barely conscious to witness the grisly scene.

They didn't bother to pick up brass, as the guns would all be shredded at a scrapyard the next day. There would be nothing left to match chamber marks, firing pin strikes, or rifling marks against, and the cartridges were all wiped free of fingerprints with solvent and triple-ought steel wool before being loaded into magazines.

That being all the gang members they expected to arrive, they initiated the next phase.

* * *

Alex and Lara stripped off their black jumpsuits. Alex donned surgical gloves, as his hands wouldn't be whatever the person who answered the door was expected to look at. He was wearing jeans and a tee shirt with the name of a heavy metal band. Alex put on baseball cap with an image of a chopper, brim pulled down low. He unsheathed a stiletto and held it with the blade behind his right wrist. Lara was wearing a sexy, low halter top, short shorts, and sturdy cross-trainers. Alex gave her an affectionate little pinch on her cute butt, and she giggled and gave him a kiss.

He took her elbow, and they walked up to the house. Alex knocked, and Riley answered the door. Lee was inside, pulling a big hit off a bong in the kitchen. Alex saw his gun on the counter, almost six feet from him. That was a relief. Plan B was to just shoot them both. Riley looked at Lara, who had her eyes down.

The thug grabbed her chin and lifted it as he grunted, "What's the matter? Don't want to party with real men? Hey, Lee, we got us a shy one."

That was all he got out as Alex's eight-inch blade entered his chin and drove straight up into his brain. Lee looked up at the three just as Lara ran straight to him and delivered a hard kick to his groin.

Lee grunted and doubled over. Lara's fist followed the kick, and she connected with the side of his head. Lee staggered back, but not before delivering a hard uppercut to Lara's stomach. It almost knocked the wind out of her.

"Who the fuck are you?" Lee shouted.

"A friend of Shirley, the young woman you raped. The one who's going to cut you open to see if you even have a heart."

Alex was standing in a shadowed corner now, suppressed Model 1911 .45-caliber semiautomatic pistol with a red-dot reflex sight trained on Lee's head. One sign of trouble Lara couldn't handle, and Lee would be dead instantly. At this range, Alex could accurately hit whichever of Lee's eyes he chose, even moving. The noise would be about the same as slamming a door hard, but the neighbors wouldn't be able to hear it from the relatively isolated house.

Lee charged at Lara, and she sidestepped his attack. He ran at her again and managed to land a blow on her arm as she executed a blocking move. She countered with a knifehand to the wrist as the impact glanced off her arm.

They traded blows and blocks for a little under a minute. Lara's arm began to bleed a bit, dripping a little blood on the sheet-vinyl floor.

Lee grabbed for her again, and Lara let him take her right wrist. She grabbed his hand with her left, rotating her right wrist and turning Lee's over at the same time, trapping it. With as much force as she could muster, Lara dropped her hands straight down. She was pleased to hear Lee's wrist crack. It was now either broken or dislocated.

Lee howled in pain. With speed she had not anticipated, though, he kicked her in the shin. She let go of Lee's wrist and hopped away from him. He rushed her, but she grabbed his arms and pulled, dropping to the floor. She rolled backward and used her leg to throw him over her as they fell. She jumped to her feet. He was just scrambling up, reaching for something in a front jeans pocket with his uninjured right hand.

Lara aimed a side-kick at Lee's right elbow. Since his right hand was in his pocket, he couldn't move it in time to avoid contact or block with the already-injured arm. The kick connected at the joint, and Lee's mouth opened in a silent scream. His head involuntarily shot back in pain. Lara delivered another knifehand to his exposed throat.

Lee went to his knees, gasping for breath. He looked at the woman before him with bewilderment. His expression pleased Lara to no end. It all but shouted, "How could a hooker get the best of me?"

Enough was enough, and Alex walked up to Lee and put the forty-five right in his right ear. Trying to keep a straight face, he growled, "Move, and I'll paint your house for you."

Lara laughed hard, which cut the tension and began to counter her adrenaline rush. She knew Alex had always wanted to use that corny B-movie line but never had the right opportunity.

With a jerk, she pulled Lee's broken arm out of the pants pocket. Lee screamed in pain as Lara quickly zip-tied his now-useless hands in front of him. She bound his feet with another tie. She and Alex lifted him onto the kitchen table. They used cords cut off appliances to anchor his neck and ankles to the table's legs. A dirty kitchen towel served as a gag.

Alex had a fanny pack under his loose tee shirt. He pulled out several items, including another pair of surgical gloves, which Lara put on, and some clotting agent.

Lara menaced over Lee and proclaimed, "Lee, you are going to die tonight. There is nothing you can do about it. You raped and killed the wrong people. They had friends. Those friends are our friends. They asked us to do them a favor. Lee, have you ever heard of Voodoo? No? Well, it's a religion practiced in Louisiana and around the Caribbean. Now we have bad news for you, Lee. Honey, would you break the bad news?"

"Yeah, Lee. What my wife just told you was true. There is bad news. And it's not that my wife just whipped your ass, either. Yeah, I know you were drunk and high and all of that, but when you get to hell, you're going to have to tell all of your friends you were bested in a fair fight by a woman. And even worse, she's going to kill you with her bare hands in a little while."

Lara gloated, "But what Alex here just said is not the worst news. Tell him the worst news, honey."

By now, Lee's eyes were wide with fear and rage. He couldn't struggle much, because they had him tied down too well, and his broken wrist and elbow were making him groan with every movement.

"Well, Lee, my soon-to-be ex-friend, she's going to make this look like you ran afoul of a Jamaican drug gang. She's going to cut out your heart. Before she cuts out your heart, though, she wants to see if something is possible. Tell him about your scientific experiment, sweetheart."

Lara got right next to his head and tweaked his nose as she excitedly explained, "Lee, the two of us have been taking karate for years. One of our instructors showed us an attacking move. It's supposed to kill a man by shoving all of the cartilage in his nose into his brain. Of course, we couldn't practice doing that because, well, that would be ridiculous. You can't just kill people in a class, after all. So tonight, I get to find out if it's possible. Isn't that interesting? You get to be part of my experiment. But first, you just lie there in pain. Our instructions are for you to die slowly."

Alex said, "Now what my lovely wife just said is true. You get to lie there in pain for a bit while I take care of my wife."

The casual back-and-forth banter was having its desired effect on Lee. He was jerking his head back and forth and trying to scream in rage.

Alex fed the flame by patting Lee on the head. He took a clotting agent packet and tore the top off, applying just a touch to the minor wounds on Lara's arm. What little bleeding there still was stopped immediately.

"Wow, sweetheart. This stuff really works. Speaking of bleeding, see what he was fishing for."

Lara reached into the pocket Lee had been going for when she broke his elbow and pulled out a folding knife with a thumb assist. She opened the knife and felt the blade.

"That'll do. Lee, I'm going to do some surgery with your own knife. Isn't that special? Maybe I can use your phone to Facebook it to your friends," she said.

Lee struggled and tried to yell again through the gag, but the pain kept him from moving much.

Lara disappeared into the kitchen pantry for a minute and returned with a pair of tongs.

"What's with the kitchen utensils, Lara?" Alex asked.

"Well, I'm not touching him with my hands!" she replied.

Alex laughed. "Like picking a hot dog out of a pot, eh? Well, okay then. Let's see what our buddy Lee has to offer. Hey, Lee, maybe she'll cut off what you were originally going to use on her when we arrived."

Lee's eyes opened wider in terror.

Lara shook her head. "No, too much chance he could bleed out, even with the clot pack. I'll go for a couple of extremities."

Alex stood by with the clot pack while Lara used the tongs and the knife. She removed a few fingers, followed by his left ear. Alex dumped clotting agent on the wounds. Lee was crying like a baby now. Lara made a few other gratuitous cuts here and there, with Alex stopping the bleeding each time.

Lee's eyes started to close. Lara slapped his face. "Lee ... Lee! Don't pass out on us yet. We're not done, are we, honey?"

She and Alex undid the cords that were holding Lee down. They dragged him to a door and tied one end of a cord around Lee's neck. They propped him against the door, and Alex pulled the line tight over the top of the door, tying it to the doorknob on the other side. Lee was barely conscious now.

Lee was facing away from the door. Lara took a stance in front of him. She looked at Alex.

He nodded as he said, "Lee, if you were one of the people who we have visited recently, we would tell you that you are screwed, and that only doing something to bring us back could make it any worse. Unfortunately for you, even though you are utterly screwed, things still can and are about to get much worse. Time to say goodnight, Lee. Go ahead, sweetheart. Remember, don't hit low, or you will cut your hand on his teeth."

That was the last earthly thing Lee ever heard. With all her might, Lara thrust the heel of her hand hard against Lee's nose in the move she had been practicing on her makiwara board. She felt her palm slap flat against his face as the nose collapsed. Lee stiffened for an instant and then fell limp against the tension of the cord. He was still breathing, though, as massive amounts of blood started coming out of his smashed face.

"Damn, Alex! It didn't work!"

"Told you so. Karate myths," Alex observed.

Lara lifted one of Lee's eyelids and looked at the pupil. It started to dilate. His breathing became ragged and red foam appeared at the corner of his mouth. He appeared to be hemorrhaging internally, and blood was entering his airway from his nasal passages. In under two minutes, he stopped breathing. She felt his carotid artery, and there was no pulse.

"Well, sweetheart?" Alex inquired.

"He's dead, honey. It didn't do it instantly, but the blow did eventually kill him. Either drowned in his own blood or just bled out."

"Close enough for me, I guess," Alex said with a laugh.

Alex pulled out a photo and put it on the table. It was a picture of a Jamaican gang murder scene from several years ago in New York. He retrieved the SUV from the cul-de-sac, took a gallon jug and a plastic bag from an ice chest and a plastic five-gallon pail from the rear. The bucket contained several items.

First, they used a flashlight of the same type that hunters use to find blood trails. They blotted any blood drops, leaving those that were obviously Lee's on the table or near his lifeless body. After they finished wiping up Lara's blood, they used a mild lye solution to go over everything that was left to destroy any remaining DNA.

Alex looked under the kitchen sink and found a can of drain cleaner. That was good news, as they didn't have to use the can from their supplies and try to get Lee's fingerprints on it. He poured some down the kitchen sink, followed by a short flush of water. He put the can on the counter and then knocked it over, spilling quite a bit on the floor.

He lifted Lee's shoes, dampened them with a wet paper towel, and dropped pellets under them so some would stick to his soles. Then Alex tossed a few random pellets around the house. That would explain the lye solution they used if it was even detected. It would look like the drunken Doyle had just spilled some and tracked it throughout the house.

They cleaned Doyle's hands, including under his fingernails, with a chemical solution to destroy any remaining DNA. Then they rinsed them and scratched the nails against Lee's own filthy, sweaty skin to load them up again before spotting his own blood all over them.

Alex took a whole, uncleaned dead chicken from the plastic bag and started spattering the jug's contents, chicken blood, around the room with the chicken's feet in the same manner as the splashes in the picture. He made a point of dripping over any blood-spill areas they had cleaned up. He drew a few of the figures he saw in the image on the walls, too. Alex used Lee's knife to cut the chicken's head off and leave it at Lee's feet.

Meanwhile, Lara took a cleaver from the kitchen to hack open Lee's chest and cut his heart out, using the tongs to handle it the same way she had dealt with the fingers and ear. She placed the heart at his feet with a candle on it and then lit the candle. She set a few other lit candles about the room. Alex looked again at the photo, and, mimicking the style of a name in the picture, he wrote the name of a deceased local Jamaican drug-gang member, Melvin Harrums, in blood on a wall. He drew a cross-and-heart symbol above the name, also as pictured. Harrums had been killed two months earlier, but a suspect had never been identified in that murder.

The pair went around the room and picked up everything they had touched, including the knife, the cleaver, the tongs, and the clotting agent packs. Doyle's knife and the cleaver were wiped clean as a precaution and then coated with Doyle's blood. The tongs, plastic bag, and clotting pack scraps went into the bucket and then back to the SUV.

They rechecked the house. The blood was spread as well as they had hoped.

***

They stopped at the car holding the prostitute. Lara opened the rear door. She pulled the gag down under the hood and asked, "What's your name, dear?"

"J—Jenny," the woman replied, visibly shaking.

"Jenny what?"

"Miller. Jenny Miller," the woman answered.

Lara opened the woman's clutch purse and looked at her ID. It was the same name. She said, "Well, Jenny Miller, that asshole Lee is dead, and so is Riley. Calm down. You're safe. We'll send the cops over to let you out in a few. When they get here, you want to tell them that you were mugged from behind and didn't see anyone. All you heard was four men with Caribbean accents talking about Lee and a man named Melvin Harrums. The men said Melvin would be avenged. Got that? Melvin Harrums. Say it."

"Four Caribbean men talking about Lee and Melvin Harrums," Jenny repeated.

"Very good. Is that a good address on your license?"

"Yes. It's where I live."

Lara admonished, "Good. If we read in the paper that the police are looking for four Caribbean men who avenged Melvin Harrums, a package will be delivered to this address with five thousand dollars. If the papers say anything else, our employers will spend the five Gs for us to pay you a visit. Now, what was that name?"

"Melvin Harrums."

"Good girl," Lara said as she reapplied the gag and shut the door. She and Alex went over their exit list one more time, and they departed. On the way, Lara put on a shirt and a skirt that covered the halter top and the short shorts.

* * *

They drove to the hotel and parked the SUV in the same spot they had found it, on the other side of a tree that blocked the hotel's security cameras. They returned to their room, and Alex cleaned Lara's cuts then applied an antiseptic and a couple of small Band-Aids. After a change of clothes, they went to the lobby bar. Lara was shaking a little. They found a booth away from other patrons. When the cocktail waitress came to take their order, they requested a couple of E.H. Taylor Single Barrel bourbons on the rocks with a splash.

"Sweetheart, you're still shaking a bit. Are you okay?" Alex asked.

"Yeah. Just adrenaline rush wearing off. I never had to do a hit like that without gloving up first."

"It wasn't the lack of gloves during the fight, sweetheart. It was the fight itself and the ending. How do you feel about killing him with personal contact?"

"Good," she said. "I mean, it was everything I thought it would be. Sure, Lee had a lot to drink, but he was tough as shit. And I took him, Alex. I took him!"

Their drinks arrived, and they both took good swigs before sitting back against the benches of the booth. Alex gave a slight smile.

"So, sex tonight should be pretty spectacular."

Lara actually blushed when she replied, "Yeah. Pretty …"

* * *

The following morning as they had a leisurely room-service breakfast, Greg returned to take care of any last-minute details Alex and Lara might request.

He greeted them, saying, "The two of you are spectacular. One of our contacts in the police department gave us a report. Mr. Arcadia laughed for half an hour over your work. He asked me to convey his appreciation."

"Thanks. By the way, here's the address to send the payoff to the hooker," Alex said as he handed Greg a piece of paper.

"We'll take care of it. Pleasant voyage," he said as he pocketed the paper.

After Greg left, the pair checked out and took the hotel's shuttle to the cruise terminal.

Chapter 22

Jamaican Ja-shmaken

Not long after Doyle met a very disappointing end, Phil stopped by Cody's cubicle and asked, "Hey, Cody. Got a minute?"

"Sure, Phil. What's up?"

"Remember Esterharken from DEA?"

"Sure. Good guy. When I was in the New York Field Office, he asked for some info on a Jamaican gang we were working on. They were doing some bank robberies."

"Yeah. That's what he said. Give him a call. He's in LA now. Here's his number," Phil said as he handed Cody a message slip.

Cody dialed the number, and DEA Agent Harold Esterharken answered.

"Harry! How's it hanging?" Cody said to his old friend.

"A little off-center these days. Been a long time, buddy. You got a minute to talk about the Jamaicans? I need to pick your brain."

"The government pays me to be here to get my brain picked. I'm yours," Cody offered.

"Great. In all your time in New York, how many cases did you see involving a ritual Voodoo murder by the Jamaicans?" Esterharken asked.

"Well, three or so. The real expert on it is a New York detective named Willie Jenkins, though. You should have seen him back in the day—dreadlocks, perfect Jamaican patois. Best of the best."

"Yeah, he's on my list of guys to call, but I know you know the Jamaicans, too," Esterharken explained.

"Well, I got involved sort of as a sideline. There was a beef between them and some Russians. I was working the latter because I speak Russian. Anyway, I worked in conjunction with Willie's team for a couple of months until we made a few arrests, and the issue died down. What kind of info do you need?"

"Just a hunch. Did you hear the news about an enforcer from a California gang called the Cruisers out of Long Beach?"

"No. Never heard of them. What happened?"

Esterharken related, "Well, the story is that he was killed by a Southern California group affiliated with the East Coast Jamaicans. It was supposed to be in retaliation for hitting one of their bosses two months ago. Badass named Lee Doyle was their target."

"Too bad for Mr. Doyle. So, what's the problem?" Cody asked.

"Problems. Plural," Esterharken emphasized. "The locals are buying the story that it was a ritual Voodoo hit by the Jamaicans. Closes the books on one murder by pinning it on Doyle and giving them political support to put more money in the kitty to go after the Jamaicans. I suspect that there are a few holes in the story, though, and that's why I called you first. You like working those weird convoluted cases, so ..."

"You mean the Qatar Card cases. Yeah. Pretty weird. So, what's the connection, Harold?"

"You know how the suspects in the domestic ones liked to leave a ton of false physical evidence?"

"Yeah, fibers, DNA samples, random fingerprints on cans and bottles. Real jokers," Cody interjected.

"Well, whoever did Mr. Doyle left the same kind of evidence, I think. The place was doused in chicken blood."

"So? Some Voodoo rituals use it," Cody said, matter-of-factly.

"Well, Cody, I would agree with you, but there was enough of it to fill several chickens. At least a quart or two of it. And there was only one chicken found at the scene. The chicken was dead and refrigerated beforehand. According to the CSI team from LAPD, the blood in the room was at least a day or two old and it also had been refrigerated. Possible anticoagulant added, too."

Cody mused, "Hmm. Interesting. Maybe the Jamaicans couldn't find a live chicken on short notice. They were in an urban setting, you know. Made a stop at Chicken-Blood-R-Us before hitting Doyle."

Harold laughed and said, "Maybe, but there are places, maybe a farmers market in an Asian area, that have live birds. No, that was odd, but the corker is the victim himself. They cut out his heart."

"So?" Cody replied. "That's been done before. They cut his chest open while he's alive and remove his heart."

"Oh, they cut out his heart, all right. Put it at his feet with a candle on top, but that didn't kill him."

"Harold, how the hell does cutting a man's heart out not kill him?" Cody asked incredulously.

Esterharken replied, "Because it was done after he was already dead. He was strung up over a door with an electrical cord. They didn't go for the heart first, though. Someone hit him hard enough in the nose to crush it and drive the cheekbones and cartilage into his sinuses. Caused massive bleeding. He was drowning in his own blood as he exsanguinated. They waited until he was dead before they cut his heart out."

Cody admitted, "That is pretty weird. Maybe they fought before the Jamaicans could subdue him and one got in a lucky blow to Doyle's snot-locker."

Harold agreed, "We think alike, pal. Yeah, some Jamaicans have taken martial arts, so I guess it's possible. The result could have been a fluke before they could get to his heart. The rest of the scene, though, makes it suspect. Here's what the PD figures. First, the perps take out five of Doyle's friends in the driveway. Clean hits to the head. They get a rifle shot from a distance that turns most of their frontal lobes to jelly. Kills all but one instantly. Then they get a couple of shots to the head from a twenty-two at close range when they are down. Insurance for the first four and the coup de grâce for the fifth. The neighbors are some distance away, and none hear a thing. It looks like suppressed weapons and subsonic ammo. Some .300 AAC Blackout casings were found near the scene and some twenty-twos.

"Next, one of Doyle's buddies answers the door, and they shiv him. Dagger of some kind straight up through the chin and into his brain. Whoever did it was powerful and extremely well trained. The asshole is down for the count and dies minutes later just inside the door. What follows is a fistfight between Doyle and at least one assailant. He has multiple bruises, a broken wrist, and a broken elbow. The perps cut him up good after they subdued him, too, just for the fun of it. Then they used clot packs to stop the bleeding."

"So? They didn't want him to bleed to death before they were ready to kill him. Torture protocol."

"Cody, these guys had guns. Why get into a fistfight with Doyle?" Esterharken asked.

"Maybe it was personal. You know, a buddy of the guy Doyle supposedly murdered," Cody offered.

"Okay, maybe, but Doyle was tough as a coffin nail. I doubt anyone would want to go toe-to-toe with him, even if it was just to impress his buddies."

"Still, some of the Jamaicans are darn tough themselves, Harold. Revenge is a strong motivation. Any DNA on his hands?"

"No. First, the fingernail scrapings just show he was scratching his own sweaty ass. Second, the chicken blood makes finding any perp blood like a needle in a haystack in the rest of the room. Third, that drunken, stoned asshole Doyle spilled a can of drain cleaner or something and tracked pellets of lye all over the place. Blood DNA is useless. But they made one error."

"What was that?" Cody asked, ears pricking up a bit.

"A foil packet that clotting agent came in. They left one tiny piece of it when they tore open the pack. It has a partial print. Not enough to run, but if we ever get a suspect, we might be able to match it. Iffy, though. Very iffy. Probably not enough to have a legal match for court."

"Any witnesses?" Cody asked.

"One. A hooker. One of the dead guys outside brought her for Doyle and his buddy to share. She said she'd been out there twice, and one time they roughed her up. She claims she was jumped from behind, blindfolded from the beginning, and only heard some Jamaicans talking. Personally, I think she just likes Doyle being dead."

"So, what's your gut tell you?"

Esterharken said, "Professional hit team, Cody. They take the guys outside and the first mook inside cleanly. Then they play with Doyle like a cat teasing a mouse. They kill him with a blow to the face and try to make it look like a Jamaican hit."

"Motive?" Cody asked.

"Several possible. It could be a power struggle in the Cruisers themselves. Someone trying to take out a rival and point the finger elsewhere. Could be a rival gang doing the same, or it could be someone getting revenge for one of the ten or twelve murders Long Beach PD thinks he's involved in but couldn't prove. Could be revenge for any of the extortion cases or murders the PD thinks the Cruisers are involved in."

"Any possibility it actually was the Jamaicans leaving a message to the Cruisers but wanting the Long Beach cops to not believe it was them?"

"Damn! I didn't think of that. Yeah, that is possible. Tweak it just enough to make it seem contrived. Good thought. Leave it to you, Cody, to wreck my best conspiracy theories."

"My pleasure. Nothing else at the scene?" Cody asked.

Esterharken replied, "Lots of tire tracks. An unaccounted-for set from a RAV4 or something else with the same wheelbase. But again, if it was the Jamaicans, they had to come in something."

"How much effort are you putting into this?"

Esterharken lamented, "I can't do much more than make a few phone calls without some leads. The Long Beach PD is sort of satisfied with the public explanation. A couple of the guys working the Jamaicans are grateful for the notoriety."

"Turning a lemon into lemonade, I guess, Harry. Well, I'll give it some thought and call you if I hear anything."

After the call, Cody thought about the case. The way the murder was committed was as intricately planned and bizarrely executed as the Qatar Card cases.

He put it on the back burner. There was more than enough to keep him busy with his own current workload, and he was too busy to think about the Long Beach caper or the Qatar cards.

It was three weeks before he got another call involving the Semyon and Gleb cases. It was from Alyosha. Again, they spoke in Russian.

"Hello, my friend. I have some interesting news from my fine city. You asked about visas for anyone named Cutter or Gutter. We had four in the time you asked me to check. All of them checked out, however. All legitimate visitors here for work or tourism."

"Any of them named Al or Alfred or anything else that can be shortened to Al?"

"Let me see. No, just three tourists, Daniel, Louise, Millie, and a pilot, Norman," Alyosha gleaned from his report.

"So, you called me to tell me there were no interesting people? You could have sent an email," Cody said, wondering if there was more.

Alyosha replied, "No, you are correct. I could have sent an email about them, but there is something else. Something I cannot send in an email. Like you, we have personnel monitoring many forms of communications. One other instance of the name Cutter or Gutter came up. It was a call between two known associates of a crime family. The voices were hard to make out, but one man mentioned the name Cutter or Gutter. Our man could not make it out exactly."

"What was the context?" Cody asked.

"I will read you the transcript. The first man says, 'Am I driving the same two that helped us get rid of the files, you know, the Cutters (or Gutters)?' The second man says, 'Shut up, moron! No names on the phone.' The second man berated the first for a while before hanging up."

"Who did those two work for?" Cody inquired.

"They are low-level employees of a local criminal affiliated with a larger organization led by what your press would call an oligarch. A very wealthy man named Kuznetsov. Maxim 'Molot' Kuznetsov."

Cody laughed because the English translation would literally be "Maximum 'Hammer' Blacksmith."

He asked, "What do these underlings do for 'the Hammer'?"

"They do driving and delivering goods and payments for one of his petty enterprises. That sort of thing. One is young and inexperienced."

"But you have no record of anyone other than your four with the Cutter name coming to Moscow?" Alex asked.

"That is correct," Alyosha answered.

"Do you have any idea what the first one meant by 'helped us get rid of the files'?"

"There are several cases that would fit. One of them you came here for."

Cody remembered the case Alyosha was talking about and exclaimed. "Oh, god! That's right! The Gleb Froylenko case. Of course, Alyosha!"

"And do you remember one later that I called you about regarding my hunch?"

"That was the … the … Semyon. It was the Semyon suicide-by-cop! Do you think they were related?"

Alyosha said, "My sources say the telephone call was intercepted three days before I shot Semyon. They did not discuss enough on the phone to give the people listening a clue what the Cutters were going to do."

"Who were the people listening? Are they with the police department?"

"Cody, my friend, I can no more tell you who they are than you can tell me who listens to conversations in America. When I started looking for people named Cutter, someone listened and told someone who told someone. One of those someones found me and they gave me the information. That is all I know."

"Yeah, well there is that, I guess. I'm going upstairs with this. This is the first actual intelligence we have that there might actually be someone named Cutter or Gutter. Thanks, my friend."

"You are welcome. I just wish I could get someone here to listen. They don't want to spend any more resources on the Semyon case. They said chasing a man who was never here is pointless," Alyosha said with the same irritated tone he used before in describing his stonewalling superiors. He added in a more positive tone, "But the light at the end of the tunnel that is not a train coming at us is that I have obtained permission to bring in the caller who mentioned Cutter. We have a tail on him now and are confident we will catch him doing something to reel this fish in in a few days."

Cody said, "That is wonderful news! Let me know when you have him."

* * *

After the call, Cody briefed Phil. He told him about the intercepted call that finally mentioned Cutter or Gutter by name and how it correlated with the Gleb and Semyon cases adding, "We can actually tie one of the Qatar Card cases to what is probably a homicide."

"The Moscow cops don't think so, Cody," Phil replied.

"Their brass is lazy, but one cop thinks there is something to it. He's an old-fashioned, hard-ass cop, too. I trust him," Cody countered.

"Let me run it by Henderson. See if he wants to bite," Phil suggested.

Four hours later, Phil called Cody to his office.

"Pack a bag, buckaroo. I don't know how he did it, but Henderson got you a ticket to see your friend. Just you. Four days, travel included as soon as you hear that they have the suspect in custody. He wants you to find any damned link you can to the Qatar Card case. No one upstairs thinks you have a prayer, and I guess this is the last gasp to get the Russian thing out of your system."

Chapter 23

Pyotr Spills the Beans After His Are Pressure-Cooked

A phone call from Alyosha and a mound of travel-authorization paperwork later, Cody stepped out of the Moscow airport and was greeted by his friend Alyosha. Sasha was in the car behind the wheel.

"Good to see you, sir," Sasha said with a smile.

"Good to see you, too, Sasha. Alyosha, any news?" Cody asked as they got into the car.

"We had a tail on the one who was heard on the telephone. Our equivalent of your customs people caught him for us, though. He was picking up a crate of what was labeled common chinaware at an air terminal, but our officials opened the crate since we had told them he was under suspicion. Inside were high-value electronics. The man was arrested for the customs violation. Our government may not be the most stringent in enforcing some laws, but when you try to cheat the government out of tax dollars, they get furious."

"Yeah, Alyosha. They couldn't get the gangster Al Capone for murder in my country, so they got him for tax evasion. Both governments are the same."

Alyosha reminisced, "Ah, yes. I remember this Al Capone from the days when he was our government's example of your government. He is very well known even in my country. Yes. Our old Soviet leaders used to say that America was full of gangsters like Al Capone. Capitalists and the politicians who supported them—all gangsters we were told. Well, we have our smuggler now, and some of my fellow detectives had a little discussion with him. They told him that we have a connection between him and a murder. We don't, actually, but he does not know this. We are … what is the English word?"

Cody answered in English, "Bullshitting him would be the term in English. Vraki or govno, I think, in Russian."

Alyosha and Sasha both laughed.

"Yes. Yes. That is what we are doing," Alyosha said. "We have him scared. We hinted that the smuggling charge could be dropped if he gives us information. He is afraid, though, that he will be killed if he tells us anything. Unfortunately, I think he is right. Could be a problem."

"Have you mentioned the name Cutter to him yet?" Cody asked.

"No. We have not."

"Want to see what happens when an American FBI agent breaks it to him the first time?" Cody suggested.

"Aha! That would indeed be interesting," Alyosha said with a grin. "I will ask if that is possible. It would certainly catch him off guard. He has counsel. Paid for by his employers, I'm sure. It is required that he have counsel present when we question him, but if you just go in and talk to him without asking anything, I think we can get away with it."

Cody asked, "Can he be questioned without his counsel being there?"

Alyosha gave Cody a look that indicated this case was being handled in a special way and said, "My superiors are concerned that this may tie into the internationally-known Qatar Card cases. If it results in its notice by the international press, they want to hold this up as a shining example of the Russian criminal justice system."

Cody just nodded, understanding that high-profile cases were handled with kid gloves in almost any jurisdiction.

Over lunch, Cody told them that this might be their last chance at confirming the Cutter name, explaining, "My boss says that the story is too thin to dedicate much more to this. Resources are as tight back home as I'm sure they are in your country. They sent me here as a favor, hoping I will finally shut up."

"If you come back with something, what will they say?" Sasha asked.

"My special agent in charge will be happy, I think. I don't know about anyone above him."

After lunch, Cody went with Alyosha to the police department, and they spent the afternoon going over everything that they knew about Cutter. They had decided that Gutter was so close to Cutter that the smuggler, Pyotr Volkov, wouldn't know the difference.

* * *

That evening Cody phoned Haley just to talk with her. The wedding was coming up in a couple of months, and he promised her he would pay attention to the details. To tell the truth, he was actually looking forward to it and all the pomp that came with it.

He told her, "I want William to be my best man. Out of all the guys I've known in the Bureau, he's my closest friend. Have you picked your bridesmaids?"

"Yes. I want my older sister, Michelle, to be my maid of honor and Maryann to be my bridesmaid. Can her husband, Ricky, be a groomsman?"

"Sure, honey. I'm dying to meet him."

She gushed, "You'll love him, sweetheart. He's so much like my sister. Like peas in a pod. Smart, athletic, loves to play games. Hey, and he speaks lots of languages. You can ask him questions about the polyglotism thing in that Qatar Card case, or are you calling it the Cutter case now?"

"We still don't have confirmation on the Cutter name, so it's still Qatar. I can't say over the phone what we have tomorrow, but it could help in deciding that very issue."

"Well, call me tomorrow night, and we'll talk about guests. I have most of the people you hang out with at the Bureau, but I need you to tell me any I've missed," she said.

They chatted about the wedding for another fifteen minutes before Cody decided he had to hit the sack. It was 4:15 p.m. in Washington, DC, but it was after midnight in Moscow.

* * *

Early the next day, Sasha was at the hotel to pick him up. Cody wanted to treat him to a breakfast of blinis, something Cody's grandmother used to make for him. Sasha knew a place that made good ones, and they sat and talked over the Russian pancakes with jam.

"Sasha, you have a great mind. Why are you a driver instead of the head of something?"

"I have no appetite for being in charge of anything. I like to read, and being a driver gives me a lot of time to do that. I live for my wife. She and my children are all to me, and I am pleased with my life. I have been to wonderful places, and I have met wonderful people such as you. How many people can say they love their life?"

Cody thought for a minute. Sasha was right. To do what one loves and to live as one chooses is the very definition of happiness. At that moment, he realized that was the reason he had never tried for supervisory special agent. He truly loved what he was doing. Now that he had Haley in his life, he felt completeness that he never knew existed. He looked at Sasha with a new appreciation and raised his glass of tea.

"Sasha, you are looking at another one. In that pursuit, we are brothers."

Sasha raised his glass and smiled back. "To brothers," he toasted in English.

Cody raised his glass and said, "Da, brat'yev."

* * *

After Sasha dropped off Cody at the police building, Alyosha and Cody met with Alyosha's commander, along with someone from the prosecutor's office and three other detective bureau members. The seven of them talked about strategy concerning Pyotr. The consensus was that the sudden arrival of an American FBI agent with what seemed to be details of the Cutter case might shake Pyotr enough to confirm those details. It was a crapshoot. If their suspicions were correct, they might hit the jackpot. If not, what they thought they knew probably wasn't correct anyway, and nothing would be lost.

Pyotr was brought to an interrogation room by Alyosha. It was similar to the one Cody had seen during the Gleb interrogation, but the fluorescent fixture above the table flickered annoyingly, and this room looked as if it hadn't been painted since Stalin died.

A CCTV camera was mounted high on one wall. On the side of the room was the same sizable one-way mirror with sound-deadening double glass. On the other side of the mirror was the observation room, where audio and video recording equipment for the CCTV system was located and where witnesses and police could watch and listen to what was happening.

Pyotr sat in the chair Alyosha pointed to and asked, "Where is my lawyer? I'm not saying anything," apparently believing that what he had been told by the police about questioning and lawyers was gospel.

"Pyotr, we don't want you to say anything. We want you to listen to a guest who is visiting Moscow. I'm going to leave you with him while I get something to eat."

Alyosha walked out without further explanation, and Cody walked in a few seconds later.

He said in Russian, "Hello, Pyotr."

"Who are you?" Pyotr asked defensively.

"Someone who wants to let you know what fascinating information about you we have."

"What do you know? Your accent is funny. Where are you from?" Pyotr asked.

"I'm from a place where your secrets are no longer secrets. Let me tell you a story. A pair of people come to Moscow. They are here to see a man about the bad things he is doing. They will expose those bad things, but the man has some files belonging to others that should not be exposed. The pair finds and destroys those files as a favor to some friends. The man is exposed, but when he talks to the police, those friends have the man killed."

He now had Pyotr's rapt, undivided attention.

Cody paused for dramatic effect then continued, "Sometime later, another man runs afoul of those same friends. The pair is called back to Moscow to escort the man to the graveyard."

Pyotr was visibly sweating.

"Now the pair who visit the second man make it look like he was shooting at the police, so the police shoot back, killing the man. The pair needs transportation to and from the crime scene. Several people are involved in this."

Cody stared into Pyotr's eyes as he said the next bit. "So, Pyotr, let me give you some names. Gleb Froylenko, Semyon Blinov, Al Cutter and his wife, and you, Pyotr."

Pyotr was gray. The blood drained out of his face, and he was trembling. "Who are you? How do you know such things?" he asked in a cracked, dry, almost-whisper.

Cody had seen suspects in this position before. To Cody's eye, Pyotr was on the verge of folding, and something unexpected, another detail or something visual, often provided the tipping point in these moments. He decided to go for the visual theatrics. He pulled out his FBI ID and flashed it in Pyotr's face, solemnly translating the large letters: "FBI Special Agent."

Cody knew that Russian media often mentioned the FBI, and not always in the most favorable light. The badge had the desired effect. He saw Pyotr sink into his chair as if he was trying to disappear through it, gripping its arms with white knuckles. He shoveled a bit more vraki at Pyotr.

"You have seen the movies, Pyotr. The American FBI sees everything. Out of all the people who transported those criminals, you were the only one to look up at the sky when you were doing it. Our satellites caught you providing the transportation, so I guess that makes you an accessory to murder. Semyon may have been a corrupt government official, but he was still a government official. You helped kill a government official, Pyotr Volkov. Now we at the FBI don't care if you confess or not. This is not our crime. We just have an obligation under international law to tell you what we told the Moscow police. This fulfills that obligation, so please have a good day, Pyotr Volkov."

With that, Cody flipped his ID closed with the snappy flourish only practice can achieve, put it in his pocket, and walked out. When he got to the viewing room on the other side of the one-way mirror, he found Alyosha and two of his fellow detectives in stitches. They were stifling laughs to the point that their faces were red.

"You did wonderfully, my drook. Look at the floor under his chair! 'The FBI sees everything?' That is Russian-class, uh, bullshit." He pointed to the other detectives and announced, "Judges give you nine-point-five."

Cody smiled at the compliment as he looked at the floor in the interrogation room and saw a spreading trickle of yellow. Pyotr's shaking had intensified to the point that the detectives in the viewing room could hear the microphone pick up his hands trembling on the metal table.

Alyosha, who had prepared in advance for his return, entered the interrogation room with paper cups of tea and a bag of ponchiki, Russian doughnut holes. He acted as if he hadn't seen Pyotr's condition.

As he walked in, he said, "I got enough for both of us. Tea and ponchiki. Do you like them?" Then pretending to suddenly notice what Pyotr had done to himself, he said, "Oh, dear, what happened? You are a mess. Let me call to get you a new jail uniform. Do you need to go to the bathroom to clean up? Here, do you want ponchiki while we're waiting for clean clothes? Do you want to talk to your mob lawyer and let him report back to your employers what we know about you?"

The rapid string of questions had Pyotr trying to answer one while being interrupted by the next. When Alyosha got to the last question, he froze.

"You look confused, Pyotr. I'll just call your lawyer and have him come down here to take care of you … I mean to advise you."

Alyosha started to leave. Pyotr began to cry. Cody watched with appreciation how the tough, experienced detective handled the young, inexperienced hood. Alyosha's last words cut through their target like a knife. Cody saw the slumped posture and confused stare at the floor. He knew Pyotr was defeated.

"No, don't call him," he sobbed. "I need to think. I need to have someone tell me what is going on."

Alyosha put the bag and a cup on the table.

"Have tea and something to eat, Pyotr. Clean clothes will be here in a minute, and you can take all the time you need to think about whether you want your lawyer or my friends in the Prosecutor General's Office. It is up to you."

"You can make a deal with me?" Pyotr asked, looking up hopefully.

"The prosecutor general certainly can. It's not up to me. You want advice. The Prosecutor General's Office can advise if you don't want to talk to your employers' lawyer. If you want to make a deal, they can appoint a government attorney to make it for you."

Alyosha left Pyotr to think about it. Someone brought him a new uniform and a plastic basin of water with a washcloth and a towel. Pyotr cleaned himself and changed clothes.

As he did so, Alyosha gave Cody Pyotr's options. "He can stay silent; in which case he thinks we have evidence making him an accessory. He believes he goes to jail, where he will probably be killed. He can tell his own attorney, but he is pretty sure that would be a death sentence, too. He would be too much of a liability to the mob he works for. He's not tattooed, so he's expendable to them. You know these tattoos of stars on the chest, churches and such?"

"Yes. I've seen a number of them," Cody replied. "When I worked a case in New York City we arrested many criminals who were heavily covered with them. Each one has a meaning, so it's like a tattooed resume."

"Good." Alyosha nodded. "So, he dies in jail. His best option would be to give testimony and hope we can send him somewhere with a new identity. Something similar to your witness protection program."

* * *

They let Pyotr sit in that room for three hours. They gave him bathroom breaks and fed him. When he asked why he was still there, the detective who brought him lunch gave him an answer that took his appetite away.

"The FBI agent is downloading more information to give to the lead detective. Those high-definition satellite pictures are some pretty big files. The Prosecutor General's Office wanted pictures showing your face better, I think."

The look Pyotr gave the detective was priceless. Cody slapped his friend on the back. "Forget the 'satellite,' Alyosha. I want a high-definition picture of his expression to take back to the FBI."

"It won't exactly be high definition, but I can have a copy of the recording made for you."

* * *

About an hour after lunch was brought to him, Pyotr sat back in his chair. His face was resolute, and he was nodding to himself. The detective who was monitoring Pyotr notified Alyosha of this new behavior.

Cody and Alyosha returned to the viewing room and watched Pyotr. The two veteran law enforcement officers knew the look. A few minutes later, Alyosha entered the interrogation room.

"Have you had enough time?" he asked.

"Yes. Whatever I do now, I'm dead unless you hide me. Get me someone from the Prosecutor General's Office. I want to make a deal."

"Very well," Alyosha said.

Cody now knew Pyotr would never have made his stars. A vor or a made member of any Russian mob would die before cooperating.

Alyosha left the room. He made arrangements with the Prosecutor General's Office earlier in case this was the outcome. The attorney that had consulted with them was still was on call. He returned within the hour and found Pyotr chatting with the two uniformed officers Alyosha's captain had assigned to protect him.

* * *

Alyosha and the attorney offered Pyotr their version of a witness protection program for all the information he could give if it was valuable. For the next three hours, Pyotr gave them everything he knew. He had nothing to lose at this point, and he knew it.

Pyotr was a young and inexperienced recruit, a friend-of-a-friend of a made member in the organization. Very little was revealed to people such as him until they proved themselves. As the police expected, he never had direct contact with the bosses, but he had enough information about some lower-level individuals to make the deal worthwhile. There was sufficient detail about a few crimes to most likely convict four low-level men. The investigatory team was disappointed that there was no one higher they could go after, but this was not unanticipated.

Pyotr said, "From kitchen conversations, I knew that there were a few old-time vory in the organization. They had joined with Kuznetsov when they were in their twenties and thirties after the Soviet Union fell. I only glimpsed an occasional tattooed vor or other made member here or there when picking up visiting guests at hotel rooms or spas. I never knew names unless I overheard someone higher than me talking."

The treasure among the chicken feed was that he did indeed drive the Cutters. He used the name Cutter, not Gutter, so that was cleared up when he talked about them.

He admitted, "I picked them up in a hotel district and drove them to the Semyon hit. I did not know Semyon's name until I saw the news footage later that day and realized Semyon was the target's name. I was only given the address and what to do.

"Months ago, when I was delivering food to a meeting, a supervisor talked about someone named Cutter doing a great service by erasing some files from the computer owned by a man named Gleb Froylenko. He was yelling at another man for not doing more to check out Gleb before giving him the files and was grateful that the Cutters' employers had the courtesy to call them to see if he was connected before taking care of Gleb.

"When my supervisor called me to tell me I had a driving assignment involving foreigners, I asked if it was the Cutters again. He was furious at me for saying the name on my phone. He said I didn't really need to know their names as I was being given an 'I heart NY' baseball cap to wear for them to recognize me."

Alyosha smiled at Pyotr's stupidity that had led the police to this moment and asked, "Describe them as best you can remember."

"It has been some time, and I was nervous during the trip, but his height was several centimeters under two meters, slim build. She was a few centimeters shorter. I picked them up again after the hit and drove them to Gorky Park."

He added, "The man wore a baseball cap pulled down. The woman wore a hat with a wide brim. Both wore large aviator sunglasses, and both constantly looked down. I never got a good look at their faces, so I don't think I could identify them if I saw them again. When they came out of Semyon's house, I was looking for police, so I didn't look at them coming."

* * *

After watching the interview through the one-way mirror, Cody called Phil and asked him to get their SAC and William on the line. It wasn't a secure line, so he was brief and circumspect.

"We now have confirmation on the name. With a C. We're going to make inquiries in the area where they may have been staying. I'll see you guys in a couple. I really can't say more on this phone. If you need more, I can go to the American embassy and use a secure line. Let me know."

Henderson thanked him and said he would pass the information up the chain.

* * *

After Cody's call, Alyosha and his team got the wheels turning. Pyotr was escorted to a safe location and kept under guard by uniformed officers trusted by the detectives. Two teams of detectives were sent out to start canvassing the hotels in the area of the pickup café. Cody went with the team Alyosha was on.

Of course, none of the hotels had a guest named Al Cutter or any variation of that name.

"That would have been too easy," Cody said at the end of the day. "None of the people named Cutter who were in the country during the crimes stayed at any of the hotels your teams canvassed today, Alyosha. Besides, none of the people named Cutter matched the descriptions Pyotr gave, anyway."

Their plan wasn't very sophisticated. The detectives called the hotels within six blocks of Pyotr's pickup point. They asked about any American couples in the twenty-five-to-thirty-five-year age range who stayed during the period that included either Cutter incident. There were fourteen such couples, with six that were there during both attacks. It was unknown where the suspects had been picked up for the Gleb attack, but the team decided to see what they could turn up for both date ranges. It never occurred to Cody that the Cutters may have driven themselves to Gleb's.

Three couples stayed for about a week after the Gleb homicide. They put that group at the bottom of the list, guessing that a hitman wouldn't stay that long after a hit. After they developed the list, detectives started interviewing hotel staff.

By the end of the day, they were sure that the eleven shorter-stay guests were legitimate. They all had airtight reasons for being in Moscow—business, booked guided tours, and other verifiable details.

The following day, Alyosha dejectedly announced to the team, "I'm sorry, but we are at the bottom of the list. We are reduced to three longshots before we are out of possibilities completely."

Of the last hotels with possible couples, Alyosha took Cody to the one with the best restaurant. After breakfast, they interviewed the hotel staff.

The concierge and desk staff remembered the couple Alyosha and Cody were there to inquire about. They said the pair was in town to sightsee and to conduct some antique business. They had to stay longer than planned because the government paperwork on some of their purchases took time to process. One of the managers remembered the couple having a guest for dinner one evening.

Alyosha and Cody called the hotel restaurant's maître d' at his residence, as he wasn't on duty until dinnertime. The man remembered the guest, an antique dealer.

The maître d' recalled, "He is the gentleman our export permit man at the concierge desk often uses for assistance. A most respected dealer."

It was another dead end, the same as the leads at the other hotels. The detectives were out of possibilities, other than the obvious one that the Cutters were staying elsewhere and simply took a cab or the Metro to the café where Pyotr picked them up.

* * *

It was time for Cody to go. He treated everyone on the task force to dinner as a thank-you for their work. With all the vodka toasts that evening, Cody was glad he picked the restaurant in his own hotel. He was too drunk to do much more than stagger back to his room. As he passed out in bed, his last sorry thought was about taking a long flight with a hangover.

As he shut off his alarm at 6:30 a.m., his worst fears were realized. He had a full orchestra playing the "Anvil Chorus" in his head. He had time for breakfast before Sasha was going to drive him to the airport, though he ate very little with his tomato juice and ibuprofen.

He was pleased to see that Alyosha was in the back of the car when Sasha pulled up. The bellman put his suitcase in the trunk, and they were off. Sasha and Alyosha appeared to be okay.

"How do you drink so much and not have a hangover?" Cody inquired.

"For Sasha and me, vodka is not an alcoholic beverage. It is liquid food. Stay in Russia for a month next time, and you will get acclimated."

"I don't think my doctor or my liver would approve. I drink a little at home, but not more than one or two an evening," Cody replied.

"How boring," Alyosha chided. "You must learn to live. These doctors don't know anything. My grandfather lived through the Great Patriotic War on potatoes, cabbage, and vodka, and he lived to be eighty-four. Anyway, if you stay longer, you can take some side trips to see the country around Moscow. It is very beautiful."

"Alyosha, you are a genius!" Cody exclaimed.

"I know this already, but why do you say this only now?" the detective replied with a laugh.

"Because that is what we all forgot to check! Could you see if any of the guests on our list of couples took side trips? Maybe in the direction of Gleb?"

"It is what you call a longshot, but I can have one of my men do that, sure. The hotels will have records of guests who left and returned. I will send you an email."

"One more thing," Cody asked as an afterthought. "See if any of the members in Kuznetsov's mob have ties to specific American mobs. Maybe I can do some looking from my end if they do."

"Sure. Now that we know who they are, our organized crime units will be happy to give us that information if they have it. I'll include it in my email."

On the flight home, Cody drank bottle after bottle of water and slept for hours. He thought about the longshot of Alyosha finding a substantial lead. Little did he know that Alyosha's clues in Moscow would eventually bring the Cutters right to Cody's doorstep.

Chapter 24

End of an Era

Three years and a month after Papa Paul's hobby had begun, he made the call he knew he would have to make someday: "Alex, can the two of you come to Nashville this weekend? Lucy and I are having a little get-together, and we'd like you to come. There are two people, in particular, we want you to meet."

"Of course, Papa Paul. We'd love to come," Alex replied.

Alex let Lara know, and she made plane reservations. They knew there was a room waiting for them at Papa Paul's anytime they wanted to stay there except Thanksgiving and Christmas, when the house would be full of their children and grandchildren.

* * *

Siggy picked them up at the airport. After lunch at a good barbecue joint, they found themselves at the door to Papa Paul's rural home.

Inviting them in, Papa Paul looked at Lara's shirt and laughed as he hugged her. "Still drowning your ribs in sauce, I see by the stains, Lara."

Lara laughed, too, as she replied, "I like enough where ten Wet-Naps are needed just to get my hands clean enough to go to the washroom."

Alex gave Papa Paul a hug, too, as Lucy entered the large front room with a tray of lemonade-filled glasses.

"Good to see you, Lucy. How are the grandkids?" Lara asked after taking a glass.

At the question, Alex reflected that Theresa and Maria were only seven and eight when he and Lara took care of Packy. Through seven years of hitting for Siggy and now three years of scammers for Papa Paul's hobby, they had watched the kids grow up. Pauli Jr.'s daughters were in high school now. Papa Paul's daughter, Connie, had two sons in college.

"They're all fine, Lara," Lucy answered. "Maria sprained an ankle on the lacrosse team, but she's better now. All are getting good grades."

She set the tray down and hugged Lara and Alex.

"Why don't the two of you settle in, and then Papa and I can have a chat with you about why you're here," Lucy suggested.

Knowing that Lucy's "suggestions" were always to be taken as canon law, Lara replied, "Sure, Lucy. Give us twenty to freshen up, and we'll join you."

They had a quick shower and a change of clothes. Both were dying to find out why they had been summoned to Nashville.

* * *

When Siggy knocked on their door, they followed him to Papa Paul's office. It was quite a change from the one he had in Chicago. Instead of dark wood and a thick oriental rug, his Nashville digs were done in country style. The office featured a rack of fishing rods and a few mounted deer heads and ducks. The furniture was casual and rustic. in the middle of the floor lay a large oval braided rag rug.

A steel vault door disguised as a bookcase led from the office to his reinforced-concrete gun room, where he had expensive shotguns and rifles displayed on the walls, a reloading bench where Papa Paul enjoyed the hobby of crafting precision ammo, and several gun cabinets. The vault door was open, and Alex and Lara could hear Papa Paul talking to someone inside.

Lucy was sitting in the office waiting for them, and she called to Papa Paul. He came out of the gun room with two other men that Alex and Lara did not recognize at first.

One was shorter than the other by a head and was a bit on the heavy side. He was wearing a tweed shooting jacket with leather elbow patches and shoulder pad. The taller, slimmer one was wearing a hunting coat with L.L. Bean embroidered over the pocket. Alex suspected that they recently returned to the house after shooting trap out back with a few of the Holland & Holland and Purdy shotguns that adorned the walls of the gun room. Both men moved with an easy confidence around Papa Paul that indicated they were old friends.

Papa Paul made the introductions, gesturing first to Alex and Lara. "Gentlemen, this is the couple you know as Lara and Alex Cutter. Lara and Alex, these are two of your biggest fans." Pointing to the taller man, he said, "This dodgy old fart is Senator Eustis Carmichael. He sits on the United States Senate Commerce Subcommittee on Communications, Technology, Innovation, and the Internet. "He pointed to the other and continued, "This overweight card sharp is Senator Claude Dubois of the Senate Homeland Security and Governmental Affairs Committee."

Alex and Lara shook their hands. They recognized the name Dubois as the senator from their parents' home state. They were somewhat taken aback to find themselves in the presence of two senators. To hear that they were fans was even more of a shock.

"Sit you two. I'll explain," Papa Paul said, motioning to a rustic loveseat.

When everyone was seated and adequately provisioned with a drink, Papa Paul turned to Alex and Lara. He raised his glass, toasting, "To the most lovable and entertaining two people who ever came into our lives, Alex and Lara."

Alex wondered why they were being introduced to the senators by their crime-family aliases, but he kept quiet and went with it.

The others raised their glasses, too. After everyone had a sip, Papa Paul looked inquisitively at Alex and asked, "Have you two ever wondered how Siggy finds the marks that Lara can't find herself?"

"Uh, Lara and I always figured he just had someone working for him who was really good at tracing Internet and phone traffic."

"He doesn't have someone. I do. Some are called the US government, to be exact. They are also known as my poker buddies and their friends. You see, there are a lot of people who have the ability to track down those assholes. They just can't do much of it legally within their official mandates, and they can't reveal how much they know. If they trace them illegally, it can't be used in court, and most of the scammers just get a slap on the wrist, if anything, before they start again. Also, they have no jurisdiction over foreign scammers. They do have a lot of contacts who are Black Hat hackers, though. As it turned out, they were our most valuable asset."

"How did this start?" a bewildered Lara asked.

"Well, one night over cards, the subject of robot dialers came up. Once every couple of months, I used to host a game here. Now it's every month. Most of the people who play are friends I've helped out through campaign contributions and the friends of those people, plus a lot of people I do business with … legitimately, that is. I've been backing these two for years."

Senator Dubois added, "And we certainly appreciate Paul's support. He's assisted us with campaign contributions and political contacts for a few decades. Good man!"

Papa Paul nodded and said, "Thanks, Claude. I like the good work that you and Eustis do. We need more like you. Anyway, these guys have connections you wouldn't believe. NSA, Justice Department, FCC, even NASA. Oh, sure, the government can catch a few scammers here and there. They can fine a few, but it's pretty much catch-and-release. Everybody wished there was someone who could actually put the fear of god into those assholes. One day I got tired of hearing them grouse about how they couldn't take action against the robodialing scammers when one call actually came in during a game. Wrecked my aces-and-eights moment."

Lara laughed. "Of course. Edward. The first one."

Papa Paul continued, "Right. Well, I told my buddies that I wished I could take the guy's phone and cram it up his ass. Lucy had just come in with a tray of drinks and snacks. She laughed when I said that."

Lucy nodded and said, "I suddenly realized that Papa had someone on the payroll who could do what he just wished for. I was half-joking when I said, 'I bet Alex and Lara could do just that.'"

Papa Paul continued, "I asked the guys … and not all are guys, by the way … if they could get me the necessary information, and they said they might be able to. The test case was tracking down old Edward."

Senator Carmichael explained, "We all knew Paul had a shady side, but that it was a pretty-much-extinct part of his empire. He admitted that he still had a slim toehold in that world and offered to let us access it. It was just too dang tempting to pass up. Hell, we have the CIA do things that make his old operation look like a kindergarten recess game. We just couldn't use the CIA or any other government agency to carry out what we wanted you two to do."

"What my esteemed colleague is trying to say," Senator Eustis interjected, "is that the two of you have provided a public service as well as providing us all some of the most entertaining shenanigans we could ever have hoped for."

Lara asked, "What was that about the Black Hats?"

Siggy explained, "Well, ordinarily Black Hat hackers don't much care for law enforcement, government people, big business, and the like. We found an exception. They are the same as everyone else who hates being robocalled constantly. Now, don't get me wrong; they have the ability—the good ones, so to speak—to punish some scammers. They take over the scammers' systems, plant viruses, or simply format their hard drives. But when they just get a sales call or one of those cardholder services calls, there's not much they ordinarily do. When the Dark Web rumor mill started spreading stories about someone who wanted to physically punish them, they were lining up to get their pound of flesh."

Alex asked, "Couldn't just the government contacts get you the information?"

Siggy explained, "Sure, we got lots of info from our government spooks, but the layers-deep chat rooms started tracing scammers for us, too, and volunteered a bunch of their own pet peeve irritants. Dozens of Black Hat hackers, from teens who just usually make mischief to serious multinational groups, became honorary White Hats for the public benefit and improvement of society."

Papa Paul said, "Toying with the computer of a fake Microsoft Help Desk jerk is fun, but knowing you just got someone to shove a phone up one of their asses is viscerally far more satisfying. Some of them even started competing to identify new targets for us. We suspect there may have been some internal revenge involved from time to time, a response to an insult, for example, but the whole thing exploded to help us. Anyway, out of all the scammers they identified, we got to pick and choose, though quite a few came from the calls that I personally received. We spread the word that we were only doing about one a month, and then the ones we did that came from our Black Hat friends became the gold standard of bragging rights in some of their communities.

"When word got out that that Russian scammer, Gleb, had used ransomware against a hospital, we had a dozen Black Hats lined up to turn him in. He broke their code. Same as the one you went to in the Czech Republic when the ransomware attacker took the money and never sent the code to free up the victim's computer. That one wasn't a morality violation. The ransomware community is relying more and more on the certainty that the victim's system will be restored to increase the percentage of ransom payments. That code violation had the potential to hit the others in the pocketbook."

Siggy shook his head at the irony of a ransomware code of conduct and said, "I guess the moral of the story is that everyone has a hot button, even the Black Hat hackers. People are people, after all, and if you robocall the wrong person, it has consequences."

Alex and Lara laughed at the explanation. Lara looked at Papa Paul and asked, "Uh, how many of you are there? I mean, how many know about Alex and me?"

"Twenty-three, Lara. There are twenty-three people in my little poker group, and eight to twelve make it to any single game. All of them are in on the deal, pun intended. No one in the group was ever allowed to meet you personally or know your real names. These two begged me to let them come here today, though. We'll get to why in a little bit. There are quite a few who know something about you two generally, but not by your real names."

"You said entertaining, Senator Eustis?"

"Yes, Lara. Entertaining beyond anything you could have imagined when you performed your little acts of service. You see, we have some top intelligence and security people in our group. We all made bets on the two of you. Bets on whether their people can track what you're doing."

Senator Carmichael explained, "Take that Ann Arbor episode. One member's agency had a team in the area. It was explained to the team as a training op. They were told there would be an objective in the area where you two were. Just a training activity they were supposed to find and track. They weren't to interfere—just to try to find you and observe your exit. They had no idea how you infiltrated the area. The car they thought brought you out was followed, but you were not in the car when it eventually parked at a motel. There were just two guys on their way to some kind of convention."

"We came on the back seat floorboards of an older couple's car. Did your people happen to see an old guy eating a hamburger while he was driving?"

"That was you?" Senator Eustis exclaimed.

"Yeah, Senator. Under a black thermal-shield tarp. They brought us in, and another car picked us up for the exfil. So did they follow the exit car south?"

"Yes. They were almost positive their training objectives were in the car they followed. A FLIR image showed two objects that just appeared suddenly in addition to the driver. The transcript said they were not there when the car entered the target zone, but there when the car exited it. The agency car had to follow you at a distance, though. They lost line of sight when the car parked at an all-night market, but it was picked up again when the car left the lot. There was the same heat signature in the car all the way to the guy's motel. How did you get out?"

"We switched cars at the grocery. Dome lights were turned off. What your guys were following was a hot rotisserie chicken and the driver from the car we switched to."

The senators laughed. Senator Eustis said, "That's a good one!"

Siggy stood and turned to the two senators, reminding them, "We promised that we would give the group details someday. You just got the first."

"Papa Paul, why didn't you tell either of us about your little cabal?" Lara asked.

"Lara, because I didn't want to skew the game. Did you and Alex ever wonder why I encouraged your plans to become ever more complex and convoluted?"

"Well, we knew you liked the game-like intrigue. You seemed to enjoy the stories," Lara replied.

"That was true, but the other reason was that I loved to one-up the pros who were betting that they could detect you. I knew that every twist and turn you put into those Rube Goldberg plans of yours would not only keep the two of you safer, but it would also win me more bets."

"How much did you bet?" Alex asked, hoping that it was thousands.

"A dollar. I only had to pay out three times the whole time you guys were active. They never ID'd you, but they figured out most of your entry or exit a couple of times. I made over thirty bucks off the two of you."

Senator Eustis remarked, "Yeah. You two had real pros chasing their tails. We were limited in what we could use, though. No retasking satellites or using helicopters and that sort of thing. All of us chipped in to make up the buck each time against Paul's. It cost me a dime or fifteen cents every time we lost. Paul made us line up and drop our coins in that jar over there on the shelf."

Alex walked over to the shelf. He turned and grinned as he held up the large jar full of loose change.

"A dollar! Look, sweetheart; we made Papa Paul a fortune!" Alex exclaimed. "Wow. We made him about a quarter a week."

Lara laughed along with everyone else in the room.

Papa Paul suddenly wasn't laughing as he explained, "Those dimes and nickels represent more to me than all the bank and investment accounts I have. It was never really about money. We made it a buck just so there would be someone who had to pay either way. It was really all about one side or the other having to admit they'd been outwitted. Lucy and I not only laughed our asses off each time you two visited a scammer, but we found immense enjoyment every time you outfoxed these two old cusses and the rest of the poker club. But everything has a lifespan of its own."

Lucy walked to his side. She had tears in her eyes as she said, "I love the two of you. Remember the promise I made you give all those years ago?"

Lara was catching on. She stood and hugged Lucy as she said, "Yeah. You made us promise that we would retire if there was a danger that our real identities could be blown. Is that it, Lucy?"

"Yes, dear. Senator Carmichael brought us some information on Monday that makes us think they are getting too close. When you made the promise, we all thought it wouldn't be more than a couple of years. It's been over three … and ten for your entire career with us. You two had a good run."

Alex asked, "What was it?"

Siggy replied, "What we always feared it would be. A weak link in an associate's organization gave your cover name to the police when he was in a bind. Russian police, to be exact. Your name was overheard in a phone conversation, and the Moscow cops squeezed a suspect on one end of the call. They had him between a rock and a hard place. It wasn't just the name, though. The idiot they caught was the guy who drove you on your last Russian assignment involving Semyon. We think he told them where he picked you up, which could lead to your true identity. They started asking questions at the hotels near the café where you met the driver. Some moron supervisor told him the Cutter name, and the driver later repeated the name. And get this: He repeated it on a cell phone!"

Lara clenched her fists and hissed, "Talk about a moron!" She turned to Papa Paul and said, "He never needed to know our names. He was given a baseball cap for us to identify him. I told you that the mook was too inexperienced to pick up take-out borscht, let alone drive us. How did you get the information?"

Senator Carmichael explained, "It was reported up the chain of command at Justice. We know who the special agent in the FBI is who's tracking your foreign cases. He made a friend in the Moscow

PD. One day our FBI guy's boss asked for travel for him to Russia. This was after most resources had been cut off for the scammer-punishment case. That meant that the travel had to be approved at a higher level than usual.

"I'm on a Senate committee that oversees a lot of law enforcement activity. One of my contacts was watching for any requests like that on the Cutter case. When the special agent came back, he reported that the Cutter identity had possibly been blown. More resources might be available to investigate that and future cases. Your true identities weren't revealed yet, but there's the danger they could be. Our information also showed that the Russian who was arrested revealed the identity of the mob he was working for. That led to discovering some American contacts who were doing business with them."

Papa Paul solemnly revealed, "Unfortunately, one of them was identified as Angelo. That was too close for comfort."

Papa Paul took their hands as he pronounced, "What the two of you have done is spectacular. You made a promise, though, and today that promise must be fulfilled. Siggy is now shutting down that last vestige of our old life. His two dried cranberry buyers are getting the golden parachute we promised them when their work was done. All operations are being turned over to former associates. But we're not risking the two of you in this move. You two are not moving with that change of management. There will be no more work for Alex and Lara Cutter."

Alex and Lara had anticipated this day. They knew that when Papa Paul said they were done, they were done. Each kissed the hand they were holding.

Alex, emotion straining his voice, vowed, "Yes, Papa Paul. We have done more already than we ever hoped to, and you have fulfilled our dreams. Thank you."

Alex and Lara also knew that "no more" meant no more lethal hit assignments, either. They just assumed that they couldn't talk about those in front of their guests. The three of them hugged, and then Lara and Alex hugged Lucy. The two senators stood and shook their hands.

Papa Paul patted the backs of the senators as he addressed Alex and Lara. "You two, that's why Eustis and Claude are here. They wanted to thank you personally, and they may have an offer for the two of you."

Senator Dubois grinned as he said, "We have been privileged to have been able to follow you. It's been better than any fantasy football league! Following the two of you around the country—indeed, the world— doing to those crooks what all of us wished we could do, well, we had a lot of fun watching. And it did some good for the little guys those crooks hurt. Of course, there were also some victim restitution instances based on the records you revealed to the police. But more than that, it boosted the spirits of anyone who's ever been scammed. Social media and the press look at the two of you as Robin Hoods."

Senator Carmichael added, "Your popularity around the county is higher than the president's. If you two could go public, either of you would be a shoo-in for Congress. I even hear that some Hollywood producer is thinking about a comic antihero movie based on your exploits."

Papa Paul invited everyone to sit again and then said, "The reason I invited the two of you to meet these fine gentlemen is that they are friends of ours."

Both Alex and Lara looked at him with incredulity.

"They are? We can talk to them freely?" Alex asked.

"Yeah, that's right. They both know what else you have done for me. Eustis, for instance, was the one who asked me for a favor with the Andrew McCormick problem."

"But that was well before Alex and I started on the anti-scamming project," Lara said.

Senator Eustis explained, "Yes, it was. Paul and Lucy have been my friends for decades. Another of my friends had invested with McCormick's financial company and was about to lose hundreds of thousands. He found out from an insider that McCormick was committing fraud on a massive scale, and he came to me. McCormick was using his legitimate companies' reputations as a front for it. There were allegations, but someone at the SEC was stonewalling the investigation. My friend's whistleblower knew there was no way he could convince the SEC that there was funny business with McCormick's books because McCormick was in bed with the right people, just as in the Madoff case.

"I knew my friend's position was just the tip of the iceberg, and I wanted to stem the tide before it got worse and began to affect pension plans and nonprofits. I was in a quandary. I came to Paul and asked for his advice and assistance. He assured me that the only way to expose McCormick was most likely going to be the way you did."

Senator Dubois asked, "So, just how did you get McCormick to write his suicide confession note? There had been no signs that he was tortured, and the handwriting was definitely proven to be his."

Alex answered, "Easy. My gal here has been studying pressure points for years. She applied a little force to a few sensitive areas. It doesn't take much. With McCormick, it was fifteen minutes of a spot on the cheekbone and pressure straight up at the philtrum."

"The what?" Senator Dubois asked.

"The little groove under your nose," Lara explained. "Senator, put the side of a finger there and push straight up."

The senator tried it and exclaimed, "Ow! Damn, that hurts. Okay, I can see that being effective."

Alex continued, "That's the idea. She applied pain without doing significant damage. Whatever was visible on the cheekbone and the nose was pretty much masked by two hundred thirty grains of hollow-point forty-five-caliber bullet going into his mouth and out through the top of his skull. Before that final event, he was broken to the point that he would have confessed to the Kennedy assassination."

Senator Dubois commented, "That persuasion was pretty effective. The cops found a list of the locations and account numbers of every bank that he'd used to stash the cash he'd siphoned off. The feds were able to recover the bulk of what he'd taken, and most investors got at least a good percentage of their original investment back."

The senator added, "I always wanted to thank you for having him add the name of the guy at the SEC who was running interference for him for bribes. The icing on the cake, as you might say. So, thanks."

Lara looked at Lucy and asked, "What happens now?"

"Sweetheart, today is the last day anyone will ever know you as Alex and Lara Cutter. From now on, we only use your real names. Senators, meet Ricky Desmêt and his lovely wife, Maryann, formerly of Savannah. If you ever need high-end antiques or collectibles, please look them up in Chicago."

Senator Dubois said, "Georgia is my state. Say, I knew a Philippe Desmêt from Savannah years ago. Any relation?"

"My grandfather, sir," Alex replied.

"Wonderful man. I knew his son, Edward, too. He told me about his son and … wait … Maryann? … Young lady, that would make you?"

"Yes, Senator. The former Maryann Briggs."

Papa Paul calmly said, "We all know that there is an itch you will miss being scratched in the future. These two gentlemen would like to know if the two of you would like a retirement job in a similar field. Your compensation from Lucy and me will be permanent, as we promised, but we thought you would like something that would really challenge your intellect and skills."

Ricky and Maryann looked at each other, and then with smiles, they turned attentively to the two senators.

Chapter 25

Trying to Nail Jell-O to a Tree

Cody read the email from Alyosha carefully. It had taken his Russian police friend weeks to track down any possible leads with the little time and resources available. He pretty much had to do it on his own time with the assistance of a couple of subordinates whom Cody guessed were doing the extra work to curry favor with their boss. Even with Pyotr's cooperation and the new information from Alyosha, no one up the Bureau's chain of command felt that it warranted the expenditure of any additional resources.

Cody begrudgingly had to agree. There weren't any useful security camera recordings ever located at the hotels. The media had long been overwritten with new video. Everyone who matched the Cutters' descriptions appeared to have legitimate business, and the one couple, identified by Alyosha as the Desmets, who made a side trip about the same time as the Gleb case had their primary hotel make arrangements for a hotel outside the city. That was hardly the act of someone trying to hide their movement. It was not even in the same direction as Gleb's house.

Alyosha said he called a friend in the Zelenograd police unit to check out the hotel as a favor to Cody. The report was simply that someone remembered the American pair coming in late, drunk as could be, and asking where to get breakfast when they sobered up. The clerk at the desk remembered this because the man gave him a wad of bills without looking at them, and it was a lot of money to tip for a breakfast suggestion. The clerk seemed to remember that the vodka bottle he waved from the elevator was almost empty.

The Moscow hotel staff also remembered going over pictures with the couple and putting names to some places in the photos after the excursion.

Alyosha said a simple phone call to the department that issued export permits showed the Desmets did have documents on file that were approved days after the Semyon incident. The Desmets left Moscow the day following their receipt of the papers.

The side trip looked legitimate, and the couple returned with lots of sightseeing pictures. Also, they did not sneak back to the hotel but came in loud and drunk. This was not the action of the typical person not wanting to be seen or remembered.

As much as Alyosha had hoped he had a pair of suspects because the Desmets fit the Cutters' general physical description, everything they were known to have done pointed the other way.

The email had some unexpected good news, though. The Russians had a list of suspected connections between Kuznetsov's mob and some American ones. Stolen or illegally shipped high-tech electronic technology and software were linked to a Los Angeles outfit. Stolen precious metals were tied to a Chicago-based mob. Human trafficking was identified with a Boston crime organization. There might be others, but these three were the only constant associations that had been found. The email gave whatever details were available, including arrests, other than Pyotr's, that had been linked to American organizations. The electronics he was picking up when he was nabbed had been export-restricted ones from the LA mob.

The email ended with Alyosha's assessment: "If an American contractor was used for Gleb and Semyon, it would probably be through Los Angeles, Chicago, or Boston. Your hunch on the way to the airport seems to have been a good one. Good hunting."

At least Alyosha hadn't given up, bless his heart, Cody thought. Cody sent an email to Phil asking for travel money again if Alyosha did uncover something, and he related the other information received from his Moscow PD friend.

Cody realized Phil sent the email up the chain of command promptly when Henderson sent back an email an hour later saying, "The powers that be say they'll send you about the same time as when the burger you get at a fast-food joint looks like the picture on the menu. On the connections to American crime organizations, contact

Chicago, Boston, and Los Angeles ASAP. Keep us posted." There was a copy to Phil.

* * *

That evening Haley read him the final guest list. There were a lot of names that Cody didn't recognize, and Haley explained who each of them was.

They also decided on gifts for the wedding party and a lot of other details.

"When are your sisters coming, anyway?" Cody asked. "You said we're putting them up here, but you didn't say when."

"The week before the wedding. We'll have five whole days to catch up. I know you're not taking time off until two days before, so it will give us girls a chance to talk."

"What about Ricky?"

"He can come with us, or he can go to the Smithsonian. He's a museum buff. Hey, maybe he can help you out at work! As I told you earlier, he's a polyglot. Maybe help you understand that Cutter guy."

Cutter cases, as they had now officially been renamed in the Bureau, had trickled off to nothing, so Haley's involvement in analyzing them had also disappeared. She hadn't had a meeting with the team in weeks. Cody considered talking to her about the information he had from Alyosha, but every lead seemed too thin. All of the possible suspects turned out to have legitimate business in Moscow, and Haley wasn't an expert on organized crime concerning the US mob leads. She had enough to think about with the wedding coming up, so he didn't bother her with the unproductive details Alyosha gave him about the case.

* * *

Cody was swamped at work with the usual constant stream of cases. He was still getting trickles from LA, Chicago, and Boston about hitters, but nothing about any known hitmen traveling to Russia. A special agent from the Chicago office called and provided one tantalizing lead from about the time of the Gleb case, though.

Special Agent Brody Farrel had been on a joint Chicago PD and FBI task force investigating a Chicago mobster named Angelo

Caparelli. Angelo had split off from the Paul Lenetti organization when Lenetti broke up his empire and allegedly quit the rackets. The operation netted a couple of small fry on loan-sharking and narcotics beefs, but their surveillance also intercepted a cryptic email fragment.

"It only said, 'Affirmative on the relationship. Partner will contact travelers with specifics.' Nothing else. It was dated just before the Cutters visited Gleb," Brody related. "Thin, but you asked anyone for anything odd about the time of the Froylenko case. Only that portion of the text had been readable, not the header, so no one knew who the recipient was. Without knowing who it was from, who it was going to, or what it was about, it might as well have been gibberish. My task force filed it in the WTF file until you made your request. I'll send you the email fragment."

Cody gave Brody the physical descriptions he had of the people Alyosha had dug up. Unfortunately, none of them matched any of the Caparelli mob's known enforcers, all of whom were decidedly Italian in appearance.

Still, Cody now had an American crime-family name connected to an email about someone traveling during the Gleb time frame. As an afterthought, he gave Farrel one more request. "Brody, see if the local PD has any incidents that relate to the Lenetti family or related mobs with bizarre details. Anything really out of the ordinary."

Cody sent Phil and Henderson an email about the message fragment Brody had found.

* * *

A week later, Cody received a phone call from Brody.

"Cody, my SAC got off the phone with the Chief of Chicago PD a few hours ago. I actually don't know if he was amused or pissed, but I just got reamed in the fallout."

"What for?" Cody asked.

"Without thinking, I put the word out that the Bureau was looking for any weird mob-related events. You know, the Caparellis or any of the asshole set with them or against them."

"So?" Cody asked.

Brody laughed and said, "Cody, this is Chicago! Asking here about weird stuff related to mobs is like asking if anyone knows anything related to Lake Michigan that might be wet. Within days, I got enough phone calls and emails to last me until my kids retire. Seems every briefing erupted in one cop trying to outdo the others with some unsolvable piece of mob crap. Their commanders said everyone was wasting time, and their chief finally told my SAC that the Bureau could go pound sand if they wanted to stir up a hornet's nest like this in the future."

"Sorry, Brody. Anything useful come out of that avalanche of crap?"

"I dunno. Their chief sent over a few intelligence guys who are specialists in mob stuff after the phone call. He said that's the last he wants to hear of it. We've been talking for an hour about anything actually related to what you asked. If you got a minute, I'll put them on a video call."

"Sure. Give me a minute to get up to Henderson's office, and I'll get us set up."

* * *

A few minutes later, Cody was in his SAC's office with William and Phil.

Brody had the six men and women from Chicago PD with him on his end. He explained what they were there for and said, "These guys are the ones their chief said could sift the nuggets out of the truckload of info the PD's officers sent me."

Henderson said, "Okay. Give us some of the most likely examples."

The PD representatives took turns around the table.

One woman identified herself only as Alice and said, "We had a case where one of Angelo's guys was found dead in a car."

"What's so unusual about that?" Phil asked.

"It was upside-down on a residential street. No skid marks, no sign the car turned or slid once it was upside-down. The victim was inside with one to the melon from a high-power rifle. No damage to any of the surrounding property and no one in the neighborhood heard a thing."

Phil asked, "So what happened?"

Alice laughed as she said, "Hell if we know. It was as if a giant picked up the car and set it down there upside-down. Never solved it. The most likely theory is that it was on a tilt-bed going to a shredder, and somehow it fell off."

Henderson said, "Okay, Cody. Pretty weird. Who's next?"

A wiry, bespectacled analyst with a high-pitched voice said, "Hi. Harry Weems here. I was working the evidence of an internal mob massacre when I came upon something odd. There was a battle between two factions of some enemies of the Lenetti family. It was about the same time that two members of Angelo's family and three guys from the Vayda mob, the ones involved in the tussle, went missing. There was a bunch of the Vayda mob in the parking lot of a rural restaurant. Big shootout with everyone dead. The problem was that three slugs didn't come from any of the recovered weapons. There was a fuzzy CCTV video from the restaurant that showed three flashes from an adjacent cornfield, but everyone said at the time they were probably just reflections or something."

Cody asked, "Could you send me a copy of the video?"

"Sure. One more thing. The witness statements and the video have one person drive off in one of Vayda's cars. He never engaged in the shootout. The guys at the scene that night said it had to have been an unarmed driver. When was the last time you heard of guys going to a mob hit and having an unarmed driver?"

"Odd? Yeah. Anything else on that one, and how did you figure the Lenetti family was involved?"

Harry replied, "I asked the other mob-intelligence guys to watch for anything. They reported that there appeared to be a truce between the Vaydas and the Lenettis shortly after the shootout. They said it was probably because Vayda's son took over from his dead hothead father, and the Lenettis were reducing their mob footprint to next to nothing at the time. They turned almost everything over to their former capos and walked away."

Another Chicago guy named Randy Summers added, "Yeah. We were watching Angelo, Papa Paul Lenetti, a capo named Peter, and a lot of others. By the third month after the massacre, Papa Paul was having almost no contact with anyone other than civilians. He got in bed with a businessman named Sigmund Fresser sometime earlier, but the IRS and SEC audited Fresser a couple of times and found he was pure legit. Art dealers, business guys, even politicians show up at Lenetti's house after that as if he was some kind of model citizen. A few former top wiseguys come over for the occasional barbecue, but they're outside, and they talk freely about everything except wiseguy stuff. Eventually, Papa Paul moves south, and we only see him when he comes to visit his kids. If that ain't weird, what is?"

"Born again?" William said with a laugh.

"Might as well have been," Randy said. "Only one I've ever seen."

The three others from the PD had equally mystifying incidents involving members of the extended Lenetti family, but none of them seemed to fit what Cody was looking for.

Henderson thanked them all for their time and told them to pass on his apologies to their chief for the can of worms Cody and Brody had opened. He ended the call.

He gave Cody a look, and Cody sheepishly said, "Sorry, boss. I never would have if I knew what would happen."

Henderson scoffed and asked, "So was this of any help?"

Cody thought for a minute and replied, "Well, the upside-down car and most of the other stuff doesn't sound like our pair, but the cornfield thing could be. I'll wait to see the video file."

Cody had a gut feeling that the next clue was within his grasp, but it was nebulous.

* * *

A couple of hours later, Cody and Phil were in Henderson's office looking at the Rossi's parking lot video. After it looked as if all but three or four of the shootout participants were down, there were three very faint flashes from the cornfield, followed by a few brighter flashes from the area of their cars. Because of the poor lighting and the distance from the restaurant, it was fuzzy and pixilated.

Someone appeared to get back in the second Vayda auto and drive to the shooting site before leaving. The driver was unidentifiable.

Before Cody could say anything, Henderson said, "I know how tempting this looks, but I don't know what we can do with it. This is a ten-year-old incident with no physical evidence except three recovered slugs with no matching weapons. Sure, there is a possibility that it could be your pair, but it looks like three shooters who each fire one shot, not two shooters. The Chicago office says that none of Caparelli's suspected hitters are either non-Italian or a married couple. In fact, they don't have any women hitters at all that they know of."

Cody held up the printout of the mystery email, but Henderson raised his hand and said, "We don't know who the email they found was to, or who sent it. Even Farrel says the email is the only piece of evidence even remotely connecting the Caparellis to the Cutter case. Maybe, just maybe, the video is useful, but beyond that, I suggest that you clear out your caseload so you can help Dr. Briggs with the details of your wedding. No one will authorize digging into a phantom email or a case that the PD closed ten years ago. Hell, maybe those were just reflections. I know what your gut tells you, Cody, but trying to piece all of this together is about as productive as trying to nail Jell-O to a tree. Sorry, but that's the way it appears to be."

Cody really couldn't give a course of action that would make any more sense with the thin leads he had gotten from Brody. It looked as if his latest hunch was going nowhere. He knew when to insist and when to go with it. At least Henderson thought enough of the clues to let Cody present them.

"Wedding details it is, guys. Thanks for at least hearing me out," Cody said as he left for his cubicle.

There was one more detail that would be revealed to him in the days leading up to the wedding. It was one he couldn't have dreamed up in a million years.

Chapter 26

Meet the Desmêts

As SAC Henderson had suggested, Cody had almost forgotten about the Cutter case as the wedding approached.

His soon-to-be in-laws were arriving in a couple of days. He and Haley spoke with Maryann and Ricky on Skype, and Ricky said he would be delighted to go with Cody to work one day.

"I want to go to the Smithsonian and the Library of Congress, but a trip to the Bureau would be fun," Ricky said.

* * *

A couple of days later, Cody heard a car pull up to the house. He went downstairs just as Haley was opening the door to let her sister in. They embraced for a minute before Haley turned to him.

"Honey, this is Maryann. And this hunk is my fiancé, Cody."

Maryann gave Cody a hug and then pointed to the man unloading luggage.

"That's my honey, Ricky."

Cody walked to the driveway and held out his hand.

"Hi, Ricky. I'm Cody. Let me give you a hand. It looks like enough luggage for a three-week stay!"

"Maryann doesn't screw around. Do the words 'Well, we may need that' mean anything to you?"

"I think it's a family trait. Haley does the same."

By the time Ricky and Maryann were settled in, it was time to pick up Michelle at the airport. She had not bothered to rent a car as she would be stuck to her sisters like glue for the next five days. Cody noticed more of a resemblance to Maryann than to Haley. Michelle was a little shorter than Haley and had the same cute button nose as Maryann. She was a bit on the plump side, but not what Cody would call fat. She was wearing a boho outfit with a sage-colored natural fabric skirt and a multicolored peasant top. She was adorned with a couple of bright colored Bakelite-style necklaces and bracelets. Cody dismissed his first impression of hippie and decided Michelle looked more a Greenwich Village hipster or a tour guide at the Smithsonian's natural history venue than a hippie.

By the end of the evening, he would discover that she was a very likable, caring free spirit.

The five of them went to dinner right from the airport. Cody and Ricky might as well have been eating by themselves. The women talked nonstop.

"Those three haven't been together in over a year," Ricky explained. "Maryann and I were on vacation in India last Thanksgiving when the families traditionally get together. We might as well be in Florida for all the attention they're going to pay to us till they get it out of their systems."

"India, hey? Did you or Maryann pick it?" Cody asked.

Ricky said without hesitation, "She did. We've gone there a few times now. It was great. We stayed at this wonderful resort and took their tours all over the place. Would you believe it, we even found an Indian single malt whiskey that is out of this world!"

"No kidding? Indian?"

"Yeah, it's called Rampur Select, and it made Whiskey Advocate magazine's top twenty a couple of years ago. Absolutely superb. If you get the chance, you gotta go there. Beautiful scenery, great food, and you have to taste some of the exotic fruit you can get there."

"I've actually gone to India a few times on Bureau business myself," Cody said. "Coordinating a case. Yeah, some of the food there is fantastic. Haley says you buy and sell stuff from all over the world. Around Thanksgiving, eh? That's about the time I was there with one of the other guys. Small world! Were you there on business, too?"

"We were there mainly on vacation," Ricky lied convincingly. "We did pick up some things for customers, too. You have to be careful there. First, there are countless fakes, and second, my customers demand that they have to be documented and have the correct government paperwork when needed. They're getting really picky about that stuff. We usually hire a reputable broker to handle the paperwork."

"Tell me about it! One of my buddies over at Customs says that they confiscate a lot of items people bring back or import, even stuff with supposed certificates. I guess it's easy to give tourists fake papers. How are you going to complain when you get back to the States, and you're eight thousand miles from that little shop where you got such a deal?" He remembered the couple at the hotel in Moscow and added, "I've run into stories about antique dealers in foreign countries who do it right. Stay the extra time to get the official export permits as you do and don't have trouble when you get back to the US."

Ricky smiled knowingly and replied, "Yeah. Someone got popped who was on the same flight as us when we came back from one of our buying trips. He bought an ivory piece that came with a certificate saying it was old enough. The guys at Customs showed him photos of twenty identical pieces they had confiscated during the previous year. Every single one had exactly the same certificate, right down to the serial number."

"It isn't limited to foreign countries, Ricky. Half the certificates of authenticity on sports memorabilia are bogus," Cody said.

Ricky replied, "We deal in art and collectibles, too. Half? Try three-quarters! I don't sell any autographs unless certified by someone such as PSA or one of the independent experts I use. Sell a couple of fake pieces, and word gets around."

Cody said, "And even handwriting experts can't always agree, either."

Ricky nodded his head as he agreed. "I hear that all the time. People come to the guys I buy from with stories about how they got the autograph personally. Sometimes the autographs check out, and sometimes they don't. Some are outright forgeries, though."

Cody pulled a face and exclaimed, "You mean there are crooks out there? Oh my god! I'll have to tell my associates we're not just wasting our time at the office."

Ricky laughed so hard he almost choked on his drink.

That got the ladies' attention and Maryann asked, "What are you two on about?"

Ricky composed himself and answered, "Cody here just discovered that there actually are crooks out there, and the government didn't hire him on a whim, honey."

Haley got in on the joke and laughed. "You mean you're actually going to have to work? I thought you FBI guys just dressed up nice so you could have press conferences about the crimes that other people solved. Hey, Michelle, ask me how long Cody has been working for the Bureau."

"I'll bite. How long has Cody been working for the Bureau?" Michelle asked with an anticipatory smile.

"Since they caught on," Haley said with a laugh.

Cody gave Haley a kiss. "That's my supportive fiancé. Always got my back. But she does even less. Consultant. Ask me what the definition of a consultant is, Ricky."

"Okay, what's the definition of a consultant, Cody?"

"Anyone with a briefcase and a PowerPoint presentation more than ten miles from home. Say hi to the professional talker."

"Hey, I resent that! It's Doctor Talker to pissant master's graduates like you," Haley said with a dramatic pose.

The table was in stitches. Haley leaned over and gave Cody a big kiss.

Cody turned to Ricky and said, "Actually, one of her presentations was the reason I wanted you to talk to the guys at work, Ricky. She said that you are a polyglot."

Haley interjected, "Dear, I actually meant that he has polyglotism. There is a difference."

"Okay, what?" Cody asked.

She answered, "A polyglot speaks many languages, but it may or may not have been easy for him to learn them. Someone with polyglotism finds it extremely easy to learn languages, though he may or may not have actually learned more than a few. So, a person with polyglotism may or may not actually be a polyglot. More often than not, he is."

"Okay, I get it. All FBI special agents are great men, but not all great men are FBI special agents," Cody said casually as if it were a well-known maxim.

"That's my lover, girls. Modest to the last," she said with a smirk.

Michelle contributed, "Cody, if you haven't discovered it yet, sarcasm is one of the professional services Haley provides at no additional charge."

"Yeah, I have noticed just a touch of it. But seriously," Cody continued, "I talked to my SAC, uh, my special agent in charge, and he cleared an hour for a Q and A tomorrow with you and whoever is in the office if you want to come. You can go to the city with me and then hit the museums afterward."

"Sure. Basically, walking distance, and I can meet you whenever. Maryann says she has the whole day planned for the gals, so it's good on my end," Ricky said with a sly smile that caught Cody's attention as a little out of place.

* * *

The next morning Ricky rode the Metro into DC with Cody. Ricky showed his ID at the building and got a visitor pass while Cody talked with a colleague who happened to be passing by just then. Cody and Ricky went to one of the conference rooms, where a dozen and a half agents filtered in. Cody introduced Ricky to the group.

"Ladies and gents, this is my soon-to-be brother-in-law, Ricky Desmêt."

Ricky smiled when Cody correctly pronounced his last name "deh-MAY" with the S and T silent. That was how it sounded when Haley pronounced it, and that was apparently the only clue Cody ever had to what his and Maryann's last name actually was. Unless they are addressing a Christmas card, how often does anybody actually see a relative's name in writing, after all?

* * *

Ricky had a lot of fun answering questions about how easy it was for him to learn new languages.

A Finnish-speaking special agent, Leo Hirsi, brought a guide to common tourist phrases in Finnish in anticipation of the meeting. In less than ten minutes, Ricky could put a few simple sentences together on his own.

One of the other agents asked Cody if he thought Cutter learned new languages specifically for each hit or if he might have chosen where to go based on what languages he already knew.

"He may already know some of the languages involved, but I strongly suspect he learns some of them for the job," Ricky insisted.

The agent continued, "Why would he bother? From what Cody says, all of the victims spoke English, too."

Ricky smiled the same smile that had caught Cody's attention the night before. He was giving this group a taste of the inside information he had on the subject. He was toying with them, and he loved it as he replied, "Well, there are several reasons. One might be that he uses it for general conversation and navigation within the country. Another is that he might be doing it for fun. Yet another might be that it's just plain scarier."

"Scarier?" Cody asked.

"Sure. If someone from Bulgaria came over here and you spoke ..., what is it that they speak?"

In unison, the agents replied, "Bulgarian."

"Of course. A Bulgarian hitman visits you. Well, even if you spoke Bulgarian as a second language, wouldn't it be scarier if the guy threatened you in your native language, English? Wouldn't that imply that he's taken the time to learn a little about you and your culture? Maybe he found out what is considered frightening in your culture? I know that if I was in that position, it would certainly make me seem scarier."

The agent with the question admitted that all three reasons were plausible.

Even SAC Henderson was having a good time, and the one-hour session went over by half an hour. When they were finished, the agents thanked Ricky for his insight and for sharing his knowledge.

"Happy to help. It was fun, and after all, I'm going to have an agent-in-law in a couple of days," Ricky said with a wink at Cody.

Cody had to get to work, but Henderson said he could get an administrative employee to give Ricky a tour of the parts of the building that were not off-limits.

"That would be wonderful. Then Cody and I can go to lunch together if he's free by then."

Ricky got the fifty-cent tour and found that Cody was ready to break for lunch on his return. They went for salads at the nearby Sweetgreen.

* * *

Cody said, "I have some interesting but disappointing news. At the meeting this morning, we talked about the suspect Cutter. Well, my buddy in Russia had a modicum of luck."

Ricky was all ears.

"He said that one of his CSI guys is a good graphic artist. He took passport photos of Cutter possibilities who even remotely fit the description of the Cutters and photoshopped hats and sunglasses on them. They showed the lineup to their witness, and he picked out two. One was a couple in Russia to buy icons, and one couple were tourists on a guided tour. The first guy is named Richard Desmet, and the second one is Hugh Eldridge."

Ricky smiled again when Cody pronounced the name "DES-meht." He had put up with that all his life. Almost no one got it right.

"Well, all you have to do is find both of them and ask them if they are Cutter, I suppose." Ricky laughed, thoroughly enjoying the inside joke.

"Yeah, right. Both there on legit business, both have airtight alibis. The identification is based on one terrified mook who needs to establish some reason for the Russians not to kick him out of their witness protection program and throw him to the dogs. Oh, and the ID is based on a couple of photoshopped photos that show how the supposed suspects look in hats and sunglasses described by the mook himself! Super reliable. I'll get around to it just after I solve the Jimmy Hoffa disappearance."

"Well, I'm off to the Smithsonian. Meet you where?" Ricky asked.

"Tell you what, I'll call you when I'm close to done, and we'll decide where to eat. Do you like seafood?"

"Cody, I'm from Savannah. They disown you if you don't like seafood down there."

"Right. I'll call you later with options."

* * *

Ricky took off walking, and Cody went back to work. That evening they met at a place in Foggy Bottom that had steamed Chesapeake blue crabs, served in a pile on newsprint with a wood mallet to crack them. They had a good time, and Cody found he liked his in-law-to-be more and more. He didn't have any siblings, and it felt pretty good to have one as interesting as Ricky. If only he had known just how interesting Ricky was.

* * *

When they got home, the ladies were knee-deep in the boxes of bridesmaid dresses and accessories freshly stored in the front room, and images of the hairstyles Haley had picked.

As Cody and Ricky passed through, Michelle was protesting that she didn't mind putting her hair up, but she wasn't going to get a perm.

Cody and Ricky went to the family room, originally the 1870s house's back parlor, and watched football. Cody thought that Ricky looked awfully smug for some reason, but he chalked it up to the fact that the Chicago Bears were whipping Washington.

Chapter 27

In-Law or Outlaw?

The following day Haley and her entourage were off to do some shopping. Cody and Ricky took the Metro into town, and Ricky got off at the Smithsonian stop. They were going to meet the ladies for dinner that evening. Cody went to work for the final time that week. After that, he was on vacation and would return to work as a married man.

About an hour after he got to his desk, Phil called. He said, "Henderson wants us up in his office. Bring William."

Cody grabbed William, and they hustled to their SAC's office.

"We have an interesting one, guys. Sit and pay attention. What we discuss may decide if we pursue a case," Henderson began.

The two special agents and their supervisor took seats.

Henderson continued, "The director just informed me he got a call from Wellbarge in the deputy AG's office."

Cody knew that Patricia Wellbarge was a highly respected former state prosecutor who now worked as one of the top assistants to the US deputy attorney general, the person directly over the FBI. Hers was a call you answered quickly and thoroughly.

"She apparently is concerned about the possible continuing expense of the Cutter case now that it has stopped producing new attacks by the Cutters and neither the local jurisdictions nor the Bureau has any suspects. She asked who was coordinating. The director called me and asked for a name. Sorry. Since you were liaison to all the foreign cases, you had the most involvement of any agent anywhere, and we pretty much had you hosting many of the teleconferences with the US field offices," the SAC explained. "You are the closest to a coordinator we have.

"She wants to meet with you to make a recommendation to the deputy AG. I think they already made up their mind, but they want us to get the last word in before they let us know what they are thinking. That being said, I want to know what you are thinking. So does the director. I think he is tired of the stonewalling from above and would like this to die a quiet death. I get the distinct impression he secretly would like to hire the Cutters to go fuck up some of the bad actors we can't get enough evidence on to convict. So, guys, what's the bottom line? Phil first, then William, and Cody last."

Phil offered, "Well, we have just about nothing except for the name. We wouldn't even have that except that Cody had a driver in Russia identify Qatar's outline and a travel agent give him the correct pronunciation. Seriously, I have better things for both of these guys to do, and I'm sure my counterparts in all the other field offices feel the same way. I say leave this to the local departments where the crimes occurred. Most of our people haven't talked to the locals about it for a while, anyway."

"William?"

"There hasn't been a foreign case in quite a stretch, and I didn't even get to go on the last one to meet with Alyosha, so my interest is pretty low, too. Besides, I agree with the director. Cutter has been doing some pretty satisfying work. If I wasn't a pure-as-the-driven-snow FBI special agent, I might consider shoving something up those assholes' assholes myself. Of course, as a dedicated employee of the Bureau, I would never consider actually doing such a thing or admitting it to anyone outside this room."

His over-the-top wink at the end had everyone laughing.

"Cody? And don't tell me you secretly admire these assholes, too."

"Sorry. I actually thought I had a possible lead to a solution in the Chicago thing, and then it turned out to be just beyond my grasp. Frustrating as hell, but we don't have the resources to chase phantoms. We've never had serial criminals of this magnitude get away so cleanly on so many events."

Cody continued, "In a perverse way, you kind of have to admire them. As Phil said, the best clues barely identified a name we don't think really exists. We only have one eyewitness who saw them without the usual disguise, and his observation turned out to be useless. They took out scammers ninety percent of the world wished they could kill themselves.

"No one seriously wants us to catch them, especially the press, and the locals stopped calling us long ago. Maybe it is time to cut our losses. We're only involved at all because of the state-to-state aspect and requests from the locals for assistance. None of these are federal crimes on their own. Unfortunately, I say we don't throw good money after bad, and we tell the locals we're putting it on hold on our end unless by some miracle one of them actually gives us a lead we can follow."

Their SAC sat back and said, "Well, thanks, guys. It looks as if we're all on the same page. Normally, someone in the director's office will see someone as highly placed as Wellbarge, but she's a longtime prosecutor. I guess she wants to watch the eyes of someone who had boots on the ground when she's getting our assessment. Ever given a report to someone at her level by yourself?"

Cody winced as he replied, "Hell no. When I see them coming, I sprint in the other direction. Having people like that admire your work only results in one thing."

Henderson asked, "What's that?"

"More work."

"Well, then trundle off to Justice and get her to hate you," Henderson joked to end the meeting.

As they began to leave, Henderson said, "William, drive Cody over and wait for him. I want the two of you back with the news as soon as possible so I can prep the director. Hopefully, I can do that before Wellbarge calls the director herself."

* * *

At the Justice Department, Cody was escorted into a conference room with an accordion partition dividing it in half. He had a seat and waited. The partition opened wide enough for Wellbarge to pass through. Cody stood and held out his hand. She shook it firmly as she introduced herself and asked him to take a seat. She seated herself across the table.

"I'm sure your SAC briefed you on what the deputy AG needs. What did SAC Henderson and your team finally conclude?" she asked bluntly.

"Well, ma'am, the consensus is that unless some local or foreign police department comes up with an actual lead, there's nothing more the Bureau can do cost-effectively. The events have apparently stopped, and the best leads we had from Moscow and Chicago were dead ends. We were hopeful for a bit, but the eyewitness folded on us in Russia, and the Chicago leads were too nebulous to make real sense of."

"Just call me Patricia here. This is informal and off the official books from here on in. You can report back to the director that we concurred. Now we need to talk. The way I asked for an agent to come here pretty much guaranteed you would be the one they sent. I want your personal feelings."

Cody had not expected this. This was too close to the if-they-like-you-it-means-more-work scenario. He decided to just roll with the punches.

"Certainly, uh, Patricia. Well, let's see. First, this case baffles me. Someone put millions of dollars into punishing trivial criminals. I have no idea who could be behind this or why. It's as if a billionaire is playing a board game with real people and real money.

"Second, the level of planning and execution of the events exceeded that of even most high-value crimes. Who plans to shove a phone up someone's ass with that kind of effort and precision? No clues are left except false ones. No trace of the suspects before or after the crimes. The playful antics of a couple of lovers who perpetrate those crimes. Just crazy. None of us have pinned down a motive.

"Finally, the Cutters have been doing things that everyone wishes they could do themselves. Whenever I get one of those stupid calls, my first instinct has been to reach through the phone line and choke the ... pardon the expression, but choke the living shit out of the caller."

"Tell me honestly, Cody, if you were not in law enforcement and you could meet the Cutters, what would you say and do?" Wellbarge asked to Cody's utter surprise.

"If I wasn't a special agent?" He sighed, knowing he sometimes secretly wished for just that when dealing with slippery criminals.

"If you weren't even a security guard. Let's say you are working flipping burgers, and the pair identifies themselves to you. What would you do?"

"Probably what the polls say most of America would do. I'd thank them and offer them a free burger. Why?" he answered.

She narrowed her gaze on an already uncomfortable Cody and said, "Because there are some very important people who want to know what your personal opinion is."

Cody was stunned, but he managed, "Why me? Because I was the one that deciphered the Al Cutter name? I don't get it."

"You will. How badly do you want to at least know who the pair is? Personally."

"Well, it would sure scratch an itch. There isn't anyone in the USA who wouldn't like to know."

"Do you have any reasonable hope of catching the Cutters?" she pressed.

Cody was wondering where this was going. She was leading him somewhere, but he couldn't guess where. Now he knew what it was like to be on the witness stand when she was prosecuting cases. Wellbarge was asking the questions without a shred of emotion revealed on her face.

"Not an ice cube's chance in hell, Patricia. I think I made it abundantly clear that the Bureau doesn't expect anyone—local police, Moscow, or the Bureau itself—to get any closer to the truth. I was personally so close I thought I could taste it, and while my gut says I might know who they work for, it's a bust officially."

"Thanks. I didn't mean to seem adversarial, but I have to be certain where we stand," she said with a slight smile that broke the tension a little.

"Sorry, Patricia. I'm in unfamiliar territory here."

"I understand," she assured him. "I only have a little more preliminary ground to cover. The reason I asked that last question was to make sure you are positive that the Cutters' true identity will almost certainly never be uncovered. You answered in the negative. With that being said, there would be no chance your itch would be scratched."

"That is a very disappointing truth," Cody honestly lamented.

"Cody, if you could discover who they are but could not do anything about it, would you want to know? I mean, you find out who they are, but you have no proof, and there's no one you can tell. Would you still like to know? Take a minute before you answer. This could be one of your more critical career decisions."

Cody had been here before. In several cases, he or his team had somehow identified a perp, but they didn't have enough evidence to prosecute, or in some cases, even enough to get an arrest warrant. It was satisfying to know "who-done-it," but very professionally disappointing to be unable to do anything about it.

Patricia's question probably meant one thing, Cody suddenly realized. Someone had done something illegal that revealed the Cutters' identity. Because of the "fruit of the poisonous tree" doctrine, they had evidence, but they couldn't use it in court. For some unfathomable reason, she was willing to share that information with him and him alone. Would it be better to know or not know?

He looked at her and asked, "Could I have a minute to think about this?"

"I was hoping you would say that," Wellbarge replied. "It's the answer of the straight-arrow special agent I was told you were. I'll be on the other side of the partition. Give me a yell when you're ready."

Cody wrestled with this dilemma for almost twenty minutes, going over every scenario he could think of. If he said yes, he would have his answer, but he would also have personal knowledge of the criminals' identities. As a law enforcement officer, could he live with not being able to act on that knowledge? He reasoned that if Wellbarge knew, the information was already known to the top echelons of law enforcement. For whatever reason—legality, political pressure, whatever—those at her level couldn't act. He knew that if he broke his word and tried to do something, it would be as effective as bailing against the tide, and it would probably end his career.

He mulled over all the cases he or his colleagues had worked where they were positive they knew the identity of a perpetrator, but could not prove it legally for one reason or another. This was another of those cases, but he was at a complete loss as to why Wellbarge wanted to read him into the file.

In Henderson's office he had decided to let this go, and that hurt. Three years of following leads and coordinating a worldwide investigation was profoundly disappointing to abandon, but that was the reality of his profession. Now he could satisfy his curiosity, but in a way he couldn't use.

It was maddening, but he finally made his decision. He called out, "I'm ready."

Wellbarge returned to the room and sat opposite him at the table, asking, "And your answer is?"

He answered almost in a whisper, "I would want to know."

She smiled and said, "Good answer."

She got up and walked around the table, sitting next to Cody. She smiled and said, "Let me tell you a story."

She told the tale of a mobster, interrupted at a card game by a scammer, who partnered with powerful friends to exact revenge on the phone pests and cybercriminals of the world.

When she got to the part about government spooks and people from private industry being involved, Cody asked, "So it was a joint effort?"

Wellbarge nodded and added, "Some other members said they could locate enough scammers to provide targets, and still others said they could run interference with law enforcement and ensure that target scammers would get prosecuted. Everything was done off the books, with a lot of it explained as training operations. Many had contacts on the Dark Web. Black Hat hackers, who could help track down the scum making robocalls. In this instance, it was a case of 'the enemy of my enemy is my friend.'"

Cody smiled weakly and said, "Yeah. That phrase has come up regarding our miscreants."

Patricia continued, "All of them had media contacts, which would make the unmasking of scammers even more enjoyable. It went from a hobby of sort to an obsession. It took on a life of its own. After the two operatives, the Cutters, became active, they provided not only retribution and satisfaction but also a rich source of other entertainment. It became its own virtual world among those sponsoring it—an alternate reality where the rules didn't have to be followed anymore, but the stakes were so low they all could rationalize the operation. After all, they were just roughing up some bad guys."

Cody was stunned, even though Haley had advanced the theory that this had been a rich man's hobby. He had trouble forming the words. "My fiancé thought it might be just this, but …"

"She was right. She nailed it. They all agreed on the name Black Hat/White Hat for the project because some Black Hats were suddenly White Hats for this task. They referred to it only as BHWH among themselves. You will never know all who were involved, but suffice it to say that you do not want to cross paths with any of them, except for two. You would find yourself assigned to the coldest, loneliest place in America to while away your time until you retired."

"So, who are the mystery couple, and why are you telling me all this? This is unfolding like a fantasy spy novel," Cody said almost out of desperation now. The tension she was building was intolerable.

"In your case, Cody, the answer is that the fallout from your discovering them on your own could be catastrophic to a number of people close to you."

"People I work with?" Cody asked incredulously.

Wellbarge thought about that for a second and replied, "I hadn't thought about that, but yes, it could affect some of them, too. I was referring to others you know, and you will understand shortly."

Cody was more confused now than he had been a minute ago. He asked, "Patricia, are you part of the group? Otherwise, how did you obtain this information?"

"Oh, I was never a part of BHWH. I accepted a role as a go-between for several members and law enforcement out of gratitude. The Cutters brought justice in the matter of a murder I was aware of. The killer was known, but the case could not be proven. The Cutters exacted justice, where the government could not. Another tidbit you will never be able to identify, let alone prove."

Cody was stunned. He thought, One of the higher officials in the Justice Department is part of … or at least knew about … a conspiracy that may have included murder. And she is telling this to an FBI special agent. He was reeling. He didn't know what to expect next.

"So, Special Agent Cody Smutters, are you now willing to agree not to reveal what you learn here today to anyone?"

Though Cody had made a decision earlier, this information put him on the horns of yet another dilemma. He decided his first instinct was the right one.

"Wow. Uh, yes. But how do you know that I won't arrest the Cutters once you identify them?"

"One, I know you are a man of your word. You have a reputation that goes far beyond the walls of the FBI. You are a rare man—honest to a fault—and a man who will not break his word no matter how it affects him later."

"Well, thanks. I didn't know I was a legend. Any other reason?"

Patricia responded as a figure appeared in the opening of the partition.

"Simple, Cody. We don't think you will arrest your fiancé's sister and her husband."

***

Cody looked at her in stunned silence, then noticed movement. Ricky, smiling, appeared at the partition opening, walked to the table, and sat across from Cody.

Cody was stunned. He almost couldn't get out a faint, "Ricky?"

"Hi, Cody. Surprised?"

"That would be an understatement. How …"

Ricky held up his hand to stop the obvious question and said, "Haley never showed you my name in writing, did she? D-E-S-M-E-

T with L'accent circonflexe at the end. You say 'deh-MAY' like Haley and I do. And Ricky is short for Richard. For most purposes, like travel, we leave the circumflex off the second E. My passport has it without the accent as an also known as. A lot of transportation company computers can't handle the accented letters, so we travel under the Americanized spelling."

"You are the Richard Desmet my friend in Moscow told me about?" Cody asked, mispronouncing the name the way he had been imagining it when he read it in Alyosha's reports. Without having seen it in writing, he had always assumed Ricky's last name was spelled something like Dumay or Demay.

"Yup, but you can't tell him. Sorry."

"And Maryann?"

"Yup."

"Where did Alex Cutter come from?" Cody asked.

"One of my gaming avatar names. I made it up when I was sixteen. Just sounded cool. And Maryann picked Lara from Lara Croft. You know, Tomb Raider? Most of the people in the life just know us by those names."

"What about the card?" Cody asked, still trying to get his head around this whole bizarre situation.

"We needed something to link the hits to scare the crap out of the scammers. No one would know if they would be next. So we had fun with the cards at our employers' suggestion. Took you guys forever to figure out what it was. We were hoping to get two years out of our little adventure before there was a slipup somewhere. We got over three."

"A Russian driver who'd been there recognized the location. I figured out the name from it," Cody explained. Ricky raised his eyebrows when Cody added, "And a Russian crook gave us a lead on the Cutter name that led back to a clue from Chicago. We just couldn't trace it back further than that."

Ricky replied, "Yeah. We heard about that. But we had a buffer there that no one in law enforcement has a clue about. I'm impressed that you got that close, though. Fantastic work. Anyway, no one expected this game to have a lifespan this long."

"And the two of you ...?"

"Cody, we've both done things you don't want to know about. You couldn't prove any of them if you did, anyway. Just suffice it to say that both of us are retired now from that line of work. We're just successful antique and collectible dealers now."

"Why tell me now?" Cody asked both Wellbarge and Ricky.

Ricky answered, "Well, at some point very soon, you were going to see my name in writing. Imagine that you are addressing a thank-you note for the wedding present we're giving you, and Haley spells our name. Or maybe you take her father to get his rental tux, and the shop clerk asks him to spell his name for the rental slip. You realize you've been pronouncing D-E-S-M-E-T wrong at work, and that you are looking at the same name as the one you got from Russia. You send your Russian cop pal our picture, and his snitch IDs us. Not a good outcome."

"The informant in Russia was shown your picture from the hotel, and he picked it out along with other possibles, but it was tenuous."

"It was only a matter of time, Cody. We have been to a lot of places, and our employers decided at the beginning that they would end the operation at the first hint of discovery."

"Yeah. I guess it was just a matter of time. Is Maryann going to tell Haley?" Cody asked.

"Hell no. She'd go ballistic. We were in no danger of her finding out ... only you."

"Unless she ever started correlating your offshore travel photos with Cutter cases. So, I have to act normal around the two of you?" Cody guessed.

"Yeah. You can do it. You've done undercover work. Just put this in perspective. Tell me you really didn't enjoy hearing about the scammers."

"I guess I did. But the others ... how could the two of you ...?"

"No kids and no one who wasn't corrupt or totally evil. For someone in the life, our standards were pretty high. We were selective."

"Damn. I've got to get my head around this. All my life I've—"

"—taken out bad guys, Cody," Ricky said. "So did we. We just did it for a lot more money. And we mostly got the ones you couldn't get."

"Are you trying to justify what you did?" Cody asked with annoyance in his voice.

"Not to you. Don't have to and don't want to. Maryann and I … well, let's leave it that we don't need to. I doubt we'll ever agree. You're finding this out today to protect Haley and because no one is ever going to let you use this information for any other purpose. Once you accept that, things will be easier."

Cody looked at Patricia, who had been looking at the exchange with obvious amusement, and then back at Ricky. He let out a heavy sigh as he said, "I don't have a choice, do I?"

Patricia answered, "No, Cody, you really don't."

Cody impulsively shot out, "You and Maryann are pretty sure of yourselves, aren't you, Ricky? All of us, including Haley, looked at the two of you as pretty arrogant. Did you two think of yourselves as smarter than all of us?"

"Not really smarter, Cody, but it's easier to play the game if you know what the other sides' cards are before you bet. We did a lot of research ourselves, but we also had experts tell us what your limitations and procedures would be. That gave our employers the freedom to tell us to be the way we were with the scammers."

Cody was still curious. "So how did you know that a correlation between a scammer hit and your foreign trips wouldn't be correlated? I mean you did travel under your own names, and all."

"We made twenty times more trips for legitimate business than we did for the Cutter cases. Needle in a haystack."

"How could you be sure?" Cody asked, convinced there had to be other weaknesses such as Pyotr.

"Tell you what, Cody. You have our real names now. We traveled under them. Contact your counterparts in India and see if they can connect us with anything but tourism and antiques." There was a pitcher of water on the table and some glasses. Ricky took one of the paper coasters from under a glass and began to write. "Here, this has my credit card number and where we ate the night Ankit got a visit. See what you can dig up. We left a paper trail in every country we've visited. Every bit of it points directly away from anything we did."

"That's a pretty bold attitude, Ricky."

"As well it should be with the help and feedback we got from the poker group. Turns out there were people in BHWH from the CIA and the NSA who were trying to track us merely for the fun of it, and they knew the dates and general areas when and where we would be active. They made bets against each other. Our employer told us what they found and heard, and we learned more from each case. After we retired, the three people we consider our employers told them how we did each hit, and now they're using what we did to train their own. Go ahead and see if anyone in India has a clue."

Cody was becoming more relaxed now. He took the coaster, looked at it, and then tossed it back with a shake of his head. He mused, "Funny. Okay, I get it. You covered your tracks so well no one could put two and two together. So, what happens now? I have two … two of whatever you two are in my wedding party and act as if nothing happened?"

"Cody, do you remember the transcripts of our customers who talked?"

"Sure. Why?" Cody asked, bewildered by the apparent non sequitur.

"I always told them that they were totally screwed to the point that only they could make it worse. I told them to relax and just accept their situation. I suggest you take that to heart."

Cody smiled, even though the phrase made his hackles rise slightly. "Yeah, I seem to have read that once or twice in the past few years about the people you visited."

Ricky nodded with a knowing smile, and said, "Pick your battles and don't even try to fight battles you know you haven't already won."

That surprised Cody and he responded, "Sun Tzu? You're well-read for a button man."

Ricky nodded and said, "Thank you. We weren't brought up in the life, you know. Didn't even know anyone in it until well after college. A happy accident got us connected and active. Turned a hobby into a career. Maybe someday after you retire, we can talk about it. We'll know each other a lot better by then."

Ricky turned to Patricia and asked, "You want to tell him now?"

Cody was getting tired of these needling surprises, and he just waved his hands in a "come on, let's have it" motion to the woman who was three or four levels above his boss. He didn't want to speak, as, by this point, he was afraid that what would come out would be rude.

She said, "Sure, Ricky. Cody, sometime in the next month or two, a pair of bodies will turn up. No, they're not going to be killed by us. We have people waiting for a John Doe and a Jane Doe who fit their general description to turn up at morgues somewhere. They won't have usable fingerprints or other identifying features. We'll have someone claim the bodies and identify one as Al Cutter and one as Lara Cutter. They'll be cremated and given obituaries, histories, birth certificates, and other documents in all the right places."

"Do I have a part to play in this charade?" Cody asked a little sarcastically.

"Yes. When we notify you, do a computer search and 'find' their names. Put that nice driver, Sasha, in for the … What was it?"

"Ten thousand dollars for just the identification, I think, Patricia," Cody answered.

She smiled, nodded, and continued, "Put him in for the ten-thousand-dollar reward and tell your superiors and the local police departments the suspects died from whatever causes the two actually did die from. That will be the final chapter on Alex and Lara."

"What do I relay to the director?" Cody honestly asked.

Wellbarge replied simply, "That my thinking was in line with yours and his. The case wasn't worth actively pursuing. I asked you about every possible angle, and we came up with nothing new that would make fiscal sense to pursue. Right now, he is getting significant pressure from some well-placed people to shut down any further attempts to find the Cutters. He will be happy. So will the deputy AG for the same reasons. I'll wait for an hour to tell my boss so you can get the word to the director first. It was nice meeting you, Cody. Congratulations on your upcoming wedding."

"Thank you, Patricia." Turning now to Ricky, he asked, "So what the hell happens now between the two of us and Maryann in this governmentally choreographed farce? Do I just show up tonight for dinner as planned and pretend none of this happened? Does Maryann know you told me? I mean this is nuts."

"You can handle it, Cody. I don't know what we would have done if it wasn't the case, but everyone who has a finger in this pie seems to think you are up to the task. And, yeah, Maryann knows. See you there."

* * *

As Cody left, he went over in his mind what had just happened. Never in a million years would he have expected this. He soon realized Ricky was right about that damned tagline. There was a certain freedom he felt. He now knew the identity of the people he'd been dying to find. His irritation wasn't because of the hits on the scammers, either. He just couldn't stand the fact that they had eluded everyone with that puzzling string of trivial assaults and that he couldn't bring closure to those slim final leads he developed. Now he not only knew who they were but also why they had been doing what they were doing.

One thing was going to bug him, though. He was about to get in-laws who were better at eluding law enforcement than he was at catching them. The only glimmer of satisfaction was that he was the one who had discovered the name, Al Cutter, and asked the right questions to find that Chicago information regarding the Lenettis and Vaydas. If he had access to the resources, he might have even been able to make a connection to the odd Long Beach incident. At least that was something.

And he knew the secret of their mistake that led to finally ending their career with the mob.

* * *

William was waiting to give him the short ride back to the office.

"Took a while, buddy," he said with a question in his voice.

Cody replied, "You don't want to know, William. She went so many places I didn't want to go that I feel like I've just had a colonoscopy. Anyway, she's satisfied with our recommendation. Looks as if the Cutter case is gone unless the unlikely happens and they start again."

When they got back to the WFO, they went to Henderson's office to brief him and Phil. Cody merely had to say, "The decision to shelf the Cutter case will be supported all the way to the top," before the SAC called the director's office at the J. Edgar Hoover Building a few blocks away to relay the message.

It took less than five minutes, and the director's reaction mirrored Henderson's, to the latter's relief.

* * *

As William and Cody walked back to their cubicles, William asked, "How do you feel about giving up on the case? Did Wellbarge give you any additional insights?"

"Just what we figured. Public opinion doesn't want us to catch the Cutters. Pressure from above and the money and time wasted on all the dead ends make it a political liability. How do I feel? I have some closure. We, at least, came up with a name and a probable connection to the Caparellis or Lenettis. Someday, they will surface, and we'll find out who they really were."

Cody didn't get much done that afternoon. He wrestled with what had happened that day. He'd said he wanted the information, even if he couldn't do anything about it. He was, in fact, told that he couldn't do anything about it. He was covered by the Whistleblower Act, but he doubted that anyone would believe such a crazy story. No, you didn't buck the tide unless you had at least a sliver of hope you could succeed.

Ricky and Maryann had gotten away with it. Some criminals never did a day in the joint, even though everyone knew they were crooks.

He knew his fiancé's sister and her husband were protected at the highest levels. That was made patently clear to him. With the help of their well-placed friends, they had beaten him. They'd won over cops from over thirty police departments in six countries, in fact, along with the Bureau.

Ricky was right when he quoted Sun Tzu. In his training as an army officer, Cody had read The Art of War. He didn't have a chance of winning this battle. He'd be remembered as the special agent who became obsessed with a crazy, unprovable conspiracy theory that got him driven out of the Bureau. Not even the National Enquirer would believe him.

On the other hand, if he went along with the plan, he would be rubbing shoulders with an admitted murderer, as Wellbarge had implied. Then there was the Semyon affair. He was pretty sure Alyosha was right, and the Cutters had set him up to be killed by the police.

Both victims had been crooks themselves. Okay, maybe there was some modicum of justice. Then there were the BHWH cases. He had to admit to himself that he found himself rooting for the Cutters, not the scammers most of the time.

By the end of the afternoon, he was mentally exhausted. He had, however, decided on a clear path.

* * *

He took the Metro to the restaurant where he was to meet everyone. The four of them were already there. Ricky looked fairly confident when he smiled at Cody, but Maryann looked a little hesitant. He walked to her and gave her a hug.

He whispered, "Don't worry. Nothing bad is ever going to happen to Haley's little sister. Not that I could actually do anything at this point."

She kissed his cheek and returned the hug. Cody gave each a hug, Haley last.

"Boy, Cody, you look worn out. Tough afternoon?"

"Yeah, honey. I was called over to Justice to talk about the Cutter case. I got picked to brief an assistant AG. We closed the active file on it. Took a lot of deliberation on everyone's part. A sip of whatever brown liquor you're drinking and a couple of unsweet ice teas will pick me up, I think."

Over dinner, he watched Ricky and Maryann. If he didn't know what they were, he would have just seen two smart, interesting people who were obviously still in love with each other after years of marriage. He hoped he and Haley would be like them ten years from now. Without the homicidal part, that is.

* * *

The next day all the parents arrived. Eddie and Jessica Briggs drove up from Savannah, and Henry and Sylvia Smutters flew in from Atlanta, where they now lived, and rented a car. Haley put them all up at the Ritz-Carlton at the north end of town. Although Henry and Sylvia could afford it, Henry being a quite successful car dealership owner, close to three hundred a night was a bit rich for a retired gunny sergeant who owned a small ice cream parlor.

Cody was glad he had taken a few days off before the wedding, as he had a chance to not only spent time with his parents but to get to know Eddie and Jessica, as well.

One opportunity came when Cody drove his father, Eddie, and Ricky to meet William at the menswear store for their tux fitting. Haley had already purchased a tux for Cody the previous month to wear at a museum fundraiser they attended, so he was just transportation, not a potential customer at the shop.

Cody decided to probe a bit. He struck up a conversation with Eddie in the car to watch Ricky's reaction. "Do you see much of Ricky and Maryann these days, Eddie?"

Eddie laughed and said, "Not as much as her mother and I would like. Since they moved to Chicago, they only get to Savannah once or twice a year now, and they missed Thanksgiving because they were off in India, of all places. Who goes to India for a Thanksgiving vacation? You'd think they would stop off more often, at least for a layover on one of their buying trips."

In the rear-view mirror, Ricky was just smiling at Cody's attempt to extract information. He winked at Cody, who decided to up the ante to see if he could get a reaction.

"How did they get into the antique business, anyway? I never did ask Haley."

Eddie thought for a moment, as if he hadn't really realized why they had switched from their college majors to the antique business. He said, "Well, Maryann was always into computers. I guess they started small, just selling on eBay, and it took off. They both really got into it. Alex could have saved a hundred thou on his college degree. I don't know what antiques have to do with electrical engineering. At least they got over that obsession with those silly hitman games. Used to drive her mother and me nuts. Always sneaking around for some assassin club tournament or watching movies about contract killers. I'm glad it was just a phase."

Ricky's smile morphed into a grin as Cody said, "Yeah. Haley mentioned that. So, they're not obsessed with hitmen anymore, eh?"

"Thank god, no," Eddie laughed. "They're far too busy with their business. Keeps 'em hopping from what they tell me. And the places they get to go. Jessica calls them the global shoppers. You should see some of the stuff they send us for Christmas and birthdays. Exotic stuff to really impressive memorabilia. They started us on a whole collection of historical memorabilia from Savannah. We love it."

Much as he tried, Cody couldn't get a hint about Ricky and Maryann's other occupation from Eddie. They did, however, get to share some stories about Quantico. Eddie was stationed there with the marines a decade or so before Cody went there for the FBI Academy.

While Haley had said she grew up mostly in the Savannah area, Eddie explained it in more detail. "Just after I married Jessica, her parents died in a car crash. They left us their house in the north end of Savannah. When I was stationed overseas, they stayed there. It was close enough to Parris Island when I was stationed there, and they could use the PX at Hunter in Savannah. They lived in Virginia with me the couple of years I was stationed at Quantico. That's where I got on the base rifle team. Never made it to Corps team, but I was pretty good."

Cody said, "Yeah. Haley said you taught her and her sisters how to shoot."

Eddie replied, "Haley is okay, and Michelle couldn't care less, but Maryann really took to it. Jessica and I always thought that might have been what got her into that silly assassin gaming. She spent a week or two's summer job salary to buy a Nerf sniper rifle. She was the bane of her club at school. Just when we thought her obsession couldn't get any worse, she met this lovable asshole, Ricky here, and it got worse. Anyway, Jessica and I are glad they got it out of their system. Maryann said they dropped it when they discovered competition shooting. Now that I can relate to."

Cody checked the rear-view mirror again, and Henry and Ricky were chatting as if nothing were happening in the front seat.

* * *

At the menswear store, Cody realized that Wellbarge's analysis had been correct. When the fitter asked Eddie for his name, Eddie had to spell his last name aloud for the rental ticket.

Whether or not it would have clicked with Cody right then or not, Cody knew that he would eventually have made the connection: Desmêt, Chicago, shooting, antique dealers, trips to Russia, India, and the other foreign destinations. It was only a matter of time, and he might have tried to do something without knowing that Ricky and Maryann were protected from on high by the gods of a mobster's poker club and their minions in the federal government. Cody realized that the reality of the situation made this the best outcome he could reasonably imagine.

The families went out to eat, took the DC Ducks tour, and did other things people do when they have visitors from out of town. They all hit it off from the outset. By the time of the rehearsal dinner, they were fast friends. Cody decided he was going to fully include Ricky and Maryann in his life for two reasons. First, he loved Haley, and she loved them. Second, there wasn't a damn thing he could do otherwise.

*****

The wedding went off without a hitch. By that time Cody was used to having the exotic pair around, and he laughed at the irony of an FBI special agent having two criminals as notorious as "Alex and Lara Cutter" in his wedding party … with the knowledge of the Department of Justice, no less.

One instant during the ceremony interrupted his moment with Haley. When it was time for Michelle to hand Haley the ring destined for his finger, Cody glanced at Maryann next to her. She was grinning at Haley, obviously pleased that her sister had finally found love. Cody realized that there was now a deep, dark secret he would never be able to share with the love of his life. He and Haley had gotten to the point where nothing was taboo or hidden from the other. But now there was this.

When Haley turned to him to put the ring on his outstretched hand, she saw his slight look of hesitation. She paused for a heartbeat until his mind returned to her. His eyes then reassured her that his love was absolute.

During the reception, the bride and groom danced with the members of the wedding party. When Cody danced with Maryann, his hand on her back felt a muscle tone that surprised him. He knew from a few hugs that she was in good shape, but she was MMA fit.

Six hours later, the reception was over and the happy couple was off to their honeymoon. Seven days at a luxury resort in the Caribbean was more romantic than either of them even hoped, and they did all the touristy things they could think of: carriage rides at sunset, snorkeling over colorful reefs, and beach barbecues. They signed up for the lot. When they returned, they were even more in love than they were before the wedding.

While life at home was better than ever, life at work when Cody returned was, unfortunately, worse.

Chapter 28

Some Really Bad Eggs

Almost simultaneous with Cody's return to work, a series of ultra-violent bank robberies began. Since then, nine people had been seriously injured and three killed in ever-escalating violence. The robbers used terror to overpower the staff, the guards, and the customers. Their MO was to pistol-whip the first person they encountered and throw him or her into the middle of the bank floor. They fired a couple of shots in the air and then emptied the cash drawers. Anyone who got even remotely in their way was beaten or shot. They didn't demand safe contents that were not already visible or anything else that would take precious time. They were in and out in a couple of minutes.

What was worse was that they had gotten away clean every time. The gang wore masks, raincoats, rubber boots, and gloves. Their getaway cars were always stolen and later found torched.

The Bureau and the local police were getting pressure from every side to solve the cases, but clues were scarce. The word on the street was that a mob run by a family named Semmons who were known for stolen cars, burglaries, and loansharking, had graduated to the big time with these robberies. No one could pin it definitively on them. Every time a possible witness was located, he or she recanted or disappeared.

The Bureau, the DC cops, and the Virginia authorities formed a joint task force. They had Mickey Semmons' neighborhood under twenty-four-hour surveillance, but even that wasn't proving productive. The surveillance team couldn't find a location with good visibility. Mickey Semmons lived in an older working-class neighborhood riddled with alleys lined with rickety fences and enormous old trees. Even with FLIR infrared scopes, it was hard to follow people going in and out of the general area, and impossible at the residence itself. The neighborhood was under the mob's control, with many residents supporting the gang since they spread money around locally and had been known by all for generations. Even their departure from small-time crimes to the new violent bank robberies didn't seem to turn the neighborhood against them.

The gang also took some aggravating measures of their own. They often moved in vans that had no windows behind the cab. One of their habits was to jump out of a van stuck in traffic and into another going the opposite way. Once in a while, they would even wave to the tailing cops stranded in traffic. They did this sort of thing when merely going to dinner just to piss off the cops. They knew every store, bar, and restaurant that had back doors or side exits. There weren't enough cops in DC to provide a useful tail or keep track of them.

They also had at least one tech-savvy member. The Bureau got lucky one day and managed to plant a bug in the Semmons house when Mickey's wife called a plumber. It wound up in the men's room of a nearby service station four hours later.

When a string of robberies occurs, senators, congressmen, mayors, and other elected officials start getting a lot of heat from worried constituents. When violent robberies take place in or near a city where those elected officials and their families do their own banking, it's the senators and congressmen themselves who start applying the heat. The Bureau and the cops in DC and surrounding cities were getting hammered to solve the case.

Chapter 29

Product of a New Career

About three months into the investigation, Haley announced, "My sister is coming to visit."

"Michelle or Maryann?" Cody asked.

"Maryann, and she's bringing Ricky. There's a big antique auction in Fredericksburg. We're less than two hours from there, so they can stay here and commute to the auction. We can put them up in one of the guest bedrooms."

Cody was curious to find out how they were doing in the non-sociopath world, so he was actually looking forward to the visit. Because Haley was so good at reading Cody's tells, he had intentionally avoided dwelling on the pair since the wedding when she was around.

"Ricky told me they are renting a car at the airport and coming to visit the day before the auction," Haley explained.

When they arrived at Haley's, Ricky handed Cody a small envelope as the ladies hugged each other. "Open the day after tomorrow. It's a little personal present for you. I think you'll enjoy it," Ricky said with a wink.

Cody put the envelope in the inside coat pocket of his suit and did his best to forget about it. If it had anything to do with their past activities, he was afraid Haley would see it on his face.

* * *

The following day, the pair left long before Cody and Haley got up. They were going to be at the auction all day, and with travel, they wouldn't be able to meet for dinner until two hours after the auction's 5 p.m. end time.

When everyone met for dinner back in Fairfax, Maryann showed Cody and Haley the auction catalog with all their purchases circled.

"You two were busy!" Cody exclaimed. "There's got to be thirty or more items you won."

Ricky rolled his eyes as he said, "Seventy-three actually. Maryann picked up more than a few things for the house in addition to the things we bought to sell. But yes, we were busy. We would have gotten more, but there were a lot of people buying for themselves. No profit left when you're bidding against people willing to pay almost retail. Still, the market here is softer than in Chicago. We like buying south of the Mason-Dixon Line."

Maryann added, "Look on page twelve. We picked up something for you, too, Cody."

Cody looked on page twelve and saw a couple of items circled. The second one piqued his interest. He looked up just as Ricky handed him a manila envelope.

"No way! Authenticated?" Cody gasped.

"Yep. It has the JSA hologram," Ricky assured him.

Cody gingerly pulled a piece of paper in a plastic sleeve from the envelope. It was a typed letter on FBI stationery from 1934, but instead of "Federal Bureau of Investigation," it merely read the then-current "Bureau of Investigation." It was addressed to the widow of W. Carter Baum, an FBI special agent who was killed by "Baby Face" Nelson during a raid in Wisconsin that year. It was signed by Director J. Edgar Hoover.

"Wow! This is getting framed and hung up in the family room. Thank you both. I'm going to show this to the guys at work, too. Letters signed by Director Hoover are cool, but one about another famous FBI agent is even better."

That set the tone for the evening, and everyone had a great time. Haley regaled the husbands with tales of her sister from high school.

"I'm not saying she was a tomboy, but there was a group that played assassin with Nerf guns and squirt guns. They usually did a last-man-standing tournament, and Maryann won way more than once. After she met Ricky at that karate class, she got him involved, too. They teamed up whenever doubles or team games were played, and they terrorized the rest of the club. It wasn't just skill with a toy gun, either. It was strategy. I told her she should have joined the CIA or something."

"Aw, Sis. I like how my life turned out," Maryann protested.

Cody was afraid that Haley might have seen the wince that comment produced, but she was looking at her sister across the table, not him. Ricky, on the other hand, winked.

Cody was well over being angry that Ricky and Maryann had outfoxed him, so he took Ricky's jab with a sense of humor and smiled back. He was pleased that he had gotten to this stage of acceptance.

"In computing and then antiques? I always thought you would go for something a bit more adventurous," Haley continued, oblivious to the exchange between brothers-in-law.

"Well, Ricky and I have hunted down a lot of valuable assets and killer deals together over the years. I guess that was exciting enough," Maryann said impishly with a sidelong glance at Cody.

Cody guessed she had seen his reaction to the first comment. He forced himself not to laugh and hid his face by gulping a good swig of wine. Maryann winked at his discomfort and returned the smile he had as he put down his glass.

* * *

The next day Cody's visitors had breakfast with Haley and Cody at about six and then left a little after seven to meet with a trucking company in Fredericksburg. They were going to ship most of their purchases to Chicago by truck. Cody went to work, only to find the bullpen almost deserted.

William spotted Cody across the room and yelled, "Big conference room. The Martellos hit the Semmonses this morning. It was a massacre!"

He and Cody arrived in the conference room ten minutes before SAC Henderson addressed the assembled staff.

"This morning, about six, Mickey Semmons's van showed up at Mickey's door. We're pretty sure its driver had been carjacked by the Martellos on the way to his boss's house, but he hasn't been located yet. As soon as the Martellos burst in, all hell broke loose. Our joint surveillance team heard World War Three and notified the PD for SWAT. They arrived shortly, and it didn't take long to figure out there was no one still moving inside that door. The video from a SWAT entry robot showed eight members of the Martello mob and ten of the Semmons mob, all dead on the kitchen and hallway floors."

"Mickey's wife and three younger kids were eventually found hiding in the basement, terrified to come out. Mickey, his twenty-year-old asshole son, Liam, and eight of his goons weren't as lucky as Mickey's wife and kids. It looks as if Mickey's crew was gearing up for a robbery. They all had guns, and the usual raincoats and other robbery paraphernalia were in an adjacent room. Apparently, some of the Semmons thugs caught the Martellos breaking in, and it became the gunfight at the O.K. Corral. Everyone but the wife and kids were so full of holes that it's going to take the DC cops a month to figure out who shot who. Coroner says the time of death was the same for all the victims."

Henderson paused thoughtfully and then said, "We knew the Martellos and the Semmonses were having problems over something, but no one knew what it was, and no one foresaw this.

"As a bonus to this morning's festivities, the PD found some of the loot from three of the bank jobs plus a Rolex that was stolen from a bank manager. And that's just the preliminary report. There will probably be more. Our suspicions were correct, and now we know for sure it was the Semmons mob doing the robberies."

What he said next resulted in a burst of laughter from everyone.

Henderson grinned with gallows humor as he said, "We would like to thank all the Martellos, who were kind enough to invade Mickey's, for solving this for us. Too bad they're all too dead to collect the substantial reward money."

Applause broke out throughout the room.

Henderson concluded the briefing with "Your supervisory special agents will assign as many of you to teams to assist the PD as necessary. We're mainly doing the bank evidence side, but we'll assist them as needed."

* * *

Cody was assigned to a team working with the DC police on one of the robberies. He spent the rest of the morning with a Washington detective matching serial numbers and bank records.

By 10 a.m., the news was on the street. The papers and broadcast media were having a field day. They had been covering the violent robberies on their front pages. Now they played up the angle that the same violence that the Semmons gang has used to terrorize the city had now been used against them by another gang. As with most news reports, after the first station came up with that angle, every station from San Diego to Maine used almost the same language.

Everyone at the Bureau and the PD found it odd that the reporters missed a significant anomaly. The two top members of the Martello mob had personally gone on the raid. Thugs at their level seldom put themselves in that much danger. Cody and William talked it over.

"Maybe they wanted to remind their crews that they were still tough guys," William surmised.

"Could be. Or maybe they just wanted to get the satisfaction of watching Mickey die."

Another strange occurrence was revealed that afternoon. The Bureau was given the transcript and taped interview with Mickey's wife, Irene, after she was treated for psychological shock and released from the hospital.

The DC detective had just asked her why she fled to the basement before the shooting started.

She answered, "I got an anonymous phone call telling me that the Martellos were on the way to kill Mickey and anyone else they found at the house. I barely had enough time to warn Mickey. He told me to get to the basement and hide. I was barely there ten seconds before I heard the shots."

The detective asked, "Did you come up after the gunfire stopped?"

"I peeked upstairs when the shots ended, but I ran back to the basement when I saw the bodies. I didn't have a phone down there and was afraid to come back up until the cops came."

Theories discussed by the DC cops and the Bureau were that the Martellos had been betrayed by one of their own when Irene was warned.

Cody told William, "Yeah. I agree that it could have happened. Personally, though, I think that it's also likely that they were set up by someone we don't know about yet. You know, one side playing the other two. But, yeah, it could have been a Martello lieutenant wanting to move up. We'll have to ask the DC guys what happens to their mob after this."

William said, "Intel doesn't show any more friction between Semmons and Martello than normal for the asshole set. Mickey's guys didn't really horn in on other gangs. They were robbers, not drug dealers or pimps. The hate between the Semmonses and the Martellos wasn't over territory. Maybe this was just something personal."

***

An hour before quitting time, SAC Henderson called everyone still in the building, including a few DC detectives who had been going over bank evidence with the special agents, back to the conference room. He had a video link to the Little Rock Field Office on the screen.

"We have a lead on the motive for the battle this morning. On the screen is SAC Denise Grefton and Special Agent Byron Knowles from Little Rock, Arkansas. Thanks for calling, Denise."

"No problem. As soon as we put two and two together, we knew we had a lead for you. Special Agent Knowles will fill you in."

"Hello, everybody," Knowles said, sitting in what could have been a mirror image of the WFO conference room. "We got word from the Hot Springs PD that a shooting yesterday evening seems to tie into what you have up there. Four people were found dead in one of their better hotels after other guests reported hearing gunfire. Give us a second. We're just getting HSPD on the call with us."

A few seconds later, the software showed another window with a Hot Springs lieutenant and some plainclothes personnel.

Knowles said, "Onscreen is Lieutenant Mel Jaspers and a few of the detectives who were at the scene. Mel, could you tell our Washington people what you explained?"

The uniformed lieutenant said, "No one thought about connections until the coroner processed the bodies. They found IDs from Arkansas and DC. The victims looked as if they were having a meeting when something set them off."

Henderson asked, "Anything about what made them start shooting?"

One of the plainclothes cops answered, "No. They just pulled guns on each other and started shooting. There were partially consumed drinks still on the coffee table and end table. The two from DC had registered under their own names, and they had round-trip air reservations. The other two drove to the hotel from their local residences, according to family members. Their vehicle was still parked in the hotel parking lot. The room was the sitting room of a two-bedroom suite on the sixth floor of the hotel. Security cameras in the elevator lobby of that floor show no one entering or exiting just before or after the shooting. We can't figure why things got unpleasant.

"When my guys ran the names, they found that one of the Arkansas residents was one Michael Martello, son of Charles Martello and nephew of Paul Martello. With him was a Martello lieutenant named Marco Ziti. The other two were Semmons's men, Danny Flynn and Patrick Floyd. We notified the Martello next of kin last night but hadn't been able to locate the Floyd or Flynn families yet."

One of the DC detectives said, "I think I might know what they were doing down there. The word on the street was that the Semmons family was planning to send someone to talk with Michael to see if he couldn't negotiate a truce between the Semmonses and the Martellos. Charles's father and uncle were known to be hotheaded, and someone was allegedly going to see if Michael down in Hot Springs could talk sense to them. Got that recently from a confidential informant we turned last March on a drug arrest."

Jaspers replied, "Thanks. We hadn't figured out what the meet was about, but some of my guys called DCPD to ask around. Seems as if everyone who knew anything about the Martellos and Semmonses was busy today with what happened at Mickey Semmons's residence. We called your Hot Springs office as soon as we put two and two together."

Special Agent Westerfield was in the WFO audience, and he offered, "Knowing Charles and his crazier brother, Paul, when they heard about Michael getting killed at what was supposed to be a peace talk, it must have put them in hyper-maniac mode. Everyone knows both those pinheads had zero impulse control. It's safe to assume they wanted immediate gratification by way of payback."

Nods and agreement bounced around all three conference rooms. By the time the videoconference call ended, both Cody and William were comfortable with the probable genesis of the two-city massacre.

Chapter 30

If the Shoe Fits

Just before leaving the office, Cody got a call from Haley. She would be twenty minutes late getting to Fiola's, the restaurant where they were meeting Ricky and Maryann. She told him what to order for her, as they were both familiar with the bill of fare.

When he arrived at Fiola's, Cody's brother- and sister-in-law were there waiting for him at the hostess station. He told them about Haley, and they decided to do what she requested rather than wait in the lounge for her.

Ricky asked the hostess, "Can we get a back booth with a little privacy?"

She responded, "Sure. It's the middle of the week. A little slow tonight. I think I can find a quiet one."

When they were seated in a back booth in the rustic restaurant, Ricky said, "I'm glad we have a little time to talk."

Without wondering what Ricky and Maryann had to discuss, Cody said, "Been there, done that with Haley and her court cases. I'll wait for ten minutes and order so that our food will arrive a few minutes after Haley."

They ordered drinks and an appetizer in the meantime.

While they were talking over an order of antipasto, Cody recounted the events of the day. "I don't know if you two ever ran into the Martello or Semmons mobs in your former line of work, but they both did the citizens of Washington a huge favor. The Martellos have been into opioid sales and human trafficking. They run hookers brought in from abroad and some US-born girls. They hook 'em on drugs and essentially turn 'em into slaves. The locals have made a few arrests, and the Bureau has had some luck with the interstate transport angle, but they start one new operation for every one we shut down. The Semmons mob ..."

Ricky interrupted with a snake-thin smile, saying, "Yeah. We know about the Semmonses. One generation after the next of brutal thugs."

"That's them, all right, Ricky. Lately, they've taken to bank robberies. Neither the locals nor the Bureau could pin anything on them, but we were pretty sure it was them. Anyway, the heads of both families took out each other this morning. Massacre at Mickey Semmons's house. Semmons, his eldest son, and both heads of the Martellos. All dead."

Cody used hand motions to indicate a timeline as he explained, "It appears so far to have started when a couple of the Semmons mob went to Arkansas for, if you can believe it, a peace meeting. Turned sour, and they turned on each other. Four dead. Paul and Charlie Martello get wind of it and go to Mickey's for revenge. They get it, but Mickey and his guys get all of the Martellos on the hit as well."

Maryann asked, "How did you feel about it?"

Cody thought for a few seconds and then shrugged as he replied, "Well, to tell you the truth, I was actually relieved. Semmons's mob had already killed some bystanders at banks and injured a lot more. We were afraid more would die before we could finally have enough to put them away—only a matter of time before they killed more bank patrons. The Martellos? Well, that was just a bonus. With Paul and Charles gone, their tenuous political influence is history. The rest of their operation will be a lot easier to shut down now."

"So, you don't mind the lot of them taking a dirt nap, then?" Ricky asked with a laugh.

"No, I don't. I won't lose a minute of sleep over it."

Lara leaned forward mock-conspiratorially with a smile and asked, "Ever secretly wish there was someone to whom you could turn to do what the Martellos did? I know you can't actually, but it's as if you're driving down the road, and someone cuts you off. You secretly wish your gearshift knob included a button to launch a missile."

Cody laughed and said, "Sure. Everyone has those thoughts. If I had a button I could push, and certain people would disappear, yeah,

I'd think about pushing it. But, hell, you two were in a position to push those buttons, and you quit pushing them. I guess it's just self-control."

Ricky offhandedly said, "That reminds me, Cody. Open my note? The one I gave you the other day?"

"No. Kind of forgot about it, to tell you the truth."

Ricky grinned. "Well, find it and read it when you get home. I think you'll find it entertaining. I can tell you about it afterward."

"Uh, I think I put it in the pocket of this suit, as a matter of fact. Uh, yeah, here it is." Cody said as he extracted the envelope.

Maryann eagerly prompted, "Open it. Maybe we have enough time to tell you before Haley gets here."

Cody opened the envelope. He didn't know it was going to spark one of the most challenging conversations he would ever have. Inside there was a printed note. It said, "Arkansas—four. Mickey, Charlie, and Paul next."

Cody looked up at Ricky and Maryann in stunned silence. Finally, he spoke. "You two ain't active again, are you? I mean, you promised me."

Maryann put a hand on Cody's and assured him, "No, silly. Where were we when the Hot Springs events happened? Right there with you and Haley. That's when we gave you the J. Edgar Hoover autograph. We were at the auction early today at eight-thirty, and we stopped off for breakfast at Denny's on the way. The auction house is two hours or more from the Semmons house, and breakfast took an hour. Both places have CCTV, and you will find our time-stamped faces on both. No, we didn't hit anyone."

"Then how did you know? The note?"

"What line of work are Ricky and I in?" Maryann asked.

"You said you were just antiques and collectibles dealers now."

"Well," Maryann said, "we may have done a little government consulting on the side since."

"What? Government spooks planned this? Set it up? Carried it out?" Cody asked, almost in a gasp.

"Government spooks didn't plan it. Ricky and I did, with others, of course. Well, I guess you're right. We never thought of ourselves as government spooks, though."

"How? ... Who?" Cody stuttered.

"Take a sip of your drink, Cody, and calm down and breathe. You look as if you're going to have a stroke. Relax, and we'll tell you. After we folded BHWH, Ricky and I were approached by some of the people who watched and helped us. Important people. Well-placed people. They liked our approach. Another group formed."

"What?" Cody blurted. "Some secret government hit squad? That's against everything I believe in. What we do at the Bureau may be frustrating and imperfect, but the alternative leads to totalitarianism. When there's no government oversight, democracy fails. It would be a hundred times worse than what you used to do. Please tell me you two aren't involved in something like that. Please."

Ricky looked him in the eye and said, "Cody, we can assure you that nothing we are involved in is like that. You are certainly familiar with the Homeland Security Act?"

"Sure. It was enacted to prevent acts of terrorism, among other things."

Ricky explained, "Well, there are many who believe that some criminal organizations are engaged in domestic terrorism. A gang invades banks, beats people up, and murders some. If they do it for political reasons, we call them terrorists. If, like the Semmonses, they do it for financial gain, we call them bank robbers. Both commit the same act. So, what's the difference between a political terrorist and a financial terrorist? If you ask the dead people's families, I don't think they would make that distinction."

Maryann added, "You surely aren't so naïve to believe that Homeland Security doesn't have some black bag operations going on here and there?"

"Well, I guess I suspected it," Cody admitted.

Maryann said, "Some of those original poker players got together with some other really scary government people. They had long discussions about domestic terrorism. The outcome was that if mobs kill each other off, that is for the police or the feds. If they kill innocent people and are caught by the police, that is also a police matter. But if the police know who these people are, but the killings go on and on because the police can't get enough evidence to make arrests stick, then that needs special attention."

"So, what makes this different from a South American death squad?" Cody argued.

"Plenty," Ricky replied. "Nothing is done that is not reviewed by a panel of magistrates, a Senate committee, and some people at the executive branch who hover around the cabinet level. Nothing is done except those acts that will prevent multiple murders or grave injuries to innocent people. And nothing is done unless it can be made to look as if it is not what it is. The American public sleeps better at night, not knowing. And nothing is done that is not funded by Congress. You won't find this operation listed in any line item on any budget, but it is paid for by Uncle Sam. It's essentially the same level of bipartisan, three-government-branch oversight as the military has when it takes out a terrorist with a drone-launched missile, and I'm sure you don't object to that. It has every check and balance its creators could think of to prevent corruption, though nothing, I guess, is foolproof."

Cody objected, "I still think it is unconstitutional."

Ricky shrugged and said, "There are some at the top who think you are right. As in spiriting people away to Guantanamo without due process. But in response to the other side saying that the need outweighs that question, the doubters agreed to let the courts decide if and when the first case becomes public. They also agreed, and this is what helps prevent corruption, that no operations are undertaken unless they are sanctioned by those in full agreement with the operation and those who are not. It did become a little less quarrelsome in one case recently, though."

"How was that?" Cody asked.

"Well," Ricky said, "such discussions result in a lot of righteous indignation and posturing on both sides when argued in the abstract. But when one of the opposition has a wife and child witness a random murder at one of the Semmons's bank robberies, the discussion seems to shift from the abstract to the concrete. That senator swung the vote on this particular operation."

Maryann added, "What oddly seems to be the deciding factor in the miniscule number of proposed cases that are finally sanctioned is the fear that social media and public opinion will fry any politician if it is discovered that they had the means, legal or not, to stop cold-blooded murders but failed to do so."

Ricky laughed and said, "Maryann and I, along with some of the other operatives, call it the James Bond syndrome. Even most constitutional conservatives and social liberals who hate the thought of operations such as ours root for James Bond when he's taking out bad guys in a manner that no free-world government would openly sanction. You observed a bit of that pressure when public opinion was part of what shut down the investigation on us, remember?"

Maryann let this sink in for a couple of seconds and then asked, "So, related topic. When are you authorized to use deadly force?"

Cody replied, "To save another from death or serious injury or to stop a fleeing felon who is likely to do such harm before being apprehended or who is likely to avoid apprehension completely after doing such harm. Why?"

Ricky asked, "Cody, do you think the police would eventually have caught the Semmonses?"

"Sure," he replied.

"When?" Maryann pressed.

"I don't know. Eventually. Everyone slips up. Maybe they would do a robbery when a cop was close enough to the bank to catch them or something."

Maryann said, "Okay. Rhetorical question: How many bank robbery murders would be acceptable to incur before solving the case and arresting the Semmons mob? There's no rational answer, is there? So, it's okay to shoot a fleeing murderous bank robber whose identity is unknown, but if you know who he is but can't prove it in court, you can't shoot him if he's not actually leaving the scene of a murder."

Cody chuckled and said, "That reminds me of my roommate at the Academy. He had a tee shirt with a cartoon on it. It showed a sniper with a fleeing suspect in his sights. The sniper's spotter has a Miranda card out, and the sniper is saying, 'No. We only have to read them their rights if we're going to arrest them, not shoot them.'"

Maryann smiled and nodded, then followed up with, "When you were at the Academy, did you happen to study Terminiello?"

"Sure. Free speech case where a minister's speech caused a riot. Supreme Court overturned his conviction on First Amendment grounds. 1940s, I think. Why?"

She replied, "Associate Justice Jackson's dissent: 'The choice is not between order and liberty. It is between liberty with order and anarchy without either. There is danger that, if the court does not temper its doctrinaire logic with a little practical wisdom—'"

"'It will convert the constitutional Bill of Rights into a suicide pact,'" Cody recited. "Yeah. That argument comes up somewhere a few times every year. So, enough people agreed, even begrudgingly, to take it to its logical conclusion, eh?"

Maryann nodded and replied, "Uh-huh. Some people decided that not removing bloodthirsty maniacs such as the Semmonses and the Martellos was tantamount to suicide. Even you were happy that they were no longer breathing air before you knew the mechanism behind their demise. Ask yourself how that knowledge changes your view of the situation."

They let Cody absorb this for another minute. These two weren't the cold-blooded thugs he had imagined in Wellbarge's conference room. They had an ordered worldview, and they were educated and articulate. He looked up at them with curiosity in his eyes.

"Yeah. Confusing to think about … uh … I mean, well, no, I meant what I said. So, what part do the two of you play? Are you part of the execution of these operations?"

Ricky answered, "No, Cody. In the symphony that is the subject of this discussion, we no longer play an instrument. We gave that up well before we revealed ourselves to you. No, in this symphony we conduct."

"Conduct?"

"Yes. What Maryann and I did with the scammers was the subject of endless amusement to some of the original group. We over planned everything to point to anyone but ourselves or our clients. Most of the time, the experts had no idea how we did what we did, including getting in and out. Do you remember Frank Abagnale, Cody?"

"Sure. Everyone in the Bureau knows about Frank. Con man and counterfeiter turned security expert. He worked for the Bureau during the last part of his sentence. Educated a whole generation of agents about the subject."

"Well, the two of us were hired for essentially the same reason. Our particular set of skills allows us to provide the operatives involved with unconventional training to carry out their missions with a very low probability of being caught and a very high probability of being successful," Maryann explained.

Cody raised an eyebrow and said, "Well, that's a new twist on criminal-government relations."

Ricky laughed. "No, it's not. It's a tried-and-true American tradition that dates all the way back to the United States' first declaration of war. In the War of 1812, Andrew Jackson gave a full pardon to the murderous pirate Jean Lafitte in exchange for Lafitte's assistance in defeating the British at the Battle of New Orleans. During the Second World War, your precious Bureau looked the other way because the mob kept the docks and trucking lines safe. And before you dismiss that as an old wives' tale, remember who we used to work for. My former employer's father got a pass from the feds after he took care of some fifth columnists and a few Reds early in the war."

Ricky suddenly looked at his watch and flagged a waiter to order, as it was now ten minutes before Haley was expected.

After they ordered, Cody asked, "Okay. Then tell me what this note was about. What did you and Maryann plan?"

Ricky said, "Sure. Happy to let you in on our little production, but we were only two of more than a dozen planners. The central players are two mobs. The Martellos and the Semmonses. Two of the most brutal collections of serial killers, drug dealers, human traffickers, and robbers you could assemble. The Bureau and the local cops know who they are and probably what they are responsible for, but the crooks are smart enough to keep just out of your grasp. Innocent people keep getting crippled and killed by both mobs. There is tension between the two mobs, however, and that could be useful. Word gets out that an emissary of one is going to meet with a relative of another."

Maryann explained, "It's trivial to set up the situation. A snitch tells the cops about the Arkansas meeting, and word gets back to us. The four men are in a hotel room drinking whiskey and talking. Suddenly a shot rings out from one of the bedrooms, wounding one of the Arkansas men. Michael Martello is injured. He and his buddy draw their guns and start firing at the Semmons men, probably thinking they planned an ambush. The Semmons guys shoot back. Those who aren't killed outright are finished off by the guys from the bedroom. Those two then drop one floor down to their own room from the balcony after leaving their guns next to the dead guys. The cops come and see two sets of dead guys who appear to have shot each other. All have gunpowder residue."

Ricky continued, "The news gets back to Paul Martello, and his sources say that Mickey Semmons is at home. In the predicted rage, he and Charlie take off to hit Mickey. Just before they get there, one of our people provides an anonymous tip to the wife, who tells her husband. Mickey tells her to go downstairs, and he gets some guys and guns to the kitchen to wait for the intruders. That they had a lot of guys in the house in preparation for a robbery is just a plus."

"How did you know that the Martellos would go to Mickey's house that morning?"

"Simple," Maryann replied. "We had a mole in the Martello's camp. The same guy the cops turned using a drug rap a while back. He goaded Paul and Charlie until they were foaming at the mouth, and then he fingered Mickey's driver using the information we supplied. After they hit the driver on the way to pick up Mickey and stole the van, our informant volunteered to take care of the driver's body. The informant is in a safe house in Gilbert, Arizona as we speak waiting for a new identity."

Ricky picked up the story: "While Semmons and company are waiting to ambush the intruders at the back of the house, they are covered by the same two guys and a woman, all in black, who tipped off the wife a minute earlier. They're already in the residence. When the door opens and the Martellos storm in, the Semmonses' ambush is disrupted by gunfire from behind them, causing confusion. The Martellos kill some Semmons men and vice versa. The survivors are quickly finished off by experts actually trained for close-quarters combat."

With wild arm movements, Maryann pantomimed as she described the scene. "There are shots all over the place, into bodies, walls, and floors. It looks like a Wild West shootout between the two sides. In the time it takes for the task force and SWAT to arrive, the guys in black simply slip away."

Again, Cody was stunned. The plan wiped out the critical members of two mobs, all of whom were serial killers. Law enforcement had been after them for years with no success.

Cody asked the million-dollar question: "If this is so secret, why are you telling me?"

Maryann answered, "A couple of reasons, actually. Ricky and I thought you would like to know, and there's no one you can tell, as you promised Wellbarge. No one would believe you anyway, and you know what kind of people we have behind us to quash any mention of an investigation."

"Yeah," Cody sighed. "The being screwed thing. There's a lot of truth to that shitty tagline of yours. But here's a switcheroo, my little in-law buckaroos. If you hadn't been protected on high by the shady gods of the underworld, you might have been screwed, yourselves, if they had given me more resources. You two are smart, but not as smart as you think."

Ricky and Maryann did, indeed, look surprised at this potential turn of the tables.

Ricky asked, "So, what do you think you know?"

Cody looked at them smugly and said, "I've been waiting for a good opportunity to tell you this, and now appears to be the time. You two did come up with some of the most untraceable operations known to man or beast, but that could have been your eventual downfall. People throughout the country knew I was coordinating your screwy Cutter card cases, and they started to call me about any cockamamie hits with bizarre MOs. My cubicle became Nutjob Central. That became your tell. Does Lee Doyle or Donat Vayda ring a bell? Semyon? Voodoo? Three unaccounted-for slugs and an internal gang struggle that no one saw coming? Death by cop?"

For a change, it was Maryann and Ricky who were silent. The look on their faces instantly conveyed the shock that Cody had gotten that close.

Ricky spoke first. "Damn, Cody, we never thought anyone could or would link those cases except for the last one. We were retired because of it and the guy Alyosha pinched as a result of it. What gave it away on the Donat one?"

Cody said, "Three blurry flashes from the cornfield on the CCTV followed by someone driving off. An unarmed driver on a hit? Give me a break! We traced US mob activity connected to Kuznetsov's organization because of Semyon and Pyotr, about whom I'm sure your blabby handlers told you everything. One of three US possibilities was Angelo. When I asked Chicago PD for odd mob cases, I got enough to fill an encyclopedia. One of CPD's analysts gave me the Donat hit as one that stood out. I guessed that either Lenetti or Angelo was the driver who got away, but I couldn't track who you two worked for. No known button men with your descriptions."

Cody explained, "They wouldn't give me the resources to dig deeper, though, so dead end. The setup was as complicated as the Cutter cases. Your trademark. A DEA guy looked at the Doyle hit and called me, again because it just looked wrong in a Malcolm Gladwell sort of way."

"Blink?" Maryann asked, referring to one of Gladwell's books on intuitive deduction.

"You two are well-read for hoods," Cody quipped. "Yeah. He looked at the scene and instantly thought there was something wrong. He called the FBI agent who handled screwy cases: me."

Maryann and Ricky had been cocky throughout the conversation, but it was apparent by their quieter expressions and less-erect postures that Cody had just taken some of the wind out of their sails.

Ricky allowed, "You could have actually had us, I guess, so I think we should tell you the missing piece. As much as we can, that is. You couldn't pin us to any of the Lenetti family branches because of how we came to be tied to him. We blundered into a hit on him and his wife and grandkids. We stopped it by taking out the three hitters ourselves, so they figured they owed us. We were farmed out, off the Lenetti family grid. They granted us permission to accept work only when it fit our sense of justice. We declined a few cases that didn't fit it. Not typical of someone in our position at all. That's why we never showed up on Chicago PD's radar, except for that Donat incident, of course. Whoever that analyst was who figured out the three shots weren't reflections or random pixilation is pretty good."

Then Cody dropped the bomb he had been waiting to drop since he and Ricky met at Wellbarge's conference room. "Maryann, you were a computer science major, right?"

She nodded, and he said, "For someone as smart as you and as trained in computers as you, you should have fixed the sole flaw in one of your visits."

Maryann appeared to be running frames of every hit and scammer-revenge case they had done. She looked up at Cody with a bewildered look and asked, "Okay. Which one?"

Cody merely said, "Gleb."

Maryann turned to Ricky, but he just shrugged. They turned back to a gloating Cody.

He said, "When you erased those four files, they were unreadable, but they left four perfect patches of white noise on the disk."

Maryann blanched and exclaimed, "Oh god! I should have overwritten the disk space, right?"

Cody nodded and said, "The fact that four files of equal size were erased on all of his hard drives led the Russian detective to dig deeper into the case. He knew you were connected somehow to a Russian mob. That's what set the whole chain of events in motion that led to the connection with Angelo."

Maryann said, "You can kill the giants and slay the dragons, but it's the stone in your shoe that will bring you down, isn't it? Of course! The blank space on a new hard drive would not seem abnormal, but on a heavily used one, like scammer Gleb's, it would stand out. Damn! That was an amateur's mistake." She turned to Ricky and said, "Sorry, sweetheart. I should have known better."

Cody smiled, nodded, and asked, "You told me one reason you wanted to read me into your little cabal. So, what's the other one you hinted at?"

"Well, the two of us have been watching your reactions. First to what we told you before the wedding and then again tonight before we told you what we were really up to. The second reason is that we have a question for you. You have a rare analytical ability and are as persistent and honest as they come. Now that we know more about what you uncovered besides the Semyon/Pyotr leak, we are even more impressed."

Cody gulped. He had an idea of what might come. He asked, "What's the question?"

Rickey asked, sotto voce, "Want in? Still get paid by Uncle Sam, retirement, seniority, and everything. Actual government job with a title, a job description, and everything. Oh, and a big pay raise. If you don't opt to do it from within the confines of the Bureau as a loaner to the program, that is. Help us identify domestic terrorists and plan their removal. And removal does not usually mean something fatal. Our preferred outcome is to have the terrorists execute their next job where a hornet's nest of cops just happens to be waiting."

Before Cody could answer, Maryann waved her hand at someone approaching.

"Haley! Over here."

Haley peered into the shadowed corner and smiled. She walked to the booth and sat down next to Cody. She gave him a kiss, saying, "Sorry I'm late. Only one juror was left to select, and the judge didn't want to make the rest of the pool come in again tomorrow. I'm bushed! Have you three been entertaining each other while you were waiting for me?"

"Yeah, Sis. We were just telling Cody about how rewarding this trip was," Maryann replied.

"You were interested in their business?" Haley asked, raising an eyebrow at Cody.

Cody did a pretty good job of recovering from the shock of Ricky's "want in?" question, answering, "Uh, yeah. It's more interesting than you might expect. Quite fascinating, as a matter of fact."

Fortunately, Haley wasn't exactly on point as a psych profiler, concentrating instead on the refreshing brown liquid in the glass Cody had ordered for her.

"Well then, the next time they're here for another auction, maybe you should take a day off and go with them," Haley suggested after a long sip.

Maryann offered, "Sure, Cody. The next time we're in town for business, we'll let you know. Only if you're interested, of course."

Cody smiled as he replied …

Acknowledgments

I would like to thank Tim Mudie, my developmental editor, and Michael Schuler, my proofreader. Together, they improved my writing style more than all of the professors I had in college. Their contributions were invaluable.

Of course, I have to thank all of the wisecracking special agents I have met since I attended the FBI National Academy in 1984. While the FBI in this tale is not the FBI as it really is, I suspect my version is what a few of them would like it to be.

About the Author

Born in 1949 and raised in East Oakland, California, Glenn Della-Monica enlisted in the US Army in 1968 as a military police officer. He started writing professionally as an army correspondent during his second and third tours in Vietnam.

After regular army service, he joined the California State Police, where he rose to the rank of captain. He commanded offices at the capitol in Sacramento and in the San Francisco Bay Area. In 1984, he was nominated to attend the FBI National Academy at Quantico, Virginia, and is still a member of the FBI National Academy Associates.

Shooting with the award-winning State Police Blue Team, he earned the pistol classification of Distinguished Grand Master, and during a hitch with the California National Guard, he won a slot on the California National Guard State Pistol Team.

When the California State Police organization was about to be folded into the much larger California Highway Patrol, Glenn switched careers. He finished his 32-year stint in civil service as the manager of the million-square-foot California Supreme Court headquarters building in San Francisco.

After retiring from state service, he moved to New Hampshire. He spent over a dozen years as an antique dealer and an appraiser for a firearms auction company.

He has volunteered for such diverse activities as portraying a gunsmith in an 1840s living history program, building a dorm for homeless boys in Fiji, chairing the planning board in Hudson, New Hampshire, and serving at COVID-19 mass vaccination sites.

Glenn has written a few stories and articles for various publications, and this is his first published novel.